Shelter in His Arms

Laurel Ridge Series, Book #10

Tara Baisden

Sterling Ridge Press LLC

Copyright

Cover designed by Sterling Ridge Press LLC

Published by: Sterling Ridge Press, LLC www.sterlingridgepress.com

ISBN: 978-1-966093-09-1 Printed in the United States of America

First Edition: May 2025

For permissions, contact: tara@tarabaisden.com or visit www.tarabaisden.com

Also by Tara Baisden

Riverbend Valley Series

#1 A Cowboy's Second Chance

#2 Wanderlust & Wild Horses

#3 Heartstrings on the Horizon

#4 Runaway in Riverbend Valley

#5 Mended Hearts

Laurel Ridge Series

#1. Season of Hope

#2. Finding Grace

#3. His Perfect Plan

#4. Love Redeemed

#5 Snowbound Blessings

#6 Sheltered Hearts

#7 Restoring Faith

#8 Love Rekindled

#9 Where She Belongs

#10 Shelter in His Arms
#11 Where Love Stands

About The Author

Tara Baisden is a Contemporary Christian Inspirational Romance author who proudly calls the beautiful state of West Virginia her home. Nestled on a sprawling mountainous property, she is surrounded by the peace and serenity of nature. Her days are happily spent in the quiet of country life, writing heartwarming stories of love, faith, and second chances. Tara also enjoys quilting, working in her garden, tending to her beloved pets, and soaking in the beauty of her surroundings.

With deep roots in West Virginia, family is everything to Tara. One of her favorite pastimes is gathering on the front porch with loved ones, sharing stories, laughter, and enjoying the simple, meaningful moments that life offers. When she's not crafting her novels, Tara can often be found exploring the rich history of her home state, visiting local historical sites, and, of course, stopping by every bookstore she passes! Her passion for reading and discovery always fuels her next adventure.

Tara is the author of the Laurel Ridges series of novels, as well as the Riverbend Valley series of novels, of which have been beloved by fans of inspirational romance. Her novels reflect her love for faith, family, and the timeless beauty of the world we live in.

Known for her sweet and clean romances, she creates characters that feel like family and settings that make readers want to visit again and again.

You can find out more about Tara and her latest releases at www.tarabaisden.com or follow her on social media for updates and behind-the-scenes glimpses of her writing process. Stay connected—you won't want to miss the heartfelt stories of love and family she has in store!

About Laurel Ridge

Welcome to the fictional town of Laurel Ridge, West Virginia!

Nestled deep in the heart of the Appalachian Mountains, Laurel Ridge is a place where time slows down, allowing visitors and residents alike to enjoy life's simple pleasures. With its quaint, brick-paved streets, historic storefronts, and the ever-present backdrop of rolling hills and dense forests, Laurel Ridge is a hidden gem that attracts tourists looking for both serenity and adventure.

A Rich History

The town was founded in the early 1800s by pioneering settlers who were drawn to the fertile land and abundant natural resources of the region. Laurel Ridge began as a small logging community, relying on the towering forests that covered the surrounding mountains. The New River, one of the oldest rivers in the world, provided an essential transportation route for lumber, as well as a lifeline for the early settlers.

As the years passed, the town evolved from a logging outpost into a thriving hub for craftspeople and artisans. By the late 19th century, it had developed a reputation for its hand-crafted furniture, textiles, and pottery, all made by skilled locals. The town's proximity to the New River also made it a destination for adventurous souls seeking to kayak, fish, or hike along the riverbanks.

A Place of Renewal

Though the logging industry faded by the early 20th century, Laurel Ridge adapted to the changing times. Its natural beauty and deep connection to West Virginia's mountain heritage drew travelers from near and far, transforming it into a beloved tourist destination. Local shops, run by generations of the same families, line the town square, offering handmade goods, locally sourced foods, and, most of all, warm hospitality.

The town's signature event, the Harvest Festival, began in the 1930s, celebrating the craftsmanship, music, and traditions passed down through the generations. Each year, visitors flock to enjoy live Appalachian music, taste locally grown produce, and witness demonstrations of old-world techniques like blacksmithing and weaving.

A Town of Faith and Community

At the heart of the town stands Laurel Ridge Community Church, a small, white clapboard building with a steeple that reaches toward the sky. Built in 1876, the church has been a pillar of faith and strength for the community for over a century. Its bell, crafted by the town's original blacksmith, has been ringing on Sunday mornings ever since, calling townsfolk to worship and reminding everyone of the enduring values of faith, hope, and love.

The church's history is intertwined with the town's, serving as a refuge in difficult times and a gathering place in moments of joy. Over the years, the church has grown to include an outreach center that supports local families and tourists in need, providing everything from free meals to spiritual counseling. The church's welcoming atmosphere reflects the town's deep sense of unity and service.

A Growing Tourist Haven

Today, Laurel Ridge has grown to a population of around five thousand people, yet it has managed to retain its small-town charm.

Dedication

To the quiet heroes among us—the caregivers, the protectors,
those who show up day after day without fanfare.
Your unwavering strength and boundless love light the darkest paths.

And to those who've built walls around their hearts:
may this story inspire you to slowly dismantle them,
brick by brick, discovering that true shelter exists not in our barriers,
but in the beautiful vulnerability that opens the door to genuine connection,
healing, and love in the most unexpected places.
Love, Tara

Contents

Chapter 1

The crunch of boots on gravel broke the predawn silence as Reed Dunbar crossed his yard toward the barn. His breath formed small clouds in the crisp mountain air, dissipating like the remnants of another restless night. A thin rim of light edged the eastern horizon, silhouetting the Appalachian peaks against a sky gradually shifting from black to deep indigo—darkness giving way to light, a daily transformation Reed still found himself counting on when his personal darkness felt permanent.

The steady burble of the river running past his property provided a constant backdrop, as much a part of his morning routine as the coffee warming his insides.

As he approached the weathered red barn, a soft nickering greeted him from inside. The corners of his mouth lifted slightly. At least someone was happy to see him at six in the morning.

"Coming, Jasper," he called.

The barn door protested with a familiar creak as Reed slid it open. The scent of hay, horses, and leather enveloped him. He flipped the light switch, and warm yellow illumination chased shadows into the corners.

Three curious faces peered over their stall doors. Jasper, his chestnut gelding, was the most vocal, pawing impatiently at the ground.

"Yeah, yeah, I know," Reed said, grabbing a lead rope from its hook. "Nobody's going to starve on my watch."

The morning routine anchored him. It had anchored him for the two years since he'd purchased this remote property outside of Laurel Ridge. There was comfort in the predictability, in knowing exactly what came next. Horses to feed and water, stalls to muck, tack to check.

Reed led Jasper out first, settling him in the small paddock before returning for the other two—Scout, a dappled gray mare, and Tango, a black gelding with a single white sock. Each horse had a distinct personality, and over time, they'd become more than just animals to care for. They were steadying presences, especially on days when the weight on his shoulders felt crushing.

As he worked, Reed's mind drifted to his schedule for the day. A morning patrol through town, afternoon paperwork, and a meeting with Sheriff Baker about the upcoming summer festival security planning at some point during the day. Simple, routine tasks, but necessary ones. Necessary for keeping Laurel Ridge safe.

Keep it together today, Dunbar.

The thought came unbidden as he forked fresh hay into Jasper's stall, his knuckles whitening around the wooden handle. Today marked exactly three years since the Davis tragedy. Three long years since he'd failed to prevent—

A familiar tightness seized his chest. The hay fork trembled in his grip.

Reed closed his eyes briefly, purposefully cutting off the memory. The faces—their faces—threatened to surface, but he'd gotten better at that, at least, stopping the replay before it fully formed. He took a deep breath that caught halfway through, exhaled in a shudder, and opened his eyes.

"Lord," he whispered, leaning his forehead against the rough wooden post, "give me strength for today. Help me serve this town like You would have me do."

It wasn't an elaborate prayer, but it was genuine. Faith had been the one constant that hadn't wavered after that night. If anything, it had deepened, becoming the bedrock beneath his feet when everything else had threatened to crumble.

Reed finished the last of the barn chores and checked his watch. Time to head in. He gave Jasper a final pat as he passed the paddock, then strode toward the cabin to shower and change.

***

Thirty minutes later, Reed navigated his department SUV down the winding gravel drive that connected his ranch to the main road. The vehicle's headlights cut through lingering shadows under the canopy of trees, illuminating the light fog hanging in pockets over the driveway. He'd chosen this property precisely for its isolation. It was close enough to town for his job, but far enough away to provide the solitude and peace he craved.

As he turned onto the two-lane highway that would carry him into Laurel Ridge, the rising sun began painting the mountains in shifting hues of purple and gold. Reed had grown up in these mountains, had known their contours and moods his entire life, yet their beauty never failed to catch his breath. Today, they offered a momentary respite from his thoughts.

The road curved and dipped through dense forests of oak, maple, and pine before beginning its gentle descent toward town. Through gaps in the trees, Reed caught glimpses of the valley below along the river, the morning mist still clinging to the buildings of Laurel Ridge like a protective blanket.

He passed the wooden sign welcoming visitors to "Laurel Ridge, West Virginia—Where Faith and Community Meet," and felt the familiar shift in his chest—the quiet pride of belonging to this place, mingled with the weight of protecting it.

The transition from country to town happened gradually. First came scattered homes set back from the road, then clusters of houses with neat yards and American flags. The speed limit dropped from fifty-five to thirty-five, then to twenty-five as Main Street appeared ahead.

Laurel Ridge looked like it had been plucked from a postcard. Brick-paved streets lined with historic two-story buildings, housing shops and businesses, many dating back to the early 1900s. Wrought-iron lampposts stood at regular intervals, each adorned with hanging baskets of early summer flowers. Even at this early hour, lights glowed in some windows as shopkeepers prepared for the day.

Reed drove slowly down Main Street, eyes scanning habitually for anything out of place. Martha's Diner was already bustling, warm light spilling onto the sidewalk. Several cars were parked outside, locals gathering for breakfast and conversation before work. The General Store's OPEN sign had just been illuminated, and Reed spotted Emma Talbot arranging a display in the window of the general store.

The steeple of Laurel Ridge Community Church rose above the rooftops a few blocks away, its white spire catching the early morning sunlight. The church bell would ring at eight, as it did every morning, a reminder of the faith that formed the town's foundation.

Reed slowed as he passed the town square with its pristine white gazebo and park benches. A community board near the entrance displayed flyers for upcoming events—the summer festival, a bake sale fundraiser for the youth group's mission trip, and a quilting circle at the church.

As he neared the Sheriff's Department, Reed's focus shifted back to the day ahead. The two-story brick building housed both the Sheriff's Department and the town hall, practical but dignified, with its American flag fluttering beside the West Virginia state flag.

Reed parked in his usual spot and grabbed his travel mug of coffee before heading inside. The familiar scent of coffee and paper greeted him as he pushed through the glass doors. Nancy, their dispatcher and administrative assistant, looked up from her computer at the front desk.

"Morning, Deputy Dunbar," she said with a warm smile. "Sheriff's waiting for you."

"Thanks, Nancy. Quiet night?"

"As a church on Monday," she replied, turning back to her computer. "Though Bill Turner called to report Mrs. Henderson's chickens in his yard again."

Reed chuckled. "I'll add that to my list of high-priority cases."

He passed through the small reception area into the main office space, a modest room with four desks, only two of which were currently occupied. Laurel Ridge's entire law enforcement consisted of Sheriff Mark Baker, Reed, and two other deputies who worked rotating shifts. It was enough for the small town, where major crime was rare.

Sheriff Baker looked up from his desk when Reed entered. At thirty-five, Mark had the weathered face of a man who spent time outdoors and the sharp eyes of someone who noticed everything. He'd been Sheriff for seven years, taking over after Reed's grandfather, Bill Dunbar, had retired.

"Reed," he greeted, gesturing to the chair across from his desk. "Coffee before we start the day?"

Reed settled into the seat, placing his travel mug on the desk. "Sounds good. What's on the agenda?"

"Nothing major. Summer festival planning this afternoon. I'd like your input on the crowd control measures, especially with the increase in tourists we're expecting."

"Sure thing," Reed nodded. "I'll patrol as usual this morning, check in on some of the outlying properties. Sam Morgan mentioned seeing some suspicious vehicles up near his place last week."

"Probably just tourists who got turned around," Mark suggested.

"Most likely, but worth checking."

Mark studied Reed for a moment, his expression softening slightly. "You doing okay today?"

The question was casual enough, but Reed knew what Mark was really asking. The Sheriff had been there that night, arriving just after everything had gone wrong. He'd seen the aftermath, had stood by Reed through the investigation that cleared him of any wrongdoing.

"I'm good," Reed said, the words automatic. Then, meeting Mark's knowing gaze, he amended, "Honestly. I'm managing it all really well."

Mark nodded, not pushing further. That was one thing Reed appreciated about the Sheriff—he knew when to ask and when to let things lie.

"Amanda mentioned she ran into you at the grocery store yesterday," Mark said, changing the subject. "Says you're still eating like a bachelor, despite her best efforts."

Reed smiled faintly at the mention of Mark's sister. "She exaggerates. I made a real dinner last night."

"Frozen pizza doesn't count as cooking."

"It had vegetables on it," Reed countered.

Mark laughed, a warm sound that filled the small office. "That's something, I suppose. Though I'm sure your mom would have something to say about it."

"Mom has opinions about everything," Reed said, his tone affectionate.

They spent the next twenty minutes reviewing incident reports, mostly minor issues typical of small-town life. A dispute between neighbors over a fallen tree. A teenager caught spray-painting behind the high school. A fender bender in the grocery store parking lot. Nothing that would make headlines, but each matter was important to someone in Laurel Ridge.

"Tourist season is starting to pick up," Mark said as they finished. "Since the magazine article about 'America's Hidden Mountain Gems,' we've had more out-of-staters than usual. Add it to your patrol to check in on some of the trailheads and picnic shelters along the river."

Reed nodded. "Won't be a problem. I'll swing by a few during my patrol today."

"Good man," Mark said, standing and stretching. "I appreciate your reliability, Reed. This department runs smoother because of it."

The compliment was genuine, and Reed felt a familiar mixture of pride and discomfort. He took his job seriously, perhaps too seriously according to his sister, but he couldn't bring himself to approach it any other way. Not when he knew firsthand the consequences of things going wrong.

"Just doing my job," he said, rising as well.

"You do it well," Mark countered.

"Alright, let's get to work."

Reed gathered his things and headed for the door.

"Reed," Mark called after him. When Reed turned, the Sheriff's expression was serious. "Remember what we talked about? You can't save everyone. None of us can. All we can do is our best."

Reed nodded once, acknowledging the words without fully accepting them.

Outside, Reed paused on the steps of the department building. The town was fully awake now, sunlight washing over the brick buildings and reflecting off storefront windows. People moved along the sidewalks. Mrs. Hanson walking her miniature poodle, Earl Smith unlocking his hardware store, and a group of mothers with strollers heading toward the park.

These were the people he'd sworn to protect. People living ordinary lives in an extraordinary place, trusting that they were safe under his watch. Reed gazed across the town square, taking in the peaceful morning scene, and felt the weight of it all settle more firmly across his shoulders.

Three years ago, he'd failed one family—a young mother and her children who had depended on him doing his job correctly. The official report had cleared him, stated there was nothing more he could have done given the circumstances, but Reed knew differently. There were always signs, always warnings, if you were observant enough to see them.

He wouldn't fail again. Couldn't allow himself that weakness.

As he descended the steps toward his patrol vehicle, Reed offered up another silent prayer—for wisdom, for alertness, and for the ability to see danger before it struck. Laurel Ridge might seem tranquil on the surface, but Reed knew better than most that tragedy could unfold anywhere, even in paradise.

He slid behind the wheel, checking his equipment one last time before starting the engine. The radio crackled to life—Nancy's voice calling in a routine check. As he responded with his position and status, his gaze lingered on a young mother walking her toddler across the square, holding the child's hand.

Reed's fingers tightened on the steering wheel. Whatever the day might bring, Deputy Reed Dunbar would be ready. It was his duty, his calling, and his penance.

And for now, as the patrol vehicle pulled away from the curb and the mother and child disappeared in his rearview mirror, that would have to be enough.

The dashboard clock flipped to 8:30 AM, and the church bells began to toll across Laurel Ridge, marking another day that Reed would spend standing guard against shadows most people in town never even noticed.

Chapter 2

Hannah Gentry jerked awake, her heart racing. The clock beside her bed read 7:42—eighteen minutes before her alarm was set to go off. She blinked at the red digits, momentarily disoriented, the remnants of an unsettling dream slipping away like water through her fingers.

Something had awakened her. A sound? A feeling?

The house was quiet. Too quiet. Usually, by this time, she could hear her mother's television playing softly from the adjacent bedroom. The morning news was Peggy's ritual, her way of maintaining a connection to the outside world.

Hannah sat up, pushing tangled chestnut colored hair from her face.

"Mom?" she called, her voice scratchy with sleep.

No response.

A trickle of uneasiness slid down her spine. Hannah swung her legs over the side of the bed, her bare feet connecting with the cool hardwood floor. The sensation anchored her to reality, dispelling the last foggy remnants of sleep.

"Mom?" she called again, louder this time.

She crossed to her bedroom door in three quick strides, pausing only to grab her faded blue robe from its hook. The hallway was dim, morning light barely filtering through the closed blinds in the living room beyond.

"Mom, do you need help?"

Hannah moved quicker now, tying her robe as she went. The house was small, the distance from her bedroom to her mother's no more than fifteen feet, but this morning it felt endless.

Peggy's door stood slightly ajar. Hannah pushed it open, the familiar smell of her mother's favorite coconut lotion wafting out to greet her.

"Mom, are you—"

The words died in her throat.

Peggy Gentry lay unnaturally still in her bed, her lined face ashen against the white pillowcase. Her right arm dangled over the edge of the mattress, fingers slightly curled, motionless.

The television was off. The remote control lay on the floor, as if it had fallen from her hand.

"Mom?" Hannah whispered, panic climbing up her throat like a living thing.

She rushed to the bedside, grasping her mother's limp hand. It was cool to the touch, but not cold. Not the terrible coldness Hannah remembered from her father's hand at the hospital after the accident.

"Mom!" Hannah's voice rose sharply as she gently shook her mother's shoulder. "Mom, wake up!"

Peggy's head lolled slightly, but her eyes remained closed. Hannah placed trembling fingers against her mother's neck, searching for a pulse, the way she'd learned in a first aid course years ago.

There it was, faint but present, a flutter beneath the skin.

Relief surged through Hannah for one precious second before fear crashed back, stronger than before. Peggy was alive, but unresponsive. Something was terribly wrong.

Hannah reached for the bedside phone with shaking hands, knocking over a glass of water in the process. Water splashed across the nightstand and dripped onto the floor, but Hannah barely noticed.

Her fingers fumbled over the keypad, missing the first time. She took a deep breath, forced herself to slow down, and dialed.

"9-1-1, what's your emergency?" The dispatcher's voice was calm, professional.

"My mother—" Hannah's voice broke. She swallowed hard. "My mother won't wake up. She's breathing, but I can't get her to respond."

"I understand. What's your address?"

"128 Elm Street, Laurel Ridge." Hannah recited automatically, her eyes never leaving Peggy's face. "Please hurry."

"Help is on the way. Can you tell me your mother's name and age?"

"Peggy Gentry. She's forty-eight." Hannah moved closer to the bed, cradling the phone between her ear and shoulder as she checked her mother's breathing again. "She has mobility issues. She's been in a wheelchair since a car accident ten years ago."

"Does she have any medical conditions?"

Hannah rattled off the list she knew by heart—hypertension, anxiety, PTSD, mild arthritis, the lingering effects of the spinal injury that had left her paralyzed from the waist down. "But she's been stable. This isn't... this has never happened before."

"You're doing great," the dispatcher assured her. "Paramedics have been dispatched and are on their way. I need you to stay on the line with me until they arrive."

Hannah nodded, then realized the woman couldn't see her. "Yes, I'll stay."

"Can you check if your mother is breathing regularly?"

Hannah leaned closer, watching the shallow rise and fall of Peggy's chest. "Yes, she's breathing, but it seems... I don't know, weaker than normal?"

"Is there any chance she could have fallen or hit her head?"

"No, she can't get out of bed by herself." Hannah's voice caught. The words were a painful reminder of her mother's dependence, of the daily reality they'd lived for ten years.

"What about medications? Did she take anything unusual last night or this morning?"

"Just her regular prescriptions last night. I give them to her myself, but she hasn't had her meds this morning yet."

The dispatcher continued asking questions, but Hannah found it increasingly difficult to focus. Her mind kept returning to her father, to the awful day when their lives had changed forever. She'd been eighteen, the summer between high school graduation and college, eager to begin her photography program at the University of Pittsburgh. The three of them had been driving back from a photography exhibit in Charleston, her father singing off-key to some old country song, her mother laughing. The memory of headlights suddenly blinding through the windshield still haunted her dreams—the drunk driver who crossed the center line and stole their future in a screech of metal and shattered glass.

Hannah had walked away with minor scrapes and bruises. Her father had been killed instantly. And Peggy, her vibrant, active mother, had awakened in the hospital to the news that she would never walk again.

"Miss Gentry? Are you still there?"

The dispatcher's voice snapped Hannah back to the present crisis.

"Yes, sorry, I'm here."

"The ambulance is about three minutes away. Can you unlock your front door so they can enter when they arrive?"

"Yes, I'll do that now." Hannah hesitated, not wanting to leave her mother's side.

"It's okay," the dispatcher said, as if reading her thoughts. "Just go quickly and come right back."

Hannah hurried to the front door, her bare feet slapping against the hardwood. She unlocked the deadbolt and the doorknob, then rushed back to her mother's room, the cordless phone still clutched in her hand.

"I'm back," she told the dispatcher, breathless. "The door's unlocked."

"Good. Now, is there anyone else home with you?"

"No, it's just me and Mom."

Hannah reached for her mother's hand again, squeezing it gently. "Mom, if you can hear me, help is coming. Please wake up. Please."

There was no response, not even a flicker of the eyelids.

Hannah's chest tightened, each breath becoming shorter and more difficult. Her fingernails dug half-moons into her palms. "What's taking them so long?" she asked the dispatcher, her voice rising to a pitch she barely recognized as her own.

"They're very close. Just stay calm and keep talking to your mother."

Hannah nodded again, pointlessly. "Mom," she said, leaning close to Peggy's ear. "The ambulance is almost here. You're going to be okay. You have to be okay."

Her voice broke on the last word. Hannah pressed her forehead against her mother's shoulder, her eyes burning with unshed tears. "Please, Mom. I can't lose you too."

In the distance, she heard the wail of a siren. The sound grew steadily louder until it seemed to fill the entire house, drowning out the thundering of Hannah's heart.

"They've arrived," the dispatcher said. "I'm going to stay on the line until they're inside with you."

Hannah nodded, her throat too tight for words. She heard car doors slamming, then quick footsteps on the front porch. A sharp knock at the door was immediately followed by a male voice calling, "Emergency services!"

"In here!" Hannah shouted, finally finding her voice. "Second bedroom on the right!"

The footsteps approached rapidly. A moment later, two emergency medical technicians appeared in the doorway, equipment bags in hand. Behind them, filling the doorway with his tall, broad-shouldered presence, was a uniformed officer.

Hannah barely registered the paramedics as they moved efficiently to Peggy's bedside, asking questions she answered automatically. Her attention was caught by the officer—by the calm authority he radiated, a stark contrast to the chaos she felt inside.

He was tall, with dark brown hair cut short and professional. His green eyes, alert and observant, scanned the room before settling on her. There was something steadying about his presence, like a rock in a stormy sea. But there was something else too, a shadow of understanding in his eyes that suggested he knew what it was to face the unexpected. Not sympathy exactly, but recognition.

"Ma'am," he said, his voice deep and measured. "I'm Deputy Reed Dunbar. Can you tell me what happened?"

Hannah realized she was still clutching the phone, the dispatcher forgotten on the other end. She murmured a quick "Thank you" before hanging up, then turned to the deputy.

"I—I found her like this when I woke up," she said, gesturing helplessly toward her mother. "She won't wake up, but she's breathing. I don't understand what's happening."

Deputy Dunbar nodded, his expression attentive. Professional, rather than pitying.

"The paramedics will take good care of her," he assured her. "Can I get you anything? Is there someone we should call?"

Hannah shook her head, hugging her arms around herself. She was suddenly acutely aware of her disheveled appearance. Her unwashed hair hung limp against her shoulders, dark circles surely shadowed her eyes, and her faded pajama pants visible beneath her robe bore a small coffee stain from yesterday. Her bare feet, with chipped lavender polish on her toenails. She must look like a complete mess.

Why she should care about that at a moment like this was beyond her, but the thought flitted through her mind, nonetheless.

"No, there's no one. It's just me and my mom." She managed a shaky breath. "I should... I should get dressed if they're taking her to the hospital."

Deputy Dunbar nodded. "There's time for that. They'll need to stabilize her first."

One of the paramedics, a woman with short blonde hair and efficient movements, was checking Peggy's vital signs while her partner prepared what looked like an IV bag.

"Blood pressure's 80 over 40, pulse is weak and rapid," she reported. "Respiratory rate slightly depressed. Skin is cool and clammy." She turned to Hannah. "Has your mother been eating and drinking normally?"

Hannah frowned, thinking back. "She didn't have much appetite yesterday, but I thought she was just tired. She drank some water before bed."

"Any vomiting or diarrhea?"

"No, nothing like that."

The paramedic nodded, continuing her assessment. "Pupils equal and reactive to light. No obvious signs of head trauma."

Her partner, a middle-aged man with salt-and-pepper hair, was now gently pressing on Peggy's abdomen. "No signs of rigidity or guarding," he noted.

Hannah watched, feeling utterly helpless, as these strangers touched and examined her mother. She'd been Peggy's only caregiver for years, had learned to anticipate her needs, had developed routines and systems to make their life work. And now, in an instant, control had been wrenched from her hands.

"What's wrong with her?" she asked. "Is it a stroke?"

The female paramedic glanced up. "We're not seeing typical stroke symptoms, but we'll need to get her to the medical center for proper tests. Has she been diagnosed with diabetes?"

Hannah blinked, surprised. "No."

"Her glucose level is critically low," the paramedic said, checking a reading from a small device. "We're going to start an IV with dextrose solution right away. This should help bring her around quickly, if that's the main issue."

The male paramedic had already prepared the IV line. Hannah watched, fascinated despite her fear, as he skillfully inserted the needle into a vein in Peggy's arm. Within moments, clear fluid was flowing through the tubing into her mother's bloodstream.

Hannah felt a presence at her side and turned to find Deputy Dunbar.

"They know what they're doing," he said quietly, not looking at her directly. "Holly, my sister, is a nurse at Laurel Ridge Medical. Best medical team in three counties, she always says."

The casual information, offered simply as reassurance, made Hannah feel marginally better.

"Thank you," she said. "For coming, I mean. I didn't expect—"

"Standard procedure," he replied. "First responders include law enforcement for medical emergencies. We're often closer than the ambulance."

Before Hannah could respond, Peggy made a soft moaning sound. Hannah's attention snapped back to her mother, heart leaping with hope.

"Mom? Mom, can you hear me?"

Peggy's eyelids fluttered, then slowly opened. Her gaze was unfocused at first, confusion evident as she took in the strangers surrounding her bed.

"Hannah?" she called, voice weak but unmistakable.

Relief crashed through Hannah like a physical force. She pushed past the paramedics to grasp her mother's hand.

"I'm here, Mom. You gave me quite a scare."

Peggy blinked several times, her gaze gradually clearing. "What happened? Who are these people?"

"You wouldn't wake up," Hannah explained, tears spilling down her cheeks. "I called an ambulance. They're helping you."

The female paramedic moved closer. "Mrs. Gentry, I'm Sarah with Laurel Ridge Emergency Services. How are you feeling right now?"

Peggy frowned slightly. "Tired. Dizzy. My mouth is so dry."

"That's normal with low blood sugar," Sarah explained gently. "We've started an IV to help with that, but we need to take you to the hospital for a full evaluation."

Fear flashed across Peggy's face. "Hospital? No, I don't need—"

"Mom," Hannah interrupted firmly. "You were unconscious. We need to find out why. Please."

Peggy's resistance visibly wavered at the worry in Hannah's voice. She sighed, a sound of resignation that Hannah knew well. "Fine. But I'll need my things."

Hannah almost laughed with relief. If her mother was concerned about her personal items, she couldn't be too badly off.

"I'll pack a bag," she promised.

The next several minutes passed in a blur of activity. The paramedics continued monitoring Peggy's vital signs, which were already improving with the IV fluids. Hannah rushed around the house, throwing together an overnight bag with her mother's essentials—medication, toiletries, a nightgown, a change of clothes. She barely registered that Deputy Dunbar had stepped outside, giving them privacy but remaining close by.

When she returned to the bedroom, the paramedics were preparing to transfer Peggy to a stretcher.

Hannah watched anxiously as they carefully lifted her mother onto the stretcher, securing her with straps. Peggy looked small and vulnerable, her silver-streaked hair splayed against the white sheet.

"Hannah," Peggy called, reaching out a hand. "My sweater. The blue one."

"I packed it, Mom," Hannah assured her, squeezing her hand. "And your moisturizer, and the book you're reading. Everything you need."

Peggy nodded. She still looked pale, but nowhere near as terrifying as she had when Hannah first found her.

As the paramedics prepared to move, Hannah suddenly remembered her state of undress. "Wait, I need to change quickly."

"Take your time," Sarah said kindly. "We need to finalize some paperwork anyway, and your mother is stable now."

Hannah hurried to her bedroom, throwing on the first things she found—jeans, a faded green t-shirt, and sneakers. She dragged a brush through her tangled hair and splashed water on her face, not bothering with makeup. Her reflection in the bathroom mirror looked back at her with wide, frightened eyes, but she didn't have time to dwell on it.

When she returned, the paramedics were wheeling Peggy through the living room toward the front door. Deputy Dunbar was holding the door open, his expression unreadable.

"I'll follow in my car," Hannah told the paramedics, grabbing her purse and her mother's overnight bag.

Laurel Ridge Community Hospital was only minutes away, one of the small mercies of living in a tourist town.

Outside, a small crowd of neighbors had gathered at the edge of the property, watching with concerned expressions. Hannah recognized Mrs. Wilson from next door and the Peterson family from across the street.

As the paramedics loaded Peggy into the ambulance, Hannah felt a presence beside her.

"Do you need someone to drive you?" Deputy Dunbar asked. "You've had a shock."

Hannah blinked, surprised by the offer. "No, I'm fine. Thank you, though."

He nodded, not pressing the issue. His radio crackled, and he turned slightly away to respond with a brief code. When he turned back, his expression remained professional, but his eyes had softened almost imperceptibly. "The hospital is—"

"I know where it is," Hannah interrupted, then winced at her abruptness. "Sorry. I just—this is a lot."

"Of course," he said simply. "I'll follow and make sure you both arrive safely."

Hannah wanted to protest that it wasn't necessary, but she found the words stuck in her throat. There was something reassuring about the deputy's calm presence, about knowing someone was watching out for them, however temporarily.

"Thank you," she said instead.

The female paramedic approached. "We're ready to go. You can ride in the ambulance if you prefer."

Hannah shook her head. "I'll follow in my car."

The paramedic nodded. "We'll see you there."

As the ambulance doors closed on her mother, Hannah felt a sudden rush of fear. What if Peggy took a turn for the worse on the way to the hospital? What if these were the last moments they had together?

"Mom's going to be okay," she whispered to herself. "Please, God, let her be okay."

It was the first real prayer she'd offered in months—perhaps years. Her faith, once a comfort, had become fragile under the weight of her burdens, a distant memory rather than a daily reality.

"Miss Gentry?" Deputy Dunbar's voice broke through her thoughts. "The ambulance is leaving."

Hannah nodded, hurrying toward her aging Toyota Corolla parked in the driveway. Her hands trembled as she fumbled with the keys.

Hannah started her car, hands gripping the steering wheel tightly as she prepared to follow the ambulance carrying her mother. The wail of the siren pierced the quiet morning as the emergency vehicle drove away.

"Please be okay," Hannah whispered, knuckles white against the steering wheel. In her rearview mirror, the deputy's patrol vehicle followed steadily, its presence inexplicably reassuring. Ahead, the ambulance carried her mother toward whatever came next, the siren's wail cutting through the peaceful morning like a reminder that life could change in a heartbeat.

Chapter 3

The antiseptic smell hit Hannah the moment the sliding doors of Laurel Ridge Community Hospital opened, sharp and astringent, scraping against her senses like sandpaper. Her stomach clenched as memories flooded back. The same chemical scent had permeated her clothes, her hair, even her dreams during those endless weeks after the accident, when she'd practically lived at the hospital in the next county over while her mother underwent surgeries and began the painful adjustment to her new reality. She'd always hated that smell.

She paused, swallowing hard against the wave of nausea that always accompanied hospital visits, and forced herself to breathe through her mouth. The fluorescent lights hummed overhead, casting everyone beneath them in the same unflattering, slightly greenish pallor that made even the healthy look ill.

The small waiting area was mercifully quiet this morning. An elderly man with gnarled worker's hands thumbed through a dog-eared fishing magazine, his weathered face a topographical map of Appalachian life. Across from him, a young mother cradled a sleeping toddler, dark circles beneath her eyes telling a familiar story of sleep-less nights and endless worry. Their presence, strangers united in the universal language of waiting, somehow made the sterile room feel less lonely. Hannah approached the reception desk, where a middle-aged woman with kind eyes looked up expectantly.

"My mother was just brought in by ambulance. Peggy Gentry," Hannah explained, trying to keep her voice steady.

The receptionist nodded. "Yes. They're getting her settled now." She pushed a clipboard across the counter. "If you could fill these out while you wait—medical history, insurance information, and that sort of thing."

Hannah accepted the clipboard and pen with a resigned nod. Paperwork. Always more paperwork. She'd become an expert at navigating medical bureaucracy over the years, and could recite her mother's medical history in her sleep.

She settled into a hard plastic chair and began the familiar process of documenting Peggy's life through checkboxes and blank lines. Date of birth. Previous hospitalizations. Current medications. Known allergies. Hannah filled in each section meticulously.

The sliding doors whooshed open again, and Hannah glanced up to see Deputy Dunbar entering, his tall frame somehow making the modest waiting room seem smaller. Their eyes met briefly before he approached the reception desk, speaking in low tones with the woman there. Hannah couldn't make out the words. She'd expected him to simply drive away once they reached the hospital—duty fulfilled, crisis averted.

Hannah returned her attention to the forms, but found it difficult to concentrate with the deputy's presence. There was something about him, not just the authority of the uniform, but a quiet intensity he carried like a physical weight.

"Miss Gentry?"

Hannah looked up to find a nurse standing before her, clipboard in hand. The woman was in her early thirties, with warm brown eyes and dark hair pulled back in a practical ponytail. Her scrubs were patterned with cheerful butterflies, a small bright spot in the sterile environment.

"I'm Nurse Holly Dunbar," she said with a gentle smile. "I'm overseeing your mother's care."

Dunbar. The connection clicked immediately. A relative of Officer Dunbar's possibly? Hannah glanced toward the reception area, but the deputy had disappeared.

"How is she?" Hannah asked, setting aside the half-completed forms.

"Stable," Nurse Dunbar replied. "We're running some tests, but she's awake and alert."

Hannah exhaled, the tension easing from her shoulders. "Can I see her?"

"In a few minutes. Dr. Roberts wants to complete his initial assessment. But I promise she's comfortable," Holly assured her. "She mentioned you might be worried, so I wanted to come update you right away."

"Thank you," Hannah said, genuinely touched by the consideration. "Did she say... does she need anything? I brought her overnight bag, but—"

"She's fine for now," Holly interrupted gently. "She seemed most concerned about you, actually. Wanted to make sure you'd eaten breakfast."

A surprised laugh escaped Hannah. "That's Mom. Barely conscious, but still mothering."

Holly smiled, the expression warming her entire face. "That's what mothers do, isn't it? They never stop worrying, no matter what."

She gestured to the forms in Hannah's lap. "How are those coming? Anything I can help with?"

Hannah glanced down. "I've got most of it. Just trying to remember the dates of her last few doctor visits."

"No rush. We may be able to pull up the dates in our system." Holly checked her watch. "I need to get back, but I'll come find you as soon as you can see your mother."

"Thank you," Hannah said again, the words feeling inadequate.

As Holly turned to leave, Hannah impulsively called after her. "The deputy...is he still here?"

Holly glanced back. "Reed? He's my brother. He had to check in at the station, but knowing him, he'll be back to follow up, I'm sure."

Hannah nodded, not entirely sure why she'd asked.

As Holly disappeared through the swinging doors leading to the treatment area, Hannah returned to the forms with renewed focus.

The next hour crawled by. Hannah completed the paperwork and returned it to the receptionist, then paced the small waiting area, too restless to sit. She checked her phone, discovered three missed text messages from Emma, her friend who ran the General Store in town.

Heard sirens this morning. Someone in town said an ambulance was at your house. Is everything OK?

Hannah? Call me when you can.

At the store all day. Let me know if you need anything.

Hannah typed a quick reply: *At the hospital with Mom. She's stable. Will call later.*

She'd barely slipped the phone back into her pocket when the swinging doors opened and Holly reappeared.

"You can come back now," she said with a smile. "Your mother's asking for you."

Hannah followed Holly through a series of short hallways. Laurel Ridge Community Hospital was a modest facility. Just one floor with an emergency department, a small wing of patient rooms, and basic diagnostic equipment. Serious cases were typically transferred to the larger hospital in Beckley, forty minutes away, but for the community's everyday health needs and minor emergencies, it was a blessing to have care so close.

"She's in here," Holly said, stopping outside a room. "Dr. Roberts will be by shortly to discuss her condition."

Hannah nodded her thanks and stepped into the room, bracing herself for the sight of her mother in a hospital bed. Despite the preparation, her heart still clenched at the image of Peggy looking small and pale against the white sheets, an IV line snaking from her arm to a bag of clear fluid hanging beside the bed.

"Hannah," Peggy said, relief evident in her voice. "There you are, thank goodness. These white coats keep patting my hand and talking about 'waiting for my daughter' like I've suddenly lost my mental faculties along with my blood sugar."

Hannah crossed quickly to the bedside, setting down the overnight bag and taking her mother's free hand. "That's because they know who really runs the show," she said, forcing a light tone. "How are you feeling?"

"Ridiculous," Peggy declared, though her voice lacked its usual vigor. "All this fuss over a fainting spell?"

"You were unconscious, Mom," Hannah corrected, the fear of those moments still too raw to dismiss. "I couldn't wake you up."

Peggy's expression softened. "I'm sorry I frightened you, dear. But I'm fine now. Just tired."

Hannah studied her mother's face. The lines etched around her eyes and mouth; the silver threading through her dark brown hair.

"What did they tell you?" Hannah asked.

"Something about blood sugar." Peggy waved her hand dismissively. "They took blood samples. I guess they ran several tests, completely unnecessary, if you ask me."

Before Hannah could respond, there was a soft knock at the door. A man in his early thirties with sandy brown hair and wire-rimmed glasses entered, a tablet computer in his hands.

"Mrs. Gentry, Miss Gentry," he greeted them with a nod. "I'm Dr. Tucker Roberts. I've been reviewing your mother's test results."

Hannah turned to face him fully, still holding her mother's hand. "What's going on with her? The paramedics mentioned something about low blood sugar."

Dr. Roberts nodded, his expression compassionate but direct. "Your mother experienced a severe hypoglycemic episode—dangerously low blood sugar. Based on the initial tests, I'm diagnosing her with type 2 diabetes."

Diabetes.

The word struck Hannah like a physical blow. The word hung in the air between them, heavy with implications Hannah immediately understood. Another medication to track. Another set of doctor's appointments to schedule around her work hours. Another expense their threadbare insurance might fight covering. Another daily reminder of how fragile their carefully constructed life really was.

"Diabetes?" Peggy's voice wavered slightly. "That can't be right. Wouldn't I have noticed symptoms?"

"Not necessarily," Dr. Roberts explained, moving closer to the bed. "Type 2 diabetes can develop gradually, with symptoms so subtle they're easy to miss, especially if you're already managing other health issues."

"What kind of symptoms?" Hannah asked, mentally reviewing the past few weeks, searching for signs she might have overlooked.

"Increased thirst, frequent urination, fatigue, blurred vision," the doctor listed.

Hannah's stomach tightened with guilt. Her mother had complained of being unusually tired lately. Hannah had assumed it was related to a recent medication adjustment for her blood pressure.

"I should have realized something was wrong," she murmured.

Dr. Roberts shook his head. "This isn't about missed signs, Miss Gentry. Your quick action this morning likely prevented a much more serious outcome. You did everything right."

Hannah nodded automatically, but the reassurance barely penetrated her self-recrimination.

"So what happens now?" Peggy asked, her voice steadier as she processed the diagnosis.

"We'll keep you overnight for observation and to stabilize your blood sugar levels," Dr. Roberts explained. "Tomorrow, we'll start education on diabetes management—monitoring blood glucose, medication, dietary changes."

Hannah's mind was already racing ahead to the practical implications—additional medical costs, dietary restrictions to implement, another layer of daily health monitoring. One more complication in their already precarious balance.

The weight of responsibility settled across her shoulders like a familiar, heavy coat she never quite took off. Each new diagnosis, each additional medication, they were stones added to pockets already full, threatening to pull her under completely.

"She'll need insulin, correct?" she asked.

"Not initially," Dr. Roberts replied. "We'll start with oral medication, combined with diet and exercise modifications. With proper management, many Type 2 diabetes patients can control their condition without insulin injections."

Hannah nodded, mentally adding "research diabetes management" to her ever-growing to-do list.

"I'll check in on you later today," Dr. Roberts continued, "and our diabetes educator will visit tomorrow morning. In the meantime, Nurse Dunbar will be overseeing your care." He offered a reassuring smile. "Try not to worry too much. This is manageable."

After he left, Hannah sank into the chair beside the bed.

"Well," Peggy said finally, her voice overly bright, "another adventure for us, hmm?"

The forced cheerfulness broke Hannah's heart a little. It was the same tone Peggy had used in the early days after the accident, when she was trying so hard to be brave, for Hannah's sake.

"We'll figure it out, Mom," Hannah promised. "We always do."

Peggy squeezed her hand. "I know, sweetheart. I just hate to be more trouble."

"You're no trouble," Hannah insisted fiercely. "Never think that."

A nurse's aide appeared with a lunch tray, momentarily interrupting their conversation. After helping her mother get situated with the meal, Hannah checked her watch.

"I should call Martha," she said, realizing she'd completely forgotten about her shift at the diner. "Let her know I won't make it in today."

"Of course," Peggy nodded.

In the quiet corridor outside, Hannah leaned against the wall as she punched in the diner's number.

"Martha's Diner, where every day starts with a smile!" The familiar greeting carried through the line, along with the clatter of plates and murmur of the lunchtime crowd.

"Martha, it's Hannah."

"Hannah!" Martha's warm voice shifted immediately to concern, the background noise fading as she presumably moved away from the counter. "Lord have mercy, I've been worried sick! Hal Jenkins came in babbling about an ambulance at your place this morning. Said he saw Deputy Dunbar there too. What's happened?"

"It's mom. She's stable. But I'm at the hospital with her. They've diagnosed her with diabetes."

"Oh, honey." Martha's sympathy flowed warmly and genuinely through the phone. "My sister's boy has that. Lots to manage, but it's not like it was in the old days. They've got good medicines now." A brief pause. "Don't you worry about your shift. Kylie can cover for you today, and we'll figure out tomorrow if needed."

"Are you sure? I know—"

"Hannah Jean Gentry," Martha cut her off with firm affection, "you hush that nonsense right now. Your mama needs you more than my customers need your coffee refills, skilled as they may be."

A surprised laugh escaped Hannah's throat, feeling foreign after the morning's tension. "Thank you. I'll keep you posted."

"You do that. And Hannah? Let us know if you need anything. Anything at all."

"I will," Hannah promised, though they both knew she wouldn't. She'd never been good at asking for help.

After ending the call, Hannah remained in the hallway, overwhelmed by the morning's events. The hospital's background sounds washed over her. The soft beeping of machines, the squeak of rubber-soled shoes on linoleum, the murmur of voices from the nurses' station. It was barely noon, but she felt as though she'd lived a lifetime since waking to the terrifying silence in her mother's room.

Hannah closed her eyes, leaning her head back against the wall. The adrenaline that had carried her through the morning was ebbing, leaving exhaustion in its wake. She needed to pull herself together, be strong for her mother, and start planning for what came next.

"Miss Gentry?"

Hannah's eyes snapped open to find Deputy Dunbar standing a few feet away.

"Deputy," she acknowledged, straightening from the wall.

"I wanted to follow up," he said. "Make sure everything is alright."

"That's... very thorough of you."

A flicker of something, perhaps amusement, crossed his face before it settled back into professional lines. "Part of the job. How's your mother?"

"Stable," Hannah replied. "They've diagnosed her with diabetes. She'll be staying overnight."

He nodded, absorbing the information. "She's in good hands here."

"Your sister seems very kind," Hannah said.

"She is," Reed agreed, a hint of pride softening his features. "Holly's always had a gift for helping people."

The simple statement revealed more about Deputy Dunbar than anything he'd said directly. There was genuine affection in his voice when he spoke of his sister, a glimpse of the man beneath the professional exterior.

Hannah was acutely aware of her disheveled appearance, her hastily thrown on clothes, her hair pulled back in a messy ponytail, and the shadows of worry were likely visible under her eyes.

"I should get back to my mother," she said.

Reed nodded. "Of course. But before you go—" He hesitated, seeming to choose his words carefully. "If you need anything while your mother's in the hospital, the department can help. Checking on your house, picking up anything you might need."

The offer surprised her. "That's not necessary. I can manage."

"I'm sure you can. But the offer stands."

Hannah studied him, trying to reconcile this thoughtful gesture with the reserved deputy who had arrived at her door this morning.

"Thank you. That's... kind of you."

He nodded once, a brief dip of his head. "I'll let you get back to your mother."

"Deputy Dunbar?"

He paused, looking back at her with those steady green eyes.

"Thank you for being there this morning. For staying with me. It helped."

Something in his expression shifted, a slight softening around the eyes. "You did all the hard parts, Miss Gentry. I just showed up."

Before she could respond, he continued down the corridor, his tall figure retreating until he disappeared around a corner. Hannah stood for a moment, watching the empty space where he had been, puzzling over the curious mix of professional distance and personal thoughtfulness he seemed to embody.

With a small shake of her head, she returned to her mother's room.

Peggy had finished her lunch and was attempting to reach the television remote on the bedside table.

"Here, let me," Hannah said, crossing quickly to hand her the remote. "How was lunch?"

"Bland," Peggy declared, making a face. "Apparently diabetes means everything tastes like cardboard."

Hannah smiled. "I'm sure we can figure out ways to make diabetic-friendly food taste better once we're home."

"Home," Peggy repeated wistfully. "I want to go home now, Hannah."

"Tomorrow, mom."

Peggy sighed, the sound heavy with resignation. "A night in a hospital bed. Isn't that something to look forward to?"

Hannah perched on the edge of the bed, careful not to disturb the IV line. "It's just one night. And it's important to make sure your blood sugar is stable before we go home."

Peggy nodded, though her expression remained discontented. She had always hated hospitals, even before the accident that had made them a regular part of their lives. "I suppose you're right. You should go home and get some rest. You look exhausted."

"I'm fine," Hannah assured her automatically. "I want to stay with you."

"At least go get something to eat," Peggy urged. "I know you didn't have breakfast."

Hannah hesitated. She was hungry. Starving, actually, now that she thought about it, but she hated to leave her mother alone.

"I've come to check Mrs. Gentry's vitals and change her IV bag," Holly said as she walked into the room. "Miss Gentry, I agree with you mom, go get something to eat. The cafeteria's serving chicken pot pie today, and it's actually pretty good."

Hannah glanced between Holly and her mother, feeling gently but firmly outmaneuvered. "Alright," she conceded. "I'll be back soon, Mom."

"Take your time," Peggy said. "Nurse Dunbar and I will have a nice chat while you're gone."

Holly winked at Hannah. "We'll be just fine. The cafeteria is down the hall to the left, then follow the signs."

With a final glance at her mother, looking small but oddly content with Holly fussing over her IV, Hannah stepped into the hallway. Her stomach growled audibly. Food first, then she could face whatever came next. The diabetes education, the medication schedules, the inevitable battles with insurance. One step, then another. It was the only way to keep moving forward when the road ahead seemed impossibly long.

Chapter 4

The lunch rush hit Martha's Diner like a summer storm. Sudden, intense, and all-consuming. One minute, Hannah had been refilling salt shakers; the next, every table was full, order tickets fluttering from the kitchen carousel like autumn leaves. Now she balanced three plates along her left arm while gripping a coffeepot in her right hand, weaving between tables with the practiced grace of a dancer who'd learned her steps through years of repetition rather than formal training. Her feet ached inside her sensible shoes, her lower back throbbed where it had never quite healed right after a high school soccer injury. The headache that had started an hour ago pulsed behind her eyes with each beat of her heart.

"Denver omelet with hash browns," she announced, setting the first plate down before a gray-haired man in overalls. "BLT with extra bacon." The second plate found its home. "And chicken salad on wheat for you, Mrs. Peterson."

"Thank you, dear," Mrs. Peterson said, patting Hannah's arm. "How's your mother doing?"

Hannah managed a smile while refilling the woman's coffee cup. "Better every day. Learning to manage the diabetes."

"Tell her the prayer circle at church is keeping her in our prayers."

"I will," Hannah promised, already turning toward the counter where three more orders waited.

It had been five days since Peggy's emergency hospitalization, four days since bringing her home with a new diagnosis and a stack of pamphlets about diabetes management. Thirty-six hours since Hannah had gotten more than four hours of sleep at a stretch. But bills didn't pay themselves, so here she was.

"Order up!" Martha's voice carried from the kitchen pass-through window. "Hannah, honey, when you get a moment, could you refill the napkin dispensers on the counter?"

"On it," Hannah called back, grabbing an empty tray to collect used dishes from a recently vacated booth.

The diner hummed with conversation and the clinking of silverware against plates. Country music played softly from the jukebox in the corner, barely audible beneath the tide of human voices. The scent of freshly brewed coffee mingled with frying bacon and Martha's apple pies cooling on the rack.

Hannah stacked dirty plates on her tray, wiping down the Formica tabletop with practiced efficiency. As she worked, her mind ran through calculations—the hospital co-pay, the new medications, the glucose monitor, test strips, and the specialized foods Dr. Roberts had recommended. Each item added to the growing mountain of expenses that already included their normal bills and everyday necessities.

"You're a million miles away," a familiar voice observed.

Hannah looked up to find Emma Talbot sliding into the recently cleaned booth, her bright smile a welcome sight. Emma's curly blonde hair was pulled into a messy bun, and her blue eyes sparkled with their usual warmth.

"Just thinking," Hannah said, tucking a loose strand of hair behind her ear.

"Dangerous pastime," Emma teased. "Got time for a quick break? I brought reinforcements." She held up a brown paper bag with the General Store logo.

Hannah glanced toward the counter, where Martha caught her eye and nodded, silently granting permission for a short break.

"Five minutes," Hannah agreed, setting her tray aside.

Emma reached into the bag and pulled out two cans of iced tea and a container of homemade cookies. "Sustenance," she declared, pushing a can toward Hannah. "You look tired."

Hannah cracked open the tea, the hiss of carbonation oddly satisfying. "I haven't been sleeping well."

"How's Peggy adjusting?"

Hannah took a long swallow of tea before answering. "About as well as you'd expect. She hates the diet restrictions, hates the finger pricks, and hates taking more pills. But she's following the program."

"And how are you adjusting?" Emma asked, her tone gentle but direct.

Hannah shrugged, reaching for a cookie. "I'm fine."

"That's what you always say, even when you're running on fumes and caffeine." Emma nudged the cookie container closer. "Seriously, Han. You look exhausted."

"Thanks a lot," Hannah huffed, though there was no real irritation behind it.

"You know what I mean. Have you had any time for yourself since this happened?"

Hannah shook her head. Between hospital visits, learning diabetes management, and adjusting Peggy's care routine, there had been no time for personal needs. Not that there had been much time before, but now even those stolen moments seemed like a distant luxury.

"I'm managing. The hospital bills are going to be tight, but Martha's giving me extra shifts, and—"

"And you're going to work yourself into the ground," Emma interrupted. "What about the medical assistance programs Holly Dunbar mentioned? Have you looked into those?"

Hannah shifted uncomfortably. "Not yet. I've been busy, and honestly, we probably don't qualify. We're not poor enough for full assistance, but not well-off enough to absorb these new costs easily. It's that frustrating middle ground."

Emma nodded sympathetically. "Still worth checking into. Holly knows the system better than most."

The bell above the diner door jangled, cutting through the ambient chatter. Hannah turned automatically, her waitress instincts kicking in even before her conscious mind registered the sound. The afternoon sunlight silhouetted two broad-shouldered figures in the doorway before they stepped inside, revealing Deputy Reed Dunbar and Sheriff Mark Baker. Hannah's stomach did an unexpected flip. She smoothed her apron with suddenly damp palms, aware of Emma's curious gaze on her face.

"Your fan club's here," Emma murmured.

"What? No, they're just—" Hannah broke off, flustered. "They're probably just here for lunch."

Emma smirked. "Uh-huh. And Deputy Tall, Dark, and Serious hasn't asked about you at the General Store twice this week."

"He has not," Hannah protested, then hesitated at Emma's expression. "Has he?"

"Just casual questions about how your mom is doing. Very professional. Very concerned." Emma's eyes twinkled with amusement. "Also very interested for someone who's 'just doing his job.'"

Hannah felt heat creep into her cheeks. "Stop it. He's just being thorough."

"If you say so," Emma singsonged as Martha approached.

"Hannah, could you take Table 3?" Martha asked, her gray-streaked hair escaping from its bun as she wiped her hands on her apron.

"Of course," Hannah said, standing quickly. She smoothed down her apron and grabbed her order pad, ignoring Emma's knowing grin.

Martha watched her with maternal concern. "You sure you're up for another few hours? You've been going non-stop. I can call Kylie in early if you need to get home."

"I'm fine, Martha, really," Hannah assured her. "Mom's got her shows to watch, and I could use the extra hours." She glanced toward Table 3, where Reed sat with his back to the wall, giving him a clear view of the diner entrance.

Martha followed her gaze, her expression softening. "Alright. But you're taking home dinner for you both tonight, no arguments."

Before Hannah could protest, Martha turned and headed back to the kitchen.

Steeling herself, Hannah approached Table 3, order pad ready. "Good afternoon, gentlemen. What can I get for you today?"

Sheriff Baker looked up with a friendly smile. "Good to see you, Hannah. How's your mother doing?"

"Better, thanks. Adjusting to the new normal." She shifted her weight, aware of Reed's steady gaze. "Today's special is meatloaf with mashed potatoes and green beans."

"Sounds perfect," Sheriff Baker said. "I'll take that with extra gravy and a sweet tea."

Hannah jotted down the order, then turned her attention to Reed. "And for you, Deputy?"

"Cheeseburger, medium well. Side salad instead of fries." His green eyes met hers briefly. "And coffee, black."

Hannah nodded, noting the order. "I'll put this order right in."

As she turned to leave, Reed's deep voice stopped her. "Miss Gentry."

She paused, looking back. "Yes?"

"How are you doing?" The question was simple, but something in his tone suggested he was asking about more than just her day.

"I'm fine," she replied automatically. "Busy, but that's nothing new."

He nodded. "Holly mentioned she provided you with some information about diabetes support resources."

"Yes, she did," Hannah confirmed, conscious of the pamphlets still sitting untouched on her kitchen counter at home. "Very helpful."

"There's a diabetes support group that meets at the church every other Thursday," Reed continued. "Holly says it's a good program, practical advice, not just medical talk."

"I'll keep that in mind."

"The Next meeting is this Thursday at seven," he added. "They provide childcare, though I guess that's not relevant to your situation."

Sheriff Baker glanced between them with barely concealed interest, the corner of his mouth twitching.

"That's... good to know," Hannah said, feeling oddly off-balance. Had Deputy Dunbar gone out of his way to research diabetes support options for her mother? "I'll put your orders in."

She retreated to the kitchen, slipping the order slip onto the carousel for the cook. Her cheeks felt warm, and she blamed it on the heat from the grill rather than the unexpected attention from Reed Dunbar.

"Well?" Martha asked from where she was crimping the edges of a pie crust.

"Well, what?" Hannah replied.

"Don't 'well what' me, young lady. What did our handsome deputy have to say?"

Hannah rolled her eyes. "He mentioned a diabetes support group at the church. Nothing earth-shattering."

"Reed Dunbar isn't exactly known for small talk. If he mentioned it, he thought it was important."

"Or his sister put him up to it," Hannah countered, reaching for the coffeepot to refill it.

"Maybe," Martha conceded. "But Reed does his own thinking. Always has, even as a boy."

Hannah paused. "You've known him that long?"

Martha laughed softly. "Honey, I've known Reed since he was knee high to a grasshopper, trailing after his grandfather with those serious eyes of his. Never was much of a talker, but always watching, always noticing things others missed."

Hannah tried to imagine a younger version of the deputy and found it oddly endearing.

"Order up!" the cook called, sliding two plates onto the pass-through counter.

Hannah grabbed them, balancing them expertly as she returned to Table 3. "Meatloaf special," she said, placing the plate before Sheriff Baker. "And a cheeseburger with side salad."

The Sheriff immediately dug in with enthusiasm, but Reed paused, studying her face with that same intensity she'd noticed at the hospital. "You look tired, Miss Gentry."

The direct observation caught her off guard. "I'm fine," she said for what felt like the hundredth time that day.

"The diabetes support group I mentioned," Reed said. "They also have information about assistance programs. Not charity," he added quickly, as if sensing her resistance. "Resources people have a right to access."

Hannah felt a surge of conflicting emotions, gratitude for his thoughtfulness, wariness about accepting help, and a touch of embarrassment that her financial concerns were apparently obvious enough for him to address.

"I appreciate the information," she said carefully. "Is there anything else I can get for you?"

"We're good for now," Sheriff Baker assured her.

Hannah nodded, turning to tend to her other tables.

For the next twenty minutes, she moved through the diner on autopilot, refilling coffee cups, delivering checks, and clearing tables. All the while, she was acutely aware of Reed's presence, though she avoided looking directly at him. Something about the deputy unsettled her, not in an unpleasant way, exactly, but in a manner that made her hyperaware of herself.

When she finally returned to their table with the coffeepot, Sheriff Baker was finishing his meatloaf, while Reed had barely touched his burger.

"Everything okay with your meal?" she asked, refilling Reed's coffee cup.

"It's fine," he assured her. "Just taking my time."

Sheriff Baker checked his watch and sighed. "Unfortunately, I can't take my time. Got that meeting with the town council in fifteen minutes." He pulled out his wallet. "This is on me today, Reed."

"Not necessary," Reed began, but the Sheriff waved him off.

Sheriff Baker laid bills on the table, including a generous tip. "Tell Martha the meatloaf was outstanding, as always."

"I will," Hannah promised. "Thanks for coming in."

The Sheriff nodded at her, then glanced at Reed. "Take your time finishing lunch. I'll see you back at the station later today."

"More coffee?" she offered Reed, gesturing with the pot.

He nodded, pushing his cup closer.

"How's your mother really doing with the diabetes management?" he asked after she'd poured.

The unexpected question—personal yet practical—made Hannah pause. "It's... an adjustment," she admitted. "The finger pricks are uncomfortable, and she hates the food restrictions, but we're figuring it out."

Reed nodded thoughtfully. "My grandfather was diagnosed with Type 2 about five years ago. Fought the changes tooth and nail at first."

"That sounds familiar," Hannah said with a small smile.

"Holly got him one of those continuous glucose monitors, eventually. It made a big difference—fewer finger pricks, better data. Insurance covers it for most people."

"I'll look into that. Thanks."

Reed took another bite of his burger, chewing thoughtfully before adding, "The resource pamphlets Holly gave you. There's information about prescription assistance programs too. Might help with the new medication costs."

"We're managing."

Reed met her gaze directly, his posture shifting forward slightly. His eyes tracked the shadows beneath hers, the tension in her shoulders, cataloging details with the same careful attention he likely gave to crime scenes. "I'm sure you are," he said, voice dropping to a lower register. "Just passing along information that might be useful." His thumb traced an absent pattern on the side of his coffee mug, the only outward sign of any uncertainty beneath his composed exterior.

"I appreciate it," she said finally, meaning it this time. "I'll take a look at those pamphlets tonight."

He nodded, seeming satisfied. "How's the photography going?"

The question came out of nowhere, catching Hannah completely off guard. "I—what?"

"Your photography," he repeated.

Hannah stared at him, stunned that he knew this detail about her life. "I haven't had much time for it lately," she admitted. "How did you know I—"

"Small town," he said with a slight shrug.

"It's just a hobby."

"Seems like more than that," Reed said. "Holly has one of your prints in her office. The sunrise over the New River Gorge."

Hannah's cheeks heated. "That's... nice to hear."

Reed finished his coffee, then carefully stacked his dishes. "The diabetes support group on Thursday," he said, returning to his earlier topic. "If transportation is an issue for your mother, I could arrange something."

"That's not necessary," Hannah said quickly. "But thank you."

He nodded, accepting her refusal without pushback. "The offer stands. For the support group or any medical appointments."

Hannah studied him, trying to understand his motivation. "Why are you doing this, Deputy Dunbar? Going out of your way to help us?"

Reed considered her question for a moment, his expression thoughtful. "It's part of serving the community," he said finally. "Connecting people with resources they might not know about."

It was a perfectly reasonable answer, and yet Hannah sensed there was more to it, something he wasn't saying.

"Well, thank you," she said simply. "I should get back to my other tables."

Reed nodded, rising from his seat. "Have a good day, Miss Gentry."

"You too, Deputy."

She watched him leave. Through the window, she saw him pause on the sidewalk, gazing across the town square for a moment before continuing to his patrol vehicle.

"So," Emma's voice came from behind her, making Hannah jump. "Just doing his job, huh?"

Hannah turned to find her friend grinning like the Cheshire cat. "Don't start."

"I'm just saying."

Hannah busied herself clearing Reed's table. "He's being nice."

"Uh-huh. And I'm the Queen of England."

"Emma—"

"Handsome, too," Emma continued, undeterred. "Those eyes? That strong, silent thing he's got going on?"

"Are you finished?" Hannah asked, fighting a smile despite herself.

"For now," Emma conceded. "But this conversation isn't over. I want details next time he comes in."

"There won't be a next time," Hannah insisted. "At least, not specifically to see me."

Emma just raised an eyebrow. "Whatever helps you sleep at night, Han."

As Emma returned to the counter where Martha was serving pie, Hannah finished clearing the table, her mind replaying the conversation with Reed. His specific offers of help, his knowledge of her photography, his mention of the resources, all of it suggested a level of thought and consideration that went beyond professional courtesy.

The question was why. Why would Deputy Reed Dunbar, known throughout town for his reserved nature and dedication to duty, go out of his way for her and her mother? What had made them stand out from all the other Laurel Ridge residents he served?

Perhaps it was nothing more than compassion from someone who understood struggle. Hannah had learned to recognize fellow members of the 'life-didn't-go-as-planned' club. They carried themselves differently, noticed things others overlooked. There was something in Reed's eyes that spoke of understanding personal battles fought behind closed doors. Or maybe she was overthinking it, finding complexity where there was only simple human kindness, because that was safer than acknowledging the flutter in her stomach when he'd mentioned her photography.

Hannah shook her head, pushing the questions aside. She had more immediate concerns, three more hours of her shift, then home to check on Peggy, prepare dinner, monitor blood sugar levels, and tackle the mountain of laundry waiting in the hamper. There was no time to puzzle over the motivations of the deputy with the observant green eyes.

And yet, as she moved through the rest of her shift, his words about the support group and assistance programs kept returning to her. Maybe she should look into them. Not because Reed had suggested it, of course, but because it was the practical thing to do. The responsible thing, for her mother's sake.

By the time her shift ended, Hannah's feet were throbbing inside her worn sneakers, each step sending jolts of pain up her calves. Her back ached fiercely, a hot band of tension that wrapped around her lower spine and squeezed until even breathing deeply felt like an effort.

The constant background noise of the diner, the clinking silverware, murmured conversations, the hiss of the grill, had burrowed into her skull, pulsing behind her eyes in rhythm with her headache.

Martha, true to her word, pressed a bag containing two meatloaf dinners into her hands.

"Don't argue," Martha said firmly.

"Martha, you really don't need to do this."

"Consider it a blessing," Martha countered. "The Lord provides, sometimes through meatloaf."

Hannah laughed softly, too tired to argue further. "Thank you."

"And Hannah?" Martha's expression grew serious. "That support group Deputy Dunbar mentioned... it's a good one. I know several people that go. They say it makes all the difference in the world to have people who understand what they're going through."

Hannah nodded, tucking the food bag against her chest. "I'll think about it."

"That's all I ask," Martha said, patting her shoulder. "Now go home and get some rest. You look dead on your feet."

Outside, Hannah walked slowly to her car, parked behind the diner, every step an effort of will. When she arrived at her car, she noticed a pamphlet stuck under her windshield wiper.

"Laurel Ridge Diabetes Support Network," the title read. Beneath it was a handwritten note in neat, precise handwriting:

Thursday, 7 PM. Church fellowship hall. No pressure, just information that might help.—R.D.

Hannah stared at the pamphlet. The gesture was thoughtful, unexpected, and oddly touching. He'd gone out of his way to make sure she had the information.

"Boundaries, Deputy Dunbar," she murmured.

Hannah tucked the pamphlet into her purse, started the car, and headed home. She had medications to administer, dinner to serve, and a mother to care for. The mystery of Deputy Reed's motivations would have to wait for another day.

But as she drove through the familiar streets of Laurel Ridge, Hannah found herself wondering what it might be like to attend that Thursday meeting. To sit in a room full of people who understood the challenges she and Peggy were facing, to perhaps find a small community of support.

And if a certain green-eyed deputy happened to check in to see if she'd taken his advice... well, that was just part of his job, wasn't it? Nothing more.

At least, that's what she told herself all the way home.

***

Reed pulled his patrol SUV to the curb, watching as Hannah walked to her car in the back lot. Even from this distance, he could see the exhaustion in her gait, the slight slump of her shoulders as she carried what looked like a takeout bag. Her chestnut hair caught the late afternoon light, the same warm color of autumn leaves after they turned colors in the fall.

He'd left the support group pamphlet on her car after lunch. Mark would give him grief if he knew, joking about police overreach for personal reasons. The sheriff had already raised an eyebrow at lunch, his knowing look saying more than words.

The thing was, Reed wasn't entirely sure of his reasons.

Yes, helping to connect citizens with resources was part of community policing. Yes, his sister had mentioned Hannah's reluctance to explore assistance programs. And yes, as a law enforcement officer, he had a duty to support vulnerable members of the community.

But there was more to it. Something about Hannah Gentry had gotten under his skin from the moment he'd responded to her 911 call. The quiet strength she projected even in crisis. The fierce independence that radiated from her despite her obvious exhaustion. The momentary glimpse of fear he'd seen in her eyes when the paramedics were working on her mother—not the panic of the moment, but a deeper dread about what came next.

Reed recognized that look. He'd seen it too many times not to know it, the face of someone carrying a burden too heavy alone, but too proud or too afraid to share the weight of it.

He watched as Hannah started her car and pulled onto the street, driving slowly in the direction of her home. Only when her taillights disappeared around a corner did Reed start his vehicle.

"This isn't about her," he told himself firmly. "It's about doing my job. Protecting the vulnerable. Nothing more."

But even as he said the words, Reed knew they weren't entirely true. Something about Hannah Gentry had awakened his protective instincts in a way that went beyond professional duty.

And that, more than anything, was what troubled him as he pulled away from the curb and headed back toward the station. Because Reed had learned the hard way that personal involvement clouded judgment, and clouded judgment led to mistakes.

Mistakes that sometimes cost lives.

His phone buzzed with a text. Holly.

Did you tell her about the support group?

He typed a one-word reply: *Yes.*

Three dots appeared, then: *And?*

Reed hesitated, then responded truthfully: *We'll see.*

"Lord," he prayed quietly as he drove, the mountains rising like sentinels in his rearview mirror, "guide my steps here. Help me serve without overstepping, care without compromising. And give Hannah Gentry the support she needs."

Chapter 5

A sharp knock at the door made Hannah jump, splattering soapy water onto her faded jeans. She'd been elbow-deep in dishes, the scent of lemon soap mixing with the lingering aroma of that evening's chicken soup. Her fingers wrinkled and reddened from the hot water. The rhythmic scrubbing had been almost meditative as she tried to restore some semblance of order to the kitchen after another chaotic day.

"Who on earth…" she muttered, drying her hands on a dishtowel. It was nearly seven in the evening.

Hannah glanced through the small window beside the front door and froze. Deputy Reed Dunbar stood on her porch, no longer in uniform but still unmistakable, with his tall frame and broad shoulders. He wore a simple navy button-down tucked into jeans. The casual clothes did nothing to diminish his authoritative presence.

Her pulse quickened unexpectedly as she smoothed her hair and opened the door, acutely aware of her disheveled appearance, worn jeans spotted with dishwater, an old t-shirt she'd never have chosen for company. A familiar tension rose within her. The instinct to protect her private world battling with a strange, unwelcome flutter of self-consciousness she hadn't felt in years.

"Deputy Dunbar," she said. "Is everything all right?"

His green eyes met hers directly, steady and clear in the fading evening light. "Everything's fine, Miss Gentry. I'm off duty now—it's just Reed." He shifted his weight slightly "I wanted to check in, see how you and your mother are doing.

Hannah blinked, momentarily thrown by both his casual appearance and the unexpected visit. "That's... thoughtful of you."

Before she could decide whether to invite him in, her mother's voice called from the living room.

"Hannah? Who is it, dear?"

Reed raised an eyebrow slightly, a silent question.

Hannah hesitated only briefly before stepping back. "Would you like to come in?"

"If I'm not intruding," he said, but his feet were already crossing the threshold, his presence immediately filling the modest entryway.

"Mom, it's Deputy Dunbar," Hannah called, leading him into the living room where Peggy sat in her wheelchair, a crocheting project abandoned in her lap. "He came by to check on you."

"Deputy! What a kind gesture. Please, sit down."

"Thank you, ma'am," Reed said, settling into the armchair across from Peggy while Hannah perched on the edge of the sofa. "And please call me Reed. I'm not here officially."

"Reed, then," Peggy smiled, straightening her cardigan with slightly trembling hands. "I must look a fright. If I'd known we were having a visitor—"

"Mom," Hannah interjected gently.

"You look fine, Mrs. Gentry," Reed said, his deep voice carrying genuine sincerity. "Much improved from our last encounter."

Peggy laughed softly. "Well, being conscious does help one's appearance, I suppose."

Hannah watched as her mother visibly brightened under Reed's attention, noting how he sat forward slightly, giving Peggy his complete focus. There was nothing perfunctory about his manner; he seemed genuinely interested in her well-being.

"How are you adjusting to the new diagnosis?" Reed asked.

"Oh, it's a bother," Peggy sighed. "All these new medications and rules. Hannah's been wonderful about it all, though—researching recipes, measuring everything." She gestured toward the kitchen. "She even tried making sugar-free cookies today."

"Tried being the operative word," Hannah added dryly. "They came out like hockey pucks."

A smile tugged at the corner of Reed's mouth, transforming his serious features. "My mom says the first batch of anything new is always a practice run."

"A very diplomatic way to put it," Hannah said, surprised to find herself smiling back.

The soft ticking of the mantel clock filled a moment of silence. Hannah suddenly remembered her manners. "Can I get you something to drink? Water or coffee?"

"Coffee would be great if it's not too much trouble," Reed said.

"It's no trouble. Mom, did you need anything?"

Peggy shook her head. "I'm fine, dear."

In the kitchen, Hannah's hands moved automatically through the familiar ritual of preparing coffee—measuring grounds, filling the reservoir, setting out the good mugs that rarely saw use. The methodical tasks gave her a moment to breathe, to steady herself. The unexpected visit had thrown her off balance, like a sudden shift in terrain on a path she thought she knew by heart. Deputy Dunbar had no obligation to check on them personally after his shift. It was a kindness she hadn't expected.

She could hear the low murmur of conversation from the living room, her mother's voice animated in a way Hannah hadn't heard in days. The diabetes diagnosis had hit Peggy hard, though she tried to hide it behind brave smiles and jokes. This was the first time since coming home that she seemed truly distracted from her worries.

Hannah poured the coffee into their best mugs and arranged some crackers on a small plate as an afterthought. When she returned to the living room, she found her mother laughing at something Reed had said.

"What's so funny?" Hannah asked, setting the tray on the coffee table.

"Reed was just telling me about a call he responded to last month. Mr. Peterson's goat got loose and ended up in Mrs. Wilson's prize garden," Peggy explained, her eyes bright with amusement.

"Ate her blue-ribbon roses right down to the stems," Reed added, accepting the coffee Hannah offered. "Thank you."

"I'm surprised Mrs. Wilson didn't demand you arrest the goat," Hannah said, settling back onto the sofa.

Reed's mouth quirked. "She tried. Told me to read it its rights."

The mental image of Reed, serious and steady, reading Miranda rights to a wayward goat, startled a genuine laugh from Hannah. "What did you do?"

"I explained that, unfortunately, the county jail lacks appropriate accommodations for goats," he said, his eyes crinkling at the corners. "Then I helped Mr. Peterson get it home after promising Mrs. Wilson I'd speak to him about reinforcing his fence."

Hannah was struck by the image of this imposing man wrangling a garden-destroying goat with the same calm authority he'd shown at her mother's medical emergency.

"That's Laurel Ridge for you," Peggy said fondly. "I miss hearing the town gossip."

A flicker of guilt crossed Hannah's face. "Mom—"

"Oh, I'm not complaining, dear," Peggy hastened to add. "You know, it's my choice to stay home. I just miss the stories sometimes."

Reed sipped his coffee, his observant gaze taking in the exchange between mother and daughter. "Speaking of the town," he said, setting his mug down, "that's partly why I stopped by."

He reached beside him and produced several neatly folded pamphlets. "I spoke with Holly a little more about resources that might be helpful. She put these together for you."

Hannah accepted the pamphlets, scanning the titles: *Diabetes Support Group—Laurel Ridge Community Hospital, Home Health Services of Fayette County, Caregivers' Connection: Monthly Meetings.*

"The diabetes support group meets twice a month at the hospital. That's a different group than the one that meets at the church," Reed explained. "Holly says it's a good mix of people—some newly diagnosed, others who've been managing for years. They share recipes, tips, that sort of thing."

Hannah felt a rush of conflicting emotions. The thoughtfulness of the gesture touched her, but it also triggered her instinctive resistance to outside help. Since the accident ten years ago, she'd learned that help often came with strings, expectations, obligations, and pitying looks that made her feel like a charity case rather than a person. Better to struggle alone than to stand beneath that weight of others' sympathy. At least that's what she'd told herself through countless sleepless nights.

"That's very kind," she said carefully, "but we're doing okay. I've been researching online, and Dr. Roberts gave us plenty of information."

"The support group could be nice, Hannah," Peggy said gently. "It might be good for you to go and talk to others going through the same thing I am."

Hannah looked at her mother, surprised.

"Would you want to go?" she asked.

Peggy shrugged. "No, you go, Hannah, and let me know what it's like."

"First and third Tuesdays at 7 PM," he replied. "And there's transportation available if needed if you would like to go, Mrs. Gentry. The hospital has a volunteer shuttle service."

Hannah felt a strange tightness in her chest.

"We'll think about it," she said, setting the pamphlets on the coffee table.

Reed nodded, not pushing further. He turned to Peggy. "My sister also mentioned a home health service that can help with the transition. They have nurses who can come by, check your blood sugar, and help with medication management until you're comfortable doing it yourself."

"That sounds expensive," Hannah said immediately.

"It's covered under most insurance plans, especially with a new diagnosis," Reed explained. "And there are county programs to cover any gaps. No one should have to manage a new health condition without proper support."

His straightforward approach lacked the saccharine pity she'd come to dread from others. There was something refreshingly direct about him, as though offering help was simply the logical thing to do, not a judgment of her capabilities. It made her wonder what kind of man he was beneath the professional exterior. What experiences had shaped him into someone who seemed to understand the delicate balance between offering support and respecting independence?

No one should have to manage without support. Wasn't that exactly what she'd been doing for years? Managing. Surviving. Going it alone because it seemed like the only option.

"We'll look into it," Hannah said, unable to outright refuse such a reasonable suggestion. "Thank you for bringing these."

Reed nodded, his eyes meeting hers briefly before he turned his attention back to Peggy. "How are you finding the blood sugar monitoring, Mrs. Gentry? My grandfather said that's often the biggest adjustment."

As Peggy launched into a detailed account of her struggles with the glucose meter, Hannah observed Reed. His posture was relaxed but attentive, his head tilted slightly as he listened to her mother. There was a genuineness to his interest that Hannah found both puzzling and compelling.

"...and then Hannah had to help me because I couldn't see those tiny numbers," Peggy was saying. "It's frustrating to need help with one more thing."

"Technology can be challenging at any age," Reed said. "My grandfather refuses to use anything with a touch screen. Says his fingers are too big and the buttons too small."

Peggy chuckled. "Does your grandfather still in the area?"

"Yes, ma'am. He lives out past the ridge, has a cabin on Laurel Creek now."

"Sheriff Dunbar," Peggy nodded in recognition. "I remember him. A good man. Very kind when..." she trailed off, her eyes darting to Hannah.

Hannah knew what her mother had stopped herself from saying. Very kind when we had the accident. Sheriff Dunbar would have been in office then, would have known about the crash that killed her father and paralyzed her mother. The realization that Reed might know about their tragedy too sent a wave of uncomfortable vulnerability through Hannah.

"He's slowed down some, but he's still as sharp as ever," Reed continued smoothly, either not noticing or tactfully ignoring the moment of awkwardness. "Still gives advice whether you ask for it or not."

"The prerogative of grandparents everywhere," Peggy smiled.

Hannah checked her watch. "Mom, it's almost time for your evening medication."

"Oh, is it that late already?" Peggy glanced at the mantel clock. "Time flies in good company."

Reed took the hint, setting his coffee mug down and rising to his feet. "I should be getting back, anyway. I've got horses waiting to be fed."

"You have horses?" Peggy asked, interest lighting her face.

"Three of them," Reed confirmed. "Jasper, Scout, and Tango. They get pretty vocal when dinner's late."

"Do you have a ranch?" Hannah asked, surprised by this glimpse into his personal life.

"A small one, just outside town," Reed said. "Nothing fancy, but it's home."

Hannah tried to reconcile this new information with her mental image of the serious deputy. Reed Dunbar, returning home to a ranch and horses after a day of enforcing the law. It added an unexpected dimension to the man standing in her living room.

"Well, don't let us keep you from your responsibilities," Hannah said, standing as well. "Thank you for stopping by. And for the information."

"It was my pleasure," Reed said, nodding to Peggy. "I hope you continue to improve."

"Thank you for the visit, Deputy—I mean, Reed," Peggy smiled warmly.

Hannah walked Reed to the door, acutely aware of his solid presence beside her in the narrow hallway. At the threshold, he paused.

"Miss Gentry—"

"Hannah," she interrupted, surprising herself. "If I'm calling you Reed, you might as well use my first name."

"Hannah, then." The sound of her name in his deep voice sent an unexpected flutter through her chest. "I hope the resources are helpful, but if there's anything else you need, don't hesitate to reach out."

Hannah nodded. "Thank you. It was thoughtful of you to bring them by."

Reed hesitated, as if there was something more he wanted to say. Instead, he simply nodded. "Good night, Hannah."

"Good night, Reed."

She watched from the doorway as he walked to his truck. Only when he'd driven away did Hannah close the door, leaning against it for a moment to collect herself.

When she returned to the living room, Peggy had a small smile playing on her lips.

"What a nice young man," she said. "And so handsome, too."

"Mom," Hannah warned, feeling a flush rise to her cheeks. "He was just being kind. It's part of his job."

"He's off duty, dear. He didn't have to come by at all, let alone bring those pamphlets. And he certainly didn't have to stay for coffee."

Hannah ducked her head, busying herself with gathering mugs, while the heat crept up her neck and bloomed across her cheeks. "He was being courteous."

"Mmm-hmm," Peggy hummed skeptically. "Courtesy doesn't usually include those kinds of looks."

"What kinds of looks?" Hannah asked before she could stop herself.

"Like he was trying to figure you out. Interested." Peggy smiled mischievously. "I haven't forgotten what those looks mean, wheelchair or no wheelchair."

"You're imagining things," Hannah said firmly, though a warmth had settled in her chest at her mother's words. "He's a deputy doing community outreach, that's all."

Peggy raised her hands in surrender, but her smile remained. "If you say so, dear."

As Hannah carried the dishes to the kitchen, she replayed moments from Reed's visit. The way he'd listened so attentively to her mother. The resource pamphlets he'd thoughtfully brought. The brief moment when he'd smiled at her joke about the cookies.

She washed the coffee mugs under the warm water, thinking about Reed returning to his ranch, caring for his horses in the quiet evening hours. There was something appealing about that image.

Hannah placed the mugs in the dish drainer and leaned against the counter, her eyes falling on the pamphlets in the living room Reed had brought.

Maybe it was time to consider accepting some help, if only for Peggy's sake. The support group might be good for her mother, a chance to connect with others facing similar challenges, if she could persuade her to go.

Chapter 6

The lunch rush had ebbed like a retreating tide, leaving Hannah alone on a sea of crumb-scattered tables and half-empty coffee cups. She rolled her shoulders, trying to ease the familiar ache that had taken up permanent residence between her shoulder blades. Three more hours until her shift ended. Three more hours of smiling through the bone-deep exhaustion that seemed as much a part of her now as her own heartbeat.

The bell above the door jingled, pulling her attention to the entrance, where sunlight briefly flooded in around a tall silhouette.

"Afternoon, Deputy," Martha called from behind the register.

Reed nodded in acknowledgment as he removed his sunglasses, tucking them into his uniform shirt pocket. His gaze swept the diner, a habit Hannah had noticed each time he entered the diner, an automatic assessment of his surroundings before settling on her.

"Miss Gentry," he greeted with a slight nod. Then, correcting himself, "Hannah."

"Reed," she replied. "Your usual table?"

A hint of surprise crossed his features, there and gone in an instant. She hadn't meant to reveal that she'd noticed his pattern over the past week, coming in around one-thirty, after the rush had cleared. Always wanting to sit in the same corner booth with his back to the wall and a clear view of both the entrance and the street beyond.

"If it's available," he said.

Hannah grabbed a menu and a glass of water, leading him to the booth by the window. "It's a slow Saturday today," she commented, setting down the items. "The high school baseball team is playing an away game, so we're missing our usual teenage crowd."

Reed slid into the booth. "Heard they're having a good season."

"Three wins, one loss," Hannah confirmed, producing her order pad. "Coffee?"

"Please."

As Hannah turned toward the coffee station, Martha caught her eye with a knowing smile that made Hannah's cheeks warm. She busied herself with the coffeepot, taking a moment to compose herself before returning to Reed's table.

"Decided yet?" she asked, pouring the steaming coffee with a steady hand.

Reed closed the menu he'd barely glanced at. "Grilled chicken sandwich and side salad."

Hannah wrote it down. In the week since their conversation at her home, Reed had come into the diner every day she'd worked the lunch shift. His order varied slightly, sometimes the burger, sometimes the chicken, but always with the healthier option of salad instead of fries.

"Coming right up," she said, tucking the order pad into her apron pocket.

As she turned to leave, Reed's voice stopped her. "How's your mom?"

Hannah paused. "Better today. The new medication seems to be helping with her energy levels."

Reed nodded. "Good. And the home health nurse?"

"Coming tomorrow for the first visit. Mom's... apprehensive."

"Understandable," Reed said. "It's hard having someone new in your space that upsets your routine."

"Exactly," Hannah agreed, relieved he understood. "I keep telling her it'll make things easier."

"But people value their independence. Sometimes accepting help feels like giving something up."

Hannah stared at him, momentarily startled by how perfectly he'd articulated the unspoken tension that had filled her home since she'd arranged the home health visits. "Yes. That's... that's exactly it."

Their eyes met for a brief moment, and Hannah felt a connection with him again, like he truly understood, not just the words she was saying, but the emotions behind them.

"Order in!" she called, breaking the moment as she hurried to the kitchen pass-through window.

As she worked through her remaining tables, an elderly couple sharing a slice of pie, and a young mother with a toddler having a late lunch, Hannah found her attention repeatedly drawn to Reed's corner. Unlike some customers who buried themselves in phones or newspapers, Reed simply observed. He watched the street outside, nodded to people he knew who passed by, and occasionally made notes in a small notebook he carried.

When she delivered his sandwich, he thanked her with that same quiet politeness he always showed. It struck her as a rare quality these days, genuine courtesy without expectation.

"Martha makes the best chicken sandwich in the county."

"I'll tell her you said so. She'll be insufferable," Hannah replied with a small smile.

"How's the photography going?"

The question caught her off guard again, just as it had during his previous visit. "I haven't had much time."

Reed nodded, accepting her answer without pressing. "There's a nice spot by Laurel Creek where the morning light hits the water just right. Thought of your photography when I drove past it on patrol yesterday."

Hannah blinked, warmth spreading through her chest at the idea that he'd thought of her. "Where exactly?"

"Just beyond Miller's Bridge, where the creek widens before joining the river. There's a clearing with some old sycamores."

Hannah could picture it immediately. Her fingers itched for her camera, a sensation she hadn't felt in months.

"Sounds beautiful," she said.

"It is. Worth seeing, if you get the chance."

Martha appeared beside her, a gentle hand on her shoulder. "Hannah, why don't you take your lunch break? I can cover your tables."

Hannah glanced around the diner. Only three tables were occupied, including Reed's. "Are you sure? I can wait until—"

"Go on," Martha insisted with a meaningful glance toward Reed. "You've been on your feet since six this morning. Take fifteen minutes."

"Alright. Thank you."

As Martha moved away, Hannah hesitated, suddenly unsure. The logical thing would be to retreat to the small break room in the back, but something made her linger.

"Would you like to join me?" he asked, gesturing to the empty seat across from him.

Hannah surprised herself by sliding into the booth. "Thanks. I don't usually take breaks out here, but..."

"But the break room smells like a mix of food and pine-scented cleaner?" Reed suggested.

A genuine laugh escaped her. "How did you know?"

"The sheriff's department break room is the same."

Hannah relaxed slightly, reaching for a napkin to fan herself. The afternoon had turned warm, and the diner's air conditioning was fighting a losing battle against the heat radiating through the front windows.

"Have you worked at the sheriff's department a long time?" she asked, realizing she knew very little about him despite his increasingly regular presence in her life.

"Since I was twenty-two," Reed replied. "Started as a rookie deputy under my grandfather, Sheriff Bill Dunbar."

"That's right," Hannah nodded. "I forgot he was your grandfather. That's quite a legacy."

"He set a high standard. He served Laurel Ridge for nearly thirty years."

"And now you're carrying on the tradition."

Reed took a sip of his coffee. "Trying to. The town's changed some since his day. Quieter in some ways, more complicated in others."

Hannah considered this. "I can see that. When I was growing up, we didn't even lock our doors. Now..."

"You still don't have to lock your doors in Laurel Ridge," Reed pointed out. "Though, as a deputy, I probably shouldn't encourage that."

"Professional advice noted," Hannah said with a small smile. "So, was law enforcement always the plan? Following in your grandfather's footsteps?"

Reed seemed to consider the question carefully. "Yes, and no. I always respected what he did, but I originally thought about wildlife management and working with the state parks service."

"Really?" Hannah leaned forward slightly, genuinely interested. "What changed?"

"Life," Reed answered simply. "My grandfather encouraged me. The department needed deputies who knew the area. It felt like the right path." He paused, turning the conversation back to her. "What about you? Was photography always your passion?"

Hannah nodded. "Since I was a teenager. Mom and dad gave me a camera for my sixteenth birthday. I took it everywhere."

"What do you like photographing most?"

"Nature, especially the mountains and animals. There's something about capturing a moment that will never exist exactly that way again." Hannah stopped herself, embarrassed by her sudden enthusiasm. Her fingers twisted in her apron. "Sorry, that probably sounds silly. Not everyone gets excited about light patterns and fleeting moments."

"Not at all," Reed said seriously. "I feel the same way about dawn on the ranch. Each one's different, the way the light hits the trees, the way the mist moves across the field. Some things you can't explain to others. You just have to witness them."

Hannah studied him, seeing beyond the uniform to the man who noticed morning dawns and mountain light. "Your ranch sounds peaceful."

"It is. It's nothing fancy. Just a cabin and a small barn with some pasture for the horses—but it's home." Reed's expression softened slightly. "So, you sell your photographs online?"

Hannah nodded, surprised he remembered that detail. "Just prints. Nothing major, but it brings in a little extra money. Mostly landscapes of the area that tourists like."

"I'd like to see your work sometime," Reed said, then immediately added, "If you're comfortable sharing it, of course."

Hannah felt a flutter of nervousness mixed with pleasure. "I have an online gallery. I could write down the website..."

Martha appeared beside their table, effectively ending the conversation as she set a plate in front of Hannah. "Turkey sandwich and a fruit cup," she announced.

"Martha—"

"Hush now," Martha interrupted with affectionate firmness. "Enjoy your lunch."

The corners of Reed's eyes crinkled as he smiled. Martha patted her shoulder and moved away.

"So," Reed said finally, "about that photography website?"

Hannah reached for a napkin and borrowed Reed's pen, carefully writing down the web address. "It's nothing special, just some local shots."

Reed accepted the napkin, tucking it carefully into his pocket. "I'll check it out. Thanks for sharing it."

They ate quietly for a few minutes, the silence surprisingly comfortable. Hannah found herself relaxing, her perpetually tense shoulders dropping slightly as she enjoyed the simple pleasure of a meal she hadn't had to prepare or rush through.

"How's the diabetes support group information working out?" Reed asked after a while. "Has your mom decided about attending?"

Hannah sighed. "She's reluctant. Says she's not ready to 'parade her illness in front of strangers,' as she puts it."

Reed nodded understandingly. "My grandfather was the same way initially. Took my sister practically dragging him to finally get him there."

"And did it help?"

"More than he expected. Turns out complaining about glucose monitors and diet restrictions is more satisfying when everyone else understands exactly what you mean." Reed's expression grew thoughtful. "The social aspect was good for him too. He'd gotten isolated, spending too much time alone with just his thoughts and frustrations."

Hannah recognized her mother's situation in his words. Peggy had become increasingly withdrawn since the accident, preferring the safety of home to the perceived judgment of the outside world.

"Maybe I'll try again," Hannah said. "Approach it differently."

"If transportation is an issue, the offer stands," Reed reminded her. "Or Holly could arrange something through the hospital volunteer service."

"Thank you," Hannah said sincerely. "I appreciate all your help, really. I'm just not used to..."

"Accepting it?" Reed suggested when she trailed off.

Hannah nodded, a rueful smile touching her lips. "Is it that obvious?"

"Let's just say I recognize the signs."

Chapter 7

Three days later, Hannah was wiping down the diner's front windows when Reed's patrol SUV pulled up outside. She'd come to expect his arrival around this time, though she tried not to acknowledge the small thrill of anticipation she felt each time she saw him.

"Afternoon," he greeted, removing his sunglasses as he stepped inside the diner. Today he seemed more tired than usual, faint shadows visible beneath his eyes.

"Rough day?" Hannah asked as she led him to his usual table.

Reed's eyebrows rose slightly at her perception. "Long night. Had to help with a search and rescue operation for some hikers who got lost up in the state park. They were found safe around dawn."

"That's good news at least," Hannah said, pouring his coffee without being asked. "You look like you could use this."

"Thanks," he said, wrapping his hands around the mug as if drawing strength from its warmth. "How's everything with you? Your mother doing okay with the nurse's visits?"

Hannah nodded. "Better than expected, actually. Nurse Ferguson is kind and has a no-nonsense personality, which is undoubtedly what mom needs. And she brought homemade sugar-free cookies that actually taste good, which immediately won Mom over."

"Smart woman," Reed commented with a hint of amusement. "Food diplomacy works wonders."

Hannah smiled, tucking a strand of hair behind her ear. "What can I get you today? Martha made meatloaf if you're hungry enough for a full meal."

"Meatloaf sounds perfect," Reed said. "And maybe keep the coffee coming."

"Coming right up."

As Hannah turned to place his order, Martha caught her eye from the kitchen pass-through, gesturing her over with a spatula.

"That poor man looks exhausted," Martha said when Hannah approached. "Heard about the hikers on the morning news. He must've been out all night."

"He mentioned it," Hannah confirmed. "Says he wants meatloaf and lots of coffee."

"I'll give him an extra-large portion," Martha said, already preparing a plate. "And Hannah, when does your shift end today?"

"Four, why?"

Martha nodded toward the wall clock, which read 3:38. "Why don't you finish up with Deputy Dunbar's order and then clock out? Kylie's already here for the dinner shift, and we're slow."

"But I still need to stock the napkin dispensers and—"

"Kylie can handle it," Martha interrupted. "You've been pulling doubles all week. Take the extra twenty minutes."

Hannah knew better than to argue. "Alright. Thanks, Martha."

By the time she delivered Reed's meatloaf, the diner had emptied, except for a couple sharing a slice of pie at the counter. Reed looked up from his phone, setting it aside as she approached.

"Thank you," he said as she placed the generously portioned plate before him. "This looks great."

"It's a customer favorite."

Reed took a bite and nodded appreciatively. "One of my favorites as well."

Hannah hesitated. "I'm actually finishing my shift early today. Would you mind if I grabbed a cup of coffee and joined you? Unless you'd prefer to eat alone."

"I'd welcome the company," Reed said, the sincerity in his voice impossible to miss.

Hannah poured herself a mug of coffee, then slid into the seat across from him after removing her apron. The simple act of sitting down after hours on her feet was blissful.

"I visited your photography website," Reed said after she'd settled.

Hannah nearly choked on her coffee. "You did?"

"Your work is impressive, Hannah. You've got a real eye for composition, especially those mountain fog shots."

The praise warmed her more than she expected. "Thank you. Those are some of my favorites."

"I can see why people buy your prints. You capture something essential about this place—not just how it looks, but how it feels to be here."

Hannah stared at him, genuinely touched by his observation. Most people commented on the "pretty colors" or asked if she'd enhanced the images.

"That's... that's undoubtedly what I aim for. To capture the feeling of a moment."

Reed nodded. "The one of sunrise over Miller's Ridge, with the light just hitting the tops of the trees while the valley's still in shadow, that reminded me of the spot I mentioned the other day."

"That's actually one of my best-selling prints," Hannah admitted. "Tourists love it, but locals buy it too. I think it reminds them of why they choose to live here, despite the economic challenges."

"It's a special place," Reed agreed. "Different from anywhere else."

They fell into an easy conversation about favorite locations around Laurel Ridge. The lookout point above the old mill, the quiet bend in the river where herons nested in spring, and the wildflower meadow that bloomed in brilliant waves of color each summer.

"I haven't been to some of those places in years," Hannah said.

"It's difficult to find time for yourself when you're caring for someone else."

"That's true," Hannah acknowledged. "Though, every time I reach for my camera, I hear this voice in my head calling me selfish. Like I'm somehow betraying Mom if I take an hour for myself when she's confined to a wheelchair."

"It's not selfish to need moments that are just for you. It's necessary."

Hannah traced the rim of her coffee mug with her finger. "That's what Emma always says—that I need to make time for myself. But there's always something more urgent, you know? Another bill, another doctor's appointment, another reason why it isn't the right time."

Reed's expression was thoughtful. "My grandfather has a saying: 'There's never a perfect time for anything important.' He claims it's ancient wisdom, but I'm pretty sure he made it up."

Hannah laughed softly. "Your grandfather sounds like quite the character."

"He is," Reed confirmed with obvious affection. "Stubborn as they come, but wise in his way."

As they continued talking, Hannah realized how much she'd come to enjoy these conversations with Reed. Just simple, pleasant conversation about places they loved and people they knew.

"I should be heading home soon," she said reluctantly, glancing at the clock. "Mom will be expecting me."

Reed nodded. "Of course."

As they both stood, Reed left money on the table to cover his meal.

They walked together to the door, Reed holding it open as they stepped onto the sidewalk. The air felt heavy with approaching rain; the clouds hanging low over the mountains that ringed the town.

"Thank you for the company," Hannah said, suddenly shy.

"I'm glad you joined me," Reed replied. "It made a long day much better."

"I should go." Hannah glanced at her watch, hesitating slightly. "Mom's nurse is coming at five."

"I'll see you tomorrow?"

Hannah tucked her hair behind her ear, that nervous habit she couldn't seem to break. "I'm working the lunch shift."

"Good." Reed's gaze held hers a beat longer than necessary, something unspoken passing between them. "Be safe, Hannah."

"You too," she replied softly. "Get some rest."

As Hannah turned to leave, the first fat raindrops began to fall, pattering against the sidewalk. She quickened her pace as she headed to the back of the diner for her car. The rain began falling more steadily, but Hannah hardly noticed, lost in her thoughts.

Chapter 8

Hannah pushed open the heavy oak door of the Laurel Ridge General Store, triggering the cheerful jingle of antique brass bells. The sound was as familiar to her as her own heartbeat, a constant since childhood when she'd rush in with pocket change clutched tightly in her small fist, eager for penny candy.

"Be right with you!" Emma's voice called from somewhere among the packed aisles.

The store hadn't changed much in the decades since Hannah's childhood visits. The wooden floors still creaked in the same spots, the ceiling fans still turned lazily overhead, and the mingled scents of coffee, beans and vanilla scented candles still permeated the air. Modern necessities had found their way onto the shelves alongside traditional staples, but the essence remained unchanged—a community gathering place as much as a business.

Hannah navigated toward the specialty foods section at the back, consulting the list in her hand. The nurse had recommended several diabetic-friendly products that might make Peggy's restricted diet more palatable. Her mother's complaints about bland food had been relentless these past two weeks.

"Hannah Gentry, as I live and breathe!" Emma emerged from behind a display of local honey, arms already opening for a hug. "It's been almost two weeks since I've seen you!"

Hannah accepted the embrace, relaxing into the familiar comfort of her oldest friend. "Has it really been that long?"

"Thirteen days," Emma confirmed, pulling back to examine Hannah's face with a critical eye. "And you look exhausted. Tell me you're not working a double shift today."

"No, I'm done working for the day." Hannah gestured to her list. "I need to pick up some things for Mom."

Emma peered at the paper. "Sugar-free snacks and stevia sweetener? How's Peggy handling the diabetes regimen?"

"About as well as you'd expect. She's convinced the whole world is conspiring to remove every small pleasure from her life," Hannah replied, unable to keep the weariness from her voice. "Yesterday she accused me of hiding cookies, as if I have time for covert sugar operations."

Emma squeezed her arm sympathetically. "The adjustment period is rough. My aunt went through similar dramatics when she was diagnosed. Now she's the self-appointed sugar police at family gatherings."

They moved together down the aisle, Emma plucking items from shelves with practiced efficiency.

"These diabetic-friendly cookies actually taste pretty good," she said, adding a package to Hannah's basket. "And this maple-flavored syrup has zero sugar. My mom uses it in her coffee. She says she can barely tell the difference."

"Thanks," Hannah said gratefully. "The nurse gave us some resources, but it's overwhelming trying to figure out what's actually edible versus technically edible."

Emma nodded understandingly. "Nurse Ferguson, right? She helped my mom after her knee surgery last year. Worth her weight in gold."

"She's been a godsend," Hannah admitted. "Mom actually looks forward to her visits now."

The bell over the door jingled again as an elderly couple entered. Emma waved, but continued helping Hannah.

"How about this almond flour? Good for baking alternatives." Emma added the package to Hannah's growing collection. "Though I'm guessing you haven't had much time for experimental baking."

"Between work shifts and Mom's appointments? I'm lucky if I remember to eat, let alone bake."

Emma's expression softened with concern. "When was the last time you had a break, Hannah? A real one, not just collapsing into bed for five hours before starting all over again."

Hannah busied herself examining a nutrition label to avoid Emma's too-perceptive gaze. "I'm fine. We're managing."

"That's not what I asked," Emma persisted gently.

The concern in her friend's voice made Hannah's throat tighten. She blinked rapidly, determined not to break down between the gluten-free pasta and the organic canned goods.

"It's just a busy time," she said finally.

"Hannah." Emma's hand on her arm stopped her nervous rambling. "You can't pour from an empty cup. Even the strongest person needs rest and support."

"What choice do I have?" Hannah whispered. "It's just me and Mom."

"It doesn't have to be," Emma countered. "That's what community is for. That's what friends are for." She guided Hannah toward the small sitting area near the coffee counter, gently pressing her into one of the comfortable armchairs. "Wait here. Don't move."

Hannah sank into the chair, suddenly aware of how much her feet ached. Emma returned moments later with two steaming mugs of coffee and placed a small plate of scones between them.

"Don't worry, they're regular scones. You're not diabetic," Emma said with a wink, pushing a mug toward Hannah. "Now drink your coffee and talk to me like we used to, before life got so complicated."

The rich aroma of the coffee washed over Hannah, and she wrapped her hands around the warm ceramic mug, drawing comfort from its heat. The first sip was heaven. Emma always made it exactly right, strong but not bitter, with just a hint of cinnamon.

"Thanks," Hannah murmured. "I forget sometimes how nice it is to just...sit."

"That's because you're always running, Hannah." Emma broke a scone in half, offering part to Hannah. "You need respite care, you know. Not just the nurse visits."

Hannah immediately shook her head. "Mom would never—"

"I'm not talking about for your mom," Emma interrupted. "I'm talking about for you. Someone to spell you for a few hours a week so you can breathe."

"That's not necessary," Hannah said automatically. "I'm handling it."

Emma fixed her with a knowing look. "Are you, though? When was the last time you picked up your camera? Or went anywhere that wasn't work or the pharmacy or the doctor's office?"

The questions stung because they hit directly at the truth Hannah had been avoiding. Her camera had gathered dust on her bedroom shelf, her photography relegated to the rare stolen moment when inspiration and opportunity aligned perfectly.

"I don't have that luxury," Hannah said quietly. "Mom needs—"

"Your mom needs you, healthy and whole," Emma cut in firmly. "Not running yourself into the ground until you break." She leaned forward, her expression earnest. "The church has a caregivers' support ministry, you know. Volunteers who provide respite care for a few hours a week. No cost."

Hannah tensed. "I haven't been to church since—"

"Since the accident, I know," Emma said gently. "That doesn't mean the church has forgotten you."

Hannah stared down at her coffee, watching the steam curl upward. The truth was, she'd stepped away from church not just because of logistics, but because of the hollow emptiness that had filled her after the accident. The questions about God's plan—why her father had been taken, why her mother had been left broken, why their family had been shattered—had overwhelmed her faith.

"I appreciate the thought," Hannah said finally. "But we're okay."

Emma sighed. "You know what I think? I think you're afraid to accept help because then you might have time to think about yourself, about what you want, about the life you've put on hold."

Hannah felt a flush of defensive anger. "That's not fair."

"Maybe not," Emma conceded. "But it's true, isn't it? You're hiding behind your responsibilities because it's safer than facing your dreams and needs."

The insight was too accurate, too painful. Hannah's eyes stung with unexpected tears. She blinked them back furiously.

"Speaking of things you've been avoiding," Emma continued, her tone gentling, "Martha mentioned you've had a certain deputy stopping by the diner regularly."

The abrupt change of subject caught Hannah off guard. "Reed? He just comes in for lunch."

"Mmm-hmm," Emma hummed skeptically. "And he just happens to time those lunches during your shifts?"

"He's being friendly," Hannah protested weakly.

"Hannah Gentry," Emma said with exaggerated patience, "that man is interested in you. And based on the blush spreading across your face right now, I'd say the feeling is mutual."

Hannah felt her cheeks grow warmer. "It's complicated."

Emma's expression softened. "Life is always complicated, sweetie."

"I barely know him," Hannah protested.

"But you'd like to know him better," Emma observed shrewdly.

Hannah looked away, unable to deny it. There was something about Reed that drew her—his quiet strength, his perceptiveness, the way he seemed to understand her unspoken struggles. The conversations they'd shared had become bright spots in her otherwise exhausting routine.

"It doesn't matter anyway," she said finally. "I don't have time for...whatever this is. Mom needs me."

"Your mom needs you to be happy," Emma countered. "And I'm pretty sure she'd be the first to tell you that if she wasn't so caught up in her own struggles right now."

"You don't understand. Even thinking about...about dating or having a personal life feels selfish. Like I'm abandoning her."

Emma reached across the small table and squeezed Hannah's hand. "It's not selfish to want connection, Hannah. It's human. And you're allowed to be human."

"I don't even know how to do this anymore. I haven't dated since senior year of high school."

"Ah, Eric Thornton," Emma said with a nostalgic smile. "Captain of the debate team and proud owner of the town's first Prius."

Despite herself, Hannah smiled. For a moment, Hannah felt like her old self, the girl who'd had dreams and plans before life had intervened so dramatically.

Emma leaned forward, her expression turning serious again. "Listen, I'm not saying you need to dive headfirst into a relationship. But allowing yourself to connect with someone? That's not betraying your mom. That's honoring the life God still wants you to live."

Hannah tensed slightly at the mention of God. "I'm not sure God's plan for me is particularly concerned with my personal fulfillment," she said, unable to keep the bitterness from her voice.

"Oh, Hannah," Emma said softly. "Of course it is. Do you think God wants you to be lonely? To put your whole life on hold indefinitely?"

"Well, He certainly hasn't made it easy to do anything else, has He?" Hannah replied, setting her mug down with more force than intended.

Emma didn't retreat from Hannah's flash of anger. "I don't claim to understand why things happen the way they do. But I do know that even in our darkest moments, God is working to bring light back into our lives. Sometimes through unexpected people."

Hannah was saved from responding by the approach of Mrs. Patterson, one of the town's most notorious gossips, who was bearing down on their table with determined speed.

"Hannah Gentry, I was just telling Betsy Wright about your mother's health troubles," the older woman announced without preamble. "My sister-in-law had the sugar too, you know. Lost three toes before she got it under control."

Hannah forced a polite smile. "Mom's doing much better with the new medication, Mrs. Patterson. Thank you for your concern."

"And I hear you've been getting extra attention from our handsome deputy," Mrs. Patterson continued, eyes glinting with curiosity. "Martha tells me he's taken to frequent lunches at the diner."

Hannah felt her face flame. "Reed is just being kind. He helped when Mom had her emergency."

Mrs. Patterson's smile was knowing. "Of course, dear. Though kindness from a man like that is nothing to brush aside. My Carlton was 'just being kind' when he offered to change my flat tire forty-two years ago." She patted Hannah's shoulder. "Sometimes the Lord works in ways we don't expect, bringing the right people to us in our time of need."

As Mrs. Patterson moved away, Emma struggled to contain her laughter. "Well, if Mrs. Patterson knows, then half the town is already planning your wedding. By Thursday, they'll have named your future children."

"I just can't deal with this right now..." Hannah gestured helplessly.

Emma's expression turned sympathetic. "Hannah... this town loves you. They remember the bright girl with the camera who was going to make it big. They want to see you happy."

"I'm not sure if I remember how to be that girl anymore," Hannah admitted quietly.

"She's still in there," Emma assured her. "She's just been buried under a lot of responsibility and worry." She paused, then added carefully, "Come to church with me on Sunday. Just once. No pressure beyond that."

Hannah hesitated. The invitation awakened a complex tangle of emotions—longing, fear, doubt, and underneath it all, a tiny flicker of the faith she'd once cherished.

"I don't know, Em..."

"Pastor Andrew's speaking about finding joy in unexpected places," Emma said. "And the coffee hour afterward has amazing cinnamon rolls. If nothing else, come for the baked goods." She smiled encouragingly. "Plus, I know at least one deputy who rarely misses Sunday service."

Hannah rolled her eyes, but a small smile tugged at her lips. "You're shameless."

"I prefer 'strategically persistent,'" Emma corrected with a grin. "So? Sunday? I'll pick you up at nine-thirty."

Hannah drew a deep breath, hovering on the edge of possibility. Part of her wanted to retreat to the safe, predictable routine of her carefully managed life. But another part, a part that had been dormant for too long, yearned to reconnect with the community, with her faith, and with herself.

"I'll think about it," she said finally.

Emma's face lit up. "That's all I ask." She squeezed Hannah's hand. "And Hannah? It's okay to let people care about you. It's okay to let yourself care about someone else. That's not betraying your mom. That's living the life God still has planned for you."

Hannah nodded, not trusting herself to speak.

They finished their coffee; the conversation turning to lighter topics of town gossip, Emma's plans to expand the store's local crafts section, and a funny story about Nurse Ferguson putting Peggy in her place.

As Hannah gathered her purchases at the register, Emma slipped an extra package into her bag.

"Chocolate-covered almonds," she explained when Hannah raised a questioning eyebrow. "Dark chocolate, no added sugar. Nurse-approved indulgence for both you and your mom." She winked. "Consider it medicinal. Good for the soul."

Hannah smiled gratefully. "Thanks, Em. For everything."

"That's what friends are for," Emma replied simply.

As she walked to her car, Hannah contemplated what Emma had said about God's plan. She'd stopped looking for signs of divine purpose in her life, convinced that her path had been irrevocably fixed on that terrible day ten years ago. But what if there was still room for unexpected blessings? What if Reed was one of them?

Chapter 9

The screen of Hannah's phone illuminated with another pharmacy notification as she turned onto her street. The diabetes supplies for her mother, test strips, alcohol wipes, and a new glucose monitor, had been processed, ready for pickup tomorrow. Another $63.42 that would stretch her already thin budget to the breaking point.

She mentally calculated how much was left in her checking account after the morning's groceries. Not enough. Not nearly enough.

The thought evaporated instantly when she spotted the sheriff's department SUV parked in her driveway, its official markings gleaming against the black paint. Hannah's heart lurched painfully against her ribs. Scenarios flashed through her mind.

Only as she skidded to a stop beside the vehicle did rational thought break through. If there was a true emergency, an ambulance would be here. The absence of flashing lights and emergency personnel meant whatever had brought Reed Dunbar to her home wasn't immediately life-threatening.

Hannah grabbed her purse and the bag of groceries, practically tumbling from the car in her haste.

"Mom?" she called as she entered the house. "Mom, are you okay?"

The sound that reached her ears made her blood run cold. The unmistakable, ragged gasping of her mother struggling to breathe. Hannah dropped the grocery bag, barely registering the crack of something breaking inside as she rushed toward the living room.

Peggy sat in her wheelchair, hunched forward, her thin shoulders heaving with each labored breath. Reed knelt before her, his uniform shirt stretched across his broad shoulders as he gently held her trembling hands.

"That's it, Mrs. Gentry. Nice and slow," he was saying, his deep voice steady and calm. "In through your nose... good... now out through your mouth."

"What happened?" Hannah rushed forward, dropping to her knees beside Reed.

Peggy's frightened eyes darted to Hannah, her face pale and glistening with sweat. "Can't... breathe..." she gasped.

"She's having a panic attack," Reed explained quietly. "It started a few minutes ago. I've been trying to help her regulate her breathing."

She reached for her mother's wrist, feeling the rapid flutter of her pulse beneath her fingertips. "Should I call an ambulance?"

Reed shook his head slightly. "I don't think that's necessary unless it continues. The breathing is helping." He turned back to Peggy. "You're doing great, Mrs. Gentry. Everything's going to be fine."

Hannah watched as her mother fixed her gaze on Reed, following his exaggerated breathing pattern. In for four counts, hold for two, out for four. Gradually, the desperate gasping eased, though Peggy's hands still trembled violently in Reed's steady grip.

"What are you doing here?" Hannah asked Reed, her voice low enough that only he could hear.

"I was on patrol and thought I'd stop by to check how you both were doing," he answered, his eyes never leaving Peggy's face as he continued guiding her breathing. "We were just talking when she became agitated. It seemed to come on suddenly."

Hannah's mind raced. Her mother had been fine when she'd left for work this morning—tired and a bit irritable, but stable. What could have triggered this?

As if reading her thoughts, Reed added, "She mentioned opening some mail today. Something about insurance."

Hannah's stomach dropped. She'd been dreading opening the insurance company's response to their appeal for extended home health coverage. They'd already denied the first request, claiming that Peggy's needs could be met with fewer nursing visits than the doctor had prescribed. Hannah had left the unopened mail that had arrived yesterday on the counter in the kitchen.

"Mom, you opened the insurance letter?" she asked.

Peggy nodded, her breathing still shallow but more controlled. She gestured weakly toward the side table, where several envelopes lay scattered.

Hannah reached for them, immediately spotting the one from Midwest Health Partners. Her hands shook slightly as she scanned the contents quickly. The clinical, impersonal language couldn't disguise the message: claim denied upon second review.

"They won't cover the additional nursing hours," she said flatly, letting the letter fall to her lap. The implications were immediate and overwhelming—either find a way to pay for the extra visits out-of-pocket or reduce Peggy's care.

"I'm sorry," Reed said, genuine concern evident in his eyes.

Peggy's breathing had slowed to near normal, though her face remained drawn with anxiety. "I'll be fine without the extra visits," she insisted, her voice thin and unconvincing. "We can't afford it, Hannah. We just can't."

"We'll figure something out, Mom. Don't worry about it right now."

"How?" Peggy demanded, sudden anger flaring in her tired eyes. "How are we going to figure it out? My medications cost a fortune." Her voice broke, tears welling. "I'm nothing but a burden to you."

"You're not a burden, mom."

Reed remained silent, but his presence was steady and calm beside them, a counterpoint to the swirling anxiety that filled the room.

Peggy closed her eyes, exhaustion etched in the lines of her face. "I'm so tired, Hannah. I just want to rest for a while."

"Of course," Hannah stood, ready to help her mother to bed, when Reed's radio crackled to life.

"Unit 3, what's your status?" The dispatcher's voice was clear and professional.

Reed unclipped the radio from his shoulder. "Unit 3, I'm at the Gentry residence on Elm Street. Conducting a welfare check following up on a medical situation from a few weeks ago. All secure, but I'll be here for approximately thirty more minutes."

"Copy that, Unit 3."

He returned the radio to its position and turned to Hannah. "Let me help get your mother to bed."

Hannah hesitated, the ingrained habit of handling everything herself making her pause.

"Please," Reed added. "I'd like to help."

Something in his tone, not pity, but genuine care, made her nod. "Thank you."

Reed moved toward Peggy, his manner gentle but confident. "Mrs. Gentry, would it be alright if I helped you to your room? You'll be more comfortable there."

Peggy looked up at him with tired eyes. "I suppose that would be fine, Deputy."

"Call me Reed, please," he said with the hint of a smile.

With an ease that surprised Hannah, Reed maneuvered the wheelchair toward the hallway. When they reached the bedroom, he positioned it next to the bed and engaged the brakes.

Hannah pulled back the covers on Peggy's bed, watching as Reed bent down to speak quietly to her mother. "I'm going to lift you now, Mrs. Gentry. Just relax and let me do the work."

He slipped one arm behind Peggy's shoulders and the other beneath her knees, lifting her from the wheelchair in a smooth motion. The ease with which he moved, supporting her mother's frail body without strain or awkwardness, spoke of experience. He laid Peggy gently on the bed, ensuring her legs were properly positioned, before stepping back.

"Thank you," Peggy murmured, her eyelids already heavy with exhaustion.

Hannah moved forward to pull the lightweight blanket over her mother's form. "Rest, Mom. I'll check on you in a little while."

Peggy nodded, her eyes closing. "I'm sorry about the panicking. I just... when I started thinking about that letter..."

"Don't worry about it now," Hannah soothed, brushing a strand of hair from her mother's forehead. "Just rest."

They retreated from the room, Hannah pulling the door partially closed behind them, before walking back to the living room, where the abandoned grocery bag still lay on the floor, a thin puddle of something seeping from its bottom.

"Oh no," Hannah hurried over.

Reed was already reaching for the bag. "Let me help clean this up."

Together, they salvaged the undamaged groceries and mopped up the spilled syrup. The mundane task gave Hannah a moment to collect herself, to push back the tidal wave of worry that threatened to engulf her.

When the mess was cleaned, Reed gestured toward the front porch. "Why don't we sit outside for a few minutes? The fresh air might do you some good."

The suggestion, simple as it was, felt like an unexpected gift. How long had it been since she'd just sat on her porch and relaxed?

"Alright," she agreed, "but just for a minute."

The porch swing creaked softly as they settled onto it, the weathered wood warm from the afternoon sun. The view was nothing special, just their modest front yard, the rural road beyond, and the distant silhouette of mountains, but the simple act of sitting in the open air with another person felt strangely freeing.

"Thank you," Hannah said after a moment of silence. "For being here when she needed help. If you hadn't been..."

"Don't go down that road," Reed advised gently. "You can't be everywhere at once."

Hannah stared out at the distant mountains, their blue-hazed peaks a constant in a world that had become unpredictable. "I used to think I could handle it all," she admitted. "That if I just tried hard enough, worked enough hours, planned carefully enough, I could make everything okay." She swallowed hard. "I'm not sure if I believe that anymore."

The swing rocked gently beneath them, its creaking rhythm soothing.

"No one can handle everything alone," Reed said.

"I'm scared," she said, the words slipping out before she could stop them. "All the time. Scared that I'll miss something important, make a mistake that hurts her. Scared that I can't keep up with the bills, the appointments, and everything she needs." She drew a shaky breath. "Scared that this is all my life will ever be."

The moment the words left her mouth, shame flooded her. What kind of daughter complained about caring for her mother? What kind of person was she to resent the life she'd been given?

"I'm sorry," she blurted. "I shouldn't have said that. I don't mean—"

"Yes, you meant it, and that's okay," Reed interrupted gently. "Feeling trapped doesn't mean you don't love your mother."

Hannah blinked rapidly against unexpected tears. "How did you know that's how I feel?"

Reed's gaze remained on the distant landscape, giving her the privacy to compose herself. "Because I recognize it. That sense of being caught between duty and dreams, between what you feel you should do and what your heart wants." He paused. "I've been there."

Hannah turned to study his profile, struck by the vulnerability in his admission. "With your job?"

He shook his head slightly. "There was an incident a few years ago. A domestic violence call that went bad."

The gravity in his voice told Hannah this wasn't a casual reference. This was something significant, something that had shaped him.

"What happened?" she asked.

Reed was quiet for so long that Hannah thought he might not answer. When he finally spoke, his voice was low and measured, as if each word was carefully chosen.

"A young couple. Two small children. The husband had been showing signs of instability for weeks. The neighbors had called in noise complaints." His jaw tightened. "I'd been to their house several times before. I noticed signs, the wife's behavior, bruises she tried to hide, but there wasn't enough for me to act on legally. I made a note to follow up, but..." He trailed off, his gaze distant.

"One night, we got a call. Possible gunshots. I was the first responder." He drew a deep breath. "By the time I arrived, the wife was already gone. Shot. The husband had fled the scene. Two terrified children hiding in a closet."

Hannah felt a chill despite the warm air. "Reed, that's terrible."

"The husband crashed his truck about twenty minutes later. Died on impact." Reed's hands, resting on his knees, curled into fists. "Two orphaned children in the space of an hour."

"But how is that your fault?" Hannah asked, bewildered. "You didn't cause any of that."

"I should have seen it coming," Reed said, the self-recrimination evident in his voice. "I should have done more. Maybe if I'd checked in more often, connected them with resources sooner... maybe she'd still be alive, those kids would still have their mother."

Hannah reached out impulsively, placing her hand over his clenched fist. "You can't know that. You can't carry the weight of 'what ifs' forever."

The irony of her words wasn't lost on her. Wasn't she doing exactly that—living in a prison of what ifs? What if she'd been driving that night instead of her father? What if she'd insisted they leave earlier, or later? What if they'd never gone to that photography exhibition in the first place?

Reed's hands relaxed beneath hers, turning until their palms met, his fingers gently closing around hers. "It's easier to give that advice than to take it, isn't it?"

The simple contact of his hand holding hers sent a warmth through Hannah that had nothing to do with the afternoon sun. When was the last time someone had held her hand? When was the last time she'd allowed herself to be comforted instead of being the comforter?

"We're quite a pair," she said with a trace of rueful humor.

"We are," Reed agreed, a small smile softening his features. "Both of us carrying more than we should, both too stubborn to ask for help."

"I'm asking now," Hannah said. "I don't know what to do about the nursing care. About any of it, really. The bills keep piling up, and I'm running out of options."

Reed's expression turned thoughtful. "Have you considered applying for additional assistance? There are programs beyond just insurance. There is state aid and nonprofit organizations that help with medical expenses."

Hannah nodded. "I've looked into some, but the application processes are overwhelming. Every form needs twenty different documents, and I just haven't had the time to gather everything."

"I could help with that," Reed offered. "My sister Holly knows the system pretty well from working at the clinic. Between the two of us, we could probably get the paperwork sorted out."

The offer was tempting, but Hannah hesitated. Accepting help had never come easily to her. It felt like admitting failure, like confirming she wasn't strong enough to handle her responsibilities. And yet, wasn't that exactly what she'd just done—admitted she was drowning?

"I don't want to burden you with our problems," she said finally.

"It's not a burden," Reed countered. "And Hannah..." he paused, meeting her gaze directly. "I care about what happens to you. To both of you."

"Why?" The question slipped out before she could stop it.

Reed seemed to consider his answer carefully. "Because when I'm with you, I feel something I haven't felt in a long time. Something I thought I might never feel again." His eyes, warm and earnest, held hers.

Hannah's heart pounded against her ribs. His words resonated with something deep inside her—a longing she'd buried beneath years of duty and sacrifice.

"I don't know if I remember how to do this," she admitted. "How to let someone care about me. How to care about someone else, beyond my mother." She drew a shaky breath. "I've been alone in this for so long."

"You're not alone now," Reed said, his voice low and certain. "Not unless you want to be."

The weight of the moment pressed on Hannah's chest, a strange mixture of fear and possibility. Part of her wanted to retreat, to pull her hand from his and rebuild the careful walls that had protected her heart for so long. But another part urged her to lean into this unexpected connection.

Before she could respond, the radio on Reed's shoulder crackled again.

"Unit 3, we have a minor traffic accident at Main and Cedar. No injuries reported, but requesting officer's presence."

Reed's face registered a brief disappointment as he released her hand to answer the call. "Unit 3 responding. ETA ten minutes."

He turned back to Hannah. "I have to go."

"I know," she said, a familiar resignation settling over her. Of course, this moment couldn't last. Reality always intervened.

Reed stood, adjusting his equipment belt. "Hannah, about what I said—"

"It's okay," she interrupted, not wanting him to feel awkward. "You don't have to explain."

"I'm not explaining," he said firmly. "I meant every word. And I'd like to continue this conversation, if you're willing."

The earnestness in his expression caught her off guard. He wasn't retreating or making excuses. He was asking for more time with her, deliberately and directly.

"I'd like that," she found herself saying.

Relief visibly washed over his features. "I was hoping you'd say that." He hesitated, then added, "Would you... would you consider joining me for dinner tomorrow night? Nothing fancy, just a meal where neither of us is working or rushing somewhere else."

The invitation hung in the air between them. A simple request that represented so much more—a step beyond the safe, isolated life she'd constructed, a chance to reclaim some small piece of normalcy.

"What about Mom?" she asked, practical concerns immediately surfacing. "I would rather not leave her alone for long, especially after today. I'll worry too much."

"Maybe Emma could sit with her?" Reed suggested. "Or Martha? I get the impression either would be happy to help."

Hannah considered this. Emma had indeed offered numerous times to spend an evening with Peggy. Hannah had always declined, unwilling to impose.

"I'll ask Emma," she decided, the words feeling both terrifying and liberating. "If she's available, then yes. I'd like to have dinner with you."

The smile that spread across Reed's face transformed his serious features, creating crinkles at the corners of his eyes and revealing a dimple in his right cheek that Hannah had never noticed before.

"I'll pick you up at six-thirty? We could go to the Ridge View Restaurant."

Hannah nodded, a flutter of anticipation displacing some of her perpetual anxiety. "Six-thirty."

Reed took a step back, as if reluctant to leave despite his duty calling. "I'll check in with Holly about those assistance programs."

The sincerity in his voice nearly undid her. "Thank you," she managed, the words wholly inadequate for the lifeline he was offering.

With a final nod, Reed descended the porch steps and returned to his vehicle. Hannah remained on the swing, watching as the SUV pulled away, its tires crunching on the gravel driveway.

Inside, the realities of her life awaited—her mother's needs, the unpaid bills, the endless responsibilities. But for this moment, sitting in the warm afternoon light, Hannah allowed herself to feel something dangerously close to hope.

Her thoughts drifted to Emma's words from earlier that day: It's okay to let people care about you. It's okay to let yourself care about someone else.

Was it truly possible? Could she find room in her carefully structured existence for something as unpredictable as feelings for Reed Dunbar?

The porch swing creaked softly as she pushed it into motion with her foot, the rhythm soothing. For the first time in years, Hannah allowed herself to contemplate a future that included more than just survival, one that might include connection, joy, and perhaps even love.

The possibility both terrified and exhilarated her.

Chapter 10

"I can't do this. I just can't."

Hannah stared at her reflection in the bathroom mirror, hardly recognizing the woman who stared back. She'd spent twenty minutes on her hair, coaxing the chestnut waves into something that looked deliberately styled. The subtle makeup she'd applied, mascara, a touch of blush, and tinted lip balm, felt foreign on her face.

The delicate silver earrings that dangled from her ears had been a birthday gift from Emma three years ago. Her blue dress, simple but flattering, had hung untouched in her closet for so long, the price tag was still attached.

"You absolutely can do this!" Emma called through the bathroom door. "And hurry up in there! Reed will be here in fifteen minutes, and I need to approve your outfit."

Hannah groaned, pressing her palms against the cool porcelain of the sink. A colony of butterflies had taken up residence in her stomach, and her pulse drummed an erratic beat against her throat. How had she allowed herself to be talked into this? What had possessed her to agree to a date when her life was already a precarious balancing act?

"Hannah Jean Gentry, if you don't come out of that bathroom in thirty seconds, I'm picking the lock," Emma threatened.

"I'm coming, I'm coming," Hannah muttered, taking one last critical look at herself before opening the door.

Emma sat perched on the edge of Hannah's bed, surrounded by discarded clothing options, and immediately straightened up. Her eyes widened as she took in Hannah's appearance.

"Oh. My. Goodness." Emma's hands flew to her mouth. "Look at you!"

Hannah fidgeted with the hem of her dress. "Is it too much? I feel ridiculous. Like I'm playing dress-up."

"It's perfect," Emma insisted, rising to circle Hannah like an art appraiser evaluating a masterpiece. "Not too formal for dinner at Ridge View, but nice enough to show you made an effort." She tugged gently at a strand of Hannah's hair. "And your hair looks amazing down like this. I'd forgotten how pretty it is when you actually let it breathe."

Hannah bit her lip, anxiety bubbling up again. "I should cancel. Call him and say Mom isn't feeling well."

"Don't you dare." Emma placed her hands firmly on Hannah's shoulders. "Your mother is fine, and you know it. I'm here. I've brought three different board games, a deck of cards, and enough snacks to survive a minor apocalypse. We're going to have a wonderful evening, and so are you."

"But what if—"

"What if nothing," Emma interrupted. "Everything is handled. Peggy took her medication. Her blood sugar is perfectly fine. I have both your cell number and Reed's programmed as favorites on my phone. I've got the clinic's after-hours number, poison control, and the direct line to Sheriff Baker himself."

Despite her nerves, Hannah laughed. "You've thought of everything, haven't you?"

"Yes." Emma's expression softened. "Hannah, it's just dinner. Two or three hours, tops. The world won't end because you dared to enjoy yourself for one evening."

Hannah sank onto the bed. "I know you're right. I just... I can't remember the last time I did something like this, just for me."

"Exactly my point. And just for the record, it's years since you've done anything for yourself." Emma sat beside her, taking Hannah's chilly hands in her warm ones. "Listen, I know this feels huge. Like you're scaling Mount Everest in stilettos. But it's actually small in the grand scheme of things. A tiny step toward reclaiming pieces of yourself."

Hannah nodded, swallowing against the unexpected knot in her throat. "And what if I don't recognize those pieces anymore? What if they don't fit back together?"

"Then you build something new," Emma said simply. "Something that honors who you were and who you've become."

From the living room, Peggy's voice called out, "Hannah? Are you ready yet? I want to see you before your young man arrives."

"Coming, Mom," Hannah called back.

She stood, smoothing her dress with trembling hands. "How's Mom been while I was getting ready?"

"Surprisingly supportive," Emma replied with a small smile. "And suspiciously interested in what you're wearing."

Hannah raised her eyebrows. "Really? When I mentioned the possibility of going out yesterday, she seemed... hesitant and irritated."

"Well, she's singing a different tune now. Go see for yourself."

Hannah checked her appearance one last time in the mirror, trying to quiet the voice in her head, reminding her of all the ways this evening could go wrong. Taking a deep breath, she stepped into the hallway and made her way to the living room.

Peggy sat in her wheelchair near the bay window, positioned to watch the driveway. She'd asked Hannah to help her change into a nicer blouse earlier, and someone—Emma, presumably—had pinned a small brooch to her collar and arranged a colorful afghan across her lap.

Her mother turned at the sound of Hannah's approach, and her expression transformed. "Oh, sweetheart," she breathed. "You look beautiful."

The simple compliment, offered with such genuine warmth, made Hannah's eyes sting. "Thanks, Mom."

"Come closer, let me see you properly," Peggy urged, gesturing Hannah forward.

Hannah moved to stand before her mother, feeling oddly shy, as if she were heading to the prom rather than a simple dinner with a man she was only beginning to know.

Peggy pointed to the delicate silver chain around Hannah's neck. "Your father gave me that necklace on our fifth anniversary," she said. "I've always thought it would look lovely on you."

Hannah's hand flew to the pendant, a small silver heart with a tiny pearl nestled in its center. "I thought it might look nice with this dress."

"It's perfect," Peggy agreed, her eyes lingering on Hannah's face. "You look so much like him. He would be so proud of you."

The mention of her father, rare and precious, made Hannah's breath catch. "I wish he was here," she admitted, the words barely above a whisper.

"Me too, sweetheart." Peggy's hand found Hannah's, squeezing gently.

Emma appeared in the doorway. "Ten minutes until Reed gets here," she announced. "Hannah needs shoes."

"The navy flats, Hannah," Peggy suggested. "The ones with the little bows. They'll match that dress perfectly."

Hannah blinked in surprise. "You remember those? I haven't worn them in years."

"Of course I remember," Peggy said. "I bought them for your high school graduation."

Emma slipped away, presumably to locate the shoes, leaving mother and daughter in a moment of rare openness.

Hannah knelt beside her mother's wheelchair, still holding her hand. "Mom, are you sure you're okay with me going out tonight? I can stay home if you'd prefer. It's no trouble."

Peggy's expression turned fierce with sudden conviction. "Hannah Marie, you listen to me. You are going out tonight, and you are going to enjoy yourself."

"But—"

"No buts," Peggy interrupted firmly. "Hannah, I…" She paused, seeming to struggle with her words. "I need to say something I should have said a long time ago."

Hannah waited, sensing the importance of the moment.

"I know what I've done to your life," Peggy said finally, her voice thick with emotion. "I know what I've stolen from you."

"Mom, no—"

"Please, let me finish." Peggy's fingers tightened around Hannah's. "Since you were eighteen years old, you haven't had a life of your own. No college experience, no travels, no… no normal young person things. No dates." Her voice wavered. "All because you've been tied to this chair with me."

"That's not true," Hannah protested. "I chose to stay. To take care of you."

"Because what choice did you really have?" Peggy's eyes glistened with unshed tears. "I've watched you sacrifice everything, your dreams, your photography career, and your youth. And I've been selfish enough to let you."

The raw honesty in her mother's voice struck Hannah like a physical blow.

"I was never strong like you," Peggy continued. "After the accident, after losing your father, I just... gave up. Let the grief and the pain consume me. Let you pick up all the pieces." A tear slipped down her cheek. "And God forgive me, but I've been angry... angry that I survived when he didn't. Angry at being trapped in this useless body."

Hannah felt tears threatening. "Mom, please don't—"

"But I've never been angry with you," Peggy pressed on. "I just feel guilty. So guilty of what my survival has cost you." She reached up to touch Hannah's cheek. "And now here's this good man, this kind man, who sees what I've always seen, how special you are. And all I can think is that it's about time the world got to see my Hannah. The real Hannah. Not just the caregiver."

Emma appeared in the doorway, shoes in hand, but stopped short when she saw the intense moment between mother and daughter. She quietly retreated, giving them privacy.

Hannah struggled to find words, overwhelmed by her mother's unexpected confession. "I never resented taking care of you," she said finally. "I love you."

"I know you do, sweetheart. And I love you too much to watch you shrink your life to the size of this house anymore." Peggy straightened in her chair, a new determination in her bearing. "So tonight, you're going to put on those pretty shoes, and you're going to go have dinner with that handsome deputy. You're going to talk about something besides medications and bills. You're going to laugh and remember what it feels like to be young and free."

Hannah managed a watery laugh. "Is that an order?"

"Yes, it absolutely is," Peggy declared, wiping away her tears with surprising briskness. "And I expect a full report when you get home."

Emma cautiously reappeared. "Sorry to interrupt, but he'll be here in five minutes."

The tension broke as Hannah stood, accepting the navy flats from Emma. She slipped them on, surprised that they still fit perfectly after all this time.

"See?" Peggy said with satisfaction. "Perfect."

Hannah took a steadying breath, smoothing her dress one more time. "I don't even remember how to have a normal conversation that doesn't involve work or caregiving."

"Just be yourself," Peggy advised. "The self you were before you became my full-time nurse."

"I'm not sure if I remember who that is," Hannah admitted.

"I do," Peggy said. "She's still in there. The girl who loved catching the first light on the mountains. Who could talk for hours about her dreams. Who laughed so easily."

Something shifted in Hannah's chest at her mother's words—a recognition, a remembering. That girl wasn't gone, just buried beneath years of responsibility and worry.

"He's here!" Emma announced, peering out the window. "And punctual, I might add. Excellent sign."

Hannah's pulse quickened. "Maybe I should change. This dress isn't really—"

"Don't you dare," Emma and Peggy said in unison.

Emma crossed to Hannah, adjusting a strand of her hair with sisterly affection. "You look beautiful, your mom is fine, and everything will be great. Now take a deep breath and try to remember that this is supposed to be fun, not a root canal."

The doorbell rang, its simple chime sending Hannah's heart into overdrive.

"I'll get it," Emma said, heading for the door.

Hannah knelt once more beside Peggy's wheelchair. "Are you sure—"

"Yes," Peggy interrupted firmly. "Now go."

Hannah hesitated, then leaned forward to kiss her mother's cheek. "I love you, Mom."

"I love you too, sweetheart. Now scoot. Don't keep that boy waiting."

Hannah stood, smoothing her dress one final time as Emma's cheerful greeting reached her ears.

"Deputy Dunbar! Right on time. Come on in."

Hannah moved toward the entryway, her nervousness giving way to a tentative excitement. She stopped, her breath catching at the sight of Reed standing just inside the front door.

He was dressed in dark jeans and a light blue button-down shirt that brought out the green in his eyes. His typically serious expression softened visibly when he saw her. He held a small bunch of wildflowers wrapped in simple brown paper.

"Hannah. You look beautiful."

"Thank you," she managed, surprised by how steady her voice sounded despite the fluttering in her chest. "You look nice too."

Reed glanced down at the flowers in his hand, then extended them toward her.

Hannah accepted the bouquet, touched by the simple gesture. The flowers were a cheerful mix of black-eyed Susans, Queen Anne's lace, and tiny purple asters—wildflowers native to the mountains around Laurel Ridge. "They're lovely. I should put them in water before we go."

"Allow me," Emma offered, stepping forward to take the flowers.

Reed smiled, a genuine, relaxed expression that transformed his typically serious features. "Thank you for staying with Mrs. Gentry tonight. I know it means a lot to Hannah."

"Please, call me Peggy," Hannah's mother called from the living room. "We'll be just fine. Emma's brought enough entertainment to keep us busy for days."

Reed moved toward the living room, nodding respectfully to Peggy. "I promise to have her home at a reasonable hour, Mrs.—Peggy."

"I trust you, Deputy. Besides, I'm pretty sure Hannah is beyond curfews," Peggy replied, her eyes twinkling with amusement. "But don't rush on our account. We've got a Scrabble tournament planned, and Emma's a sore loser who demands rematches."

"I resent that entirely accurate characterization," Emma retorted, returning from the kitchen, where she'd presumably arranged the flowers in water.

Hannah watched the easy interaction between them, a strange sense of disorientation washing over her. This felt like a scene from someone else's life: the supportive mother, the teasing best friend, and the handsome date waiting patiently. Not her life of rushed meals, medication schedules, and perpetual exhaustion.

Reed turned back to Hannah, offering his arm with old-fashioned courtesy. "Shall we?"

The simple gesture grounded her, pulling her back to the present moment. This was happening. She was going on a date with Reed Dunbar.

"Yes," she said, slipping her hand into the crook of his arm. The solid warmth of him beneath her fingers felt reassuring.

"Have fun, you two," Emma called, making shooing motions toward the door.

As Reed guided her toward the door, Hannah glanced back once more at her mother and best friend, both watching with expressions of such transparent joy that it made her heart ache in a strangely pleasant way.

Outside, the early evening air was cool and sweet with the scent of honeysuckle from the vine that climbed the porch railing. Reed's truck, not his department SUV but a well-maintained dark blue pickup, was parked in the driveway. Hannah noticed a small cooler in the truck bed, alongside what looked like a folded blanket.

"I thought maybe after dinner, if you're not too tired, we could drive up to Archer's Point," Reed explained, following her gaze. "The moon's supposed to be almost full tonight, and the view of the valley is pretty spectacular. But no pressure," he added quickly.

"That sounds nice, actually."

Reed opened the passenger door for her, waiting until she was settled before closing it. As he walked around to the driver's side, Hannah took a deep breath, willing her racing pulse to steady.

This wasn't leaping off a cliff, she reminded herself. It was dinner. Conversation. Perhaps a moonlit view afterward. Small, normal things that people did every day.

Yet as Reed slid into the driver's seat beside her, his clean, woodsy scent enveloping her in the close confines of the truck cab, it felt monumental.

"Ready?" he asked, his deep voice tinged with what might have been a hint of nervousness.

"Ready."

As Reed started the engine and backed carefully down the driveway, Hannah glimpsed movement at the living room window. Emma and her mother watching their departure, twin expressions of delight visible even through the glass.

The sight made her smile. For all her worry about leaving, there was something unexpectedly freeing in this moment.

"Something amusing?" Reed asked, noting her smile as they turned onto the main road.

"Just my cheerleading squad back there," Hannah replied, gesturing toward the house now receding behind them. "They're more excited about this date than either of us, I think."

Reed's mouth quirked in that almost-smile she'd come to recognize. "I don't know about that. I've been looking forward to tonight since you said yes."

"Me too," she confessed. "Once I got past the panic, anyway."

Reed glanced at her, his eyes reflecting understanding. "Second thoughts?"

"About a dozen, but not because of you. It's just... been a long time since I did anything like this."

Reed nodded, returning his attention to the road. "I understand. It's been a while for me, too." He paused, seeming to choose his words carefully. "Whatever happens tonight, whether it's just a nice dinner between friends or something more, I'm glad you said yes, Hannah."

"I'm glad too," she said.

Chapter 11

Hannah laughed as she set down her fork, the rich chocolate cake half-finished on her plate. "You're making that up. There's no way Sheriff Baker actually got stuck in the town's Christmas display."

"Hand to God," Reed insisted, his eyes crinkling at the corners as he recalled the memory. "It was his first year as sheriff. The department was helping set up the nativity scene in the town square, and Mark decided the stable needed reinforcement. Except he used the wrong supports and the whole thing collapsed with him inside it." Reed took a sip of his coffee. "Picture our esteemed sheriff crawling out from under a pile of wooden beams with a plastic sheep stuck to his back."

Hannah covered her mouth, trying to stifle another burst of laughter. The elderly couple at the nearest table glanced over, smiling at her obvious enjoyment.

"The worst part was the timing," Reed continued. "The elementary school choir was just arriving to practice their Christmas carols. Twenty third-graders got a good laugh that day."

Hannah could barely catch her breath. The mental image was too vivid. It felt strange to laugh this freely, like exercising a muscle long neglected. Her cheeks actually ached from smiling.

The Ridge View Restaurant hummed with quiet conversation around them, its rustic elegance creating a comfortable backdrop for their dinner. White tablecloths draped over sturdy oak tables and wall sconces cast a warm amber glow over the dining room. The large windows overlooked the valley and river below, the mountains now shadowed silhouettes against the deepening twilight sky.

Their initial awkwardness had dissolved somewhere between the appetizers and entrees, conversation flowing more naturally than Hannah had dared hope. Reed was different outside his uniform, still reserved, but with an underlying warmth that emerged more freely. The way he spoke about his family, his ranch, the town he'd sworn to protect, it all revealed a depth to him that intrigued her.

"What about you?" Reed asked, sliding his empty dessert plate aside. "Any embarrassing stories from your waitressing adventures?"

Hannah grimaced. "Too many to count. My first week at Martha's, I tripped and dumped an entire milkshake down Principal Webber's back."

"Chocolate or vanilla?"

"Strawberry. It looked like he'd been wounded." Hannah shook her head at the memory. "Martha rescued me, of course. She somehow convinced him it was a new spa treatment. 'Very expensive in the big cities,' she said."

Reed chuckled, the sound warm and genuine. "Martha's quite the force of nature."

"She is," Hannah agreed. "Martha has been a good friend to me. I don't know what I would've done without her these past few years." She traced the rim of her water glass, memories surfacing. "After the accident, when everything fell apart, she just... showed up. Brought casseroles, helped with paperwork, and she was just always there. She offered me a job when I needed it most."

Reed's expression softened. "You were young to take on so much responsibility."

"Eighteen," Hannah confirmed. "Just graduated from high school a couple of months before. I had everything planned out, and a scholarship to study photography at the University of Pittsburgh."

Hannah took a breath, her fingers fidgeting with her napkin. It was strange to discuss this aloud. Most people in town already knew the story, and new acquaintances rarely got close enough to ask.

"The car accident changed my life," she said finally. "Dad was driving. Mom was in the front passenger seat, and I was behind her. We were coming back from a photography exhibit in Charleston, which was one of my graduation presents." The bittersweet memory tightened her throat. "Dad died instantly. Mom's spine was injured. I walked away with scratches and bruises."

Reed reached across the table, his hand covering hers where it rested beside her water glass. The warmth of his touch anchored her to the present.

"You don't have to talk about it if you don't want to," he said.

Hannah shook her head. "It's okay. It was ten years ago." She turned her hand beneath his, their palms meeting. "Everything changed overnight. My college plans shelved. I became Mom's caregiver. The house needed modifications, medical bills piled up..." She glanced up, meeting his eyes. "You adapt. You do what needs doing."

Reed nodded, understanding in his gaze. "But you kept your photography."

"As much as I could," Hannah said. "More of a hobby now than a career path. Stolen moments between responsibilities."

"Your work shows genuine talent," Reed said.

The genuine appreciation in his voice warmed her. "Thanks."

Their conversation shifted to lighter topics as their server approached with the check.

Hannah relaxed back in her chair, taking in the quiet elegance of the restaurant. The Ridge View was several steps up from her usual haunts: Martha's Diner and the occasional fast food drive-through between errands. The last time she'd been here was for her high school graduation dinner, her parents beaming with pride across the table, and her future spread before her like an open road.

How different everything had turned out.

"You look thoughtful," Reed observed as the server returned with his credit card.

"Just remembering the last time I was here," Hannah admitted. "With my parents, after graduation. Everything seemed so certain then."

"Life has a way of taking unexpected turns."

"It does," Hannah agreed. "Though I'm starting to think maybe that's not always a bad thing." She met his gaze directly, feeling a flutter of nervousness at her boldness.

A smile spread across Reed's face, transforming his features.

As they rose to leave, Reed helped Hannah with her jacket, his fingers brushing against her shoulders. The simple courtesy made her feel strangely cherished.

Outside, the night air carried the crisp scent of late spring blossoms. The restaurant's exterior lights illuminated the stone pathway to the parking lot, where Reed's truck waited.

"Would you like to go up to Archer's Point? The view of the valley at night is something special. But I completely understand if you need to get back to your mom."

Hannah hesitated. The thought of extending the evening was tempting, but responsibility tugged at her.

"Let me call Emma and check in," she said, pulling her phone from her purse. Hannah punched in the number as she turned slightly away.

Emma answered on the second ring.

"Spill it. Are you having a magical evening? Is he as dreamy up close? Has he kissed you yet?"

"Emma!" she hissed, glancing at Reed, who politely pretended to be fascinated by something in the distance. "I'm just calling to check on Mom. Is everything okay?"

"Everything's fine, Hannah." Emma's voice softened. "We had dinner, played two rounds of Scrabble—I won both, for the record—and now we're watching that British baking show she loves. Her blood sugar is perfectly stable."

Relief washed through Hannah. "Thank you. I just wanted to make sure—"

"You wanted to make sure you could stay out longer," Emma interrupted, her tone knowing. "Which you absolutely should. In fact, I packed an overnight bag, so I'm fully prepared to sleep on your couch if it gets too late. Your mother has already agreed to this plan, by the way."

Hannah blinked in surprise. "You packed an overnight bag? That's a bit presumptuous, don't you think?"

"Enjoy your evening, Hannah. Take your time. Be a normal twenty-something for once."

Hannah glanced at Reed, who now leaned against his truck, patient and steady in the soft lamplight. The prospect of more time with him made her pulse quicken.

"You're sure it's no trouble?" she asked one last time.

"The only trouble will be if you cut your date short unnecessarily," Emma replied firmly. "Now go have fun, and I want details later."

Hannah ended the call and returned to Reed's side, a smile playing at her lips. "Everything's fine at home."

"Emma's a good friend," Reed observed.

"The best," Hannah agreed. She took a deep breath, feeling strangely liberated. "So... Archer's Point?"

Reed's face brightened. "If you're up for it?"

"I am," Hannah said, surprising herself with how much she meant it.

Chapter 12

The drive to Archer's Point took them up winding mountain roads that curved through dense forest before opening to higher elevations. Reed handled the truck with confidence, navigating the twists and turns of the road while maintaining a comfortable conversation about the history of the area.

"This used to be a lookout point during Prohibition," he explained as they climbed higher. "Folks would watch for revenue agents coming up the valley. There are still old moonshine stills hidden in these woods if you know where to look."

"How do you know that?" Hannah asked, genuinely curious.

Reed's mouth quirked in that almost-smile. "My grandfather has some... colorful stories about his dad and when he was a child. The sheriff's badge came later in his life."

Hannah laughed, enchanted by this glimpse of Reed's family history. "So, law enforcement... it's a family thing?"

Reed slowed as they approached a small turnout. "My grandfather, his father, and my dad. Though dad didn't keep it as a career for long.

He worked for the state police briefly before he and mom opened the bookstore and inn. Law enforcement runs in the blood, I guess."

He pulled into the gravel area that marked the lookout point, positioning the truck, so its headlights illuminated a rustic wooden picnic table at the edge of the clearing before switching them off. The sudden darkness was momentary, soon replaced by the silvery glow of the nearly full moon rising above the eastern ridge.

"Oh," Hannah breathed as she stepped from the truck. The valley spread before them like a velvet blanket, pin-pricked with the distant lights of Laurel Ridge. Above, the night sky blazed with stars, more than seemed possible, their brilliance undimmed by city lights.

"Worth the drive?" Reed asked, coming around to join her.

"Absolutely," Hannah said. The view awakened the photographer in her, fingers itching for her camera to capture the moonlight and shadow across the landscape.

Reed retrieved the cooler and blanket from the truck bed, setting them on the picnic table. "Coffee?" he offered.

"Please."

He poured the steaming liquid into two insulated cups, the rich aroma mingling with the scent of pine and mountain air. Hannah accepted hers gratefully, the warmth seeping through the cup into her chilled fingers.

Reed unfolded a thick plaid blanket, draping it around Hannah's shoulders before she could protest. The weight of it was comforting, the fabric carrying a hint of his scent.

"Thank you," she said, pulling it closer.

"The temperature drops quickly up here after sunset," Reed explained, settling beside her on the bench. "Views like this deserve to be captured."

"I haven't been up here in years. Not since..." she trailed off, calculating. "Not since senior year, probably."

"That's a shame," Reed said quietly. "It's one of my favorite places."

"Do you come here often?"

Reed's expression turned contemplative. "When I need to think. Or just... breathe." He glanced at her. "After the Davis incident, I spent many evenings up here."

The mention of the tragedy that had shaped him hung in the air between them. Hannah sensed there was more he wanted to say and waited, giving him space to find the words.

"I kept replaying it," Reed continued after a moment, his voice low. "Every detail, every decision. Wondering what I could have done differently. The department psychologist said it's common, the 'what-ifs' after a traumatic event. But knowing that didn't make them stop."

Hannah understood that particular torment all too well. "After the accident, I did the same thing," she admitted. "If we'd left earlier or later, if we'd taken a different route, if I hadn't been given that gift to the exhibit..."

Reed turned toward her, his expression somber in the moonlight. "It wasn't your fault, Hannah."

"And what happened to that young mother wasn't yours," she countered gently.

A sad smile touched his lips. "Easier to say than believe, isn't it?"

Hannah nodded, throat tight. "Does it ever go away? The guilt?"

Reed considered this. "I don't think it will... Not entirely. But it... changes. It becomes less sharp-edged with time, at least it has for me. My faith helped me. Trusting that even in the darkest moments, God had a purpose, even if I couldn't see it."

Hannah tensed slightly at the mention of faith, old wounds stirring. "That's been... harder for me," she confessed. "After the accident, I couldn't understand why God would take my dad, leave my mom suffering." She wrapped her hands tighter around the coffee cup. "Everyone at church had these ready answers—'God's plan,' 'everything happens for a reason.' But none of it made sense when I was eighteen and suddenly responsible for everything."

"That's completely understandable," he said after a thoughtful pause. "Empty phrases don't help when you're in pain."

"No, they don't," Hannah agreed. "Eventually, it was easier to stop going to church and stop asking questions that had no answers."

"Do you still believe?" Reed asked, his tone curious rather than judgmental.

Hannah stared out at the valley, considering the question. "I don't think I ever stopped believing in God," she said. "I just stopped believing He was particularly concerned with the details of my life."

Reed nodded, seemingly understanding. "I've had times like that, too. After the Davis tragedy, I was angry. Felt abandoned, like my prayers had gone unheard." He sighed. "But then something strange happened. Not all at once, but gradually. I started noticing small moments of grace in the middle of the pain. People showing up when I needed them. Strength appearing when I thought I had nothing left."

His words resonated with Hannah, echoing experiences she'd never articulated. The way Martha had appeared with meals when the pantry was empty. How Emma had shown up for no reason at all throughout the past several years. The unexpected insurance adjustment that covered the wheelchair ramp off the front porch.

"I think," Reed continued thoughtfully, "that sometimes God speaks most clearly in the little ways people take care of each other.

Not in big dramatic interventions, but in the everyday kindnesses that keep us going."

"That makes more sense to me than anything I've heard in a long time," she admitted.

Reed smiled, the expression gentle in the moonlight. "Well, I'm no preacher. Just someone who's stumbled through his own valley of doubt."

Hannah found herself drawn to his honesty, his willingness to acknowledge the struggle without diminishing its reality. Most people in her life avoided deeper topics, treating her mother's condition and Hannah's sacrifices as uncomfortable subjects best glossed over.

"Thank you," she said.

Reed looked surprised. "For what?"

"For not trying to fix everything. For just... listening."

"Sometimes that's what we need most, isn't it? Not solutions, just presence."

Hannah nodded. They lapsed into silence again, but it felt comfortable now, filled with mutual understanding rather than awkward gaps.

The moon climbed higher, casting silver light across the valley. A gentle breeze stirred the pine trees surrounding the lookout, the sound like a natural lullaby.

"Look," Reed said softly, pointing toward the eastern horizon. "Shooting star."

Hannah followed his gesture just in time to catch the brief, brilliant streak across the night sky. "Did you make a wish?" she asked.

"Maybe," Reed answered, a hint of playfulness in his voice. "You?"

"I might have," she admitted with a small smile.

Reed shifted, turning toward her. "Hannah, I want to thank you for coming out tonight. I know it wasn't easy to arrange, to step away from your responsibilities."

"I'm glad I did," she said sincerely. "It's been... I can't remember the last time I enjoyed myself this much."

Reed's expression softened. "I'd like to do it again if you're willing. Not just dinner or coffee at the diner, but... getting to know each other. Properly. Maybe you could come out to my place. We could ride my horses or even go on a hike sometime."

The simple request made Hannah's heart flutter.

"I'd like that," she said.

Reed's smile lit his face, the depth of his pleasure at her answer warming her more than the blanket around her shoulders. He stood and offered his hand. "There's something I'd like to show you. Just a short walk from here."

Hannah hesitated only briefly before placing her hand in his. His fingers closed around hers, steady and warm, as he helped her to her feet. The blanket slipped from her shoulders, but Reed caught it deftly with his free hand, draping it back around her.

"This way," he said, leading her toward a narrow path that disappeared into the trees beside the lookout. "Watch your step. The trail's a bit uneven."

Hannah followed, their hands still joined, as Reed guided her carefully along the path. The blanket whispered against the forest understory, moonlight filtering through the pine branches to create dappled patterns on the ground before them.

"Should I be worried you're leading me into the woods?" she teased, surprising herself with the lightness in her voice.

Reed chuckled. "Sheriff's deputy, remember? Sworn to protect and serve."

"That's what all the serial killers say in movies," Hannah countered, enjoying the easy banter.

"Fair point," Reed conceded. "But I promise the view is worth it. Just around this bend."

The path curved sharply, and then suddenly the trees opened up to reveal a small rocky outcropping that jutted even farther over the valley than the main lookout. A simple wooden bench, weathered by years of exposure, occupied the center of the clearing.

"Oh," Hannah breathed, stopping in her tracks. From this vantage point, the entire valley spread before them, the town of Laurel Ridge a glittering jewel nestled in the protective embrace of the mountains. The moon's light silvered the New River as it wound through the landscape, a ribbon of liquid brightness against the darker terrain.

"My grandfather built this bench," Reed explained, leading her to it. "Called it his thinking spot."

They sat side by side, closer now than they had been at the main lookout. Hannah could feel the solid warmth of Reed's shoulder against hers through the blanket.

"It's beautiful," she said softly. "So peaceful up here."

Reed nodded. "When I was a teenager, Grandpa brought me here after my first big disappointment. I didn't make the baseball team I'd tried out for. Told me that mountains had a way of putting human troubles into perspective."

Hannah smiled at that piece of wisdom. "Smart man, your grandfather."

"He is," Reed agreed. "He taught me most of what matters in life." He paused, his expression turning reflective. "He also told me that the right view can restore a person's soul. I think that's why photography speaks to me so much. The idea of an artist capturing those soul-restoring moments."

Hannah felt a surge of connection at his words. "That's why I fell in love with photography in the first place. Finding those perfect moments when light and landscape come together to reveal something... transcendent."

"I'd like to see that someday—you in your element, camera in hand, capturing those moments."

"Well, I'd like for you to bring me back here in the near future so I can do just that."

Something shifted between them, the air suddenly thick with unspoken possibilities. Hannah was acutely aware of his proximity, of the gentle rise and fall of his breathing, of her heartbeat quickening in response.

"You're remarkable, Hannah Gentry," he said. "Do you know that? The strength it takes to do what you do every day, the way you've put others first for so long..." He shook his head slightly, his admiration evident. "And yet, there's still this spirit in you, this... light that shines through."

"I don't feel very remarkable most days," she confessed. "Just... stretched thin, trying to keep everything together."

"That's exactly what makes you remarkable," Reed insisted gently. "The fact that you keep going, keep giving, even when it's hard." He took her hand, entwining their fingers. "But Hannah, you deserve to receive, too. To have someone care for you the way you care for others."

The simple truth of his words threatened to undo the careful control she'd maintained for so long. A tear escaped before she could stop it, trailing down her cheek.

Reed brushed it away with his thumb, his touch infinitely gentle. "I didn't mean to make you cry."

"Good tears," Hannah assured him, managing a watery smile. "I'm just not used to someone seeing... me. The real me, beyond the responsibilities."

"I see you," Reed said simply. "And I'd like to keep seeing you, if you'll let me."

Hannah looked into his eyes, finding sincerity there that couldn't be mistaken. Despite the practical complications, despite the voice of caution that had governed her decisions for years, she found herself wanting to step into the possibility he offered.

"I really would like that."

He leaned forward and pressed a soft kiss on her hand.

They stayed on the bench for a while longer, hands entwined, sometimes talking quietly about inconsequential things, sometimes simply sharing the companionable silence of the mountain night. Hannah couldn't remember the last time she had felt so peaceful, so present in a moment instead of worrying about the next task, or the next responsibility.

Eventually, the chill in the air deepened, and Reed suggested they should head back. The walk to the truck seemed shorter, their hands remaining linked as they navigated the moonlit path.

As they drove back toward town, Hannah found herself watching Reed's profile, admiring the strong line of his jaw, the way his expression softened when he glanced her way at stoplights. Something had shifted between them tonight, a connection formed that felt both exhilarating and terrifying in its potential.

When they arrived at her house, the porch light glowed welcomingly, and a lamp still burned in the living room window.

Reed walked her to the door, their pace unhurried, as if both were reluctant for the evening to end.

"Thank you for tonight," Hannah said as they reached the porch steps. "For dinner, the view... everything. It felt good to be out like a normal person."

"I hope this is just the first of many evenings together."

Hannah smiled up at him, feeling a lightness she hadn't experienced in years. "I'd like that."

"I'll call you tomorrow?" he asked as they parted.

Hannah nodded. "Sounds good."

With a final smile, Reed stepped back, watching as she unlocked the front door. Hannah turned to wave once more before stepping inside, closing the door softly behind her.

In the dimly lit hallway, she leaned against the door, her eyes closing as she replayed the evening in her mind. The dinner, the conversation, the breathtaking view from Archer's Point, and most of all, the gentleness in Reed's eyes when he looked at her, as if she were something precious and worthy of care.

Hannah felt the stirring of something that felt dangerously like hope—hope that perhaps her life hadn't narrowed permanently to the confines of caregiving and survival. That perhaps there was still room for joy, for connection, and for her own happiness alongside her responsibilities.

It was a fragile feeling, tender as a new shoot pushing through the soil toward the sun. But as Hannah moved deeper into the quiet house, toward the soft murmur of the television where Emma waited to hear about her evening, she held that feeling close, protecting it like the treasure it was.

Chapter 13

Reed drummed his fingers against the clinic's front desk, stealing glances at his watch while the receptionist finished her phone call. He'd arrived at Laurel Ridge Medical barely ten minutes after his shift began.

"She's with a patient now, Deputy Dunbar, but Nurse Holly said to tell you she'll be free in about five minutes if you'd like to wait." The receptionist, Anna, smiled at him kindly. "There's fresh coffee in the waiting area."

"Thanks, Anna." Reed moved to the modestly furnished waiting room, bypassing the coffee station. His thoughts had raced all night, replaying every moment of his evening with Hannah.

The mint-green walls of the waiting area displayed local artwork, including a stunning landscape photograph of the New River Gorge at sunrise. Reed paused before it, noticing the small card tucked into the corner: "Photography by Hannah Gentry." The image captured the fog lifting off the gorge, soft morning light breaking through the mist to illuminate the river below. There was something haunting about it—beauty tinged with loneliness.

"That's one of my favorites," Holly's voice came from behind him.

Reed turned to find his sister watching him with an all-too-knowing smile. She wore purple scrubs with small teddy bears printed on them, her dark hair pulled back in a ponytail.

"Hey sis. How's your day going?" he asked.

"Fairly well," Holly said. "But you didn't stop by this morning for small talk now, did you? Come on back to my office before my next patient arrives."

Reed followed his sister down the hallway, nodding to familiar faces as they passed. Holly's office was actually a small consultation room with a desk wedged into the corner, but she'd made it her own with family photos and a small potted plant that somehow thrived despite the lack of natural light.

"So," Holly said, settling into her chair and gesturing for Reed to take the seat near her desk. "I heard you had quite the evening."

Reed raised an eyebrow. "News travels fast."

"Emma texted me as soon as Hannah went to bed," Holly admitted, without a hint of embarrassment. "She said you two went out to Archer's Point after dinner. Very romantic, big brother."

"Boy, sounds like the gossip train was alive and well last night," Reed said with a chuckle. "Anyway... we had a nice evening together."

"Emma said Hannah practically floated into the house and couldn't stop smiling."

The thought of Hannah feeling happy sent warmth spreading through Reed's chest. He'd lain awake half the night, replaying their conversations.

"I like her, Holly," he admitted. "More than I expected to... I'm actually falling pretty hard."

Holly's expression softened. "That's huge, Reed. And it's about time." She studied him for a moment. "But I'm guessing you didn't come here to get my blessing. What's up?"

Reed leaned forward, resting his elbows on his knees. "I need your help... for Hannah, actually. She's drowning, Holly. Trying to manage her mother's care, work enough hours to pay the bills, and still have some semblance of a life. The insurance company denied her appeal for additional nursing care, and I can tell she's at her breaking point, though she'd never admit it."

Holly nodded, her expression shifting to professional concern. "I suspected as much. Peggy is a... challenging patient sometimes, and Hannah takes on a lot of responsibility. What kind of help were you thinking?"

"That's where I was hoping you'd have ideas. Support groups? Volunteers? Resources through the hospital?" He ran a hand through his hair, frustration edging into his voice. "There has to be something available that she doesn't know about."

Holly considered this, tapping a pen against her desk. "There are options, but the real issue might run deeper than just finding practical help."

"What do you mean?"

"Hannah's been caring for her mother for what—ten years now? That's her entire adult life, Reed. She's built her identity around being Peggy's caregiver. And Peggy, from what I've observed during her visits here, has become accustomed to that level of attention."

Reed frowned. "You're saying Peggy's taking advantage of her?"

"Not intentionally," Holly clarified. "But there's definitely a... dynamic there. Peggy's physical limitations are real, but they're not as debilitating as Hannah treats them. From a medical standpoint, many people with similar paralysis lead quite independent lives."

This perspective gave Reed pause. He'd noticed how competent Peggy seemed during his visits, how she managed her upper body mobility well. Yet, Hannah hovered, anticipating needs before they were expressed.

"You think Peggy could be more independent than she is?" he asked.

Holly nodded slowly. "I think both of them have settled into roles that may have been necessary initially but have become restrictive over time. Hannah needs to understand she can't do everything herself, and Peggy needs to reclaim some independence where possible."

Reed absorbed this, thinking about Hannah's exhaustion, the dark circles under her eyes that even her happiness last night couldn't completely erase. "So, what can we do?"

"Several things," Holly said, shifting into problem-solving mode. "First, yes, I can help connect her with resources. The hospital partners with a local volunteer organization that provides respite care—a few hours each week when a trained volunteer could stay with Peggy, giving Hannah regular breaks."

"She'd never ask for that herself," Reed noted.

"Which is why someone else needs to present the option," Holly said pointedly. "Second, I think we need to address the financial strain. Did you know the county has a work-from-home program for disabled individuals? Data entry, virtual customer service, that kind of thing."

Reed sat up straighter. "You think Peggy could qualify?"

"I don't see why not. Her upper body mobility is good, her mind is sharp. She might actually benefit tremendously from having meaningful work. It could provide not just income, but purpose, which is something I suspect she's been missing."

The idea resonated with Reed. He recalled how alert Peggy had seemed when discussing Hannah's date, how engaged she became when given something to focus on besides her limitations.

"That sounds perfect," he said. "Would you be willing to make some calls, find out what's available?"

"Already planning to," Holly assured him. "But Reed, these are just bandages on a deeper wound. Hannah needs to come to terms with the fact that she can't do everything alone, and Peggy needs to understand her daughter deserves her own life."

Reed sighed, rubbing his jaw. "That's more complicated than finding volunteers."

"Relationships usually are." Holly's expression turned thoughtful. "You know, I've wondered for years why Hannah never sought more help. At first, I thought it may be a time or financial constraint, but now I think it's something else."

"What do you mean?"

"I think she's afraid," Holly said simply. "Not just of her mother being hurt or neglected, but of who she is if she's not a caregiver. She's postponed her life for so long that starting it must seem terrifying."

The insight struck Reed as profoundly true. Hannah's hesitation when he'd asked her to dinner, the way she'd seemed almost disoriented by having an evening to herself—these weren't just the reactions of someone unused to dating. They were the responses of someone who had forgotten how to prioritize her own happiness.

"So, how do we help with that part?" he asked.

Holly smiled. "That's where you come in, big brother. You've already started, whether you realize it or not. Last night was probably the first time in years Hannah allowed herself to just be a woman enjoying an evening with a man she likes, not a daughter with responsibilities."

Reed felt a strange mixture of hope and pressure at his sister's words. "I don't want to push her or make things harder."

"Just being there matters, Reed. Being consistent. Showing her that caring for herself doesn't mean abandoning her mother." Holly glanced at her watch. "I've got a patient in five minutes, but I have one more thought. Why don't we both go over to their house this evening? We can talk through some of these resources and ideas with Hannah and Peggy together."

Reed considered the suggestion. Having Holly there would lend professional weight to the conversation, potentially making it easier for Hannah to accept help.

"Would seven work?"

"Perfect," Holly confirmed, standing as her office phone buzzed. "I'll bring information about the respite program and the work-from-home opportunities. And Reed?"

"Yeah?"

"This is a good thing you're doing. For both of them and for yourself."

Reed nodded, rising to leave. "Thanks, Holly. I appreciate it."

"Anytime." She paused at the door. "And Reed? I haven't seen you this invested in someone in a long time. It looks good on you."

Reed smiled, surprised by how natural it felt. "She makes it easy."

Chapter 14

Hannah tucked a strand of hair behind her ear as she laughed at Reed's story about his morning patrol. The diner was quiet, the lunch rush already over.

"So there I am," Reed said, leaning forward slightly, "trying to explain to Mrs. Willoughby that feeding the bears is actually illegal, and she's standing there with her grocery bag full of day-old pastries, insisting that 'her bear' needs the carbohydrates for proper hibernation."

Hannah covered her mouth, trying not to laugh too loudly. "In June? Hibernation in June?"

"Exactly." Reed's eyes crinkled at the corners. "And when I pointed that out, she informed me very seriously that 'her bear' is preparing early this year because it's going to be a harsh winter."

"How could she possibly know that in June?" Hannah asked, taking a sip of her iced tea.

"Apparently, her bunions are already acting up, which is a sure sign." Reed's deadpan delivery broke as his smile emerged.

Hannah shook her head, enjoying the easy flow of their conversation.

Reed took a deep breath. "I spoke with Holly this morning at the clinic."

"About?" Hannah asked.

"About both you and your mom. Hannah, I've seen how stretched thin you are, trying to manage everything alone. I asked Holly about resources that might be available to help—things the insurance company might not have mentioned."

Hannah's expression softened. "That was... very thoughtful of you."

"Holly has some good ideas," Reed continued, encouraged by her response. "She wondered if you'd be open to us stopping by this evening to talk about them."

Hannah's fork paused halfway to her plate. "Tonight?"

"Around seven, if that works. Nothing formal—just to walk through some options." Reed watched her carefully. "She thinks there are programs that could really make a difference for both you and your mom."

Hannah's gaze dropped to her plate. "What kind of programs?"

"For one, there's a respite care volunteer network through the hospital. Trained volunteers who could stay with Peggy a few hours each week, giving you regular breaks."

"I don't know..." Hannah began.

"And there's something else Holly thought might be perfect for your mom," Reed continued gently. "The county has a work-from-home program for individuals with disabilities. Data entry, customer service—flexible hours and training provided."

Hannah's eyes widened. "Work for Mom? I'm not sure if that would—"

"Hannah, listen, your mom is a very capable person. It could be a way for her to feel good about herself, to give her something to fill the time during the day." Reed watched her reaction carefully.

Hannah picked at her sandwich, her expression thoughtful. "Mom hasn't worked since before the accident. I'm not sure if she'd even consider it."

"It might be worth a try bringing it up," Reed suggested. "Holly can explain the program better than I can."

Hannah took a small bite of her sandwich, chewing slowly as she considered his words. "Mom barely leaves the house anymore," she said finally. "She doesn't even like going to her medical appointments. The thought of working, even from home... I'm not sure."

"Why doesn't she like going out?" Reed asked gently.

Hannah sighed, setting down her sandwich. "It's complicated. At first, right after the accident, it was the physical challenges—learning to navigate in the wheelchair, the embarrassment of needing help with basic things."

Reed nodded encouragingly.

"But over time, I think it became... safer to stay home." Hannah's voice grew quieter. "She hates the way people look at her, the awkward conversations, the pity. And honestly, I think she's afraid of running into old friends who knew her... before."

"Before the wheelchair," Reed supplied.

Hannah nodded. "She was so active—community theater, church committees, and the hiking club. Now she compares who she was then to who she is now, and..." she trailed off, blinking rapidly.

Reed reached across the table, covering her hand with his. "And she sees what she's lost, not what she still has."

Hannah met his eyes, grateful for his understanding. "I'd love for her to be more active, more engaged with life. I've tried suggesting things like a book club, or the adaptive yoga class at the community center. She always has a reason why it won't work."

"That must be frustrating for you," Reed said.

"It is, but it's harder for her." Hannah turned her hand beneath his, their fingers interlacing naturally. "I understand her reluctance. I just don't know how to help her past it."

"Maybe this work opportunity could be a first step. Something she can do from the comfort and safety of home, but that connects her to the world again."

Hannah's expression turned thoughtful. "A way to ease back into the world without the pressure of public interaction."

"Exactly. And the program provides training and equipment. Holly said they're very supportive."

"What about the respite care?" Hannah asked, her voice uncertain. "I'm not sure Mom would accept another stranger coming into the house."

Reed sipped his water, considering. "What if it wasn't a stranger? What if it was someone from church or the community that she already knows?"

Hannah's eyes lit up slightly. "That might work. Emma already sometimes helps, but I hate to always impose on her."

"You'd be surprised how many people would be willing to help if they knew what you needed," Reed said gently.

Hannah's smile was tinged with sadness. "I've never been good at asking for help."

"I've noticed," Reed teased lightly, squeezing her hand. "But accepting help isn't weakness, Hannah. It's wisdom."

She looked down at their intertwined fingers. "My dad used to say something similar. He called it 'letting love in.' Said that sometimes the greatest gift we can give others is allowing them to give to us."

"Your dad sounds like a good man," Reed said.

"He was. He would have liked you, I think."

"I wish I could have met him."

They ate in companionable silence for a moment, the diner's ambient noise flowing around them.

"So," Reed said finally, "is seven o'clock okay for Holly and me to come by? No pressure—just to talk through options."

Hannah hesitated, then nodded. "Seven works. Mom usually watches her game shows then, so she'll be in a good mood."

"Perfect." Reed grinned.

Hannah's expression softened. "You don't have to do all this, Reed."

"I know. I want to."

She studied him for a moment, as if trying to reconcile his actions. "Why?"

The question caught Reed off guard with its directness. "Why what?"

"Why are you doing this? Getting your sister involved, researching programs, wanting to help us." Hannah's voice was genuinely curious, not accusatory. "I imagine most men would run in the opposite direction from someone with as much baggage as I have."

Reed set down his burger, giving her question the consideration it deserved. "First, I don't see your life as baggage. Your dedication to your mom, your resilience—those things make you who you are. I admire them."

Hannah's expression remained skeptical.

"And second," Reed continued, his voice growing more serious, "I care about you, Hannah. When I see you struggling with something that might have solutions... how could I not try to help?"

"I'm not used to having someone in my corner like this."

"Well, get used to it," Reed said lightly, though his eyes conveyed his sincerity. "I'm not easily discouraged."

Hannah smiled, a genuine smile that reached her eyes. "I'm starting to see that." She took another bite of her sandwich, then asked, "What does Holly think about all this? About you getting involved in our... complicated situation?"

"Are you asking if my sister approves of you?"

"Maybe," Hannah admitted, her tone playful despite the vulnerability behind the question.

"She thinks you're amazing," Reed said honestly.

Hannah looked startled. "She said that?"

"Mm hmm," Reed affirmed, finishing the last bite of his burger. "And she's right."

Before Hannah could respond, Reed's department radio crackled to life.

"Unit Three, this is dispatch," came a female voice.

Reed unclipped the radio. "Unit Three, go ahead."

"Minor traffic accident at the intersection of Maple and Third. No injuries reported, but we need an officer on scene for the report."

Reed pressed the button. "Copy that. I'm at Martha's Diner. ETA five minutes."

"10-4, Unit Three."

He clipped the radio back to his belt with an apologetic smile. "Duty calls."

"Of course," Hannah said, understanding in her eyes. "I'll see you tonight?"

"Seven o'clock," Reed said.

"Be safe out there, Deputy."

"Always am."

Chapter 15

"I just don't understand why we need to have this conversation at all," Peggy said, her hands fidgeting in her lap as Hannah arranged the throw pillows on the couch. "We've been perfectly fine with our arrangement for ten years now."

Hannah took a deep breath, trying to keep the frustration from creeping into her voice. She'd started this conversation twenty minutes ago, hoping to prepare her mother for Reed and Holly's visit, but they seemed to be going in circles.

"Mom, we're not perfectly fine. We're surviving. Your diabetes diagnosis changed things. The medical bills are piling up. I'm working as many shifts as Martha can give me, but it's not enough."

Peggy's lips pressed into a thin line. "So, this is about money?"

"It's about more than money." Hannah perched on the coffee table across from her mother, their knees almost touching. "It's about you having something of your own again. About both of us having lives that aren't just... existing."

"I don't know what I can possibly offer an employer," Peggy said finally, her voice small. "I haven't worked in over a decade, Hannah. The world has changed. Everything's computers now."

Hannah reached for her mother's restless hands, stilling them between her own. "You were an executive assistant before the accident, Mom. That experience hasn't just disappeared."

"It might as well have," Peggy muttered. "Along with everything else."

The bitterness in her mother's voice made Hannah's chest ache. This was the wall she kept hitting, Peggy's conviction that her life had ended the day of the accident, that nothing worthwhile remained possible.

"Remember last month when Emma's computer crashed, and she brought over those files for you to reorganize?" Hannah prompted gently. "You had everything sorted and categorized in a system that made perfect sense in just a few hours. Emma said you saved her days of work."

A flicker of pride crossed Peggy's face before disappearing. "That was different. Emma's a friend."

"Your organizational skills are still there, Mom. Your attention to detail. Your way with words." Hannah squeezed her mother's hands. "Those skills didn't disappear. They're still part of you."

Peggy withdrew her hands. "I just don't see the point in getting my hopes up. Who's going to hire someone like me?"

"That's what Holly wants to talk about. Programs specifically designed for people in situations like yours. Will you at least listen? For me?"

Peggy sighed, adjusting the lap blanket across her legs. "Reed will be coming too?"

"Yes, Reed and Holly both."

A small smile tugged at the corner of Peggy's mouth. "I like Reed. He seems like a good man."

"I believe he is mom."

"And he cares about you," Peggy continued, her eyes softening. "I can see it when he looks at you. The way your father used to look at me."

The comparison squeezed Hannah's heart.

"Your father asked me to marry him after just three months. Everyone thought we were rushing, but when it's right, it's right."

Hannah stood, needing to move. "Let's stay on subject, mom. Tonight is about finding ways for us to move forward together. We're stuck in a rut, mom, and I don't know how to get out."

"You mean finding ways for me to be less of a burden," Peggy said quietly.

Hannah turned back, dismay flooding her face. "Mom, no. That's not—"

The doorbell chime cut through her protest. Hannah glanced at her watch—6:58. Reed was punctual, as always.

"That'll be them," she said, smoothing her shirt nervously. "Please, just keep an open mind, okay?"

Peggy nodded reluctantly, running a hand through her hair. "I'll listen. That's all I can promise."

Hannah hurried to the door, taking a steadying breath before opening it. Reed stood on the porch, Holly beside him. Both wore casual clothes. Reed in jeans and a forest green button-down that brought out his eyes. Holly in a cheerful yellow blouse and white capris.

"Right on time," Hannah said, stepping back to let them in. "Mom's in the living room."

Reed's warm smile eased some of her tension. "Thanks for having us over."

"I brought cookies," Holly added, raising a cloth-covered plate. "My famous snickerdoodles. They're sugar free, but I promise you can't tell the difference."

Hannah accepted the plate with genuine gratitude. "That's so thoughtful, thank you."

She led them into the living room, where Peggy's expression was carefully neutral, the social mask she wore for visitors firmly in place.

"Hello, Peggy," Reed said. "It's good to see you."

"Deputy Dunbar," Peggy replied, her tone softening slightly. "Nice to see you again."

"Please, it's just Reed."

Holly stepped forward, her smile professional but friendly. "It's good to see you again, Mrs. Gentry."

Hannah moved to the kitchen to prepare coffee and arrange Holly's cookies on a plate, grateful for the momentary escape. Through the doorway, she could hear Holly engaging her mother in small talk, her professional warmth putting everyone at ease.

By the time Hannah returned with the coffee tray, Reed had taken a seat in the armchair, and Holly was explaining her role at the clinic.

"I help coordinate individuals with several community programs," Holly was saying. "That's actually part of why we wanted to speak with you both about tonight."

Hannah distributed mugs of coffee and set the cookies on the coffee table before taking a seat next to Holly on the couch.

"Hannah mentioned that," Peggy said, her hands wrapped around her coffee mug. "Something about work opportunities?"

"Yes," Holly confirmed. "But before we get into specifics, I'd like to understand a bit more about your background, your interests. What kind of work did you do before your accident, Peggy?"

Peggy straightened slightly, a reflexive professionalism emerging. "I was an executive assistant at Blue Ridge Insurance for twenty years. I started as a receptionist right out of high school and worked my way up."

"That's impressive," Holly said sincerely. "What aspects of the job did you enjoy most?"

Hannah watched as her mother considered the question, something sparking in her eyes that Hannah hadn't seen in a long time—professional pride.

"I was good at anticipating needs," Peggy said finally. "Keeping everything organized, making sure deadlines were met. I enjoyed the problem-solving aspects, finding ways to make systems more efficient." She paused, a wistful expression crossing her face. "I liked feeling necessary."

The last admission hung in the air, its simple truth striking Hannah deeply. Necessary.

"Those are undoubtedly the kinds of skills that are in high demand for virtual work," Holly said, leaning forward slightly. "The county has partnered with several companies that hire remote workers for administrative support, customer service, and data management. Many of these positions are specifically reserved for individuals with mobility challenges."

Peggy's expression remained skeptical. "Everything's so computerized now. I haven't used anything beyond basic email and web browsing in years."

"The program includes paid training," Holly assured her. "They provide all the necessary equipment and software, and they offer one-on-one virtual instruction until you're comfortable."

"So, I don't have to leave my home?" Peggy repeated, glancing at Hannah.

Holly nodded. "Correct. Virtual instruction while you are comfortable here at home. After that, you'd work remotely, like many professionals do these days."

Reed, who had been quietly observing, spoke up. "Our cousin works remotely for a publishing company in New York. She never has to leave her house and enjoys working from home."

"What kind of hours would this involve?" Hannah asked.

"That's one of the best parts," Holly said. "Many of these positions are extremely flexible. Some allow you to set your own hours completely, while others might require certain core hours but offer flexibility around those. It depends on the specific role."

Peggy's fingers tightened around her mug. "And they really hire... people in wheelchairs?"

The vulnerability in her mother's question made Hannah's throat tighten.

"Absolutely," Holly said firmly. "In fact, that's the specific purpose of this program—to connect employers with talented individuals who have life challenges but also have valuable skills to offer."

"I don't know," Peggy murmured. "It's been so long since I've been part of the workforce. The idea of starting over at my age..."

"Mom, you're only forty-eight," Hannah said gently.

"And starting over isn't always a bad thing," Reed added. "My grandfather took up woodworking at sixty-five. Now he sells custom pieces at craft fairs across three states."

Peggy shook her head slightly. "That's different. He's not..."

"In a wheelchair?" Holly supplied when Peggy trailed off. "Peggy, I understand your hesitation. But I also see someone with valuable professional experience and skills that shouldn't go to waste. The wheelchair is just a means of transportation. It doesn't define what you can contribute."

Hannah watched her mother absorb Holly's words, a complicated mix of emotions playing across her face—hope, fear, doubt.

"What if I try and fail?" Peggy asked, her voice barely above a whisper.

"Then you try something else," Reed said simply. "No one succeeds at everything on the first attempt."

"I'll be right here every step of the way," Hannah said.

Peggy looked up, her eyes meeting Hannah's. "With your work schedule?"

"Martha's always been flexible when I've needed time off for your appointments, mom. I can't imagine this would be any different."

A silence fell over the room as Peggy seemed to wrestle with the possibility being presented. Hannah held her breath, recognizing the familiar signs of her mother's internal struggle. The slightly furrowed brow. The way she absently rubbed her thumb against her fingers.

"Could I..." Peggy began hesitantly, "could I possibly speak with someone who's gone through this program? Someone in a situation similar to mine?"

Holly brightened. "That's an excellent idea. There's a woman named Catherine who completed the program last year. She uses a wheelchair as well, and now she works as a virtual executive assistant for a tech company. I'm sure she'd be happy to speak with you about her experience."

"That would help," Peggy admitted. "To know it's actually possible."

"I'll arrange it," Holly promised. "And there's absolutely no commitment at this stage. We're just exploring options."

Hannah felt a flicker of hope at her mother's cautious engagement. It wasn't enthusiastic acceptance, but it wasn't outright refusal either, and with Peggy, that counted as significant progress.

"There's something else I wanted to mention," Holly continued, taking a sip of her coffee. "The hospital also coordinates a respite care program. Trained volunteers who can provide companionship and basic assistance for a few hours each week, giving primary caregivers a much-needed break."

At this, Peggy frowned. "Hannah doesn't need a break from me. We manage just fine."

Hannah bit her lower lip, avoiding her mother's gaze. This was the part of the conversation she'd been dreading—anything that made Peggy feel like a burden always triggered defensiveness.

Reed cleared his throat softly. "If I might offer a perspective, Peggy—it's not about Hannah needing a break from you. It's about her having time to pursue her own interests, like her photography."

"You take beautiful photographs," Holly added, turning to Hannah.

"Thank you. I haven't had much time for photography lately."

"That's precisely my point," Holly said gently, turning back to Peggy. "Respite care is about ensuring everyone in the family has space for their own wellbeing."

Peggy's expression remained troubled. "I don't like the idea of strangers in our home."

"What about people you already know?" Reed suggested. "The program coordinates with local churches. I believe Emma mentioned she's volunteered with them before."

"Emma?" Peggy looked surprised. "Well, she wouldn't be a stranger. But she already does so much..."

"The program has many volunteers," Holly explained. "It wouldn't just be Emma. But they try to match people who might be compatible, and they take your preferences into account."

Hannah watched her mother process this information, relief washing through her at how the conversation was being framed—not as Peggy being a burden, but as a restructuring that could benefit them both.

"Could I think about that part?" Peggy asked finally. "The work program sounds... it might be worth exploring. But having people in our home regularly... that's a bigger... I don't know, it makes me nervous."

"Of course," Holly said warmly. "There's no rush. We can take this one step at a time." She reached into her handbag and pulled out a folder. "I've brought some information about both programs for you to look over. And my direct number is in there if you have any questions."

Peggy accepted the folder, placing it on the side table next to the couch. "Thank you. You've given me some things to think about."

Holly set her coffee mug down. "Now, if you're open to it, I'd like to ask a few more questions about your specific skills and interests. It would help me identify which positions might be the best fit for you."

As Holly guided Peggy through a casual skills assessment, Hannah felt herself relaxing. The conversation flowed more naturally now, with Peggy gradually opening up about her professional background. Hannah found herself learning things about her mother's work life that she'd never known—how Peggy had computerized the filing system at her company, how she'd coordinated complex executive travel arrangements, and how she'd been known for defusing difficult client situations with her calm efficiency.

Reed moved to sit beside Hannah on the couch as Holly and Peggy talked.

"This is going better than I expected," Hannah whispered.

Reed nodded, his voice equally low. "Holly has a way with people. And your mom clearly has a lot of untapped potential."

Hannah watched her mother gesture as she described a particularly complex project she'd managed, animation lighting on her features. "I haven't seen her like this in... I can't remember how long."

"Purpose is powerful," Reed murmured. "We all need to feel useful, and needed."

The truth of his words settled in Hannah's heart. Wasn't that exactly what she'd been missing these past years? A sense of purpose beyond caregiving, a reason to wake up in the morning that was about creating a life rather than just maintaining it?

As the conversation continued, Peggy grew more animated, her initial reluctance giving way to cautious interest. Holly expertly drew her out, identifying skills and suggesting specific roles that might utilize Peggy's strengths.

"Your organizational abilities would be perfect for virtual office management," Holly was saying. "Or, with your customer service background, you might enjoy working with a company that needs phone support from at home agents."

"I always enjoyed helping people solve problems," Peggy admitted. "Getting to the heart of what they really needed, even when they weren't sure themselves."

"That's a rare skill," Holly said sincerely. "Company's value that kind of emotional intelligence highly."

Reed glanced at his watch. "We've been talking about work for quite a while. Maybe we should shift gears for a bit? Tomorrow's Saturday, and the weather's supposed to be perfect. I wondered if you'd both like to come out to my place. You know, see the ranch, maybe meet the horses. Holly can come too."

Hannah blinked in surprise. "Your ranch?"

Reed nodded, a touch of warmth coloring his cheeks. "It's nothing fancy, but it's peaceful. I thought you might enjoy getting out, maybe bring your camera, Hannah. The wildflowers are blooming all along the river on my property."

Hannah's pulse quickened at the thought of capturing the spring wildflowers in their prime, of spending time with Reed in his personal space. Then reality intruded. "I don't know if that would work with Mom's wheelchair. The terrain might be too difficult."

"Actually," Reed said, "the main areas of the property are quite accessible. The path to the paddock area is packed gravel. Even the river lookout is reachable by a solid path. And there is already a ramp up to the back porch of my cabin."

Holly nodded. "It's really lovely, Peggy. Very peaceful."

"You should go, Hannah," Peggy said firmly. "Take your camera. I'll be fine here for a day."

Hannah shook her head. "No. Either we both go, or neither of us does."

"Hannah—" Peggy began, frustration evident.

"I mean it, Mom." Hannah's tone left no room for an argument. "Let's go and enjoy a beautiful day away from home. When was the last time you spent an afternoon outdoors, just appreciating nature?"

Peggy's mouth opened, then closed. She seemed to be calculating.

"Your last doctor's appointment, and then I drove to the park, and we sat in the car and enjoyed the view," Hannah supplied when her mother didn't answer. "And you admitted afterward that you had enjoyed yourself, despite your initial objections."

Peggy sighed, her resistance visibly weakening. "There wouldn't be... many people around?"

"Just the four of us," Reed assured her. "Holly, me, you, and Hannah."

"And the horses," Holly added with a smile. "But they're excellent company."

Peggy's fingers worried at the edge of her lap blanket. "I'm not sure if I have anything nice to wear. All I have are casual clothes."

Hannah recognized the excuse for what it was—her mother's social anxiety finding a new outlet. "We can find something tonight," she said gently. "This isn't a formal occasion. Right, Reed?"

"Not at all," Reed confirmed. "Comfortable clothes you don't mind getting a little dusty are perfect. I usually end up with horse hair on me by the end of any given day."

Peggy seemed to be running out of objections. Her gaze moved to the window, where the evening sky was painted in soft pinks and purples. "I suppose... it might be nice to see something besides these four walls."

The tentative admission sent a surge of hope through Hannah. "It really would, Mom."

"And if you get tired or uncomfortable, I'll bring you right back home," Reed promised. "No questions asked."

Peggy nodded slowly. "Alright. But Hannah, you have to promise to bring your camera. Don't use me as an excuse not to do something you love."

Hannah reached over to squeeze her mother's hand. "I promise."

"Wonderful," Holly said brightly.

Reed stood, his expression pleased. "I can pick you both up around ten tomorrow morning, if that works? That gives us plenty of daylight."

"Ten is perfect," Hannah confirmed, rising to see them out.

As they moved toward the door, Holly hung back briefly to speak with Peggy, confirming details about connecting her with Catherine from the work program. Hannah and Reed stepped onto the front porch, the evening air cool and sweet with the scent of honeysuckle.

"Thank you," Hannah said quietly. "For all of this. Holly was wonderful with Mom."

Reed smiled, his eyes crinkling at the corners. "Holly has that effect on people. But your mom deserves credit too. She was willing to listen, to consider new possibilities. That takes courage."

"She surprised me," Hannah admitted. "I expected much more resistance."

"Sometimes people just need to be reminded of their own capabilities," Reed said. "To be seen as more than their limitations."

The truth of his words resonated within Hannah.

Holly joined them on the porch. "Peggy and I were just discussing some specifics about the training program. She seems genuinely interested, Hannah. I think this could be really positive for both of you."

"I hope so," Hannah said, a cautious optimism blooming within her.

"So, ten o'clock tomorrow?" Reed confirmed, his hand briefly touching Hannah's elbow in a gentle gesture that sent warmth through her.

"We'll be ready," Hannah promised.

Chapter 16

Reed's pickup crunched over the last stretch of gravel as he guided it down his driveway. Beside him in the passenger seat, Hannah leaned forward, her camera already in hand, eyes bright with anticipation. In the back seat, Peggy gripped the door handle, her knuckles white despite the easy pace of their drive.

"Well, ladies," Reed announced, steering the truck around a gentle curve where the trees opened to reveal his homestead, "welcome to Dunbar Ranch."

Hannah's soft intake of breath was audible over the truck's engine. "Reed, it's beautiful."

The cabin sat nestled against a backdrop of tall trees, its honey-colored logs warmed by the late morning sunlight. A wraparound porch hugged the front and sides of the structure, adorned with simple rocking chairs and hanging baskets overflowing with red geraniums. Beyond the cabin, a red barn stood sentinel beside a fenced paddock where three horses grazed contentedly.

Behind them, Holly's silver sedan appeared, following their path up the drive.

"I didn't realize it would be so..." Hannah trailed off, her fingers tightening around her camera.

"Remote?" Reed offered, pulling to a stop in front of the cabin.

"Peaceful," she finished. "Like something from another time."

In the back seat, Peggy relaxed her grip on the door. "The air smells different out here," she observed, rolling down her window further. "Sweeter somehow."

Reed nodded, cutting the engine. "That's the wild honeysuckle. It grows all along the back fence line."

He stepped out of the truck and moved to the rear passenger door, opening it for Peggy while Hannah climbed out on her own, already positioning her camera toward the horses in the distance.

"Let me get your chair, Mrs. Gentry," Reed said, reaching into the truck bed for the folded wheelchair.

"Peggy, please," she reminded him, watching as he expertly unfolded the chair beside the truck. "You've certainly done this before."

Reed positioned the wheelchair carefully. "I've had plenty of practice."

Holly parked beside them and emerged from her car, stretching. "Perfect day for this," she called, approaching with a large tote bag slung over her shoulder. "Not too hot, not too cold."

Reed helped Peggy into her wheelchair with practiced ease, maneuvering her away from the truck once she was settled.

"How about a tour?" he suggested, gesturing toward the packed gravel path that led to the cabin. "We can start with the house, then see the horses if you're up for it."

Peggy adjusted her position in the chair. "I'd like to see everything if that's all right. It's been ages since I've been anywhere like this."

The simple admission, delivered without her usual defensiveness, made Hannah's heart squeeze. She lowered her camera, moving to her mother's side.

"The path looks good," Hannah noted, eyeing the smooth, packed surface. "Not too much of a slope."

Reed nodded. "I had it redone last summer. The original was getting bad."

Holly fell into step beside Peggy's chair. "Wait until you see the view from the back porch. The river bends right behind the property. It's postcard-perfect."

As they approached the cabin, the sound of soft nickering carried from the paddock. One of the horses, a chestnut gelding with a white blaze, trotted to the fence line, head raised attentively.

"That's Jasper," Reed explained. "He's curious about visitors. The black one hanging back is Tango. He takes longer to warm up to new folks. And the dappled gray mare is Scout."

"They're gorgeous," Hannah said, lifting her camera again. The click of the shutter captured Jasper's alert posture, ears pricked forward in interest. "How long have you had them?"

"Two years for Jasper and Tango. Scout joined us about eighteen months ago." Reed said as he guided them toward the back of the cabin.

The ramp was wide and sturdy, with a gentle incline leading to the spacious back deck.

Once on the deck, they all paused, taking in the vista that spread before them. The cabin perched on a natural rise, offering a commanding view of the river below and the mountains beyond. Morning mist still clung to the distant peaks, creating an ethereal quality to the landscape.

"Oh my," Peggy breathed, her earlier tension visibly melting. "It's like a painting."

Hannah was already moving to the deck railing, camera raised. The morning light painted everything in soft hues, and the river caught glints of silver as it wound through the property.

"This is why I bought this place," Reed said, coming to stand beside her. "The First time I saw this view, I knew I was home."

Hannah lowered her camera to meet his eyes. "I can see why."

Reed's gaze held hers a beat longer than necessary before he turned back to Peggy.

"Would you like to see inside, or would you prefer to enjoy the view a while longer?"

"Actually," Peggy said, surprising them all, "I'd love to see those horses up close if that's possible. It's been so long since I've been near animals."

Reed brightened. "Of course."

As they made their way back down the ramp, Holly fell into step beside Peggy's chair. "I brought some carrots for the horses," she said, patting her tote bag. "They're absolute suckers for treats."

"I haven't fed a horse since..." Peggy's voice faltered. "Well, I can't remember how long it's been."

The packed gravel path curved around the cabin and across a stretch of open yard to the fenced paddock area. Jasper watched their approach with interest.

"She knows visitors usually mean extra attention," Reed explained, reaching the gate first and unlatching it. He swung it wide, making sure there was ample room for Peggy's wheelchair.

Once inside, Reed approached Jasper, stroking his neck and murmuring soft greetings. The mare nuzzled his chest affectionately.

"She's beautiful," Hannah said, raising her camera to capture the bond between man and horse.

Holly reached into her bag and produced several carrots. "Would you like to feed her, Peggy?" she asked, offering one.

Peggy hesitated, staring at the carrot in Holly's hand. "I don't know... she's so large."

Peggy reached for the carrot, her hand trembling slightly.

"Here," Reed said, leading Jasper closer. "Hold your hand flat out flat with the carrot in the palm of your hand."

Peggy extended her palm with the carrot resting on it. Jasper approached, lips velvety soft as she delicately took the treat. A startled laugh escaped Peggy as the horse crunched the carrot.

"Her mouth is so soft!" she exclaimed, a genuine smile transforming her face.

Hannah quickly captured the moment—her mother's delight, Reed's gentle guidance, the horse's attentive posture. The shutter clicked several times in rapid succession.

"Would you like to try brushing her?" Reed asked, retrieving a curry brush from a box mounted on the fence post. "She loves the attention."

"Could I?" Peggy asked.

"Absolutely," Reed assured her. He demonstrated the circular motion on Jasper's shoulder. "Just like this. Nice and easy."

He handed the brush to Peggy and guided her wheelchair closer to the horse. With tentative movements, Peggy began brushing Jasper's shoulder. The horse leaned into the contact, clearly enjoying it.

"You're a natural," Reed told her.

"Look at her," Holly said quietly to Hannah. "When's the last time you saw her this animated?"

Hannah shook her head, throat tight with emotion. "Years. Maybe since before the accident."

As Peggy continued grooming Jasper, the other two horses approached.

"Would you like to meet them too?" Reed asked Peggy.

"I think I would," Peggy replied.

Reed beckoned Tango closer with a soft clicking sound. The horse approached cautiously, neck extended.

"He's more reserved," Reed explained, "but just as gentle once he knows you."

Holly offered another carrot to Peggy, who took it with far less hesitation. She held it out to Tango, who delicately accepted it, his dark eyes watching her with calm intelligence.

"They're so different," Peggy observed. "Like people."

Reed nodded. "Each with their own personality. Tango here was mistreated before I got him. It took months to earn his trust."

"But you did," Hannah said, watching the interaction between man and horse.

Reed met her eyes over Tango's back. "Patience and consistency. Most wounded creatures respond to that, eventually."

Holly clapped her hands together. "I don't know about all of you, but I could use some refreshments. I packed a cooler with lemonade and snacks. It's in Reed's truck."

"Perfect," Reed agreed.

"I'd like to stay with the horses a little longer," Peggy said, surprising them all with her assertiveness. "If that's all right."

"Of course," Reed assured her. "Holly, would you mind staying with Peggy while Hannah and I fetch the refreshments?"

"Happy to," Holly agreed readily.

Hannah followed Reed back toward the truck, where a cooler waited in the bed. As they walked side by side along the gravel path, Reed's hand brushed against hers, the brief contact sending a ripple of awareness through her.

"Your mother seems to be enjoying herself," he said, reaching the truck and lifting the cooler with ease.

"I can't believe it," Hannah admitted, taking a smaller bag of supplies from the truck bed.

"Sometimes a complete change of scenery helps," Reed suggested.

They made their way toward the cabin. Hannah found herself hyper-aware of him beside her. The sunlight catching the hints of auburn in his dark hair, the easy strength in his movements, the way his presence felt steady and grounding.

"You know," Reed said as they reached the cabin, "I was worried about today. I wanted everything to be perfect for you both."

Hannah glanced at him. "Everything is perfect," she assured him. "Your place is wonderful, Reed. I can see why you love it here."

They continued around to the back deck, where Reed set the cooler on a large wooden table. "My grandfather helped me build this table," he explained, running his hand over the smooth surface. "Said a man needs a place where friends can gather."

Hannah set down her bag and began unpacking plastic cups and napkins. "I'd like to meet your grandfather."

"You will," Reed said, opening the cooler to reveal a pitcher of lemonade nestled among ice packs. "I think you'll like him."

After arranging the drinks and a container of sliced fruits, cheese, and crackers, they walked back to the paddock, where they found Peggy still engaged with the horses. She was speaking animatedly to Holly about something while Jasper nuzzled at her wheelchair.

"Refreshments are ready," Reed said as they approached. "We can sit on the deck and enjoy the scenery."

Peggy turned toward them, her cheeks flushed with more color than Hannah had seen in years. "Actually, I think I'd like to see the inside of your home. Holly's been telling me about the fireplace."

"Of course, Peggy," Reed said immediately. "Whatever you want to do... the day is completely yours."

As they made their way back toward the cabin, Hannah fell into step beside her mother's wheelchair. "Having a good time?" she asked.

Peggy reached up to squeeze her daughter's hand. "It feels good to be somewhere different. Somewhere beautiful." She paused, then added, "And to see you enjoying yourself."

Hannah hadn't realized how visible her enjoyment had been, but she couldn't deny it.

Back on the deck, Reed held the screen door wide as Holly maneuver Peggy's chair over the threshold. The interior of the cabin was even more inviting than its exterior promised. An open living space with high ceilings, exposed beams, and a massive stone fireplace was its focal point.

"This is lovely," Peggy said, wheeling herself further into the room. The hardwood floors allowed her chair to move easily across the space. "So much light!"

Large windows framed the mountain views, while comfortable leather furniture created conversation areas. Bookcases lined one wall, filled with a mix of practical guides, historical volumes, and the occasional thriller. A few family photographs were displayed simply on the mantelpiece.

"It's not fancy," Reed said, "but it suits me."

"It's perfect," Hannah replied honestly, taking in the space. It was undeniably masculine in its simplicity, yet welcoming and warm—very much like Reed himself.

Holly brought the refreshments inside and set them on a coffee table near the largest window. "Let's eat with a view," she suggested.

They settled into a comfortable arrangement. Peggy positioned by the window where she could see both the room and the mountains beyond. Reed poured lemonade while Hannah distributed plates.

"So, how did you find this place?" Peggy asked, accepting a glass from Reed. "It seems so tucked away."

"It belonged to an older couple who were moving closer to their grandchildren in Ohio," Reed explained. "I wasn't even looking to buy property at the time, but Mark—Sheriff Baker—heard they were selling and thought of me." He paused, taking a sip of lemonade. "The moment I stepped onto that deck out back and saw the view..."

"You knew," Hannah supplied, understanding immediately.

Reed nodded, meeting her eyes. "Some places just speak to you."

"The photographs on your mantel," Peggy noted, gesturing toward them. "Family?"

"Yes," Reed confirmed. "My parents, grandparents, Holly and me at various ages. Just snapshots of moments that mattered."

Peggy's expression softened. "Family is precious," she said quietly. "So easy to take for granted until..." she trailed off, the unspoken loss hovering between them.

Reed's response was gentle but direct. "Until you lose someone who can never be replaced. Yes, I understand that."

The simple acknowledgment of shared grief created a moment of connection. Hannah watched her mother's face as she recognized the genuine understanding of Reed's words.

"Your ranch is beautiful," Peggy said after a moment. "How much land do you have?"

"Twenty acres," Reed replied. "Most of it wooded, with the river forming the southern boundary. There's a trail that follows the water for almost half a mile before it turns back through the forest."

"Is it accessible?" Holly asked, glancing meaningfully at Peggy's wheelchair.

Reed considered this. "Parts of it are fairly smooth, but there are sections that would be challenging."

"Perhaps another time," Peggy said, but without her usual resignation. It sounded more like an actual plan than a dismissal.

As they enjoyed their refreshments, the conversation flowed. Holly shared stories from the clinic and humorous moments that came with healthcare work. Reed described his grandfather's woodworking projects, which included some of the furniture in the cabin.

When they'd finished eating, Reed collected their plates. "Hannah, would you like to explore a bit? There's a spot by the river I think you might appreciate. Great photography potential."

Hannah glanced at her mother.

"Go," Peggy said firmly. "Holly and I were just discussing a book we both read. We'll be fine here."

Holly nodded encouragingly. "Take your time. The view is spectacular."

Hannah hesitated.

"Really, dear," Peggy insisted. "I'm perfectly fine. And Holly is a nurse, for heaven's sake. I couldn't be in better hands."

"Okay, but if you need anything—"

"We'll manage," Holly interrupted kindly but firmly. "Go enjoy yourself."

Reed was already waiting by the door, Hannah's camera in hand. "Ready?"

With a last glance at her mother, who was now gesturing animatedly to Holly about something, Hannah nodded. "Lead the way."

Chapter 17

They stepped out of the cabin into the midday sunshine, the air warm but pleasant against Hannah's skin. Reed led her along a narrow path winding between tall trees alongside the river.

"Watch your step here. The tree roots can be tricky," he said.

Hannah followed, inhaling deeply. The scent of pine needles and rich earth filled her lungs, so different from the artificial fragrances of cleaning products and air fresheners that dominated her home.

"I didn't realize how much I needed this," she admitted as they ducked under a low-hanging branch. "To be outdoors, I mean. To just... breathe."

Reed glanced back at her, understanding in his eyes. "Nature has a way of restoring perspective. At least it does for me."

"Is that why you moved way out here? For perspective?"

Reed's pace slowed as the trail narrowed further. "Partly," he acknowledged. "After the Davis tragedy, I had a hard time. I needed space to think and get my life back in order. I wanted some place quiet to pray… someplace that I felt closer to God. I wanted to be able to come home and leave work far behind."

"I understand that. After the accident, I was constantly surrounded by people and noise at first. I had no space to think or breathe. Then life settled in and suddenly, it was just mom and me. I felt lonely in an odd sort of way, and angry. I felt like God had abandoned us. I believe in God, but it's… complicated. Sometimes it feels like I'm talking to someone who might not be listening."

"Yet you keep talking."

"I do, sometimes," she replied. "Even when I'm angriest, part of me is still reaching out. Still hoping for an answer."

Reed nodded. "That's faith, Hannah. Maybe the truest kind—persisting despite the silence."

The trail opened suddenly into a small clearing beside the river. The water rushed past, tumbling over smooth stones with a sound like gentle music. Wildflowers dotted the grassy bank, purple and yellow blooms nodding in the slight breeze.

"Oh," Hannah breathed, lifting her camera instinctively.

"Thought you might like it," Reed said, stepping aside to give her space.

Hannah moved toward the water's edge, adjusting her camera settings as she went. The play of light on the moving water created sparkling patterns that changed constantly. She crouched, finding an angle that captured both the dynamic river and the stillness of the surrounding woods.

Reed settled on a large flat rock nearby, content to watch her work. Hannah's awareness of him faded as she fell into the rhythm of photography. The world narrowing to light and shadow, composition and movement. She moved along the bank, finding different perspectives, different stories within the same setting.

Time slipped past unnoticed until Reed's voice gently broke her concentration. "Find anything interesting?"

Hannah lowered her camera, suddenly aware of how absorbed she'd become. "Sorry, I tend to lose track of time when I'm shooting."

"Don't apologize. It's nice to see you doing something you love."

Hannah returned to where he sat, settling beside him on the flat rock. "I haven't done a good photo expedition in... I can't even remember how long."

"Too long, probably. You're very talented, Hannah."

A flush of pleasure warmed Hannah's cheeks. "It's just a hobby at this point really—"

"No," Reed interrupted gently. "It's more than that. You have a gift for seeing beauty in ordinary moments."

"I always dreamed of doing it professionally," she admitted.

Reed was quiet for a moment, watching the river flow past. "Dreams don't have expiration dates, you know."

Hannah stared at the water, seeing not the current but the limitations of her reality. "Some dreams require freedom I just don't have."

"Yet," Reed added quietly. "Freedom you don't have yet."

The simple addition of that word—yet—opened a possibility Hannah had a hard time considering. What might be possible in her future where her mother's care was shared with someone else? Where both she and her mom had more independence?

Reed stood and offered his hand. "I have something else to show you, if you're interested."

Hannah took his hand, her palm fitting naturally against his as he helped her up. "Lead on."

They followed the river a short distance further until they reached a bent old willow tree whose branches created a natural canopy over the bank. Beneath it stood a simple wooden bench, weathered by years of exposure but still solid.

"Another of my grandfather's creations," Reed explained. "He said every thinking spot needs a place to sit."

Hannah ran her fingers over the smooth wood, worn silky by time and use. "He's right."

Reed gestured for her to sit, then joined her on the bench. From this vantage point, they could see both upstream and down, the river curving gently before disappearing around a wooded bend.

"I come here when I need to make important decisions," Reed said, his voice blending with the river's song. "Or when the memories get too loud."

Hannah glanced at him, seeing the shadow of old pain in his profile. "The Davis case?"

Reed nodded, his gaze fixed on the middle distance. "Among other things."

"Does it help? Coming here?"

"Usually," he said, turning to meet her eyes. "The constant movement of the water reminds me that nothing stays the same forever. Not pain, and not guilt."

"Not joy either," Hannah added.

Reed's expression gentled. "No, but joy has a way of leaving echoes we can return to. Like memories of your father."

The insight struck Hannah deeply—how she'd preserved certain moments with her dad like photos in her heart, returning to them when she needed his guidance or comfort.

"You're right. I still have those memories and cling to them."

They sat in companionable silence for a time, the river's music filling the space between them. When Reed finally spoke again, his voice was thoughtful.

"I wanted to ask you something, Hannah."

A flutter of nervous anticipation stirred in her chest. "Yes?"

"Would you like to try riding one of the horses? Just in the paddock, nothing challenging. Jasper is as gentle as they come."

The question wasn't what she'd expected, and Hannah blinked in surprise. "Riding? A horse? I've never..."

"New experiences are good for the soul." His smile was encouraging, without pressure.

Hannah considered it, picturing herself astride the chestnut mare. The image was both intimidating and oddly appealing. "I wouldn't know what to do."

"I'd be right beside you," Reed assured her. "And we'd take it very slow. Just around the paddock."

Hannah bit her lip, weighing the unfamiliar against the appeal of trying something new. How long had it been since she'd deliberately stepped outside her comfort zone?

"Okay," she said finally. "I'll try."

Reed's smile broadened. "You'll love it, I promise."

They made their way back along the river trail; the walk seeming shorter on the return journey. As they approached the cabin, they could see Holly and Peggy on the deck, engaged in what appeared to be an animated conversation.

"Should we check on them first?" Hannah asked reflexively.

Reed studied her face, then nodded in understanding. "Of course. But Hannah?"

"Yes?"

"Your mother seems to be doing just fine with Holly. Better than fine, actually."

Hannah followed his gaze to where Peggy was laughing at something Holly had said, her head thrown back in genuine mirth. It was a sight so unexpected and precious that Hannah felt her throat tighten.

"She does, doesn't she?"

They climbed the ramp to the deck, where Holly greeted them with a wave. "Perfect timing! I was just telling Peggy about the time Reed tried to be a vegetarian and nearly starved, because all he knew how to cook was hamburgers."

Reed groaned good-naturedly. "That was a three-week experiment in college, and I did learn to make stir-fry, eventually."

Peggy's eyes were bright with amusement. "Holly's been telling me all sorts of stories about you two growing up. I had no idea you were such a mischief-maker, Deputy Dunbar."

"Don't believe everything my sister tells you," Reed warned with mock severity.

"Oh, but the photo evidence doesn't lie," Holly countered, holding up her phone to reveal a teenage Reed with what appeared to be a spectacularly failed haircut.

Hannah couldn't help laughing at his expression of betrayal. "What happened there?"

"Holly convinced me she could cut hair right before senior homecoming," Reed explained, wincing at the memory. "I had to wear a hat for weeks."

"Worth it," Holly declared. "Best twenty dollars I ever earned on a bet."

The easy sibling banter highlighted a dynamic Hannah had rarely experienced—the teasing affection of family who had grown up together, who shared memories that stretched back through childhood.

"I was going to take Hannah riding," Reed said, changing the subject. "Just around the paddock. Would you ladies like to come watch?"

"Absolutely," Holly agreed immediately.

Peggy's expression registered surprise. "You're going riding, Hannah?"

Hannah nodded, suddenly feeling self-conscious. "Just in the paddock. Reed says Jasper is gentle enough for a beginner."

Instead of the worry Hannah had expected, Peggy's face lit with an encouraging smile. "You should absolutely try it. I used to ride when I was younger... nothing serious, just trail rides at summer camp, but I loved it."

This was a detail Hannah had never known about her mother. "You did? You never mentioned that."

Peggy shrugged, a wistful look crossing her face. "Just another memory." She brightened again. "But I'd love to watch you try it. You used to be so adventurous as a child."

She had been adventurous once, climbing trees and exploring creek beds, always pushing boundaries. When had that part of herself disappeared?

"Let's do it," she said with newfound determination.

They made their way back to the paddock, Peggy insisting on wheeling herself rather than being pushed. At the gate, Reed slipped inside first and approached Jasper, who had been dozing in the afternoon sun.

"I'll need to saddle him," he explained, grabbing a lead rope from the fence post. "Wait here, and I'll bring him to the barn."

Hannah watched as he approached the gelding, speaking softly as he slipped the rope over her head. Jasper followed him willingly, their easy rapport evident in every step.

"He's good with them," Peggy observed from beside her.

Hannah nodded. "He's patient."

"With everyone," Holly added meaningfully. "It's one of his best quality."

A few minutes later, Reed emerged from the barn leading Jasper, now sporting a simple Western saddle with a convenient handle on the front.

"The mounting block is over here," he called, guiding the horse to a sturdy wooden step near the fence.

Hannah approached cautiously, suddenly aware of how large Jasper seemed up close. The gelding watched her with liquid brown eyes, ears pricked forward with interest.

"She can sense nervousness," Reed explained gently, "but she's not bothered by it. Just move slowly and talk to her a bit."

"Hello, Jasper," Hannah said, feeling slightly foolish but taking Reed's advice. "You're very beautiful. Please don't throw me off."

Reed chuckled. "Perfect introduction. Now, I'll hold her steady while you mount. Left foot in the stirrup, hold the saddle horn with your right hand, and swing your right leg over."

Hannah hesitated, glancing at her mother. Instead of caution, she saw Peggy lean forward in her wheelchair, eyes bright with encouragement.

"Go on, Hannah," Peggy called. "You can do it."

Drawing strength from her mother's unexpected support, Hannah moved to the mounting block. Reed stood at Jasper's head, one hand on the bridle, the other extended toward Hannah.

"I've got you," he promised.

Hannah took a deep breath and placed her left foot in the stirrup. Gripping the saddle horn tightly, she pushed off with her right foot and swung her leg over, settling somewhat awkwardly into the saddle. The height was startling. She was at least four feet off the ground.

"That's it," Reed said, his steady voice calming her racing heart. "Sit up straight, heels down in the stirrups. How does it feel?"

"High," Hannah replied honestly, adjusting her seat. "But... exciting."

The gelding stood perfectly still, seemingly unbothered by the novice on her back. Hannah gradually relaxed her death grip on the saddle horn, growing accustomed to the feel of the powerful animal beneath her.

"Ready to walk a bit?" Reed asked, still holding the bridle.

Hannah nodded, finding her nervousness transforming into anticipation. "I think so."

"I'll lead her first," Reed explained. "Just focus on your balance and getting comfortable."

He began walking, guiding Jasper in a slow circle around the paddock. The mare followed with smooth, even steps, her gait surprisingly comfortable once Hannah found her balance. The initial strangeness gave way to a growing sense of accomplishment as they completed the first circuit.

"You're a natural!" Holly called from the fence.

"How does it feel?" Peggy asked, wheeling closer to the paddock rail.

"Amazing," Hannah replied truthfully, a smile spreading across her face.

Reed looked up at her. "Want to try holding the reins yourself?"

Hannah's confidence had grown enough to nod. "Show me how."

Reed patiently explained the basics—how to hold the reins, how gentle pressure directed the horse, how to signal Jasper to stop. He remained close as Hannah took the reins herself, his hand occasionally brushing her leg as he guided her through the process.

"That's it," he encouraged as she successfully directed Jasper to turn. "You're getting it."

Hannah couldn't remember the last time she'd learned something entirely new, the exhilaration of mastering even this basic skill refreshing her spirit. She guided the gelding around the paddock several times, growing more confident with each circuit. From the fence, Peggy watched with pride shining in her eyes.

After about twenty minutes, Reed suggested they take a break. "Don't want to overdo it your first time," he explained, helping Hannah dismount. Her legs felt strangely wobbly as her feet touched the ground.

"That was wonderful," she said, beaming up at him. "Thank you for encouraging me to try."

"You did the hard part," Reed replied, his hand lingering at her elbow. "Saying yes to something new."

They returned to where Peggy and Holly waited by the fence, Hannah still buzzing with the excitement of the experience.

"You looked as if you belonged up there," Peggy said, reaching for Hannah's hand. "I was so proud watching you."

The simple words, so freely given, warmed Hannah deeply. "Thanks, Mom. It was incredible."

"Would anyone else like to ride?" Reed asked, looking between Holly and Peggy.

"I'll pass," Holly said. "I've got years of childhood memories of Reed making me ride double with him."

"Not my fault you always lost at rock-paper-scissors," Reed countered with a grin.

Peggy shook her head, but without bitterness. "Not today. But it was lovely watching Hannah."

Reed nodded, then led Jasper back to the barn to remove her saddle. When he returned, he glanced at his watch.

"I don't know about all of you, but I'm getting hungry. How about I order some pizzas? There's a place in town that delivers, even out here."

"That sounds perfect," Holly agreed readily.

Peggy hesitated, and Hannah automatically prepared to make their excuses, assuming her mother would want to return home. To her surprise, Peggy spoke before she could.

"I'd like that," Peggy said. "If... if that's okay with you, Hannah? I'm truly enjoying myself today."

The simple request—her mother asking permission rather than assuming limitations—caught Hannah off guard.

"Of course, Mom," she replied warmly. "You don't have to ask."

Relief and pleasure mingled in Peggy's expression. "Then pizza sounds wonderful. I haven't had delivery in ages."

Reed smiled, pulling out his phone. "Any preferences or restrictions I should know about?"

As they discussed topping options, Hannah watched the scene with a sense of quiet wonder. Her mother, animated and engaged. Reed thoughtfully, including everyone in the planning. Holly, watchful but treating Peggy as a person first, patient second.

This was what normal felt like, Hannah realized. This was what was possible when responsibility was shared, when caregiving didn't define every interaction, and when enjoyment was allowed equal footing with necessity.

She caught Reed watching her, a question in his eyes. She smiled in response, a genuine, unguarded smile that conveyed what words could not yet articulate. His answering smile held understanding, patience, and something that looked remarkably like love in its earliest, most tender stage.

Chapter 18

"Shall we say grace?" Reed asked, extending his hands to Hannah on his right and Holly on his left.

The four of them sat at the large wooden table on Reed's back porch, the late afternoon sun casting a warm light over the weathered boards. Steam rose from the three pizza boxes arranged in the center—one pepperoni, one vegetable, and one half-Hawaiian, half-meat lovers that had sparked good-natured debate when it arrived.

Hannah slipped her hand into Reed's, the simple contact sending a pleasant warmth up her arm. She reached for her mother with her other hand, completing the circle. Peggy's fingers trembled slightly in hers, but her mother's eyes held a contentment Hannah hadn't seen in years.

"Lord," Reed began, bowing his head, "we thank You for this food and for the gift of friendship. Thank You for this beautiful day, for the new experiences, and for bringing us together. Bless this meal and the hands that prepared it. Amen."

"Amen," the others echoed.

"Oh my goodness," Peggy exclaimed after taking a bite, "this is delicious!"

"Sue's Pizza is the best," Reed said, helping himself to a slice of the meat lover's half. "Their crust is made from a sourdough starter."

"I can taste the difference," Hannah agreed, savoring the tangy, chewy crust.

"So, Peggy," Holly said, wiping her fingers on a napkin, "Tell me more about when you worked with Blue Ridge insurance. What was that like?"

Peggy seemed surprised by the question. "I loved it, actually. I worked for the regional manager at Blue Ridge Insurance. It was challenging. He managed six different offices, and I coordinated everything from his travel schedule to quarterly reports."

Hannah listened, fascinated. Her mother rarely spoke about her past career, and never with this spark of enthusiasm.

"The best part was solving problems," Peggy continued, warming to the subject. "Finding efficient systems, anticipating needs before they became issues. There was such satisfaction in having everything run smoothly."

"That's a genuine talent," Reed commented. "The department would fall apart without our administrative staff. They're the ones who actually keep things running while we're out in the field."

"Exactly!" Peggy nodded vigorously. "Everyone thinks the executives are running the show, but really, it's the support staff making sure they can do their jobs effectively."

Holly grinned. "Same at the clinic. Our office manager, Judy, is the one who literally keeps the lights on."

"Hannah practically grew up in the office I worked in. Back then, my boss never had a problem when I couldn't find a sitter for her. She came to work with me whenever needed. I used to bring Hannah to the office on the occasional school holiday, too. She'd sit at an empty desk with coloring books or homework."

"I remember that," Hannah said, the memory surfacing with surprising clarity. "You'd give me special office supplies, those fancy gel pens and markers and sticky notes shaped like apples."

Peggy laughed. "And you'd arrange them by color on the desk blotter, just so. Even then, you had an eye for composition."

"Did you always like photography?" Holly asked Hannah, reaching for another slice of pizza.

"For as long as I can remember," Hannah replied. "Dad got me my first professional camera when I was sixteen. I carried it everywhere."

"She documented everything," Peggy added with affectionate exasperation. "Every family dinner, every neighborhood walk. We have albums full of photos of our old cat from every conceivable angle."

"Mr. Whiskers," Hannah recalled, smiling. "He was so patient with me and my camera."

"Unlike your father," Peggy chuckled. "Paul would duck behind doors whenever he saw her coming with that camera."

"Which only made me more determined to catch him," Hannah added, the memory bringing unexpected warmth rather than the usual ache. "I have a whole series I called 'Dad Escaping.'"

Reed laughed. "I'd love to see those sometime."

"I'll show you the next time you come over," Hannah said.

Holly took a sip of lemonade. "What kinds of photography do you enjoy most?"

"Nature, mostly," Hannah replied. "Landscapes, and wildlife when I can capture it. I like finding the extraordinary in ordinary moments."

"Like today by the river," Reed said. "She found angles I've never noticed, and I've lived here for three years."

"Photography is about seeing differently," Hannah explained, feeling a faint blush at Reed's praise. "Noticing what others might miss."

"Hannah won the regional high school photography competition her senior year," Peggy said proudly. "Her portfolio was displayed at the community college gallery."

Hannah blinked in surprise. "You remember that?"

"Of course I do," Peggy said.

As they continued eating, the subtle sound of the river provided a gentle background rhythm, occasionally punctuated by birdsong. The mountains in the distance caught the afternoon light, their ridges standing in sharp relief against the clear blue sky.

"Hannah, do you remember when you tried making me breakfast for Mother's Day when you were twelve?" Peggy asked.

"Yes, I remember that," Hannah said.

Peggy burst into laughter, covering her mouth with her napkin. "She decided to make me pancakes, completely unsupervised. She'd watched me do it dozens of times, so she was confident."

"I dumped flour everywhere," Hannah admitted, chuckling at the memory. "And I was so sure a quarter cup of vanilla extract would make them taste better."

"My little perfectionist," Peggy said fondly. "She brought me this plate of... well, I can only describe them as soggy vanilla sponges, so proud of herself."

"Did you eat them?" Reed asked, looking horrified yet amused.

"I did. While Hannah sat there watching me, her face so hopeful. I've never tasted anything so awful in my life."

"Mom!" Hannah protested, laughing. "You told me they were delicious!"

"What else could I say?" Peggy reached over to pat Hannah's hand. "You'd worked so hard. Besides, the orange juice was perfectly fine, and the flowers you picked from the neighbor's garden were lovely."

"Mrs. Wilson's prize tulip," Hannah groaned, covering her face. "She was so mad."

"She got over it when I sent you over with an apology card you made yourself," Peggy said. "You were always good at making things right."

"You're a wonderful mother, Peggy," Reed said.

"I tried," Peggy said, her expression sobering slightly. "After the accident... well, it hasn't been easy for either of us."

"Life rarely follows the path we expect," Holly offered gently. "What matters is how we navigate the detours."

"Some detours feel more like dead ends," Peggy admitted. "But today... today has reminded me there might still be roads worth exploring."

Hannah felt her throat tighten with emotion. "Mom..."

"Don't mind me," Peggy said, waving away the moment of vulnerability. "This view is just making me philosophical." She turned to Reed. "You chose a magnificent spot for us to share lunch."

Reed accepted the change of subject gracefully. "I can't take credit for the view, that's God's handiwork. But I do love waking up to it every morning."

"Do you ever get lonely out here?" Hannah asked.

"Sometimes," he acknowledged honestly. "But most days, I appreciate the quiet. It gives me space to think, to pray, to put the day's challenges in perspective."

"Reed has always been comfortable with solitude," Holly said, gathering empty plates. "Even as a kid, he'd disappear for hours with a book or just go exploring the woods."

"While Holly was organizing neighborhood talent shows and starting clubs," Reed added. "She once founded a detective agency and recruited all the kids on our street."

"We solved the Mystery of Mrs. Abernathy's Missing Garden Gnome," Holly said proudly. "Turned out the Anderson twins had borrowed it for a school project."

"Borrowed without asking," Reed said.

"They returned it with a handmade afghan their mother made, and they apologized," Holly countered. "I call that a happy ending."

Hannah laughed, enjoying the siblings' easy rapport. "You two are close, aren't you?"

"We've had our moments," Reed admitted. "But yes, especially after our dad got sick when we were in high school."

"Your father was sick?" Peggy asked.

"Yes," Holly confirmed. "Heart attack at forty years old. Scared us all half to death, but it was the wake-up call he needed. He completely changed his lifestyle—diet, exercise, stress management. He and Mom now live in and run the bed-and-breakfast in town, The Laurel Ridge Inn."

"Mom, The Laurel Ridge Inn is so pretty," Hannah said. "It's a beautiful Victorian on Cedar Street with a wrap-around porch?"

Reed nodded. "It is a stunning place. My parents bought it as a fixer-upper. They also own The Book Nook next door, my mother's own personal extension of her library. She and Dad are also authors."

"Authors?" Peggy asked, her interest piqued.

"Yep, dad writes under the name M.J. Dunbar and writes cozy mysteries, mostly. And mom, Loretta Dunbar, writes romances."

"I've read his books!" Peggy exclaimed, her face lighting up with genuine excitement. "The Orchard Grove Mystery series, with that retired teacher who solves crimes?"

"That's Dad," Reed confirmed. "He's working on book eight now."

"I love those books," Peggy said, her expression animated.

"I'll have to tell him," Holly said, smiling. "He loves meeting his readers, if you'd like to visit him sometime."

"Oh, I couldn't possibly..." Peggy began, her enthusiasm dimming quickly.

Hannah recognized the familiar retreat, the way her mother pulled back from any suggestion of social interaction outside their small circle.

"Maybe someday," Reed said easily, not pressing the issue. "Or we could arrange for him to sign one of his books for you."

Peggy relaxed visibly at this compromise. "That would be lovely."

The conversation flowed naturally from there, moving through topics both light and meaningful. Reed described his grandfather's woodworking projects, including the table where they sat. Peggy, to Hannah's continued surprise, contributed actively to the conversation, her quick wit emerging more as the afternoon progressed.

Throughout it all, Hannah found herself repeatedly drawn to Reed. The way he listened intently to whoever was speaking, his gentle humor, and how he subtly ensured everyone was included. Several times, she caught him watching her with an expression that made her heart beat faster.

As the late afternoon began its slow transition toward evening, Holly began gathering the remaining pizza into one box.

"We should probably take the leftovers inside," she suggested. "The evening breeze is picking up."

Reed nodded, standing to help collect their plates and glasses. "I've got some coffee brewing inside, if anyone's interested."

"That sounds perfect," Hannah said, rising to assist with the cleanup.

They moved indoors, the cabin's warm interior a welcome contrast to the cooling air outside. Reed busied himself in the kitchen while Holly helped Peggy navigate into the living room.

Hannah paused by the large windows, taking in the view of the mountains now tinged with the golden light of the approaching sunset. She felt Reed's presence before he spoke, a subtle shift in the air that made her skin tingle with awareness.

"Penny for your thoughts," he said, coming to stand beside her.

"Just thinking about how peaceful it is here," she replied honestly. "Like a different world from our regular lives."

"It doesn't have to be so separate," Reed ventured, his voice careful. "This peace is something you could have more often."

Hannah turned to face him, struck by the open vulnerability in his expression. "What are you saying, Reed?"

He seemed to consider his words carefully. "I'm saying I'd like you to be part of my life. You and your mother. I'd like to get to know you both better."

"I'd like that," Hannah admitted.

From the living room, Peggy called Hannah's name, breaking the moment.

"We should join them," Reed said. "Before Holly reveals any more embarrassing childhood stories about me."

They carried mugs of coffee into the living room, where Holly and Peggy were discussing the diabetes support group that met at the church.

"It's very informal," Holly was saying as they entered. "More like a social gathering with helpful information mixed in. A few people from the congregation who have diabetes or care for someone who does, sharing experiences and tips."

Peggy looked skeptical, but not dismissive. "And it's at the church? On Sundays?"

"Thursday evenings, actually," Holly corrected, accepting a mug from Reed. "But speaking of Sundays, services at Laurel Ridge Community Church are really lovely. Pastor Whitman gives thoughtful sermons."

Hannah tensed slightly, anticipating her mother's automatic rejection of anything involving public appearances.

Reed settled into an armchair, his posture relaxed. "Actually, I was going to ask if you both might like to join us for church tomorrow. I could pick you up."

Hannah held her breath, waiting for her mother's refusal. To her surprise, Peggy didn't immediately decline.

"What time are services?" she asked instead, her fingers fidgeting with the hem of her blouse.

"Ten o'clock," Holly replied.

Peggy was quiet for a moment, and Hannah could almost see her weighing options, calculating risks and potential embarrassments.

"I don't think I'm ready for that," Peggy finally said, her voice carrying an apologetic note. "Not yet."

Hannah nodded in understanding, feeling both disappointed and relieved. "That's all right, Mom. Maybe another time."

"But you should go, Hannah," Peggy added unexpectedly, her gaze direct and earnest.

Hannah blinked in surprise. "Without you?"

"Yes," Peggy said firmly. "I'll be fine at home for a few hours."

"I haven't been to church in a long time. Not since before the accident. Not regularly, anyway. I've gone on Easter or Christmas occasionally with Emma."

"All the more reason to come with us," Holly suggested. "No pressure, of course."

"I used to find such comfort there," Peggy said quietly, surprising them all. "I miss that sometimes."

Hannah hesitated, torn between her own complicated relationship with faith and the unexpected opportunity her mother was offering—permission to step away, to reconnect with something she'd once valued.

"It's been a while," Hannah said, uncertainty clear in her voice. "But I think I would like to go."

Reed's smile was like sunlight breaking through clouds. "I can pick you up around nine-thirty?"

"I'd like that," Hannah agreed, feeling strangely nervous yet relieved.

Peggy reached for her daughter's hand, squeezing it gently. "I'm glad, Hannah. You've given up so much for me."

The simple statement, delivered without drama or excessive emotion, struck Hannah deeply. For years, she'd viewed caring for her mother as an all-or-nothing proposition, a total sacrifice that left no room for her own needs or spiritual life. But perhaps there was another way, one where caring for Peggy didn't mean abandoning herself entirely.

"Peggy, would you mind if I borrowed Hannah for the day tomorrow?" Reed asked, a hopeful smile playing at the corners of his mouth.

Hannah's eyebrows shot up. "The entire day?"

"I thought we could start with church," Reed explained, "then enjoy a picnic lunch before exploring some local trails, maybe even go horseback riding again if you're up for it."

"Oh, Hannah, you definitely have to go," Peggy urged, her eyes brightening.

"But Mom—" Hannah began to protest.

Peggy raised her hand, cutting her off. "Don't 'but Mom' me. I'll be perfectly fine on my own."

"I have nothing planned for tomorrow other than church," Holly mentioned, glancing toward Peggy. "Would it be alright if I came over?"

"I'd love that," Peggy replied warmly. "Perhaps you could teach me more about computers? Show me some essential skills... you know... just in case?"

"I'd be happy to," Holly assured her with a nod.

Reed looked around at the group, smiling. "Sounds like we've all got a perfect day lined up. What do you think, Hannah?"

Hannah glanced between her mother, Reed, and Holly, noting their expectant smiles. "Count me in!"

Chapter 19

Hannah's fingers trembled slightly as Reed opened the truck door, the cheerful Sunday bells of Laurel Ridge Community Church echoing across the town square. The white clapboard building gleamed in the morning light, its green shutters and tall steeple creating a picture-perfect scene that stirred memories long buried.

"Second thoughts?" Reed asked.

Hannah met his eyes and found unexpected courage there. "Not second thoughts. Maybe twentieth thoughts," she admitted with a nervous laugh. "I'm nervous. But I'm still here."

She reached for his hand, his warm fingers closing firmly around hers as she stepped down from the truck. The simple contact steadied her, grounding her against the anxiety fluttering in her chest.

"I haven't been to church in so long," she confessed, adjusting the simple blue dress she'd agonized over that morning. "I feel like everyone will know."

"Know what?" Reed asked, his thumb brushing reassuringly across her knuckles.

"That I'm a fraud. That I've been angry at God. That I've barely prayed in years except to ask 'why us?'"

Reed's expression softened. "Hannah, churches aren't for perfect people. We're all carrying something. Some of us just hide it better than others."

An elderly woman with silver hair approached, her smile warm and welcoming.

"Reed Dunbar, right on time as always," she declared, patting his arm before turning curious eyes to Hannah. "And you've brought a guest! How wonderful."

"Mrs. Parker, this is Hannah Gentry," Reed introduced. "Hannah, Edith Parker, has been playing the organ here since before I was born."

"Thirty-seven years this October," Mrs. Parker confirmed proudly. "Though these fingers aren't as nimble as they once were." She reached for Hannah's free hand. "We're so pleased to have you with us today, dear."

"Thank you. That's very kind."

"Not kind at all—just truth," Mrs. Parker insisted, before turning back to Reed. "Your sister's already inside, Reed, saving seats in your usual pew."

As Mrs. Parker moved to greet other arrivals, Hannah and Reed made their way up the walkway. With each step, Hannah became increasingly aware of curious glances and friendly nods directed their way.

"Small towns," Reed murmured close to her ear. "Everyone notices everything."

"Great," Hannah muttered. "No pressure."

Reed chuckled, squeezing her hand. "They're just pleased to see me with someone. The rumor mill had me pegged as destined for eternal bachelorhood."

"Deputy Dunbar!" A young boy of about eight darted across the lawn toward them, narrowly avoiding a collision with an elderly couple. "Did you bring your handcuffs today? You promised to show me next time!"

Reed laughed, ruffling the boy's hair. "Not today, Tyler. I'm off duty. But maybe next week, if your mom says it's okay."

Tyler's gaze shifted to Hannah, curiosity evident. "Are you Deputy Dunbar's girlfriend?"

Heat rushed to Hannah's cheeks. "I'm—"

"This is my friend, Hannah," Reed interjected smoothly. "Hannah, this is Tyler Matthews, future sheriff of Laurel Ridge, according to him."

Tyler puffed out his chest. "I'm gonna catch bad guys, just like Deputy Dunbar."

"A worthy ambition," Hannah replied, charmed despite her embarrassment.

"Tyler! Stop bothering people and come help your sister." A harried-looking woman juggling a toddler and a diaper bag called from nearby.

"Gotta go," Tyler announced importantly. "But don't forget about the handcuffs, Deputy Dunbar!"

As the boy scampered off, Hannah smiled. "Quite the admirer you have there."

"One of many," Reed admitted with a self-deprecating shrug. "The uniform makes an impression on kids."

They reached the church steps, where more greetings awaited them. Hannah recognized several faces from the diner, regular customers whose coffee preferences she knew by heart. Each greeted Reed warmly and welcomed Hannah with a genuine smile that eased her anxiety further.

The interior of the church was just as Hannah remembered from the past: simple wooden pews arranged in neat rows, sunlight filtering through stained-glass windows to cast colored patterns across the hardwood floor. The air held the faint scent of polished wood, well-worn hymnals, and something floral—fresh arrangements at the altar, Hannah realized.

Holly waved from a pew about halfway down the center aisle, her bright smile lighting up her face as she motioned them over. Reed guided Hannah with a gentle hand at the small of her back.

"You made it!" Holly whispered as they slipped into the pew beside her. "I was beginning to think you'd changed your mind."

"We got held up by Tyler's interrogation," Reed explained, an affectionate note in his voice.

"That boy," Holly chuckled. "He's been asking about your handcuffs for weeks."

Hannah settled onto the wooden pew, as an unexpected rush of memories filled her mind—Sunday services with her parents, her mother's floral perfume and her father's deep voice singing hymns slightly off-key. The recollection brought both comfort and an echo of grief.

Reed must have sensed the shift in her mood because his hand found hers on the pew between them, his fingers threading gently through hers. She glanced at him and smiled.

The organist began playing, and Mrs. Parker's skilled fingers coaxed a rich, resonant sound from the instrument. The hymn tugged at Hannah's heart, the melody unchanged from her childhood.

As the congregation rose for the opening hymn, Reed passed Hannah a hymnal, opened to the correct page. His shoulder pressed against hers as they stood side by side, his deep baritone joining with the surrounding voices.

"Amazing grace, how sweet the sound, that saved a wretch like me..."

Hannah's voice emerged hesitantly at first, the words rustier than she expected.

"Through many dangers, toils, and snares, I have already come. 'Tis grace hath brought me safe thus far, and grace will lead me home."

Reed's hand found the small of her back again, warm and steady, and Hannah leaned slightly into his strength as the music swelled around them. At that moment, surrounded by voices raised in harmony, Hannah felt a sense of belonging.

As they sat following the hymn, a tall man with kind eyes approached the pulpit. Pastor Andrew Whitman, Hannah presumed, based on Reed's description.

"Good morning," he greeted warmly, his voice carrying easily through the sanctuary. "What a beautiful day the Lord has given us to gather together."

The service progressed with a comfortable rhythm—prayers, scripture readings, and another hymn that Hannah remembered from her youth. Throughout it all, Reed remained a steady presence beside her, his shoulder occasionally brushing hers, his hand finding hers during prayers.

She watched him during quieter moments, the way his expression grew thoughtful during readings, how he nodded slightly at points that resonated, and the genuine ease with which he participated in the service. Faith clearly wasn't just a Sunday obligation for Reed, but a living, breathing part of his identity.

Hannah tried to focus on the pastor's words about finding strength in community and God's presence during life's trials. But her mind kept drifting, alternating between the awareness of Reed beside her and her own complicated relationship with faith.

"Faith doesn't mean we don't struggle," Pastor Whitman was saying, his voice passionate but conversational. "Job questioned God. David lamented. Even Jesus asked why He had been forsaken. Questions and doubts aren't the opposite of faith—they're often part of faith's deepest journey."

The words penetrated Hannah's wandering thoughts, striking a chord that resonated. She'd always felt her anger and questions made her faithless, unworthy of the comfort others seemed to find in religion. But what if those very questions were part of a deeper connection?

"When we walk through valleys," Pastor Whitman continued, "God walks beside us, sometimes carrying us when we cannot take another step."

Hannah felt Reed shift beside her, his hand finding hers again, as if the pastor's words had stirred something in him too. She glanced at his profile, noting the slight furrow between his brows, the attentive set of his jaw. Whatever valleys he had walked, they had left their mark.

As the sermon concluded and the congregation rose for the closing hymn, Hannah felt more engaged than she had expected to be. The pastor's words had neither magically dissolved her doubts nor made her suddenly comfortable with the faith she'd distanced herself from. But they had created a small opening, a crack in the wall she'd built between herself and spirituality.

"Be Thou my Vision, O Lord of my heart," the congregation sang, the familiar Irish melody rising toward the rafters. "Naught be all else to me, save that Thou art."

Reed's voice blended with hers, their harmony imperfect but sincere. His fingers remained intertwined with hers, warm and strong, as they sang the last verse together.

As the service concluded with a benediction, Hannah felt a curious sense of both exhaustion and renewal, as if she'd completed some emotional journey in the space of an hour.

"You okay?" Reed asked quietly as people began gathering their things and moving toward the aisles.

Hannah nodded, finding the question easier to answer than she'd expected. "I am."

His smile warmed his entire face. "I'm glad. We usually gather outside for a bit after the service. The weather's perfect for it today."

"I'd like that," Hannah replied, surprising herself with her willingness to extend the social interaction.

They made their way outside, where the congregation had indeed spilled onto the lawn in clusters of animated conversation. Children darted between groups, their Sunday clothes already showing signs of play. An elderly man set up a folding table near the steps, and a woman was arranging trays of cookies and a large dispenser of lemonade.

"Reed, there you are!" A slender woman with stunning blond wavy hair approached, her cream-colored dress complementing her warm complexion perfectly. Beside her walked Pastor Whitman, his clerical collar now loosened slightly.

"Lily, Andrew," Reed greeted them both with genuine warmth. "I'd like you to meet Hannah Gentry. Hannah, this is Pastor Andrew Whitman and his wife, Lily."

"We're so pleased you could join us today," Lily said, taking Hannah's hand in both of hers. "Reed has spoken of you a lot recently."

Hannah shot Reed a curious glance, which he met with a sheepish smile.

"All good things, I promise," Pastor Whitman added with a chuckle. "It's wonderful to meet you, Hannah. I hope you found something meaningful in the service."

"I did," Hannah admitted. "Your sermon... it gave me a lot to think about."

Andrew's expression was kind, but free of the condescension Hannah had feared. "That's all any pastor can hope for. Questions and reflection are sacred things."

"Hannah works at Martha's Diner," Reed explained. "Best waitress in Laurel Ridge, according to Martha herself."

Hannah felt her cheeks warm at the praise. "Martha's biased."

"Martha's a gem," Lily countered. "If she says you're the best, I believe it. Andrew and I have breakfast there most Saturdays. I'm almost embarrassed to admit how predictable we are."

"Blueberry pancakes for her, eggs and hash browns for me," Pastor Whitman confirmed with a grin. "We're creatures of habit."

"Saturday morning, corner booth by the window," Hannah nodded, placing them immediately.

"See? You clearly are an excellent waitress," Lily said warmly. "You remember everyone."

The conversation flowed easily from there, touching on the diner, the recent weather, and the upcoming community festival. Hannah relaxed into the exchange, the initial anxiety of returning to church fading with each friendly interaction.

More church members approached, each greeting Reed with obvious affection and Hannah with welcoming smiles. Many knew her from the diner, but none mentioned her long absence from church or asked uncomfortable questions about her mother. Instead, they simply folded her into conversations.

"Reed Dunbar, don't you dare sneak past me without saying hello!" An elderly woman with a cane and a formidable purple hat made her way determinedly toward them.

Reed's face lit with genuine delight. "Mrs. Henderson! I wouldn't dream of it. Your eyes are sharper than my department-issued binoculars."

The older woman harrumphed, but her eyes twinkled with obvious affection. "Flattery won't save you, young man. You missed last week's service."

"I was on duty," Reed explained. "Sheriff Baker had the flu."

"Hmm. Well, I suppose that's acceptable." Mrs. Henderson turned her keen gaze to Hannah. "And who might this lovely young lady be?"

"Hannah Gentry, ma'am," Hannah introduced herself, charmed by the woman's directness.

"Ah, yes. Martha's girl. You always remember my coffee with a splash of cream, no sugar." Mrs. Henderson studied her appraisingly. "You look gorgeous outside that diner uniform. Blue suits you."

"Thank you," Hannah replied, oddly touched by the compliment.

"Does your mother still enjoy reading?" Mrs. Henderson asked. "Peggy always had good taste in books."

"Yes, she does."

"Excellent," Mrs. Henderson nodded approvingly. "You tell her Harriet Henderson says hello, will you? We served on the library committee together years ago."

"I will," Hannah promised, a lump forming in her throat at this glimpse of her mother as others had known her, not as a wheelchair-bound invalid but as a vibrant community member with interests and connections.

Mrs. Henderson patted Reed's arm. "You take care of this one," she said with a meaningful look. "She's got gentle eyes. Like her mother."

"Mrs. Henderson doesn't mince words," Reed said with a chuckle once Mrs. Henderson was out of earshot. "But she's rarely wrong about people."

"She knew my mother well, from the sounds of it?"

Reed nodded. "Laurel Ridge has a long memory. Your mother was very involved in the community before the accident, from what I've been told. People haven't forgotten that."

The realization that her mother hadn't been erased from the community's memory touched something deep in Hannah's heart.

More conversations followed as they made their way around the church lawn. Hannah met Reed's parents, Mitch and Loretta Dunbar, who greeted her with such genuine warmth that she immediately understood where Reed and Holly had learned their easy compassion.

"You must join us for Sunday dinner soon," Loretta insisted. "Nothing formal—just family gathering around the table."

"I'd like that," Hannah replied, meaning it. "Maybe... maybe sometime my mother could join us too, if that wouldn't be too complicated."

"We would be delighted to have you both."

"We'll make it happen," Mitch added with a decisive nod that reminded Hannah strongly of Reed.

As the crowd gradually thinned, Hannah stood at the edge of the church lawn with Reed, watching the remaining congregants say their goodbyes. Holly had left earlier, heading to Hannah's home to spend time with Peggy, as promised.

"So," Reed said, his voice carrying a note of cautious hope, "did you enjoy yourself this morning?"

"I did. Everyone was so welcoming."

"Good. That's what church is supposed to be. A community supporting each other through life's ups and downs. Not always what it is, but what it's meant to be."

"I've felt so disconnected from everything for so long," Hannah confessed, watching a family with young children make their way toward the parking lot. "Not just church, but community in general. It's like Mom and I have been living in our own little world."

"Caregiving can be isolating. But it doesn't have to be all-consuming."

"I'm starting to see that," Hannah agreed. "Especially after yesterday at your place. Seeing Mom interact with Holly, with you and with the horses... it was like catching a glimpse of whom she used to be."

"Who she still is. Just under different circumstances."

Hannah nodded, grateful for his perspective. "You're right. Who she still is."

The late morning sun warmed the summer air around them. Birds called from the maple trees lining the church property, and somewhere nearby, children laughed.

"I'm glad you came today. I know it wasn't easy for you."

"It was easier with you," she admitted. "Having you beside me made it... easier."

They began walking toward Reed's truck, their hands linked naturally between them. The church bells chimed noon, the simple notes ringing across the town square.

"So," Reed said as they reached his vehicle, "I promised you a full day, and I intend to deliver." He opened the passenger door with a flourish. "How do you feel about a picnic by Whispering Falls?"

"Whispering Falls?" Hannah repeated. "I haven't been there since high school."

"Then it's long overdue," Reed declared, his eyes crinkling with pleasure at her clear interest. "I packed our lunch in a cooler. Nothing fancy—sandwiches, fruit, and some brownies Holly made."

"You thought of everything," Hannah said, touched by his thoughtfulness.

"I tried. I know today was a big step, going to church again. I want the rest of the day to be pure enjoyment."

Hannah settled into the passenger seat, and she felt a sense of anticipation. A day stretching ahead with no responsibilities, no schedule to maintain, no medications to administer—just open hours to be filled with conversation.

Reed closed her door and rounded the truck, sliding into the driver's seat. Before starting the engine, he turned to her with a smile that held equal parts excitement and tenderness.

"Ready for our next adventure?" he asked, extending his hand across the console.

Hannah laced her fingers through his, her heart light with possibilities she was only beginning to recognize.

"More than ready," she replied, and meant it with her whole heart.

Chapter 20

"The last spot!" Reed said as he steered his truck into a vacant space at the trailhead parking lot. "Sunday afternoon at Whispering Falls is always popular. But completely worth it."

He cut the engine and turned to Hannah. "You ready for this?"

Hannah nodded, feeling a flutter of anticipation in her stomach. How long had it been since she'd done something purely for enjoyment? The morning at church had already pushed her beyond her normal boundaries, but she found herself eager for more.

They climbed out of the truck, and Reed reached into the truck bed to retrieve a small blue cooler and a rolled-up quilt. Hannah grabbed her camera from the seat, slinging it around her neck without a second thought.

"The trail's about a mile long," Reed explained as they approached the wooden signpost marking the trailhead. "Mostly easy walking, but there are a few steeper sections. That okay?"

"More than okay," Hannah replied, inhaling deeply. The scent of pine and damp earth filled her lungs, instantly transporting her back to childhood hikes with her father. "I used to love hiking. I've missed it."

Reed offered his free hand, and Hannah took it without hesitation. His palm was warm against hers and gentle in its strength.

The trail stretched before them, a ribbon of packed earth winding between tall trees and flowering rhododendrons. Sunlight dappled the path through the canopy overhead, creating shifting patterns that danced across the ground with each breeze.

"Look," Reed said softly, pointing to a spot just off the trail where a doe and her fawn grazed quietly, seemingly unconcerned by their presence.

Hannah instinctively raised her camera, adjusting the settings quickly before capturing the tender scene. The mother deer's ears flicked toward the subtle sound of the shutter, but she continued grazing calmly.

"Beautiful shot," Reed commented, peering at the preview screen.

"I love being out in nature and capturing moments like this," Hannah admitted, lowering the camera.

They continued along the trail, the path gradually narrowed, forcing them to walk closer together.

"So, tell me something I don't know about Deputy Reed Dunbar," Hannah said, stepping carefully over a gnarled tree root that crossed the path.

Reed considered this as he navigated a slippery section of trail. "Let's see... I can play the guitar, but not well enough for public consumption."

"Really?" Hannah glanced up at him with interest. "I never would have guessed that."

"My grandfather taught me," Reed explained. "He believed every man should know how to play at least one instrument. Said it was good for the soul."

"Does he play still?"

"Not as much anymore. His hands give him trouble with arthritis." Reed's expression grew thoughtful. "But sometimes on quiet evenings, if you ask him, he'll still pick out a tune or two."

They rounded a bend in the trail, and Hannah could hear the distant sound of water rushing over rocks.

"Your turn," Reed prompted. "Tell me something about Hannah Gentry that I wouldn't know."

Hannah bit her lower lip, considering. "I used to write poetry in high school. Nothing serious, just thoughts and feelings I needed to get out."

"Do you still write?"

She shook her head. "No. After the accident, it was like... like the words dried up. Everything became about surviving each day, making sure Mom had what she needed." She paused, realizing how negative that sounded. "I'm sorry. I don't mean to be a downer."

"You're not," Reed assured her, squeezing her hand gently. "You're being honest. There's a difference."

The trail began to descend gradually, the sound of falling water growing louder with each step. Sunlight sparkled through the trees ahead, hinting at an opening in the forest.

"Almost there," Reed said, his voice lifting with excitement. "First view is just around this corner."

They turned the final bend, and Hannah caught her breath as Whispering Falls came into view. A curtain of water cascaded over a rock face about thirty feet high, splashing into a crystal-clear pool below. Sunlight created rainbows in the mist rising from the base of the falls, and moss-covered boulders surrounded the pool like nature's seating arrangement.

"Oh, Reed," Hannah breathed, momentarily speechless. "It's even more beautiful than I remembered."

"Worth the hike?" he asked, his eyes on her face rather than the scenery.

"Absolutely."

Several other hikers were scattered around the area, some sitting on rocks eating lunch, others wading around the shallow edges of the pool. Reed scanned the scene before pointing to a relatively secluded spot beneath a large hemlock tree.

"How about there? Enough privacy, but still a good view."

Hannah nodded, and they made their way carefully down the last section of trail to the clearing. Reed spread the quilt on a level patch of ground, its blue and white pattern bright against the green grass.

"This is perfect," Hannah said, settling onto the quilt while Reed placed the cooler between them.

"I can't take credit for the location, but I did pack a pretty decent lunch." He opened the cooler with a flourish. "We have turkey and Swiss on sourdough, pasta salad made with Grandma Dunbar's secret recipe, fresh strawberries, and Holly's delicious brownies."

"You weren't kidding about being prepared," Hannah said, genuinely impressed. "This is no sad sandwich and chips picnic."

"I told you—I wanted today to be special." Reed's voice carried a hint of vulnerability that tugged at Hannah's heart.

He handed her a sandwich wrapped in wax paper.

"Thanks... for all of this."

"You're welcome."

The sound of the waterfall created a peaceful backdrop as they ate. A light breeze carried the spray from the falls occasionally, cooling the surrounding air.

"May I ask you something?" Hannah ventured after finishing half her sandwich.

Reed nodded, setting down his water bottle. "Anything."

"Why have you been so kind to me, Reed, honestly? From that first morning with Mom's emergency, you've gone above and beyond." She hesitated. "I'm just... not used to someone putting this much effort into... well, into me."

Reed was quiet for a moment, his expression thoughtful. When he finally spoke, his voice carried a depth of sincerity that made Hannah's chest tighten.

"At first, it was just about helping someone in need. That's part of who I am, part of my job. But then..." He looked at her directly, his gaze unwavering. "Then I got to know you, Hannah. I saw your strength, your dedication to your mother, the way you pour yourself into caring for others without asking for anything in return."

He drew a deep breath. "The more time I spent with you, the more I wanted to be around you. Your smile, your honesty, the way you see beauty in ordinary moments through your camera lens—it all drew me in."

Reed's hand found hers on the quilt between them. "I've fallen hard for you, Hannah. Maybe the timing isn't ideal with everything you're dealing with, but there it is. I care about you... very much."

Hannah felt her heart hammering in her chest, a mix of elation and fear coursing through her. She'd had crushes in high school, even dated briefly, but nothing had prepared her for the intensity of emotion Reed's words evoked.

"I don't..." she began, then faltered. "I'm not sure if I remember how to do this, Reed. Dating, relationships—they haven't been part of my life for so long."

"We don't have to label it," Reed said. "We can just be two people getting to know each other, seeing where it leads."

Hannah looked down at their joined hands, his so much larger than hers, yet holding hers with such care. "I feel something for you too," she admitted. "Something I haven't felt... maybe ever. But it scares me."

"What scares you about it?" His question held no judgment, only genuine interest.

Hannah considered this, trying to organize the tangle of emotions into coherent thoughts. "For one thing, I'm terrified of disappointing you. My life is complicated. I have responsibilities that won't just disappear."

"I don't want them to disappear," Reed assured her. "I care about your mother, too. She's part of who you are."

"And then there's the fact that I've spent so long just... surviving. I'm always in survival mode," Hannah continued, needing to be completely honest. "I'm afraid I've forgotten how to truly live. I don't know how to be in a relationship. What if I'm no good at it?"

"I think that's a fear many people have, whether they admit it or not. We're all just figuring everything out as we go along."

A spot of sunlight broke through the trees, illuminating Hannah's face. Reed reached up, gently tucking a strand of hair behind her ear, his fingers lingering on her cheek.

"I'm not looking for perfection, Hannah. Just a chance to see where this might lead. One day at a time."

Hannah leaned slightly into his touch, drawing courage from his steadiness.

"So," he said, his tone lightening, "what else would you like to know about me? Fair warning—I'm an open book."

Hannah laughed, grateful for the slight easing of emotional intensity. "Okay, let's see... what's your favorite memory from growing up in Laurel Ridge?"

Reed didn't hesitate. "Summers with my grandfather. He taught me to fish, to track animals, and to identify bird calls. Those are the moments that shaped me." He smiled at a particular memory. "One summer when I was about twelve, we tracked a black bear for three days, just to observe it. When we finally spotted her with two cubs, it was like witnessing something sacred."

"Wow, that sounds interesting," Hannah said, trying to picture a young Reed, wide-eyed with wonder at nature's mysteries.

"What about you?" Reed asked, passing her a container of plump strawberries. "Favorite childhood memory?"

Hannah accepted the fruit, considering the question. "Road trips with my parents. Dad loved driving. He knew all these little back roads and scenic spots. Mom would pack these elaborate picnics, and we'd just... explore. Find a creek to wade in or a field of wildflowers."

She smiled at the memory. "One summer we spent three days following the Blue Ridge Parkway, stopping whenever something caught our eye. No schedule, no reservations, just... freedom."

"Sounds perfect."

"It was. I miss that sense of spontaneity."

Reed popped a strawberry into his mouth, chewing thoughtfully. "Maybe that's something we can recapture, bit by bit."

Hannah nodded, allowing herself to imagine possibilities beyond the carefully managed routine of her current life.

"May I?" Reed asked, gesturing to her camera. "I'd love to see what you've captured so far today."

Hannah handed him the camera, a small flutter of nervousness in her stomach. Sharing her photography felt oddly intimate, like showing someone pages from a private journal. Reed handled the camera with respect, carefully scrolling through the recent images.

"These are incredible, Hannah," he said, genuine admiration in his voice. He paused on a particular shot of sunlight filtering through pine branches. "This one especially—you captured something ordinary in a way that makes it extraordinary."

A warm flush of pleasure spread through Hannah at his praise. "It's just... how I see the world, I guess."

"It's a gift," Reed insisted, returning the camera. "One you shouldn't hide away."

They finished their meal as the conversation continued to flow, touching on favorite books, music preferences, and childhood misadventures. Hannah laughed more than she had in years, especially when Reed described an ill-advised attempt to build a treehouse that resulted in a broken arm and his grandfather's equal measures of sympathy and "I told you so."

After they'd packed away the lunch remains, Reed stretched out on the quilt, propping himself up on one elbow to face her. "Can I ask you something potentially difficult?"

Hannah nodded, drawing her knees up to her chest. "Go ahead."

"Do you ever resent having to put your life on hold for your mother?"

The question was direct, but not unkind. Hannah appreciated that Reed didn't tiptoe around difficult topics.

"Sometimes," she admitted after a thoughtful pause. "Not resent her, exactly, but... resent the situation. The unfairness of it all. Then I feel guilty for even thinking that way."

"Why guilty?" Reed asked gently.

"Because she's my mother. Because she lost even more than I did. Because she'd do the same for me without hesitation." Hannah shrugged. "Take your pick."

Reed considered this, his expression thoughtful. "I think it's possible to love someone deeply and still acknowledge that caring for them comes with real sacrifices. That doesn't make you selfish or ungrateful. It makes you human."

Hannah looked at him, struck by how he managed to articulate things she'd felt but never fully allowed herself to acknowledge.

"Caring for someone you love is beautiful. But sacrificing everything about yourself in the process isn't sustainable or healthy for either person," he said.

A comfortable silence settled between them, the sound of the waterfall a soothing backdrop. Hannah watched a group of children splashing in the shallow edge of the pool, their laughter carrying across the clearing.

"What do you dream about, Hannah?" Reed asked suddenly. "If circumstances were different, what would you want for your life?"

The question made her pause. It had been so long since she'd allowed herself to think beyond the immediate future, beyond the next doctor's appointment or prescription refill.

"I used to dream about going to college and then traveling," she said finally. "Not exotic places necessarily, just... seeing more of the world. Taking photographs of landscapes and people, capturing special moments." She smiled wistfully. "I wanted to study photography, and eventually photojournalism. I guess, to put it simply, I dream about having more freedom. I want more than what I have now. I want to enjoy life."

"Even your past dreams are still possible, you know. Dreams don't have expiration dates."

Hannah remembered him saying those exact words by the river on his property. The repetition made her wonder if he truly believed that her deferred dreams weren't dead, just waiting.

"What about you?" she asked. "Did you always want to be in law enforcement, or was there something more you wanted?"

Reed nodded. "Pretty much. I've always enjoyed helping and protecting people. I saw how my grandfather made a difference in people's lives. How he was a steady presence in tough situations. I've always wanted to do the same."

"You have for mom and I. You've really gone above and beyond to help us both."

Their eyes met, and Hannah felt that now-familiar flutter in her chest, a sensation both terrifying and exhilarating. Reed reached out, his fingers brushing hers on the quilt, the simple touch grounding her.

A family with young children settled nearby, their excited voices breaking the intimate bubble that had formed around Hannah and Reed. He glanced at his watch, then back at her.

"We've been here almost two hours," he said, sounding surprised. "Time flies."

"I've been enjoying myself too much to notice the time."

"The day's still young," Reed pointed out. "What would you like to do next? It's your choice."

Hannah blinked, momentarily thrown by the question. "My choice?"

"Absolutely. We could head back to my place, maybe do some more riding if you're up for it. Or we could take the ATV for a trail ride—there are some wonderful views accessible only by ATV. Or..." he hesitated, then added, "I've got a small boat we could put in on the river. It's a beautiful day for being in the water."

Hannah realized she was being offered a luxury she rarely experienced—the freedom to choose based solely on what she wanted, not what was necessary or practical or easiest for someone else.

"I'm not used to having options or someone asking what I want to do."

"Then maybe that's something else we need to practice," he suggested gently. "Finding out what Hannah wants."

The simple statement touched her deeply.

"The boat idea sounds nice," she said finally.

"The boat it is, then."

They packed up their picnic supplies, carefully folding the quilt and securing the cooler. As they prepared to head back down the trail, Hannah reached for Reed's hand.

"Thank you," she said, her voice quiet but earnest.

"For what?"

"For reminding me that I still get to have choices. That what I want matters too."

Reed lifted their joined hands, pressing a gentle kiss to her knuckles that sent a shiver up her arm. "What you want does matter, Hannah. It always will."

Chapter 21

Hannah stared at her reflection in Reed's bathroom mirror, almost startled by the woman looking back at her. Sunlight streamed through the small window, highlighting features she hadn't paid attention to in years. She'd been so focused on functioning, on getting through each day, that she'd stopped really seeing herself.

Her hair fell in soft waves past her shoulders. There was color in her cheeks. And her eyes... when had they last held this sparkle?

She leaned closer to the mirror, examining the freckles scattered across her nose. The tiny laugh lines at the corners of her eyes told stories of a day filled with more smiles than she could count.

"Who are you?" she whispered to her reflection.

Emotion welled unexpectedly in her throat as she changed into the fresh t-shirt and shorts she'd packed that morning.

A sudden, overwhelming surge of feeling joy caught her off guard. She was happy. Genuinely, unreservedly, happy at this moment.

Tears threatened, and Hannah quickly fanned her face with her hands. "Not now," she murmured to herself. "Pull it together."

She took a deep breath, straightened her shoulders, and shoved her dress into her bag. One more glance in the mirror revealed a woman transformed, not by makeup or fancy clothes, but by something far more profound: hope.

Hannah opened the bathroom door and stepped into the hallway, her heart beating a rapid rhythm against her ribs. She slipped her feet into her tennis shoes by the back door and stepped onto the porch.

The late afternoon sun cast a warm and vibrant light across Reed's property. She spotted him immediately, kneeling beside a small aluminum boat at the river's edge. Two orange life jackets lay on the grassy bank beside him.

"Hey there," Reed called, looking up with a smile that made her stomach flutter. "Feel better after changing?"

"Much," Hannah replied, making her way down the gentle slope toward him. "Sorry I took so long."

"No need to apologize. I just pulled the boat out of storage." He gestured to the small craft. "Nothing fancy, just an old john boat my grandfather and I used to fish from."

The simple aluminum boat looked well-maintained despite its obvious age. Two wooden bench seats crossed the width, with oars secured along the sides.

"It's perfect. Would you mind if I called to check on Mom before we head out? I know Holly's with her, but..."

"Of course," Reed replied immediately. "Take all the time you need. Reception can be spotty on the river, so it's a good idea to call now."

Hannah pulled her phone from her pocket. Reed busied himself with final preparations for their excursion.

She dialed home, the phone ringing twice before Peggy answered with a slightly breathless, "Hello?"

"Hi, Mom. Just checking in to see how you're doing."

"Hannah!" Peggy's voice brightened immediately. "We're fine here. Holly's been teaching me all sorts of things on the computer. Did you know there are entire forums dedicated to mystery novels?"

Hannah smiled, relieved to hear the enthusiasm in her mother's voice. "No, I didn't. That sounds like something you might enjoy. What else have you two been up to?"

"We had lunch—Holly brought sandwiches from a new deli in town. And she showed me how to use video chat. We face-timed with her mother, and I got to see the inside of The Book Nook. It was lovely."

"Sounds like you're having a good day," Hannah said, a weight lifting from her shoulders.

There was a brief pause before Peggy asked, "And you? How has your day been?"

"Amazing," Hannah answered honestly. "We went to church, had a picnic at Whispering Falls, and now we're about to take Reed's boat out on the river."

Another pause, longer this time. "Mom?" Hannah prompted. "Everything okay?"

"Yes, of course," Peggy replied quickly—too quickly.

Hannah frowned, recognizing the forced lightness in her mother's tone. "Mom, what is it? Is something wrong?"

A soft sigh came through the line. "Nothing's wrong, dear. I just... I find myself missing you, that's all. Silly, isn't it? You've only been gone a few hours."

Hannah's chest tightened with a familiar mixture of guilt and responsibility. "It's not silly at all."

"I was hoping you'd call," Peggy admitted quietly. "I wanted to hear your voice, to know you were all right. It's strange, isn't it? For years,

I've been the one you worried about, and here I am, worrying about you."

"Mom..."

"No, don't you dare feel guilty, Hannah Gentry," Peggy said firmly. "This is good—for both of us. I need to remember how to exist in the world without you hovering, and you need..." Her voice softened. "You need to remember how to live."

Hannah leaned against a nearby tree, emotion threatening to overwhelm her again. "I'm having a really good time, mom," she confessed. "I can't remember the last time I felt this... free." She took a deep breath. "I need this day, Mom. And honestly, I don't want it to end."

"Then don't let it," Peggy replied simply. "Stay out as long as you like."

"Are you sure?"

"Absolutely sure. Enjoy yourself, sweetheart. God knows you've earned it." Peggy's voice warmed. "And Hannah? I like really like Reed."

Hannah glanced toward the riverbank, where Reed waited patiently. "Me too, mom."

They said their goodbyes, and Hannah tucked her phone away. When she rejoined Reed by the water, he looked up with questioning eyes.

"Everything okay at home?"

"Yes," Hannah replied with a genuine smile. "Better than okay, actually. Mom and Holly are getting along great. Apparently, they've discovered online mystery forums."

Reed chuckled. "Holly's always been good at finding common ground with people. Is your mom having fun?"

"She is. She actually encouraged me to stay out as long as I wanted."

"Did you mean it?" Reed asked, his tone casual, though his eyes were intent.

Hannah tilted her head. "Mean what?"

"What you said to your mom. About not wanting today to end."

Heat crept into Hannah's cheeks as she realized he'd overheard her conversation. But instead of embarrassment, she felt a curious boldness, as if the day's experiences had awakened something long dormant inside her.

"Yes. I meant every word."

Something shifted in Reed's expression—a softening around the eyes, a slight parting of his lips. He stepped closer, close enough that she could catch the faint scent of his cologne mingled with sunshine and river water.

"Then we'll make sure it's a day worth remembering," he said, reaching for one of the life jackets. "Safety first, though."

He held the orange vest open for her, and Hannah turned, slipping her arms through the openings. Reed's fingers brushed against her shoulders as he adjusted the straps, sending tiny shivers down her spine despite the afternoon warmth.

"Too tight?" he asked, his voice close to her ear.

Hannah shook her head, not trusting herself to speak. When she turned to face him, their proximity stole her breath momentarily. Reed seemed equally affected, his gaze dropping briefly to her lips before he stepped back.

"Your turn," Hannah said, finding her voice as she reached for the second life jacket.

Reed smiled, shrugging into the vest with practiced ease. "Ready to set sail? Well, not sail exactly, but you know what I mean."

Hannah laughed. "Ready when you are, Captain."

Reed grinned and stepped into the shallow water, holding the boat steady against the current. He extended his hand to Hannah. "Watch your step—the rocks can be slippery."

Hannah took his hand, carefully navigating the rocky riverbank. His grip was firm and reassuring as she stepped into the boat, wobbling slightly before settling onto the middle bench seat.

"Not too tippy, is it?" Reed asked, pushing the boat further into the water before climbing in himself.

"Nothing I can't handle," Hannah assured him, feeling a small thrill at the gentle rocking motion beneath her.

Reed unshipped the oars, positioning them in the oarlocks with practiced movements. With a few strong strokes, he guided them away from the bank and into the current.

The river stretched before them, a ribbon of blue-green water winding between tree-lined banks. Sunlight danced across the surface, creating patterns of light and shadow that shifted with each ripple. The air here carried the clean scent of water and earth, with occasional sweet notes from flowering shrubs along the shoreline.

"This is breathtaking," Hannah said, reaching for her camera. She focused on a great blue heron standing motionless in the shallows, its reflection perfect in the still water near the bank.

"The river changes constantly," Reed remarked, rowing with smooth, even strokes that barely disturbed the water's surface. "Different every time I come out here, depending on the season, the weather, the time of day. This never gets old."

Hannah captured the heron just as it struck, its long beak disappearing beneath the water's surface to emerge with a small fish. "Got it!" she exclaimed with childlike delight.

Reed paused his rowing to watch her, a smile playing at the corners of his mouth. "You look so natural with that camera. Like it's an extension of you."

"It feels that way," Hannah admitted, lowering the camera to her lap. "When I'm shooting, everything else falls away. It's just me and what I'm seeing through the lens." She smiled ruefully. "I haven't felt that kind of focus, that kind of... presence in a long time. Normally, I just steal moments in my backyard whenever I can, but it's not the same."

"What kind of photography did you want to study most when you were younger? Before..." Reed let the question trail off delicately.

"Photojournalism," Hannah replied, trailing her fingers through the cool water alongside the boat. "I wanted to tell stories with images. Not just pretty landscapes, but meaningful moments." She smiled at a memory. "My high school art teacher said I had an eye for finding hope in unexpected places."

Reed navigated them around a gentle bend, where the river widened slightly. Willows draped their branches toward the water on the far bank, creating secluded pools of shadow.

"What was your favorite subject in school?" Hannah asked, turning the conversation toward him.

Reed considered this as he guided them past a partially submerged log. "History. I loved learning about how people lived in the past, and the challenges they overcame, the societies they built and lost." He grinned. "I was that weird kid who actually looked forward to museum field trips."

Hannah laughed. "I can picture that so clearly, a young Reed Dunbar, probably taking detailed notes while everyone else complained about sore feet."

"Guilty as charged," he admitted. "Although, in my defense, Laurel Ridge's field trips were usually pretty interesting. The perks of growing up near so many historical sites."

The boat drifted now, Reed having shipped the oars to let the gentle current carry them. Birds called from the trees along the shore, and somewhere in the distance, a fish jumped with a quiet splash.

"This feels like being in another world," Hannah observed, closing her eyes briefly to simply absorb the sensory experience—the gentle rocking of the boat, the sun warm on her skin, the distant calls of wildlife, the earthy scent of the river.

"That's why I love it out here," Reed said. "Helps put things in perspective."

Hannah opened her eyes to find him watching her, his expression soft with something that made her heart beat faster.

"What?" she asked, suddenly self-conscious.

"Nothing," he replied, though his smile suggested otherwise. "Just thinking how natural you look out here. Like you belong. You're beautiful."

Hannah blushed. "May I ask you something personal again?"

Reed nodded. "Of course."

"After the Davis tragedy... how did you find your way back from the guilt and pain of the situation?" She hesitated. "To hope?"

Reed was quiet for a long moment, his gaze shifting to the distant mountains visible between the trees. When he spoke, his voice carried the weight of hard-won wisdom.

"It wasn't a straight path," he admitted. "There were days I was so angry—at myself, at God, at the world—that I could barely function. I questioned everything, including whether I should remain in law enforcement."

Hannah listened intently, recognizing echoes of her own struggle in his words.

"My grandfather was the one who helped me the most," Reed continued. "Not by offering simple answers or telling me to 'just have faith,' but by sitting with me in the darkness. By acknowledging that sometimes terrible things happen, we can't prevent or understand."

He trailed his fingers in the water, watching the ripples spread outward. "He told me that faith isn't about having all the answers. It's about continuing to seek God even when—especially when—we don't understand His plan."

"That's beautiful," Hannah said.

Reed met her eyes. "It's also really hard. But I found that taking small steps helped. Praying, even when I wasn't sure anyone was listening. Finding purpose in helping others. Allowing myself to experience joy without guilt."

The boat drifted into a patch of dappled shade; the temperature dropping slightly as they moved out of direct sunlight.

"I'm trying to work on the guilt part," Hannah confessed. "Every time I enjoy something, every moment I'm not actively caring for Mom, there's this voice in my head telling me I'm being selfish."

"I understand that. But consider this—are you a better caregiver when you're exhausted, emotionally drained, and resentful? Or when you're rested, fulfilled, and at peace?"

Hannah sighed. "When you put it that way, it seems so logical."

"Emotions rarely follow logic," Reed pointed out with a wry smile. "That's what makes us human."

They drifted along the river, carrying them past rocky outcroppings and sandy shallows where small fish darted in the clear water.

"I've never told anyone the full story," Reed said suddenly. "About that night."

Hannah looked up, recognizing the significance of what he was offering. "You don't have to—"

"I want to," he interrupted gently. "If you're willing to listen."

Hannah nodded, understanding intuitively that this sharing was important—not just for her to understand Reed better, but for him to release part of the burden he carried.

Reed took a deep breath. "It was a domestic disturbance call. Not unusual in itself—we get them regularly. But this one... I'd been to the Davis house before. Isabelle Davis had bruises that she had tried to hide under makeup, the children who were too quiet, too watchful. All the warning signs were there."

He stared at his hands, as if seeing them covered in an invisible stain. "I urged her to leave, to take the kids to the shelter. She said she would think about it. I gave her resources, phone numbers. But I didn't push harder. I didn't insist. I respected her decision." His voice hardened. "And two weeks later, she was dead."

Hannah's heart ached for him, for the burden of what-ifs he carried. "Reed, you couldn't have forced her to seek help."

"I know that. Logically, I know that," he acknowledged. "But I still wonder if I could have said something different, done something more. I still to this day wonder if I would have just made their home more of a regular stop during my patrols." He looked up, meeting her eyes. "Anyway, when I arrived that night, the front door was partially open. I could hear the children crying. Michael Davis had already shot his wife. It was horrible, but the kids gutted me. The looks on their faces... that is what will haunt me forever. I'll always question what if I had done this or that? What if I had stepped in beforehand? I'll never forget the look in their eyes. Those children broke me. It was the saddest, most pitiful thing I have ever experienced."

Hannah reached across the space between them, placing her hand on his knee. She didn't offer placating words or easy reassurances, just the simple comfort of human connection.

"The children were hiding in a closet," Reed continued, his voice growing quieter. "They'd heard everything. Seen everything. Their faces... I still see them in my dreams occasionally. What those children witnessed and had to live through... It was something no child should ever have to experience."

"What happened to them?" Hannah asked.

"They went to live with their aunt in North Carolina. I check in periodically through social services. They're doing... as well as can be expected." Reed covered her hand with his own. "That night changed me forever. Made me question whether I was cut out for this job, whether I had what it takes to protect the people of this community. I distanced myself from relationships for quite a while. I haven't dated since that horrible day."

"Because you're afraid of failing someone?"

"Yes," he admitted after a moment. "If I don't let people get close, I can't fail them. Can't lose them."

"But you might have missed the chance to love someone special," Hannah pointed out.

Reed's smile was tinged with sadness. "Someone once told me I was choosing fear over faith."

"Smart person."

"Yes, I agree." Reed squeezed her hand.

The boat had drifted into a small, sheltered cove where the water was exceptionally clear, revealing stones and small fish beneath them. Reed maneuvered them closer to the bank with a few careful strokes of the oars.

"This is one of my favorite spots," he said, securing the oars and reaching below the bench for a small anchor, which he dropped over the side. "The water's so clear here, you can sometimes see trout resting in the shadows."

Hannah leaned carefully over the side, marveling at the underwater visibility. "It's like looking through glass," she murmured, spotting a small school of minnows darting beneath the boat.

"I've spent hours here," Reed admitted. "Just watching the water, thinking, praying."

"I can see why," Hannah said, sitting up to take in the surrounding beauty. The cove was framed by overhanging trees, creating a natural sanctuary. Wildflowers dotted the bank, and a pair of cardinals flitted among the branches above.

"I appreciate you sharing this with me," she said. "Not just this place, but... everything. Your story. Your struggles. I will never forget this day."

Reed's expression grew serious. "I've never told anyone all of that before. Not even Holly or my parents know every detail."

"Why me?" Hannah asked, genuinely curious.

"Because you understand what it's like to have your life changed in an instant. To carry a burden, you didn't choose but can't put down." His eyes met hers with startling intensity. "And because when I'm with you, I feel like maybe I don't have to carry it alone anymore."

The vulnerability in his admission touched Hannah deeply. "I feel the same way," she confessed. "Like, maybe I don't have to be strong all the time. Like it might be okay to lean on someone else occasionally."

"It is okay," Reed assured her, moving carefully in the boat until he was seated beside her on the middle bench. "More than okay."

Their shoulders touched, a simple point of contact that nonetheless sent warmth spreading through Hannah's body. The boat rocked gently beneath them, secure in its sheltered cove.

"Hannah," Reed said, his voice low and earnest. "I know we've only really known each other a short time, but I feel... I feel something with you I've never felt before."

Hannah's heart hammered in her chest. "Me too."

Reed reached up, his fingers brushing a strand of hair from her face with infinite gentleness. "I'd very much like to kiss you right now."

Hannah's breath caught in her throat. "I'd very much like that too."

Reed leaned forward slowly, giving her ample time to change her mind. But Hannah had never been more certain of anything. She met him halfway, and when his lips touched hers, soft and questioning, she felt something unfurl inside her. Something long dormant suddenly blooming into life.

The kiss was gentle, almost reverent, Reed's hand coming up to cradle her cheek as if she were made of the most precious material. Hannah's eyes fluttered closed, every sense heightened—the warmth of his palm against her skin, the faint scent of his aftershave, the soft splash of water against the boat's hull.

When they finally parted, Reed rested his forehead against hers, his breath mingling with her own. "Wow," he murmured.

Hannah laughed softly, the sound bubbling up from a place of pure joy. "Wow, indeed."

Reed smiled, his thumb tracing the curve of her cheek. "Worth waiting for."

"Definitely," Hannah agreed, marveling at how natural this felt, how right, despite the unfamiliarity. It was as if some part of her had recognized him long before her conscious mind caught up.

A fish jumped nearby, the splash breaking the stillness. Reed reluctantly straightened, though he kept his arm around Hannah's shoulders.

"The light's starting to change," he observed, nodding toward the sky, where the afternoon blue was deepening toward evening. "We should probably head back soon."

Hannah nodded, though part of her wished they could stay in this perfect moment forever, suspended in time like insects in amber. "Probably," she agreed.

"But not quite yet," Reed added, correctly reading her reluctance. "We can stay a little longer."

Hannah leaned against him, her head finding the perfect resting place on his shoulder. They sat in comfortable silence, watching the light shift and change across the water's surface, listening to the river's quiet music.

"What are you thinking?" Reed asked after a while, his voice a gentle rumble she could feel through his chest.

Hannah considered the question, trying to sort through the tangle of emotions and realizations swirling within her. "I'm thinking that I'd forgotten what it feels like to be Hannah," she said finally. "Not just Mom's caregiver or Martha's waitress, but... me. The person I was meant to be."

Reed's arm tightened around her. "And who is that person? Who is Hannah Gentry when she's fully herself?"

The question might have been intimidating once, but now it felt like an invitation—a space opened for her to step into her own truth.

"She's someone who finds beauty in ordinary moments," Hannah said slowly, the words coming from a deep, honest place. "Someone who loves deeply and isn't afraid to show it. Someone who does have faith even when the path isn't clear, and I didn't realize that until now."

She took a deep breath. "Someone who's ready to start living again, not just surviving."

Reed pressed a kiss to the top of her head. "I'd very much like to know that Hannah better."

"I think she'd like that too," Hannah replied, turning her face up to his.

"We really should head back now."

"Five more minutes," Hannah bargained, not ready to leave their sanctuary just yet.

Reed laughed, the sound echoing across the water. "Five more minutes," he agreed, tightening his arm around her. "And then we'll head home."

Home. The word resonated within Hannah in unexpected ways. For years, home had been a place of duty and responsibility. Today, it felt like a promise instead.

Chapter 22

Hannah balanced three plates along her arm with practiced ease as she weaved between the tables at the diner. The breakfast rush had finally subsided, leaving behind the comforting clatter of dishes being cleared and the rich aroma of coffee that perpetually hung in the air.

"Here you go, Mr. Wilson. Denver omelet with extra peppers, side of hash browns, wheat toast." She set the first plate in front of the elderly man who'd been coming in for the same breakfast every Wednesday without fail for as long as she'd worked at the diner.

"Thank you, honey," he replied, immediately reaching for the hot sauce.

"And for you ladies," Hannah continued, setting down the remaining plates, "one short stack with blueberry compote and one egg white veggie scramble. Can I get you anything else?"

"This looks perfect," Mrs. Chambers said, adjusting her reading glasses to inspect her breakfast. "But I wouldn't say no to a coffee refill when you get a chance."

"Coming right up," Hannah promised with a genuine smile that reached her eyes.

It had been three days after her Sunday with Reed, and she still felt like she was walking on air.

"Well now, don't you look like the cat that got into the cream," Martha commented as Hannah retrieved the coffee pot. The older woman's keen eyes missed nothing.

Hannah felt warmth creep into her cheeks. "It's just a good day, I guess."

"Mmm-hmm," Martha hummed knowingly, wiping down the counter with practiced swipes. "Wouldn't have anything to do with a certain deputy, would it?"

Hannah's blush deepened as she filled Mrs. Chambers' coffee cup and made her way back to the counter. The diner had emptied considerably, with just a handful of lingering customers nursing their coffee and reading newspapers or scrolling through phones. The mid-morning lull had officially begun.

"Maybe," Hannah admitted, setting the coffeepot back on its warmer.

Martha's smile was warm and knowing. "Come on back and help me sort through this delivery while you tell me all about it. Kylie can handle the front for a few minutes."

Before Hannah could protest, Martha was already heading toward the stockroom, clearly expecting Hannah to follow. With a small smile and a shake of her head, Hannah untied her apron and hung it on a hook before pushing through the swinging door that led to the back of the diner.

The stockroom was neat and organized, with shelves of canned goods, bags of flour and sugar, and other supplies lining the walls.

A delivery of fresh produce sat in crates near the door, waiting to be sorted and stored.

"Start with the tomatoes," Martha instructed, handing Hannah a small crate. "Check each one and set aside any that are too soft."

Hannah began the familiar task, turning each tomato in her hands to inspect it. The smooth, firm skin and fresh, earthy scent were oddly soothing.

"So," Martha said, not looking up from the lettuce she was examining, "how are things with Deputy Dunbar?"

Hannah couldn't help the smile that spread across her face. "Good. Wonderful, actually."

"I can see that," Martha chuckled. "You've been practically floating around the diner the past few days. It's nice to see."

"We spent all day Sunday together," Hannah confessed, setting a slightly bruised tomato in the discard pile. "Church, then a picnic at Whispering Falls, then boating on the river by his property."

"Sounds lovely."

"It was," Hannah agreed, a slight catch in her voice. "Martha, it's been so long since I've enjoyed myself as much as I did this past Sunday—not worrying about schedules or medications or bills. It felt almost..." she searched for the right word, "...decadent."

Martha set down the head of lettuce she'd been inspecting and gave Hannah her full attention. "That's not decadence, honey. That's just a normal life—you deserve that."

Hannah nodded, focusing intently on a particularly perfect tomato. "I know. At least my head knows it. My heart is still catching up."

"And speaking of catching up," Martha said, skillfully changing the subject, "are you nervous about this afternoon? Holly mentioned something about a work opportunity for your mother when she stopped in for coffee yesterday."

Hannah set down the tomato she'd been inspecting and exhaled slowly. "Yes. Holly's bringing a work coordinator to meet with Mom today. Something about a remote customer service position that might be perfect for her skills."

"That sounds promising."

"It is."

"But?" Martha prompted, accurately reading Hannah's tone.

"But I'm a little worried she'll back out," Hannah admitted, the words tumbling out in a rush. "She gets so anxious about new situations and about people seeing her in a wheelchair. And this would be such a big change for both of us. I want it so badly for her—for both of us, really—but what if she panics? What if it's too much for her?"

Martha wiped her hands on her apron and placed them firmly on Hannah's shoulders. "Listen to me, Hannah Gentry. Your mother is stronger than you give her credit for. Yes, she's been through a terrible ordeal, and yes, she's grown comfortable in her isolation and dependence on you. But I remember Peggy from before. She was always determined, always capable."

"I know," Hannah said. "I've seen glimpses of that person lately. It's like she's slowly waking up after a long sleep."

"And sometimes waking up is uncomfortable. It's disorienting. But that doesn't mean we should stay asleep."

Hannah considered this, absently rolling a tomato between her palms. "I just don't want to push her too hard."

"There's a difference between pushing and encouraging. You need to be positive but firm. This opportunity would be good for both of you."

"I appreciate you letting me have the afternoon off to be there for her," Hannah said, returning to the task of sorting tomatoes.

"Of course. Family comes first," Martha reassured her. "Besides, Wednesday afternoons are always slow."

They worked in comfortable silence for a few minutes, the only sounds being the rustle of produce being sorted and the distant clatter from the main dining area.

"You know," Martha said eventually, "I've known you for a long time, Hannah. Watched you carry burdens that would have crushed most people your age."

Hannah looked up, touched by the emotion in Martha's voice.

"You've been so focused on being strong for your mother that I sometimes wonder if you remember how to be strong for yourself," Martha continued, her eyes kind but direct.

"What do you mean?"

"I mean that today, if your mother hesitates or tries to back out, you need to stand firm. Not just for her sake, but for yours. Sometimes love means giving someone a gentle push toward something that scares them, but will ultimately help them grow."

Hannah thought about this, recognition dawning in her eyes. "Like Reed did for me with church on Sunday. He didn't pressure me, but he didn't let me hide either."

Martha nodded approvingly. "And look how well that turned out."

"It did turn out well."

"So be that person for your mother today. Be encouraging but firm. Remind her of who she was, who she still is beneath all that fear and pain."

"I'll try," Hannah promised.

Martha gave her an appraising look. "You know, God never wastes a hurt. Sometimes our deepest pain becomes the very thing that helps us connect with and help others."

Hannah tilted her head, considering this. "You think that's what's happening with Mom? That her experience might eventually help others?"

"I think it's possible," Martha nodded. "Maybe not today or tomorrow, but someday. The work opportunity Holly found—wouldn't that put your mother in touch with other people, even if just by phone?"

"Yes," Hannah confirmed. "It's some kind of customer service position."

"Well, then. That's a start, isn't it? A way for her to use her skills and experience to help solve problems for others. Maybe even talk to people going through their own difficult times."

"I hadn't thought of it that way."

"That's because you've been too close to it all," Martha said gently. "Sometimes we need a step back to see the bigger picture."

They finished sorting the produce, each lost in their own thoughts. As they worked, Hannah felt a gradual strengthening of her resolve. This afternoon wasn't just about a job opportunity; it was about helping her mother reclaim a part of herself that had been buried beneath years of pain and isolation.

"There," Martha said, dusting off her hands as they finished storing the last of the produce. "All done, and still plenty of time before you need to leave."

Hannah nodded, checking her watch. "A little over an hour. I should get back out front and help Kylie with the lunch prep."

As they moved toward the door, Martha placed a gentle hand on Hannah's arm, stopping her. "Before we go back out there, would you mind if I prayed with you?"

The request surprised Hannah, though it shouldn't have. Martha had never hidden her faith.

"I'd like that," Hannah said.

Martha took both of Hannah's hands in hers, her grip warm and reassuring. "Lord," she began, her voice quiet but firm, "we come to You today asking for Your wisdom and courage. Be with Hannah and Peggy this afternoon as they face this new opportunity. Give Peggy strength to step out of her comfort zone and embrace the gifts and talents You've given her. Give Hannah the words to encourage without pushing too hard. Help them both to see Your hand at work in their lives, drawing them toward healing and purpose. In Jesus' name, amen."

"Amen. Thank you, Martha."

"Any time, honey," Martha smiled. "Do you want me to pack up some lunch for you and your mom? Maybe one of her favorites?"

Hannah felt a rush of affection for this kind-hearted woman who had been more than just an employer over the years. "That would be wonderful. Mom loves your chicken salad on croissants."

"Two chicken salads on croissants coming right up," Martha promised. "With extra pickles on the side for Peggy."

Hannah walked back to the dining area, where Kylie was refilling coffee cups and chatting with the remaining customers. The late-morning sun streamed through the windows, casting warm patches of light across the checkered floor.

Hannah resumed her duties, clearing tables and preparing for the lunch service. As she worked, her mind kept returning to the afternoon ahead and Martha's words about being strong for both her mother and herself.

By the time noon rolled around, the diner was filling again with the lunch crowd. Hannah had just delivered an order to a table of construction workers when Martha emerged from the kitchen with a paper bag and a knowing smile.

"Here you go," she said, handing the bag to Hannah. "Two chicken salad croissants, extra pickles on the side for Peggy, and I threw in a couple of slices of apple pie for good measure. Sweet things make tough conversations easier."

Hannah accepted the bag with a grateful smile. "You're the best, Martha. Truly."

"I know," Martha replied with a wink. "Now scoot on out of here. Go help your mama find her way back to herself."

Hannah untied her apron and hung it on its hook. "Are you absolutely sure, the lunch rush—"

"Will happen whether or not you're here," Martha finished for her. "Kylie and I have it covered. You focus on what matters today."

Hannah nodded, gathering her purse from beneath the counter. "I'll let you know how it goes."

"You do that," Martha agreed. "And Hannah? Remember what we talked about? Be strong, not just for her, but for yourself too."

"I will," Hannah promised.

As she headed for the door, Martha called after her, "And tell that handsome deputy of yours hello for me."

Hannah felt her cheeks warm as several customers looked up with interest. "I'll tell him," she called back, hurrying through the door before Martha could embarrass her further.

Outside, the summer day was gloriously warm, the sky a deep, clear blue with just a few wispy clouds. Hannah took a deep breath, filling her lungs with the fresh air scented with blooming flowers from the planters lining Main Street.

As she walked to her car behind the diner, Hannah's phone buzzed with a text message. It was from Reed.

"Thinking of you and your mom today. Call me later to let me know how it goes? Praying it all works out."

A warm sensation spread through Hannah's chest as she read his words. How was it possible that just three weeks ago, Reed Dunbar had been just another face around town? Now his support felt essential, a steady presence she relied on.

She typed a quick reply: *"Will do. Thanks for the prayers. They're needed!"*

His response came almost immediately: *"God's got this. So do you."*

Six simple words, but they steadied her like a hand on her back.

God's got this. So do you.

Chapter 23

Hannah pushed open the front door of her home, the paper bag of Martha's chicken salad croissants clutched in one hand.

"Mom? I brought lunch from the diner. It's your favorite!" Hannah called, closing the door behind her. "Holly and Ms. Tanner will be here in about an hour!"

The house answered in silence. No wheelchair moving across the hardwood floors, no television playing in the background, none of the usual sounds that showed her mother was in the living room or kitchen.

Hannah set the bag of food on the counter, a faint tickle of unease creeping up her spine. "Mom? Are you awake?"

Still nothing.

Hannah moved toward her mother's bedroom, her steps quickening.

"Mom? Everything okay?" She tapped lightly on the partially open door before pushing it wider.

The sight that greeted her made her stomach drop. Peggy sat in her wheelchair beside her bed, face buried in her hands, shoulders shaking with silent sobs. All around her, discarded clothing lay scattered on the bed and floor, a colorful testament to what must have been multiple attempts to find an outfit.

"Mom! What's wrong?" Hannah rushed to her mother's side, kneeling beside the wheelchair.

Peggy lifted her face, revealing red-rimmed eyes and tear-stained cheeks. Her hair, which she'd obviously attempted to style, stuck out at odd angles where she'd run frustrated hands through it.

"I can't do this," Peggy choked out. "I just... I can't."

The moment Peggy saw Hannah's concerned face, something inside her seemed to crack further. Her breathing quickened, coming in short, sharp gasps that Hannah recognized immediately.

"I c-can't breathe," Peggy gasped, clutching at her chest. "They'll s-see me like... like this. They'll p-pity me or think I'm... I'm incapable."

Hannah took her mother's trembling hands, keeping her own steady despite the alarm rising within Peggy. The panic attack had escalated quickly, her mother's face now pale with fear.

"Mom, look at me," Hannah instructed, her voice calm but firm. "Right at me. That's it."

Peggy's frightened eyes found Hannah's, seeking an anchor in the storm of her anxiety.

"Now breathe with me, okay? In through your nose—one, two, three, four." Hannah demonstrated, drawing in a slow breath. "Hold it—one, two. Now out through your mouth—one, two, three, four, five, six."

Peggy struggled to follow, her first attempt shallow and quick.

"That's okay," Hannah encouraged. "Try again with me. In—one, two, three, four."

They continued the breathing pattern, Hannah counting steadily, never breaking eye contact. Gradually, Peggy's breathing began to synchronize with Hannah's, the desperate gasps slowing to more controlled inhalations.

"That's it," Hannah murmured. "You're doing great. Keep breathing with me."

After several minutes, the worst of the panic attack had passed. Peggy's breathing, while still slightly ragged, had normalized, and some color had returned to her cheeks.

"I'm sorry," Peggy whispered, closing her eyes in embarrassment. "I thought I could do this, but when I tried to get ready, I just..."

"It's okay to be nervous," Hannah assured her, squeezing her hands gently. "This is a big step."

Peggy shook her head, fresh tears welling. "It's not just nerves, Hannah. It's... everything. I haven't had a job interview in years. I haven't been seen by professional people since before the accident. What if they take one look at me in this chair and decide I'm not worth the effort?"

Hannah felt a surge of protectiveness, mixed with a newfound resolve that surprised her with its strength. Martha's words from earlier echoed in her mind: Be strong, not just for her, but for yourself, too.

"Mom. Look around you. Look at this room, at our home. For ten years, we've been hiding away in here, telling ourselves we're managing just fine on our own."

Peggy started to protest, but Hannah pressed on.

"But we're not fine, Mom. We're surviving, but we're not living. I've watched you these past few days—at Reed's ranch with the horses, speaking with Holly about books, even just seeing your face light up when Mrs. Henderson sent that message through me at church. There's so much more to you than this room, this house and this chair."

"I'm scared," Peggy admitted, her voice small.

Hannah nodded. "I know. I'm scared too. But I also know that the woman who raised me is one of the strongest people I've ever met. The woman who taught me to stand up for myself, to never back down from a challenge—she's still in there."

Hannah shifted, taking her mother's face gently between her hands. "Please do this for me, Mom. I never ask anything of you, but I need this. You need this."

Peggy's eyes widened slightly at Hannah's directness.

"We both deserve a chance at something more," Hannah continued, her throat tight with emotion. "I need to know that you'll be okay—that you have something of your own, something that makes you feel useful. And you need to remember who you are beyond this chair and these walls."

Peggy was silent for a long moment, searching Hannah's face.

"When did you get like this and where is my daughter?" she finally asked, a hint of her old wry humor creeping into her voice.

"I had a good teacher," Hannah replied with a small smile.

Peggy took a deep, shuddering breath. "I'm still terrified. I'm not sure if I want to do this."

"That's okay. Being brave isn't about not feeling fear. It's about feeling it and moving forward, anyway. You are going to do this."

Peggy nodded slowly, something shifting in her expression—a subtle strengthening, like steel beneath silk. "Alright. I'll try. For both of us."

"We have about forty minutes before they arrive. Let's find you something to wear that makes you feel confident."

Hannah stood, surveying the clothing scattered around the room. She spotted a powder blue blouse she'd bought for her mother's birthday two years ago, still with the tags attached.

"How about this one?" she suggested, retrieving the blouse from where it had fallen beside the bed. "The blue will bring out the color of your eyes."

Peggy eyed the garment uncertainly. "It's too nice for just sitting around the house."

"This isn't 'just sitting around the house,'" Hannah pointed out. "This is an interview. You deserve to look and feel your best."

After a moment's hesitation, Peggy nodded.

Hannah helped her mother change into the blouse, which flowed elegantly over her slender frame. The soft material draped perfectly, and the color indeed brought out the blue in Peggy's eyes, making them appear brighter despite the redness from crying.

"You look beautiful, Mom," Hannah said truthfully. "Now, let's do something with your hair."

She fetched a brush and began gently working through the tangles in her mother's shoulder-length hair.

"Remember how you used to brush my hair every night before bed?" Hannah asked, working out a particularly stubborn knot. "A hundred strokes, you always said."

Peggy smiled at the memory. "You'd sit so patiently, even when there were tangles. You never complained."

"That's because you told me stories while you brushed," Hannah reminded her. "I didn't want the stories to end."

"You always loved stories. Always seeing the world through that artistic eye of yours."

Hannah continued brushing, letting the rhythmic motion soothe them both.

"You're very talented," Peggy said quietly. "I've always thought so, even when I didn't say it enough."

Hannah's hands stilled momentarily, touched by the unexpected compliment. "Thanks, Mom. That means a lot."

She resumed brushing, then gathered her mother's hair back, securing it with a simple clip that allowed some strands to frame Peggy's face softly.

"There," Hannah said, stepping back to admire the effect. "Beautiful and professional."

Peggy glanced at her reflection in the vanity mirror across the room.

"You are still you," Hannah reminded her gently. "The accident changed your circumstances, not your essence."

The sound of a car pulling into the driveway reached them.

"They're here," Hannah said, feeling her pulse quicken. "Ready?"

Peggy took a deep breath, smoothing her hands over the blue blouse. "I don't know."

Hannah moved behind the wheelchair, guiding it out of the bedroom and down the hallway toward the living room, which she'd tidied that morning before leaving for work. The afternoon sun flooded the space through the open curtains, making it appear brighter and more welcoming than usual.

"One last thing," Hannah said, reaching for a light floral perfume on the side table—another unused gift. She spritzed it lightly in the air around her mother. "Perfect."

A knock sounded at the door just as Hannah positioned her mother's wheelchair near the couch.

"Coming!" Hannah called, taking one last moment to squeeze her mother's shoulder reassuringly before moving to answer the door.

Holly stood on the porch, dressed in blue nursing scrubs. Beside her was a woman, Hannah guessed to be in her mid-forties, with a warm smile and a professional appearance in a crisp pantsuit.

"Hannah, hi," Holly greeted with a smile. "This is Linda Tanner from Accessible Workforce Solutions. Linda, this is Hannah Gentry."

"Pleased to meet you, Hannah," Linda said, extending her hand with a firm, confident grip.

"Thank you both for coming," Hannah replied, stepping back to usher them inside. "Please, come in."

Hannah led them into the living room, where Peggy sat with her hands clasped tightly in her lap, chin lifted in what Hannah recognized as her mother's attempt at projecting confidence.

"Mom, this is Linda Tanner, from Accessible Workforce Solutions."

Peggy extended her hand, and Hannah noted with pride that it was steady. "Hello, Ms. Tanner. Thank you for coming to meet with me today."

"Please, call me Linda," the woman replied, taking a seat on the couch. "And thank you for considering our program. Holly has told me wonderful things about your background in insurance."

Holly settled beside Linda, offering Peggy an encouraging smile. "Linda's already reviewed your resume that we worked on this past Sunday, Peggy."

Linda nodded, pulling out a folder from her sleek messenger bag. "I was quite impressed with your experience at Blue Ridge Insurance. You've had quite a few years in customer service and claims processing, which is very impressive."

Hannah observed her mother's posture gradually relaxing as the conversation progressed. She moved quietly to the kitchen to prepare a tray with glasses of iced tea, listening intently to the exchange in the living room.

"I haven't worked in over ten years," Peggy was saying, her voice tight with honesty. "I'm sure a lot has changed in the industry since then."

"Technology changes, procedures evolve, but the fundamentals of good customer service remain the same," Linda replied. "And our program includes comprehensive paid training on all the current systems and protocols. We'd never expect you to jump in without proper preparation."

Holly chimed in. "That's what impressed me most about AWS when I researched programs for the clinic's patients, Peggy. They understand that returning to the workforce after an absence, for whatever reason, requires support and training."

Hannah returned with the tray of drinks, setting it on the coffee table and taking a seat in the armchair beside her mother's wheelchair. She noticed that Peggy's hands were no longer clasped quite so tightly. Her shoulders had lowered from their defensive position.

"Could you tell me more about the position?" Peggy asked, accepting a glass of iced tea from Hannah with a grateful nod.

"Of course," Linda replied, taking a sip of her drink before continuing. "The role is with Mountaineer Insurance Group, handling customer service calls and basic claims processing. All work is done remotely from home, with equipment we provide—computer, headset, secure internet connection, everything you need."

"Hours are flexible within reason," she continued. "The company needs coverage Monday through Friday from 8 AM to 7 PM, but representatives can select shifts that work for their situations, as long as they maintain a minimum of twenty hours per week."

Hannah glanced at her mother, noting the spark of interest in her eyes. Twenty hours a week would be a manageable start, providing structure and purpose without being overwhelming.

"And... the issue of my disability?" Peggy asked, her voice catching slightly on the word.

Linda's expression remained professional but kind. "Mountaineer Insurance is committed to creating an inclusive workforce. Your disability is only relevant, as we need to ensure you have the proper accommodations to perform your job effectively. Your experience and skills are what matter for the role itself."

Peggy nodded slowly, absorbing this information. "What would the training process involve?"

"Two weeks of virtual training, approximately four hours per day for five days, then you would have two days off. Then we'd repeat five days of training, four hours a day," Linda explained. "We break it into manageable sessions with plenty of opportunity for questions and practice. After that, you'd have a mentor for your first month on the job. Someone you can reach out to anytime you need assistance or clarification."

Holly leaned forward slightly. "The clinic has worked with several patients who've gone through this program, Peggy. The feedback has been overwhelmingly positive. They've really thought through the process of reintegrating people into the workforce."

Hannah observed a subtle transformation in her mother as the discussion continued—a straightening of her spine, a lifting of her chin, an animation in her features that had been absent for so long.

When Linda asked about Peggy's strengths in her previous role, Peggy's response came with increasing confidence. "I was known for being thorough but efficient. I could explain complex policy information in ways clients could easily understand."

"That's precisely the skill set we're looking for," Linda affirmed.

The conversation flowed naturally from there, with Peggy asking increasingly specific questions about the job responsibilities, training process, and expectations. Hannah felt a growing sense of hope as she watched her mother engage professionally, glimpsing the competent, assured woman who had existed before the accident.

At one point, when Linda asked about potential challenges, Peggy hesitated. Hannah noticed the momentary flicker of doubt crossing her mother's face.

"I worry about…" Peggy began, her voice faltering slightly.

Holly gently interjected. "If you're concerned about managing the physical aspects of the job, Peggy, remember that AWS specifically designs workspaces for individuals with mobility challenges." She turned to Linda. "Maybe you could explain how that works?"

Linda nodded. "Absolutely. We send an ergonomic specialist to assess your home workspace and provide all necessary adaptations—adjustable desk, supportive chair if you would like, properly positioned monitors, voice-activation software if needed. Everything is customized to your specific needs."

Hannah watched her mother's expression clear as this concern was addressed. The gentle but firm way Holly had steered the conversation back toward solutions rather than obstacles was masterful, preventing Peggy from falling into a spiral of doubt.

"That sounds… remarkably thorough," Peggy admitted.

"We've found that when we remove the physical barriers, our associates can focus entirely on what they do best—using their expertise to help customers," Linda explained.

The meeting continued for nearly an hour, covering compensation, which was better than Hannah had dared hope, benefits that included health insurance that would supplement Peggy's current disability coverage, and next steps in the application process.

"Based on our conversation today and your background, I'd like to recommend you for a formal interview with the hiring manager at Mountaineer Insurance," Linda said, closing her folder with a satisfied expression. "Would you be comfortable with that?"

Peggy glanced at Hannah, a mix of excitement and nervousness in her eyes. Hannah gave a subtle, encouraging nod.

"Yes," Peggy said, her voice steady. "I would be very interested in moving forward."

"Excellent," Linda smiled, reaching into her bag for a business card. "The interview would be virtual, of course, so you wouldn't need to travel. I'm thinking Friday morning, if that works for your schedule?"

"Friday would be perfect," Peggy confirmed, accepting the card. "Thank you for this opportunity, Linda. I really appreciate it. You made me feel good about myself today... needed."

"The pleasure is mine," Linda replied, rising to her feet. "Candidates with your experience and people skills are undoubtedly what our client companies are looking for. I'll email you with all the details for Friday's interview, along with some preparation materials that might be helpful."

Holly stood as well, her expression warm with approval. "I think this is going to be a wonderful fit, Peggy. And remember, I'm just a phone call away if you have any questions or concerns before Friday."

Hannah walked them to the door, Linda shaking her hand firmly at the threshold.

"Your mother is quite impressive," Linda said quietly. "Her experience speaks for itself, of course, but her poise and professionalism today were remarkable. Many people are nervous in initial meetings, but she handled herself beautifully."

"Thank you," Hannah replied, emotion catching in her throat.

After a few more pleasantries, Linda headed out to the car while Holly lingered on the porch a moment longer.

"That went so good," Holly said, her voice low.

"I can't thank you enough for arranging this," Hannah said, impulse driving her to give Holly a quick hug.

Holly returned the embrace warmly. "This is just the beginning, Hannah. For both of you."

After Holly departed, Hannah returned to the living room, where her mother sat staring at Linda's business card with an expression of wonder.

"Mom?"

Peggy looked up, her eyes shining with tears. "I can't believe I did that," she said. "I can't believe I remembered how to do that—to be professional, to... to be seen as something other than a burden."

"You are not a burden," Hannah insisted, kneeling beside the wheelchair. "Never."

"But I feel like one," Peggy admitted, tears now flowing freely down her cheeks.

Hannah reached for her mother's hand, squeezing it gently. "You would have done the same for me."

"Yes, but that doesn't make it right," Peggy said, her voice stronger now despite the tears. "I let fear turn into habit, and habit into a prison—for both of us."

She lifted her gaze to meet Hannah's directly. "Today felt... it felt like stepping out of that prison. Like remembering there's a real person inside me, and I might still have something to offer the world."

"You have so much to offer, Mom," Hannah affirmed, her own eyes growing damp. "So much wisdom, so much experience. You amazed me today."

Peggy dabbed at her tears with a tissue from her pocket. She looked around the living room; her gaze was thoughtful. "This house has been my sanctuary for so long, but I think... I think maybe it's time it stopped being my hiding place."

Hannah squeezed her mother's hand again, a wave of hope washing through her. "I think so, too. And this job could be just the beginning."

"I never thought I'd work again," Peggy admitted. "Never thought anyone would see past this chair to the person still inside it."

"Linda did," Hannah pointed out. "Holly did. They see what I've always seen—that you're still you, still capable, still valuable."

Peggy was quiet for a moment, then asked, "Would you call Reed for me?"

Hannah blinked in surprise. "Reed? Why?"

"I want to thank him," Peggy explained. "None of this would have happened if he hadn't come into our lives that morning. If he hadn't connected us with his sister, if he hadn't shown such kindness..." She shook her head, emotion overwhelming her again. "I want him to know what a difference he's made."

Hannah's heart swelled with affection for her mother and for Reed, whose quiet intervention had set so much in motion.

As she dialed, Peggy brushed away the last of her tears, a new determination settling over her features.

"Actually," Peggy said suddenly, "put it on speaker."

Hannah nodded, pressing the speaker button as the phone rang twice before Reed's warm voice answered.

"Hannah, hi. How did it go?"

"It went wonderfully," Hannah replied, smiling at her mother. "Actually, Mom wanted to speak with you. You're on speaker."

"Reed?" Peggy's voice was clear and steady. "I wanted to thank you personally. What you did—coming into our lives, connecting us with Holly, showing us kindness without pity—it's changed everything."

There was a brief pause before Reed responded, his voice gentle with emotion. "Mrs. Gentry, that means more to me than you know. But the courage to take these steps came from you."

"Now, Reed... you must call me Peggy," she insisted. "And I disagree. Sometimes we need someone from outside to show us possibilities we've stopped seeing for ourselves."

"Well, then I'm honored to have been that person for you both," Reed replied. "So, the job prospect looks promising?"

"Very," Peggy confirmed. "I have a formal interview Friday. I'm nervous, but... excited too. I haven't felt excited about the future in a very long time."

"That's wonderful news. I know you're going to impress them, Peggy."

"Thank you," she replied. "For everything. Would you like to come over for dinner tonight? Nothing fancy, just a small celebration."

"I'd like that very much," Reed answered, the smile clear in his voice.

After arranging the details and ending the call, Hannah looked at her mother with a mixture of love and newfound respect.

"That was a surprise," she commented. "Inviting Reed for dinner."

"It feels right," she said simply. "Now, let's figure out what we're making for dinner."

Hannah felt a surge of joy, so intense it was almost painful. "I'd like that very much."

Chapter 24

"You have to turn it this way—no, not like that," Peggy directed from her wheelchair, gesturing animatedly at the golden-brown roast chicken sitting on the cutting board. "The breast side should face you when you carve."

Reed adjusted the bird, a look of good-natured concentration on his face as he positioned the carving knife. "Like this?"

"Perfect," Peggy nodded approvingly. "Now slice downward along the breastbone—that's it."

Hannah carried a steaming bowl of garlic mashed potatoes to the table, smiling at the scene unfolding in their small dining area. The room felt different tonight—warmer, livelier, and filled with conversation and savory aromas that made it feel more like a different home.

"You know, I've helped in investigations across several counties, but this chicken has me genuinely intimidated," Reed confessed, carefully separating a wing from the breast.

Hannah laughed, returning to the kitchen for the green beans. "It's just a chicken, Deputy Dunbar. Surely, you've faced worse criminals."

"Yes, but those criminals weren't being judged on their presentability by two discerning Gentry women," Reed replied with a grin.

"Now you're getting it," Peggy encouraged, wheeling herself closer to inspect his work. "My husband, Paul, used to make a mess of carving. The poor man tried his best, but we'd end up with chicken shrapnel rather than slices."

Hannah placed the green beans on the table, completing their modest feast. The dining table, rarely used for actual dining these days, had been cleared of mail and miscellaneous items. It was set with their better dishes and adorned with a small vase of wildflowers Reed had brought, along with a bottle of sparkling apple cider.

"Everything looks delicious," Reed said, stepping back to admire his carving handiwork before washing his hands at the kitchen sink. "You didn't have to go to all this trouble."

"It's not every day we have something this important to celebrate," Hannah replied, moving to help her mother into position at the table.

"Would it be all right if I said grace?" Reed asked, glancing between Hannah and Peggy after he seated himself at the table.

"Please," Peggy replied, while Hannah nodded her agreement.

They bowed their heads as Reed's deep voice filled the room. "Heavenly Father, we thank You for this food and for the hands that prepared it. We thank You for bringing us together and for the new opportunities You've placed before Peggy. Please bless this meal and our time together. Guide us as we move forward in faith, trusting Your plan for our lives. In Jesus' name, amen."

"Amen," Hannah and Peggy echoed.

Reed poured the sparkling cider into each glass, then raised his in a toast. "To Peggy, for her courage, her determination, and what I'm certain will be a successful interview on Friday."

The crystal glasses clinked together, the sound bright and festive in the small dining room.

"And to new beginnings," Peggy added.

They passed dishes, filled plates, and for several minutes focused on enjoying the meal. Hannah had spent most of her afternoon preparing, wanting everything to be perfect. The chicken was tender, the potatoes creamy with just the right hint of garlic, and the green beans still had a satisfying snap to them.

"This is delicious," Reed said appreciatively after his first few bites. "Martha would be impressed."

"I've learned a lot working at the diner," Hannah admitted. "But these are actually Mom's recipes. She is the real cook in the family."

Reed took a sip of his cider. "So, Peggy, are you feeling prepared for Friday's interview?"

Peggy nodded, setting down her fork. "Linda sent over some more preparation materials this afternoon. Sample questions, company information, that sort of thing. It's been so long since I've done anything like this... I'm nervous, but in a good way."

"Like butterflies rather than hornets?" Reed suggested.

Peggy laughed—a genuine, unguarded sound that made Hannah's heart lift. "That's exactly it. Butterflies, not hornets."

"Holly mentioned the training would be about four hours a day for two weeks," Hannah said, reaching to refill her mother's water glass. "Do you think that's manageable, mom?"

"I think so," Peggy replied thoughtfully. "The materials mentioned, they break it up with plenty of rest periods and different activities to keep it engaging. And four hours is much less intimidating than a full eight-hour day right off the bat."

Reed nodded. "Sounds like they've put a lot of thought into making the transition back to work accessible."

"They really have," Peggy agreed. "The position itself sounds perfect, too—customer service for an insurance company. It's very similar to what I used to do, just updated for today's technology."

Hannah watched her mother talk animatedly about the job requirements, her hands gesturing to emphasize points, her eyes bright with purpose. This was the woman Hannah remembered from her childhood—engaged, intelligent, and confident in her abilities.

"If this works out, and I'm earning again," Peggy continued, turning to Hannah, "you could cut back on your hours at the diner. Maybe even go to school part-time to get a degree in photography."

The chicken Hannah had just forked into her mouth suddenly felt difficult to swallow. She reached for her water, taking a moment to compose herself. The suggestion had caught her completely off guard.

"That's not a bad idea," Reed said.

Peggy nodded eagerly. "For years, I've been... well, I've been your responsibility, Hannah."

"Mom—"

"Let me finish, please," Peggy interrupted, her voice firm but kind. "I've been dependent on you, and while I'll still need some help, this job could change our dynamic considerably. It would mean my own income, that will help pay the bills. And it would free you to pursue some of the dreams you set aside."

Hannah felt a complex swirl of emotions—hope mingled with anxiety, excitement tempered by the fear of change. For so long, her identity had been wrapped up in caring for her mother. Who would she be if that wasn't her primary purpose?

"I don't know. It feels premature to make plans before you've even had the interview."

"Sometimes hope requires a little planning ahead," Reed suggested, his green eyes warm as they met hers across the table. "There's nothing wrong with considering possibilities."

Hannah managed a small smile. "I suppose you're right. It's just... a lot to take in and think about."

"I understand," Peggy said, reaching to touch her daughter's hand. "But promise me you'll at least think about it? You've put your life on hold long enough."

"I promise," Hannah agreed, squeezing her mother's hand gently.

The conversation shifted to more practical matters—where they might set up Peggy's home office, what equipment she would need, and how her schedule might work around Hannah's shifts at the diner if need be.

"The ergonomic specialist Linda mentioned would be key," Reed said, helping himself to more green beans. "They'll make sure your workspace is completely adapted to your needs."

"That part makes me a bit nervous," Peggy admitted. "Having strangers come in, evaluating our home..."

"They're not judging," Reed assured her. "They're problem-solving. And I could be here when they come, if that would help."

Hannah glanced at him, touched by the offer. "You'd do that?"

"Of course," he replied simply, as if it were the most natural thing in the world. "That's what... friends do."

The slight hesitation before the word "friends" wasn't lost on Hannah. They were more than friends, but exactly what they were, remained undefined—a tender, growing connection that didn't yet have a label.

"Speaking of your workspace," Hannah said, turning back to her mother, "I was thinking the small bedroom might work better than the living room. More privacy, fewer distractions. It would be your own space."

"And it has good lighting," Peggy added thoughtfully. "The morning sun comes in so nicely through that east window."

As they continued discussing logistics, Hannah found herself actually engaging with the idea of having more time for herself. What would she do with that freedom? The possibilities stirred a long-dormant excitement within her.

"Well," Peggy announced after they'd finished dessert, "I think I'll retreat to my room and review those interview materials Linda sent over again. Gotta to be prepared for Friday."

Reed rose to help clear the dessert plates. "Is there anything I can help you with, Peggy?"

"I'm fine, thank you," she replied with a genuine smile. "Hannah set everything up on my tablet earlier."

As Reed moved to help her maneuver away from the table, Peggy placed a hand on his arm. "Reed," she said, "I just want you to know how glad I am that you're in our lives. Both of our lives."

A slight flush crept up Reed's neck, but his smile was steady. "The feeling is mutual, Peggy."

Hannah watched this exchange with a tightness in her throat. Her mother's approval meant everything, and this simple acknowledgment of Reed's place in their lives felt monumental.

After helping Peggy to her room and making sure she had everything she needed, Hannah returned to find Reed already at the sink, sleeves rolled up, washing dishes.

"You don't have to do that," she protested, reaching for a dish towel.

"I know," he replied, handing her a clean plate to dry. "I want to help."

They fell into an easy rhythm—Reed washing, Hannah drying and putting away.

"Your mom seems really excited about this job prospect," Reed commented, scrubbing at a stubborn spot on the serving platter.

"I haven't seen her like this in so long," Hannah admitted. "It's wonderful, but also a little... unsettling."

"Change usually is. Even a positive change."

They worked in comfortable silence for a moment before Reed spoke again, his voice taking on a more serious tone.

"I had a domestic violence call yesterday," he said, keeping his eyes on the dish in his hands. "Young couple, and children. Neighbors called it in."

Hannah stilled, recognizing the weight of this revelation. "Was everyone okay?"

Reed nodded slowly. "This time, yes. But there were signs... similar to the Davis case. The same patterns. The woman denied everything, of course. Said she fell. The children were too quiet, watching everything with those eyes..." He swallowed hard.

Hannah set down her towel, giving him her full attention.

"I did things differently this time," he continued. "I made sure a female deputy was present. We separated them completely for the interviews. I spoke to the children alone. And I've already scheduled follow-up visits, coordinated with Child Protective Services, for a welfare check."

"That sounds very thorough," Hannah said.

"I'm not leaving anything to chance," Reed said, his jaw tightening slightly. "Not again. I've personally flagged their address in our system. Any call from that location gets immediate priority response."

Hannah gently touched his forearm, feeling the tension in his muscles. "You're doing everything you can, Reed."

"I hope it's enough," he said quietly. "The woman refused to press charges, refused to go to a shelter. Legally, there's only so much we can do until..."

"Until something worse happens," Hannah finished, understanding the terrible bind he was in.

Reed nodded, returning his attention to the dishes. "I've been praying for them. For wisdom to know what to do, how far to push without making the situation worse."

After a moment, he changed the subject, his tone lightening.

"So... your mom's suggestion about photography courses. What do you think?"

Hannah resumed drying a glass, considering the question. "Honestly, I hadn't thought much about myself in all this. I've been so focused on what this job would mean for Mom."

"But?" Reed prompted.

"But the idea of having time to actually focus on photography again is... appealing," she admitted. "More than appealing. Exciting. Terrifying."

Reed smiled. "Want to look at some options?" He dried his hands and pulled out his phone. "Let's see what's available online. Maybe something you could work around your schedule at the diner."

They moved to the couch, sitting close together as Reed searched for photography programs. The warmth of his shoulder pressed against hers felt comforting and right.

"There's a lot out there," Reed commented, scrolling through search results. "Certificate programs, full degrees, specialized courses in different types of photography..."

Hannah leaned closer, genuinely interested. "I'm almost entirely self-taught. I wonder if formal training could help me take it to the next level."

"Do you need a formal degree, though?" Reed asked thoughtfully. "Your work is already exceptional. Maybe specific courses in areas you want to develop would be more practical than a full degree program."

Hannah considered this. "That's... actually a good point. Maybe I should focus on business type of classes—marketing, pricing, building a client base. Those are the areas where I feel least confident. And perhaps a few specialty photography courses to advance my current skills."

Reed nodded. "Build on your strengths, and develop the areas where you need more knowledge."

Hannah felt a rush of possibilities opening before her. "I could expand my online presence, maybe even approach galleries throughout the state or businesses about displaying my work."

"Now you're thinking like a business owner, not just an artist."

They spent the next half hour exploring options, bookmarking courses and resources, and discussing practical steps Hannah could take even before her mother's job situation was settled.

Eventually, Reed set his phone aside and glanced at the darkening window. "It's getting late. I should probably head out soon."

Hannah followed his gaze, surprised to see twilight settling over the landscape outside. The kitchen clock confirmed it was nearly nine.

"I didn't realize how late it had gotten," she said, suddenly reluctant for the evening to end.

Reed turned to face her more fully on the couch. "Before I go... there's something I've been thinking about all evening."

"What's that?" Hannah asked, noting the thoughtful expression in his eyes.

"Seeing all these positive changes happening for you and your mom... it makes me think about God's timing. There's a verse I've held onto since the Davis tragedy: 'For I know the plans I have for you, declares the Lord, plans to prosper you and not to harm you, plans to give you hope and a future.'"

Hannah recognized the passage from Jeremiah. "I used to find comfort in that verse," she admitted. "But after the accident, it was difficult to see the hope and future part. It felt like empty words."

Reed nodded understandingly. "Faith is hardest when we're in the valley. But look at what's happening now—your mom's job opportunity, your photography, us..." He gestured between them. "It's like watching puzzle pieces fall into place. Nothing has been wasted, even the difficult years."

Hannah considered his words, feeling their truth resonate with her in a way that surprised her. "I think my faith is starting to come back," she said quietly. "Not all at once, but in small ways. Being at church on Sunday, praying with Martha yesterday, seeing these new possibilities open up... it's like remembering a language I used to be fluent in."

Reed reached for her hand, his fingers warm as they entwined with hers. "That's a beautiful way to put it."

Reed stood. "I really should go. Early shift tomorrow."

Hannah walked him to the door, where his jacket hung on the hook. As he shrugged it on, she felt a curious mix of contentment and reluctance—happy for the evening they'd shared, yet wishing it didn't have to end.

Reed turned to her at the threshold, his expression soft in the dimmed entryway light. "Thanks for including me in your celebration this evening."

Reed reached up, gently tucking a strand of hair behind her ear, his fingers lingering against her cheek.

"I could get used to evenings like this," he said, his voice low and warm.

Hannah leaned slightly into his touch. "So could I."

He drew her into an embrace then, his arms strong and secure around her. Hannah rested her head against his chest, listening to the steady rhythm of his heart beneath his shirt, breathing in the clean scent of his aftershave mixed with the faint aroma of fabric softener.

"I'll see you tomorrow, lunch at the diner?"

"I'll save you the best table," Hannah promised with a smile.

Reed's eyes held hers for a long moment. "Goodnight, Hannah, and sweet dreams."

"Night, Reed."

She stood in the doorway, watching as he walked to his truck. He turned once to wave before climbing in.

Hannah remained there long after his taillights had disappeared down the road, the cool evening air washing over her, carrying the sweet scent of honeysuckle from the bush by the porch steps. The night insects had begun their symphony, a gentle background to her thoughts.

So much had changed in just a few short weeks. The rhythm of her life was shifting beneath her feet like sand in an outgoing tide. New possibilities stretched before her, exciting and terrifying in equal measure.

What would it be like to have time for herself again? To pursue photography not just in stolen moments, but as a legitimate focus? What would it mean to her relationship with her mother if they were more equal partners, rather than caregiver and dependent?

And then there was Reed, bringing a new dimension to her life she'd never expected to find. The tenderness between them was growing into something solid and real, a shelter in the midst of all these changes.

Hannah wrapped her arms around herself. Change was coming—had already arrived, in fact. Embracing it meant letting go of the safe, familiar constraints that had defined her existence for ten years. The prospect left her breathless with both anticipation and anxiety.

Chapter 25

Hannah wiped the counter with brisk, efficient strokes, stealing another glance at the diner's entrance as the bell remained stubbornly silent. The lunch rush had ended thirty minutes ago.

"Table six needs bussing," Kylie called as she balanced a tray of dirty dishes on her forearm.

"On it," Hannah replied, tucking a wayward strand of hair behind her ear as she moved from behind the counter.

She gathered plates and glasses from the recently vacated booth, arranging them on her tray. Her eyes drifted to the corner table by the window. Reed's usual spot. It remained empty.

This wasn't like him. For the past several weeks, Reed had come in for lunch every day she worked, usually around one. It was now nearly 1:45, and there was no sign of him. No text, no call. Nothing.

Hannah told herself not to worry. His schedule could be unpredictable. There were countless reasonable explanations for his absence.

Yet the knot in her stomach tightened. She'd be leaving in a few moments to help her mother prepare for the virtual interview with

Mountaineer Insurance. Today was a pivotal moment for Peggy, and Hannah needed to focus on that, not on the fact that Reed hadn't shown up for lunch.

"Earth to Hannah," Martha's voice broke through her thoughts. "You've been wiping that same spot for two minutes."

Hannah blinked, realizing she'd been absently rubbing the same section of counter while staring at the door. "Sorry. I was just thinking."

Martha's knowing eyes softened. "About a certain deputy? I'm sure he's just tied up with work. The sheriff's department has been busy with that string of break-ins over in Pine Ridge."

"You're probably right. He's just busy."

"When are you heading out to help your mom get ready for her interview?"

Hannah checked the clock. "In a few minutes. The interview's at three."

"How's she feeling about it?"

"Nervous but excited. She's been practicing answers to potential questions every day."

"That's wonderful," Martha said warmly. "I'll be praying it goes well for her."

"Thanks, Martha. That means a lot."

The older woman studied Hannah's face for a moment. "And what about you? How are you feeling about all these changes?"

Hannah paused, considering the question. "Hopeful. And a little scared. If she gets this job, our whole dynamic will shift."

"Change can be frightening, even good change," Martha nodded. "But I have a feeling this is going to be positive for both of you."

The bell above the door jingled, and Hannah's head snapped up automatically. Her shoulders fell slightly when an elderly couple entered instead of Reed.

Martha patted her arm. "Why don't you handle the new customers? I'll finish setting up for the afternoon."

Hannah forced a smile and reached for her order pad. As she greeted the couple and led them to a table, she tried to silence the worried voice in her head. But her eyes kept drifting to the empty corner table by the window, and her phone remained stubbornly silent in her pocket.

Hannah moved through her tasks mechanically, while her mind spun with scenarios to explain Reed's absence.

She'd sent him a text earlier, a casual "Missed you at lunch today. Everything ok?" But there had been no response.

Later, as she untied her apron and hung it on the hook in the back room, Martha followed her. "Try not to worry about Reed. I'm sure he's fine."

"I just can't help thinking something's wrong. He always texts if he's going to miss lunch."

"You really care about him, don't you?"

"I do."

Martha smiled. "It shows. And from what I've seen, the feeling is mutual." She held the back door open for Hannah. "Now go take care of your mama. And let me know how the interview goes!"

"I will," Hannah promised, stepping out into the warm afternoon sunshine.

As she drove home, Hannah tried to focus her thoughts on her mother's upcoming interview. Peggy had worked so hard preparing for this opportunity. Today was about her, not about Hannah's worries over Reed's absence.

She pulled into the driveway of their small home and shook off her worries over Reed.

"Mom?" Hannah called as she entered the house. "I'm home!"

She found Peggy in her bedroom, surrounded by clothing options spread across the bed. Her wheelchair was positioned before the mirror, and she was holding up two different blouses, her expression tense with indecision.

"Which one do you think?" Peggy asked. "The blue brings out my eyes, but the burgundy looks more professional."

Hannah set her purse down and considered both options. "The burgundy," she decided. "It will look crisp on camera during the virtual interview."

Peggy nodded, setting aside the blue blouse. "That's what I was leaning toward, too. I've been practicing all morning, going over the company information Linda sent and rehearsing my answers."

"You're going to do great."

"I hope so. It's been so long since I've done anything like this. What if I freeze up? What if I've forgotten how to be professional?"

Hannah knelt beside her mother's wheelchair, taking her hands. "Mom, you haven't forgotten anything. You've been practicing your answers, and you've researched the company. You're more than prepared."

"But what if they see me and only notice the wheelchair?"

"Then they'd be missing out on an incredible employee," Hannah replied firmly. "But from everything Holly and Linda have said about this company, they're looking for skill and experience, not physical ability."

Peggy squeezed Hannah's hands, drawing strength from her daughter's confidence. "You're right. I know you're right." She took a deep breath, squaring her shoulders. "I can do this."

"Yes, you can," Hannah affirmed, standing up. "Now, let's finish getting you ready. We want to make sure the computer is set up properly and test the video connection well before the interview starts."

Hannah helped her mother with the final preparations, styling her hair in a neat, professional updo, applying subtle makeup to enhance her features without looking overdone, and making sure the laptop was positioned at the most flattering angle. She pushed her worries about Reed to the back of her mind. This moment belonged to her mother.

"There," Hannah said, stepping back to assess the results. "You look fantastic."

Peggy studied her reflection, a mixture of nervousness and determination in her eyes. "Professional enough for the corporate world?"

"Absolutely," Hannah assured her. "You look capable, confident, and ready to impress."

At that moment, Peggy's tablet chimed with an incoming email notification. "That's probably Linda with the final interview details," she said, reaching for the device.

As her mother reviewed the email, Hannah couldn't resist checking her phone once more. Still no message from Reed. The knot in her stomach tightened, but she forced herself to set the phone aside. She couldn't let her worry distract from her mother's moment.

"The interview link is here," Peggy announced. "We should load it up and make sure everything's working properly."

For the next twenty minutes, Hannah and Peggy tested the video connection, adjusted the lighting in the room, and made sure the background looked tidy and professional. They positioned the wheelchair at the perfect distance from the computer, making sure Peggy appeared framed properly in the video window.

"How do I look on camera?" Peggy asked, sitting up straighter in her wheelchair.

"Perfect. Professional and poised."

Peggy nodded, taking a deep breath. "Twenty minutes until the interview. I think I need some water."

"I'll get it. Try to relax. You've got this, Mom."

In the kitchen, Hannah filled a glass with water and added a slice of lemon, a small touch to help soothe her mother's nerves. As she did so, she couldn't help glancing at her phone once more. The blank screen stared back at her, offering no reassurance.

Hannah returned to the bedroom with the water, finding Peggy reviewing her notes one last time.

"Lemon water," Hannah said, placing the glass within easy reach. "Just like you used to have before important meetings at Blue Ridge Insurance."

Peggy looked up in surprise. "You remember that?"

Hannah smiled. "Of course. I remember picking you up from work sometimes, and you'd always have water with lemon on your desk after big meetings."

"It settled my nerves," Peggy admitted, taking a sip.

"Some things don't change," Hannah said.

They spent the remaining time in quiet preparation, Peggy occasionally murmuring key points about the company or job requirements, Hannah offering encouragement and last-minute adjustments to ensure everything was perfect.

The computer chimed with an incoming call. Peggy straightened, smoothing her blouse one last time.

"This is it," she said, her voice tight with nervousness.

"Remember, be yourself. Your experience speaks for itself."

Peggy nodded, drew a deep breath, and reached for the mouse to accept the call. "Wish me luck."

"You don't need luck," Hannah replied, squeezing her mother's shoulder gently. "You've got this."

As the video window expanded to fill the screen, Hannah stepped out of camera range but remained in the room.

"Mrs. Gentry? I'm James Wilson, Hiring Manager for Mountaineer Insurance," said a friendly-looking man in his fifties, his image clear on the screen. "And this is Diane Clark, our Remote Workforce Coordinator."

"It's a pleasure to meet you both," Peggy replied, her voice steady and professional. "Thank you for this opportunity."

Hannah leaned against the wall, watching with pride as her mother transformed before her eyes. Gone was the uncertain, anxious woman of moments before. In her place sat Peggy Gentry, an insurance professional, her posture confident and her voice assured as she answered questions about her previous experience, her approach to customer service, and her understanding of the company's products.

The interview proceeded smoothly, with James and Diane asking thoughtful questions and Peggy responding with clear, articulate answers that highlighted her experience and problem-solving abilities. There was a natural flow to the conversation, punctuated by occasional smiles and even a shared laugh over an industry-specific joke that Peggy understood immediately.

When James asked about her extended absence from the workforce, Peggy addressed it directly.

"The accident changed my circumstances, but not my capabilities. I've retained my knowledge of insurance principles, and I'm a quick study of new technologies. I'm eager to apply my experience in a new environment and contribute to Mountaineer's reputation for excellent customer service."

Hannah felt a swell of pride at her mother's composed response.

"That's refreshing to hear," Diane commented. "Many candidates try to gloss over employment gaps, but your straightforward approach shows character."

The interview continued for another fifteen minutes, with discussions about specific scenarios Peggy might face in the role and questions about her availability for training. Throughout it all, Peggy maintained her professional demeanor, answering with confidence and asking thoughtful questions of her own about the company culture and performance expectations.

Finally, James leaned slightly toward the camera. "Well, Mrs. Gentry, I have to say this has been one of our more impressive interviews. You've clearly prepared thoroughly, and your experience aligns perfectly with what we're seeking."

Peggy's hands clasped tightly in her lap, but her voice remained steady. "Thank you. I've researched Mountaineer Insurance extensively, and I'm genuinely excited about the opportunity to be part of your team."

"We feel the same way," Diane chimed in with a warm smile. "We'd like to offer you the position."

Hannah had to stifle a gasp of delight as her mother momentarily froze on the screen.

"Right now?" Peggy asked, clearly caught off guard by the immediate offer.

James chuckled. "We know what we're looking for, and you're it. The training cohort begins next Monday. Would you be able to start, then?"

Peggy collected herself quickly, her professional composure return-ing. "Yes, absolutely. I'd be delighted to accept the position and begin training on Monday."

"Excellent!" James beamed. "Diane will email you all the necessary paperwork and details about the training schedule by the end of today. The equipment for your home office will be delivered early next week, with the ergonomic specialist scheduling a visit once we confirm a suitable time."

"Thank you both so much for this opportunity," Peggy said, her voice steady despite the emotion Hannah could see building behind her eyes. "I'm looking forward to becoming part of the Mountaineer Insurance team."

After a few more minutes of details and pleasantries, the call ended. Peggy sat motionless for a moment, staring at the blank screen. Then she turned her wheelchair slowly toward Hannah, tears welling in her eyes.

"I did it. I got the job," she whispered, as if saying it too loudly might make it disappear. "They didn't even need to think about it. They just... offered it to me."

Hannah rushed to her mother, kneeling beside the wheelchair to embrace her. "Because you are spectacular! I'm so proud of you, Mom."

Peggy's tears spilled over, running down her cheeks as she held her daughter tightly. "I did it," she said, her voice stronger now. "I really did it."

"You absolutely did," Hannah confirmed, pulling back to look at her mother's face, shining with tears and triumph. "This calls for a celebration."

"I can't believe it," Peggy laughed through her tears. "After all these years... I have a job."

The reality of the moment settled over them both. The significance of this step, this return to something Peggy had believed was lost forever.

"We should call Holly," Hannah suggested, wiping at her tears. "She'll want to know right away."

Peggy nodded, reaching for her phone. "And Linda. She put so much faith in me."

As her mother made the calls, sharing her exciting news with those who had helped make it possible, Hannah slipped into the kitchen to prepare a special dinner. This was a moment worth commemorating.

She opened the refrigerator, surveying its contents while mentally planning a celebratory meal. As she worked, pulling out ingredients and setting them on the counter, she felt a complex mixture of emotions, pride in her mother's achievement, excitement for the changes ahead, and relief at this positive development.

And beneath it all, a persistent worry about Reed that she couldn't quite shake.

Hannah pulled out her phone, checking it once more. Still no message. Biting her lip, she sent another text:

"Mom got the job! They offered it on the spot. Wish you could be here to celebrate with us. Hope everything's okay with you."

She set the phone down and returned to meal preparations, trying to focus on the joy of the moment rather than her growing concern.

An hour later, with a special dinner of chicken Marsala—Peggy's favorite—coming together nicely on the stove, Hannah heard her mother's voice from the living room.

"Hannah? Could you come here a minute?"

Hannah turned down the heat on the saucepan and wiped her hands on a dish towel before heading into the living room. "What's up, Mom?"

Peggy was facing the window, her expression thoughtful. She turned her wheelchair as Hannah entered. "I just got off the phone with Loretta Dunbar."

Hannah paused, surprised. "Reed's mother? I didn't realize you had her number."

"Holly gave it to me," Peggy explained. "I wanted to thank her for all she and her family have done for us, especially Reed's support. I had to thank her for raising such wonderful children. All of this happening in my life wouldn't have been possible without Reed and Holly." She hesitated, then continued. "Hannah, there was an incident today. That's why Reed missed lunch."

Hannah's heart seemed to stutter in her chest. "What kind of incident? Is he hurt?"

"No, he's not hurt. But Loretta said he had a situation with a family Reed was concerned about. Something about a domestic violence case? Reed responded to the call. It was... difficult for him, Loretta said."

Relief that Reed wasn't physically injured mingled with fresh concern.

"Did she say anything else? About how Reed is doing?" Hannah asked, sinking onto the couch.

Peggy shook her head. "Just that he was processing it. She thought I should tell you, since she knew you'd be worried when he didn't show up for lunch."

Hannah nodded, grateful for the information, yet still concerned. "I should call him..."

"Give him a little space," Peggy suggested gently. "Men like Reed sometimes need to work through difficult situations in their own way first."

Hannah considered this. "Maybe you're right. I'll give him some time." She stood, forcing a smile. "The chicken Marsala is almost ready. Your favorite, to celebrate your new job."

"It smells wonderful. I haven't had your chicken Marsala in ages."

They ate dinner together; the conversation focused on Peggy's new job, the training schedule, the equipment she would need, and their plans for converting the spare bedroom into her home office. Throughout the meal, Hannah maintained an enthusiastic demeanor, genuinely happy for her mother's success, while a small part of her mind remained preoccupied with thoughts of Reed.

After dinner, Hannah insisted that Peggy relax in the living room while she cleaned up. "You've earned a rest after all the preparation and excitement today," she told her mother.

Alone in the kitchen, Hannah moved through the ritual of washing dishes and wiping down counters, finding comfort in the routine tasks.

The dishwater grew cool as she finished the last pot, her thoughts still circling around what might have occurred with the family Reed had been so concerned about. Had the situation escalated to another tragedy? Was he blaming himself again?

She dried her hands and reached for her phone, checking it one more time. Still nothing from Reed.

Hannah sighed, setting the phone down on the counter. She would respect his need for space, as her mother had suggested. But it was hard not to worry about him, not to want to reach out and offer comfort.

She was wiping down the stove when her phone chimed with an incoming text message. Hannah's heart leaped as she quickly dried her hands and reached for the device.

The message was from Reed:

Sorry I missed lunch and didn't respond sooner. Had a difficult call today. Everyone is physically safe now, but it was challenging. Mom told me your great news—congratulations to Peggy! I'm so happy for both of you. Can we talk tomorrow? I could use a friendly voice.

Hannah read the message twice, relief flooding through her. He was okay. Not unaffected, clearly, but at least he had reached out.

She typed a quick reply:

So relieved to hear from you. I was worried. Mom is thrilled about the job—you should have seen her during the interview! She was wonderful. Of course, we can talk tomorrow. Anytime. Take care of yourself tonight, Reed. I'm here when you need me.

Hannah sent the message, then gently set the phone down. She finished cleaning the kitchen, her mind calmer now that she'd heard from Reed.

As she turned off the kitchen light, Hannah glanced once more at her phone, seeing Reed's simple response:

Thank you. See you tomorrow.

As she headed toward the living room to join her mother, Hannah felt the weight of a revelation: this was what it meant to truly love for someone, to worry when they were absent, to rejoice in their presence, and to offer comfort in their pain.

"Comfort in their pain," she whispered to herself as she crossed the threshold into the living room.

Peggy looked up from her book, her reading glasses perched on the edge of her nose. "Did you say something, dear?"

"Would you be alright by yourself for a couple of hours? There's something I need to do."

"Of course." Peggy's brow furrowed slightly. "Is everything okay?"

Hannah offered a small smile. "Nothing's wrong, I don't think. I just... I need to check on Reed."

Chapter 26

Hannah stepped out of her car, the evening air wrapping around her like a warm blanket. She'd driven to Reed's home on instinct.

"Reed?" she called, eyes scanning the property.

The cabin stood silent, windows dark. No movement in the paddock where his three horses usually grazed. The barn door was closed. His truck and the sheriff's department SUV were parked in the driveway.

Hannah made her way to the porch. She knocked on the solid door; the sound echoing in the stillness.

"Reed? It's Hannah."

Nothing.

She knocked again, louder this time, straining to hear any movement inside the cabin. Only silence answered.

A flutter of worry stirred in her chest. His vehicles were here, yet he wasn't answering. Hannah tried the door handle, finding it locked. She stepped back, considering her options.

Then she remembered the bench he'd shown her, his thinking spot by the river. The place he went when he needed to reflect or make decisions. Without hesitation, Hannah descended the porch steps and circled the cabin, finding the narrow footpath that led toward the sound of flowing water.

The trail wound gently through a stand of tall trees. As she rounded a bend in the path, the river came into view, its surface burnished with the fading light of day. And there, on the simple wooden bench positioned to face the water, sat Reed.

Hannah paused, not wanting to startle him. He sat with his back straight, bible open in his hands, head bowed slightly. The tension that had gripped her since she'd heard about his difficult day eased at the sight of him.

He looked so peaceful, his strong profile outlined against the backdrop of river and trees. His posture suggesting not defeat but surrender, a man finding solace in faith after a challenging day. The sight of him like this, vulnerable yet strong, made Hannah's heart swell with an emotion so powerful it caught her by surprise.

A twig snapped beneath her foot as she shifted her weight, and Reed's head came up, his gaze immediately finding her among the trees.

"Hannah?" Surprise colored his voice as he closed his bible and set it beside him on the bench.

"I'm sorry to disturb you," she said, stepping forward onto the small clearing beside the river. "I was worried."

Reed's expression softened as he rose to his feet. "You're not disturbing me." He extended his hand toward her. "Come sit with me?"

Hannah crossed the remaining distance between them. She took his offered hand and settled beside him on the bench.

"I know you said we'd talk tomorrow," she began, searching his face for signs of distress. "My mom spoke with your mom on the phone earlier. Mom told me about your day today... I couldn't stop thinking about you."

Reed's gaze returned to the river, his thumb absently stroking the back of her hand. "Your mom and my mom chatting about me. I'm not sure if I should be worried." A small smile played at the corners of his mouth, though it didn't quite reach his eyes.

"They're just looking out for you. Like I am."

Reed nodded, the tension in his shoulders visibly easing. "I'm sorry I missed lunch and didn't answer your texts. Today was very busy at work. I was on a call that lasted from late morning until mid-afternoon. After everything that happened... I needed some time."

"Do you want to talk about it?" Hannah asked. "Or would you rather just sit together for a while?"

Reed's hand tightened slightly around hers. "I'd like to talk about it if that's okay. I've been sitting here thinking and praying."

Hannah nodded.

"Remember I told you about that family I was concerned about? The Millers?" Reed began, his voice steady but quiet. "I've been checking in on them, making sure the wife and her kids are safe. All the signs were there, Hannah. The same patterns I'd seen with the Davis family."

He paused, looking down at their joined hands.

"This morning, one of the neighbors called in a disturbance—shouting, things breaking. When we arrived, the husband was in a rage. He'd been drinking, and the wife had a bruise forming on her cheek."

Hannah felt her chest tighten, imagining the scene, and understanding immediately why this situation would have triggered Reed's deepest fears.

"She finally admitted he'd hit her," Reed continued. "The children were huddled in a corner of the living room, terrified. I saw those same wide eyes, the same silent fear I'd seen in the Davis children."

He took a deep breath, his gaze fixed on the flowing water before them.

"For a moment today, I was back there again—in the Davis house. I felt that same panic rising, that certainty that I was about to fail another family."

Hannah squeezed his hand, offering silent support.

"But then something different happened," Reed said, his voice strengthening. "The wife looked at her children, and something changed in her face. She straightened up and said she wanted to press charges. She said she wanted help to get to a shelter."

He turned to Hannah, a mix of relief and hope playing across his features.

"We arrested the husband. Mom and the children are safe now at the New Beginnings Shelter in Beckley. She's agreed to file for a restraining order, and she's already talked with a victim's advocate about next steps."

"Reed, that's wonderful," Hannah said softly. "You helped them."

"That's just it," he replied, running his free hand through his hair. "I didn't save them. She saved herself—and her children. She made the choice that Isabelle Davis never got the chance to make."

"And that's why you needed time to process."

Reed nodded. "I've spent years carrying the weight of the Davis tragedy, convinced I should have done more, should have been faster, should have somehow prevented what happened. But today showed me something different."

He shifted on the bench to face her more directly, his green eyes intent on hers.

"We're not meant to save everyone, Hannah. We can offer help, support, resources—but ultimately, people have to make their own choices. The mother today chose safety for herself and her children today. All my checking in, all my vigilance—it created an environment where she felt she could make that choice. But the choice was hers."

Hannah heard the dawning realization in his voice, the sound of a burden being, if not lifted entirely, at least shared.

"I've been sitting here thanking God that they're safe," Reed continued. "But also thinking about how I approached this situation differently because of what happened before. I didn't try to handle it alone. I involved other deputies, victim's advocates, and child services. I created a safety net instead of trying to be the only support."

"That's wisdom, Reed," Hannah said. "Learning from experience."

"It's more than that," he replied, his gaze warming as he looked at her. "It's learning to let others in. To accept that I can't control everything. To trust."

The word hung between them, weighted with meaning beyond this one situation.

"While I was sitting here, I realized something," Reed said, his voice softer now. "The Davis tragedy changed me. It made me withdraw from everyone for quite some time, made me afraid to get too close to anyone. I told myself I was protecting others, but really, I was protecting myself from more pain."

Hannah listened, sensing he needed to voice these thoughts that had been forming during his solitary reflection.

"These past few weeks with you, and with your mom..." Reed shook his head slightly, a look of wonder crossing his face. "You've shown me what I've been missing. What true connection and love feel like."

Hannah felt her heart quicken at his words.

Reed's eyes searched hers. "Today was a reminder of how quickly life can change. How fragile everything is." He paused, swallowing hard. "When I finally had a moment to breathe after everything that happened with that family today, all I could think about was you. About how I'd missed seeing you at lunch, how I wanted to share this with you—both the challenges and the victories."

He released her hand only to gently touch her cheek, his fingers warm against her skin.

"I don't want to waste any more time, Hannah. From connection. From... from love."

Hannah's breath caught at the word. "Love?"

Reed nodded, his expression open and vulnerable in a way she hadn't seen before. "I've been falling in love with you since that first morning in your home, when you were so fierce in your concern for your mother. I just wasn't ready to completely admit it to myself."

Hannah felt tears prick behind her eyes, a swell of emotion rising in her chest.

"The way you care for your mom, the way you've fought to keep going despite everything life has thrown at you," Reed continued, his voice husky with emotion. "Your strength, your compassion, even your stubbornness—" he smiled softly "—it's all part of what makes you who you are. And I love who you are, Hannah Gentry."

A tear escaped, sliding down Hannah's cheek. Reed caught it with his thumb, his touch infinitely tender.

"I know you have so much going on with your mom's new job and all the changes that will bring. But I needed you to know how I feel."

Hannah took a shaky breath, overwhelmed by the sincerity in his eyes, the vulnerability of his admission.

She placed her hand over his where it rested against her cheek.

"You are an incredible man, Reed. You helped me remember the woman I used to be, the dreams I used to have. And somewhere between all the dinners, and conversations, and moments by the river... I fell in love with you too."

The joy that spread across Reed's face made her heart swell. He leaned forward, resting his forehead against hers.

Hannah laughed softly, the sound mingling with the gentle gurgle of the river beside them. "Are you gonna kiss me or what, deputy?"

Reed smiled.

The kiss was tender and unhurried. Hannah felt herself melting into it, into him, the warmth of the connection spreading through her body like sunshine.

When they parted, Reed kept his arms around her, holding her close as the last light of day faded around them. Hannah rested her head against his chest, feeling the steady thump of his heart.

"What happens now?" Hannah asked eventually, not lifting her head from its place against his chest.

Reed's hand stroked gently up and down her back. "Now we take each day as it comes. Together."

"Together," Hannah repeated, liking the sound of it. "I like the sound of that."

"You're not alone anymore," Reed said firmly. "Whatever comes next—with your mom's job, with your photography, with anything—we face it together."

Hannah lifted her head to look at him.

"We'll figure it all out together, you and me," he said. "Remember what Pastor Andrew said in his sermon? About faith being a journey of small steps forward, not giant leaps."

Reed smiled. "I think that applies to more than just faith. Relationships, dreams, healing—they all happen one step at a time."

Hannah leaned back slightly to study his face in the fading light. "You seem different tonight. More... at peace."

Reed considered this. "I think I am. Today was difficult, but it was also healing in a way. Seeing Mrs. Miller make a choice, knowing they have a chance at a different outcome than the Davis family... it helped me realize I don't have to be defined by that one past failure."

"It wasn't a failure, Reed," Hannah said gently. "You did everything you could."

"I'm starting to believe it. That's progress, right?"

Hannah smiled, reaching up to touch his face. "Definite progress."

Reed turned his head to press a kiss to her palm. "I meant what I said about not wasting time. Life can change in an instant. Today reminded me of that. Life is precious. I want to make the most of every day God gives me. I want to build something real with you, Hannah. Something that lasts."

The depth of feeling in his voice made Hannah's heart swell with emotion. This was real—what they were building together. Not some fleeting romance or temporary comfort, but something solid and enduring.

"I want that too," she said, her fingers tracing the line of his jaw.

<h1 style="text-align:center">Chapter 27</h1>

Hannah struggled to fit the portable laptop desk over Peggy's wheelchair, the plastic legs catching on the armrest for the third time.

"Maybe we should try a different angle," she suggested, adjusting her grip on the unwieldy contraption, while Peggy sighed with barely contained impatience.

"This contraption is ridiculous. The dining table will work fine," Peggy countered, wheeling herself backward a few inches.

Hannah persisted, finally managing to click the desk into place. "But this is designed specifically for wheelchairs. The height is adjustable, and it'll be more comfortable during four hours of training."

Peggy tested the surface with a skeptical tap of her fingers. "It wobbles."

"Just a little," Hannah admitted, tightening one of the plastic knobs. "There, that's better."

The early morning sunlight streamed through the spare bedroom window, transforming the hastily arranged workspace into something almost professional. Hannah had spent much of the previous evening clearing out old boxes and rearranging furniture to create a makeshift office until the proper equipment arrived from Mountaineer Insurance.

"What time is it?" Peggy asked, smoothing her burgundy blouse, the same one she'd worn for her interview, now deemed her "lucky" top.

"Seven thirty-five," Hannah replied, checking her watch. "Still plenty of time before your eight-thirty login."

Peggy nodded, reaching for the tablet. "Let's test the connection again."

Hannah stood back, watching as her mother navigated to the training portal with growing confidence. Peggy had made remarkable progress with the tablet, moving from hesitant pokes to smooth, purposeful gestures. The change wasn't just in her technical skills but in her entire demeanor—shoulders straighter, voice more assertive, and eyes brighter with purpose.

"Connection looks good," Peggy declared, setting the tablet aside. "Now, run through the schedule with me one more time."

Hannah leaned against the wall, crossing her arms. "Training starts at eight-thirty sharp. First break at ten, for fifteen minutes. Then back until eleven-thirty for lunch—"

"For thirty minutes," Peggy continued, clearly having memorized the schedule herself. "Then afternoon session until one-fifteen. I think I've got it."

"I know you do. I've put a sandwich, cut fruit, and some cheese and crackers in the refrigerator. Your water bottle is full, and there's an extra one chilling in the fridge as well. Your medication is in the little pill container marked with the times—"

"Hannah," Peggy interrupted. "I've been taking my medication for years. I think I can manage to remember it for one day."

"You're right. I'm hovering."

"Like a helicopter," Peggy confirmed, a bit agitated.

Hannah's phone vibrated in her pocket. She pulled it out, her heart doing a little flip when she saw Reed's name on the screen.

"Reed?" Peggy asked, not missing the smile that sprang to Hannah's lips.

Hannah nodded, scanning the message. "He wants to know how the morning preparations are going." She quickly typed a response, then looked back at her mother. "He's still planning to pick me up at nine thirty."

"Remind me what you two are doing today?" Peggy asked, adjusting her position in the wheelchair.

"He won't tell me. Just that it's a surprise and I should dress nicely."

Peggy's eyes twinkled. "Mysterious. I like that in a man."

Hannah laughed, slipping her phone back into her pocket. "He said it's something special, but that's all he would share."

"Well, whatever it is, I'm glad you're going. You deserve some time to enjoy yourself."

"Are you sure you'll be okay? It's your first day of training, and—"

"And I'll be on a video call with professionals who are there to help me succeed," Peggy finished. "If I have questions, I'll ask them." She wheeled herself closer to Hannah, reaching for her hand. "Honey, we both need to get used to this new normal. You can't be here every minute, and I need to learn to be more independent. But... this is hard... it's really hard for me."

Hannah squeezed her mother's hand, acknowledging the truth in her words. "I know. It's just..."

"Hard to break a ten-year habit?" Peggy suggested gently. "For both of us."

Hannah nodded, suddenly feeling emotional. For so long, her identity had been wrapped up in caring for her mother. As necessary as these changes were, they still left her feeling somewhat untethered, uncertain of who she was, if not primarily a caregiver.

"I'm proud of you, Mom," she said, pushing these thoughts aside. "You know that, right?"

"I know. And I'm proud of you too, more than you can imagine. Now, help me finish getting ready so I can try to dazzle these training people."

Hannah grinned, moving to help her mother with the final preparations. As she adjusted Peggy's hair and made sure everything was within easy reach, her phone buzzed again with another message from Reed.

This time, his words made her pause.

Can't wait to see you. This is going to be a special day for you—I promise. Dress professionally!

Professionally? That was a new detail. What exactly did Reed have planned?

***

Hannah was in the kitchen preparing a second pot of coffee when her phone rang. Reed's name flashed on the screen, and she answered immediately.

"Hey there," she greeted him, cradling the phone against her shoulder as she measured the coffee grounds.

"Morning, beautiful," Reed's warm voice came through the speaker. "How's your mom doing? All set for her first day?"

"All set and surprisingly calm," Hannah replied, glancing toward the hallway that led to the spare bedroom. "I think she's more ready for this than I am."

Reed chuckled. "That doesn't surprise me one bit. Your mom's a strong woman, she just needs to believe that herself."

"Takes one to know one. So, are you going to tell me what we're doing today? And why do I need to dress professionally?"

There was a pause, and Hannah could almost see Reed's expression as he considered his words.

"I probably should give you more of a heads-up," he finally said. "I don't want you walking in completely unprepared."

Hannah set down the coffee scoop. "This sounds serious."

"It's a good serious. Remember how I told you I was looking at your photography website?"

"Yes..." Hannah said cautiously.

"Well, I might have shown it to my dad, who showed it to a friend of his who runs the Beckley Arts Collective gallery. And that friend might have been extremely impressed, especially with your landscape series."

Hannah's breath caught. "Reed, what did you do?"

"I got you a meeting with Elaine Mercer, the gallery owner," he said, excitement evident in his voice. "Today at one-thirty. She rarely takes these kinds of meetings without a formal submission process, but she made an exception after seeing your work. She's interested in potentially featuring you in their 'Emerging Artists of Appalachia' showcase next month."

Hannah sank onto a kitchen chair, her knees suddenly weak. "You're serious? A real gallery? In Beckley?"

"Very serious," Reed confirmed. "It's a respected venue—regional artists, good foot traffic, connections to larger galleries in Charleston and beyond. Dad says Elaine has an eye for talent, and she was genuinely impressed with your portfolio."

"But I'm not—I mean, I've never—" Hannah stammered, her mind racing. "I sell prints online, Reed. I've never been in a real gallery."

"Everyone starts somewhere. Elaine specifically looks for undiscovered talent. She wants to meet you, see more of your work, and discuss possibilities."

Hannah's thoughts whirled. A gallery showing had been a distant dream, something she'd tucked away along with so many other aspirations when her mother's care became her priority. To have it suddenly presented as a real possibility was both thrilling and terrifying.

"I don't know what to say," she admitted. "This is... it's incredible. But today? With Mom's first training session?"

"I know the timing isn't ideal. But Elaine only had today available before she leaves for a conference in New York. The next opening in her schedule isn't for over a month."

Hannah bit her lip, torn between excitement and concern. "Mom's just starting her training. What if she needs help? What if something goes wrong with the technology?"

"I understand. If you don't feel comfortable leaving today, we can try to reschedule. But Hannah... this is a genuine opportunity. The kind that doesn't come along often."

Hannah looked toward the hallway again, thinking about her mother preparing for her own new beginning. Hadn't Peggy just been encouraging her to pursue her dreams? To reclaim parts of herself that had been set aside?

"Let me talk to Mom," she decided. "I'll call you right back."

After ending the call, Hannah carried a fresh cup of coffee to the spare bedroom, finding Peggy reviewing her training materials on the tablet. Her mother looked up with a questioning expression.

"That was Reed?" she asked, noting Hannah's flustered appearance.

Hannah nodded, setting the coffee on the desk. "He's arranged something incredible, Mom. A meeting with a gallery owner in Beckley who's interested in my photography... for a real exhibit."

Peggy's eyes widened, genuine delight spreading across her face. "Hannah! That's wonderful news!"

"It is. But it's today. This afternoon, during your training. I'll be gone most of the day."

"And you're worried about leaving me."

Hannah nodded, conflicted. "It's your first day, and I'll be pretty far away. What if something goes wrong? What if you need help with the technology or—"

"Then I'll have to figure it out," Peggy interrupted firmly. "Or I'll ask the trainer for assistance. That's literally their job, right? I mean... if something happens where I need help... it's probably happened before, I'd imagine? They would know what to do."

"But—"

"No buts," Peggy said, raising a hand to halt Hannah's protests. "This is exactly what we were just talking about. We both need to adjust to our new normal. You can't put your life on hold forever because of what-ifs."

Hannah sank into the chair beside the desk. "It just feels like I'm abandoning you on an important day."

"You're not abandoning me. You're pursuing an opportunity that you've earned through years of talent and hard work." She reached for

Hannah's hand. "Do you know how long I've waited to see you follow your dreams again? Please, don't miss this chance because of me."

Hannah studied her mother's face, seeing only sincerity and encouragement there. "You're sure?"

"Absolutely certain," Peggy replied, squeezing Hannah's hand. "Now call that handsome deputy back and tell him yes."

Hannah leaned forward to hug her mother, throat tight with emotion. "Thank you, Mom."

"Don't thank me," Peggy said as they separated. "Just bring me back every detail about the gallery and what they say about your work."

***

By nine, Hannah had selected her outfit—a simple gray dress that managed to look both professional and artistic, paired with a turquoise necklace that added a pop of color near her face. She'd spent extra time on her makeup and hair, wanting to look polished but not overdone for the gallery meeting.

She was in the kitchen preparing a late breakfast for herself when Peggy's voice called out from the spare bedroom, an edge of frustration evident.

"Hannah? Can you come here a minute?"

Hannah set down the knife she'd been using to slice an apple and hurried to the bedroom. "What's wrong?"

Peggy was frowning at the tablet screen, annoyance clear in her expression. "The audio cut out, I think, and now I can't get it back. The little speaker icon has a red line through it."

Hannah moved to her mother's side, examining the screen. "Did you tap the icon?"

"Of course I did," Peggy replied, exasperation creeping into her voice. "Three times. Nothing's happening."

Hannah took the tablet, navigating to the settings menu. "Let's check the system's audio settings."

As she worked, Peggy sighed heavily. "I feel so stupid. Basic technology troubleshooting should not be beyond me. I used a computer every day at my old job."

"Technology changes," Hannah reminded her gently. "And tablets are different from desktop computers."

"Still," Peggy muttered. "I feel helpless. I'm frustrated. Why can't this one simple thing go right for me?"

Hannah found the audio settings, noting that the tablet had somehow switched to Bluetooth output despite no Bluetooth devices being connected. She tapped the appropriate options to reset it to the internal speaker.

"Try it now," she suggested, handing the tablet back to Peggy.

Peggy tapped the unmute button, relief washing over her face as the sound returned. "Thank you. I don't know how that happened."

"Probably just a glitch," Hannah assured her. "Technology hiccups sometimes."

Peggy's brow remained furrowed. "What if this happens while you're gone this afternoon? What if something more complicated goes wrong?"

Hannah felt her earlier concerns resurface, stronger now. "I can stay. The gallery opportunity is wonderful, but if you're not comfortable—"

"No," Peggy interrupted firmly, though Hannah could see the momentary indecision in her eyes. "I just... hate feeling like this."

Hannah understood her mother's frustration all too well. Peggy had once been fiercely independent, managing a department at an insurance company, raising a daughter, running a household. The accident had robbed her of so much, including the everyday competence most people took for granted.

"How about this?" Hannah suggested. "I'll write down some basic troubleshooting steps for common issues. And you have the training coordinator's direct number if something goes seriously wrong."

Peggy nodded, visibly gathering herself. "That makes sense. I'm just being silly. One little audio problem and I'm acting like the world is ending."

"It's not silly. This is all new. But you've got this, Mom. I know you do."

Peggy managed a small smile. "You're right. I do have this. And you have a gallery meeting to prepare for."

"I'll make that troubleshooting guide before Reed arrives," Hannah promised.

As she worked, Hannah couldn't help the anxiety gnawing at her edges. Excited as she was about the gallery opportunity, leaving her mother during this vulnerable new beginning felt risky. What if something else went wrong? What if Peggy became overwhelmed or discouraged without Hannah there to support her?

By the time Reed's truck pulled into the driveway, Hannah had worked herself into a state of divided excitement and worry, her emotions pulling her in opposite directions.

She was just completing the troubleshooting guide when the doorbell rang. Checking her appearance one last time in the hallway mirror, Hannah took a deep breath and opened the door.

Reed stood on the porch, looking handsomely professional in charcoal slacks and a light blue button-down shirt that intensified the green of his eyes. His smile at the sight of her was immediate and warm.

"Wow," he said simply, his gaze taking in her dress and carefully styled hair. "You look beautiful."

Hannah felt a flutter in her stomach despite her anxiety. "Thank you. You clean up pretty nicely yourself, Deputy."

Reed grinned, gesturing toward the small portfolio case tucked under his arm. "I brought this for your photographs. Dad said it's more professional than just carrying loose prints."

Hannah accepted the sleek black case, touched by his thoughtfulness. "Thank you. That's perfect." She stepped back. "Come in for a minute? I'm just finishing up some notes for Mom."

Reed followed her inside, closing the door behind him. "How's the first day of training going?"

"Generally good," Hannah replied, leading him to the kitchen. "There was a small audio issue earlier, but we got it sorted out. I'm just making a troubleshooting guide before we leave."

Reed's expression turned thoughtful. "If you're worried, we don't have to go. Family comes first."

"No, Mom insists that I go. And she's right, we both need to adjust to our new circumstances."

"Still. I know this is a big transition for both of you."

"It is," Hannah admitted, finishing the last bullet point on her list. "But it's necessary. Good, even. Just... not without its challenges."

Reed nodded, leaning against the counter. "Change is usually challenging, even positive change."

Hannah set down her pen and looked up at him. "Thank you for understanding. And for arranging this opportunity. It's incredible, Reed. I'm just... a little nervous about the timing."

"Understandable. We'll make it work." He glanced at his watch. "We should probably leave by ten to reach Beckley, with enough time to spare."

Hannah nodded, gathering her courage and excitement. "Let me just say goodbye to Mom and give her this guide."

She headed down the hall to the spare bedroom, finding Peggy deeply engaged in her training session, making notes on a legal pad as the trainer spoke on screen. Hannah waited for a pause before softly announcing her presence.

"Mom? Reed's here, and we'll be leaving in a few minutes."

Peggy looked up, her expression brightening. "Reed's here? Send him in to say hello."

Hannah motioned to Reed, who had followed her down the hall. He stepped into the doorway with a warm smile.

"Good morning, Peggy. How's the training going?"

"So far, so good," Peggy replied cheerfully. "They've been reviewing the company history and core values this morning. The real technical training starts after lunch."

Reed nodded. "That sounds promising. You look gorgeous, by the way."

Peggy beamed at the compliment, smoothing her burgundy blouse. "Thank you. And thank you for creating this wonderful opportunity for Hannah. It means the world to her... to both of us."

"The opportunity was already there in her talent," Reed replied, glancing at Hannah with unmistakable pride. "I just made a connection."

Hannah felt herself flush under his admiring gaze. She handed the troubleshooting guide to her mother. "Here's that list I promised. Basic solutions for common tech issues. And remember, my cell will be on if you need me."

"I won't need you. I've got this." She shooed them with a wave of her hand. "Now go, before you're late. And Hannah, remember to breathe when you're talking to the gallery owner. You tend to speak too fast when you're nervous."

Hannah laughed despite herself. "Yes, Mom. Any other tips?"

"Just be yourself," Peggy said, her expression softening.

"I will. Good luck today, mom."

"We'll both have good news to share tonight."

As Hannah turned to leave, Reed stepped forward unexpectedly.

"Peggy, before we go, would it be alright if I add my cell number to that troubleshooting guide? Just in case you run into something technical that's not covered."

Peggy looked surprised, but nodded. "That would be very kind, thank you."

Reed took the paper, quickly jotting down his number at the bottom. "I'm pretty good with tech issues. If Hannah doesn't answer, feel free to call me directly."

Hannah felt a subtle shift in the room—something in the way Reed so naturally offered his support, the way Peggy accepted it with genuine appreciation. It was a small moment, yet significant. Reed wasn't just her boyfriend; he was becoming a part of their family system, a person they both could rely on.

"Thank you, Reed," Peggy said.

As they left the room, Hannah felt some of her anxiety ease. Between the troubleshooting guide, the training coordinator's number, and now Reed's backup support, her mother had resources if problems arose. She could focus on this opportunity without quite so much worry.

"Ready?" Reed asked as they reached the front door, Hannah's portfolio in one hand, his truck keys in the other.

Hannah nodded, drawing a deep breath. "Ready."

Chapter 28

Hannah looked out the passenger window at the passing landscape. Lush green mountains rising on either side of the road, sunlight filtering through the summer foliage, creating a dappled pattern on the asphalt ahead. The beauty of West Virginia's mountains had always calmed her, even on her most anxious days.

"I'm feeling so many things at once," she admitted. "Excited about the gallery opportunity. Nervous about making a good impression. Worried about Mom's training going smoothly." She paused, turning to look at Reed's profile as he drove. "Grateful to you for making this happen."

Reed glanced at her briefly before returning his attention to the road. "You made it happen, Hannah. Your talent did. I just made a phone call."

"Still," Hannah insisted. "It means a lot that you saw something in my work worth sharing."

"The world deserves to see your work, Hannah."

"Do you really think the gallery owner will feel the same way?"

"Dad says Elaine has an extraordinary eye for authentic work," Reed replied. "And she was genuinely impressed with your online portfolio. She specifically mentioned your river series and said it captured both the timelessness and the constant change of Appalachian waterways."

Hannah smiled, remembering the hours she'd spent along various creeks and rivers, waiting for just the right light, the perfect reflection.

"May I ask you something?" Reed said eventually, his tone thoughtful.

"Of course."

"Are you worried about both today's meeting and leaving your mom, or are you mostly worried about leaving your mom?"

"Mostly the latter," she admitted. "The gallery meeting will be nerve-wracking, but in an exciting way. Leaving Mom during her first training day just feels... I don't know, almost wrong somehow."

Reed nodded, understanding in his expression. "Like you're abandoning her."

"Yes," Hannah sighed. "Which is ridiculous, I know. She's a grown woman who managed entire departments before her accident. She doesn't need me hovering over her for a basic training session."

"It's not ridiculous. You've been her primary support for a decade. That created patterns that are difficult to break for both of you."

Hannah glanced at him, struck once again by how well he seemed to understand her situation. "Breaking patterns is hard, even when you know it's necessary."

Reed was quiet for a moment, seemingly gathering his thoughts. "My grandfather went through something last winter, so I kind of know how you are feeling right now."

"He lives alone in his cabin, right?"

Reed nodded. "Has for a few years ever since Grandma passed. But last winter, he fell on some ice and broke his hip. Suddenly, this man who'd been entirely self-sufficient needed help with everything... bathing, dressing, and cooking."

"That must have been difficult for him."

"It was," Reed agreed. "But it was also hard for my dad and me. We took turns staying with him during his recovery, and he resented every minute of it. Not because he didn't appreciate us, but because he hated needing us."

"I can understand that feeling."

"The hardest part," Reed continued, "was knowing when to help and when to step back. There were days I'd watch him struggle with something simple and every instinct in me wanted to just do it for him. But Dad taught me something important during that time."

"What was that?" Hannah asked.

"That sometimes the most loving thing you can do is to let someone struggle a little. Let them figure it out and let them build back their confidence and independence. Be available if they truly need you, but don't rob them of the dignity of solving their own problems."

Hannah absorbed his words, recognizing the wisdom in them. "So you're saying I should let Mom fumble with technology a bit?"

Reed smiled. "I'm saying there's a difference between abandoning someone and giving them space to grow. Your mom is embarking on a new chapter in her life. One where she's more than just a recipient of care. She's becoming a professional again, a contributor. And honestly, she's creating a new version of herself. Part of that journey involves learning to solve problems on her own."

"Even if it's harder for both of us in the short term."

Reed nodded. "And from what I've seen of Peggy, she's more than up for the challenge. She strikes me as a woman who's kind of floating between the old and the new. She welcomes the opportunity to reclaim her independence and yet, she's leaving behind the person she had become due to her circumstances. It has to be very frightening for her."

Hannah thought about her mother's insistence that she attend the gallery meeting, her determined "I've got this" attitude despite the earlier technical hiccup. "You're right."

As they approached the outskirts of Beckley, Hannah felt a subtle shift in her perspective. Her absence today wasn't an abandonment, but a vote of confidence in her mother's capabilities. The worry was still there, but it was tempered now by understanding and respect for Peggy's journey toward greater independence.

"I sincerely appreciate you Reed, thank you," she said, placing her hand on Reed's arm.

He glanced at her, eyebrows raised. "For what?"

"For helping me see this more clearly. For understanding."

"That's what love is, Hannah. Seeing each other clearly and supporting each other's growth, even when it's complicated."

Love.

That word was so powerful and true. These past weeks had transformed everything Hannah thought she knew about relationships. With Reed, love wasn't just romantic feelings or physical attraction, though those were certainly present. It was this more profound understanding, this partnership of minds and hearts facing life's challenges together.

As Reed navigated through Beckley's downtown area, Hannah found herself sending up a silent prayer of gratitude. *Thank you, Lord, for bringing this man into our lives. For showing me that love doesn't have to mean choosing between my mother and my heart. For teaching me that sometimes the most loving thing to do is to let go a little.*

"Here we are," Reed announced, pulling into a parking space across from a streamlined modern building with large display windows. "Beckley Arts Collective."

Hannah gazed at the gallery entrance, her excitement rushing back full force. Behind the glass, she could see tastefully arranged artwork, warm lighting, and what appeared to be an engaging exhibition in progress.

"Ready for this?"

Hannah took a deep breath, nodding. "Ready."

Reed stretched his hand out toward her, and she took it.

He bowed his head, still holding her hand. "Lord, we thank You for this opportunity You've created for Hannah. We ask for Your presence in this meeting that Hannah would have clarity and confidence as she shares her talent. Guide her words and open doors according to Your perfect plan. Help her to trust that while she's here pursuing this dream, You are watching over Peggy. In Your name, we pray, amen."

"Amen," Hannah echoed, feeling a calm certainty settle over her.

Together, they exited the truck and crossed the street, Hannah's portfolio tucked securely under her arm, Reed's steady presence beside her a tangible reminder that she wasn't facing this new opportunity alone.

Chapter 29

The Beckley Arts Collective gallery was larger than it appeared from outside, with an open, airy layout and polished concrete floors that gleamed under carefully positioned lighting. The main exhibition space showcased what appeared to be local artists' interpretations of industrial history—paintings and sculptures that transformed coal mining imagery into unexpectedly beautiful contemporary art.

A receptionist at a minimalist desk greeted them as they entered. "Welcome to Beckley Arts Collective. How can I help you today?"

"Hello, I'm Hannah Gentry," Hannah replied, summoning her most professional voice. "I have an eleven-thirty appointment with Elaine Mercer."

Recognition flickered in the young woman's eyes. "Of course, Ms. Gentry. Ms. Mercer is expecting you. If you'll follow me?"

They were led through the main gallery to a corridor that opened into a smaller exhibition space, currently empty between shows. At the far end, a door marked "Director" stood ajar, revealing glimpses of a well-appointed office.

The receptionist knocked lightly. "Ms. Mercer? Hannah Gentry is here for her appointment."

"Wonderful! Send her in, please." The voice that responded was warm and energetic.

Hannah exchanged a quick glance with Reed, who gave her an encouraging nod. Drawing a deep breath, she stepped into the office.

Elaine Mercer was not what Hannah had expected. Instead of the austere, black-clad gallery director of her imagination, she found a vibrant woman in her early sixties with a silver pixie cut and a flowing tunic in brilliant crimson over black leggings. She rose from behind her desk with an enthusiastic smile, extending her hand.

"Hannah! Delighted to meet you in person. And this must be Reed Dunbar, Mitchell's son?"

Reed nodded, shaking her hand. "Thank you for making time in your schedule, Ms. Mercer. This means a great deal to us."

"Please, it's Elaine," she insisted, gesturing toward a seating area in the corner of her office. "And the pleasure is mine. I've been captivated by Hannah's work since Mitch told me about her."

As they settled into comfortable leather chairs around a low table, Hannah felt her nervousness begin to transform back into excitement. There was something immediately disarming about Elaine's straightforward enthusiasm.

"I brought a selection of prints," Hannah said, opening the portfolio Reed had provided. "These include some from the river series, plus a few newer pieces I haven't uploaded to my website yet."

Elaine leaned forward eagerly. "Let's see them."

For the next fifteen minutes, Hannah laid out photograph after photograph as Elaine examined each with careful attention. The gallery director asked thoughtful questions about Hannah's techniques, her inspiration, and the locations captured in the images. With each response, Hannah found her confidence growing, her passion for her work overriding her initial nerves.

"Your eye for composition is remarkable," Elaine observed, studying a particularly striking image of morning mist rising from the New River. "You find these perfect visual moments that tell a complete story without a single word."

"That's precisely what I aim for," Hannah replied. "I want people to feel something when they look at my photographs... not just see a pretty landscape, but experience the emotion of the place."

Elaine nodded appreciatively. "That's what separates documentation from art. Anyone can take a picture of a mountain or a river. Not everyone can capture the spirit of it the way you do." She set the print aside carefully. "Tell me, Hannah, what's your background in photography? Where did you study?"

Hannah hesitated, suddenly self-conscious. "I'm self-taught, actually. I've taken some online courses and workshops, but never formal training."

Instead of disappointment, Elaine's expression showed increased interest. "Fascinating. Occasionally, the lack of formal constraints allows for more authentic expression. Your technical skills are certainly professional caliber."

Relief and pride mingled in Hannah's chest at this validation. "Thank you. I've worked hard to develop skills on my own."

"It shows," Elaine assured her, returning her attention to the photographs. After examining a few more, she sat back in her chair, her expression thoughtful. "So, our Emerging Artists of Appalachia program opens in five weeks and will run for two months. We typically feature four to five artists, giving each a dedicated wall in our secondary exhibition space—the room you walked through to reach my office."

Hannah's heart quickened. "And you're considering including my work?"

"More than considering," Elaine replied decisively. "Based on what I've seen today and on your website, I'd like to offer you a spot in the showcase."

Hannah blinked, almost unable to process the words. "You would?"

"Absolutely," Elaine confirmed. "Your river series, in particular, would make a compelling exhibit. We'd need eight to ten of your strongest pieces, professionally matted and framed. We handle the installation, promotion, and sales. Our standard commission is forty percent, with sixty percent going to the artist."

Reed, who had been quietly supportive throughout the meeting, leaned forward slightly. "That's a very generous split."

Elaine smiled. "We believe in supporting our artists, especially those early in their careers. This showcase has launched several regional photographers and painters into wider recognition."

Hannah's mind was racing, excitement building with each detail Elaine shared. A real gallery exhibition. Something she'd dreamed about for years but never truly believed would happen.

"I don't know what to say," she admitted, her voice slightly unsteady with emotion. "This is an incredible opportunity."

"Say yes," Elaine suggested with a grin. "Then we can discuss the practical details."

Hannah laughed, feeling lighter than she had in years. "Yes. Definitely yes."

"Excellent!" Elaine clapped her hands together once, then reached for a folder on her desk. "I have some paperwork for you. Just standard agreements about the exhibit terms, delivery dates for your work, and so forth."

As Elaine explained the details, Hannah found herself alternating between focused attention on the practical matters and moments of pure, disbelieving joy. This was really happening. Her photographs would hang in a respected gallery, would be seen by people who appreciated art, and might even launch a more serious career in photography.

She was so engrossed in the discussion that she nearly missed the soft vibration of her phone in her purse. Only when it buzzed a second time did she become aware of it.

"I'm sorry," she said, reaching for her bag. "I need to check this. It might be important."

Elaine nodded understandingly. "Of course."

Hannah pulled out her phone, seeing two text notifications from Peggy. Her heart immediately tightened with concern as she opened the messages.

The first read: *Having trouble with the training platform. Keeps freezing during videos. Tried your troubleshooting tips, but no luck.*

The second, sent five minutes later: *Never mind! Texted Reed's number, and he talked me through a full system restart. All fixed now. Enjoying the afternoon session. Hope your meeting is going well!*

Hannah stared at the messages, relief washing over her. She glanced at Reed, who was engaged in conversation with Elaine about framing options.

Somehow, Reed had managed to help her solve the problem without disrupting Hannah's important meeting. The consideration of his actions, the thoughtfulness behind his offer to provide his number to Peggy in the first place, touched Hannah deeply.

"Everything okay?" Reed asked, noticing her attention on the phone.

Hannah nodded, a warm smile spreading across her face. "Everything's perfect."

As they continued discussing exhibit details with Elaine, Hannah found herself occasionally glancing at Reed, seeing him with new eyes. His steady presence beside her, his evident pride in her accomplishments, his thoughtful integration of himself into both her professional opportunity and her family responsibilities—all of it spoke of a man who understood what it meant to love someone wholly, complexities and all.

By the time they left the gallery, agreements signed and her exhibit spot secured, Hannah felt as though she were floating on air. The late afternoon sun cast long shadows across the street as they returned to Reed's truck.

"So," Reed said as they buckled their seatbelts, "on a scale of one to ten, how are you feeling right now?"

Hannah laughed, the sound bubbling up from a place of pure joy. "About a fifteen. I still can't believe this is happening. A real gallery exhibit, Reed!"

"I can believe it," he replied, his expression warm with pride. "Your work deserves to be seen, Hannah."

Hannah reached across to touch his hand as he started the engine. "Thank you. Not just for the introduction, but for everything today. Including helping Mom with her technical issue."

Reed looked momentarily surprised, then slightly embarrassed. "You knew about that?"

"She texted me," Hannah explained. "Said you walked her through a system restart."

Reed nodded, pulling onto the main street. "It was nothing, just a simple fix."

"It meant a lot to me."

Reed glanced at her, his expression thoughtful. "That's what matters to me, Hannah. Finding ways to support you both, not making you choose between your responsibilities and your dreams."

As they drove back toward Laurel Ridge, Hannah felt a deep sense of contentment settle over her. The excitement of the gallery opportunity, the relief of knowing her mother had managed successfully with minimal help, the growing certainty about her feelings for Reed—all of it combined into a profound gratitude.

"What are you thinking about?" Reed asked.

Hannah smiled, watching the familiar landscape pass by. "Just how much has changed in such a short time. A few months ago, my life felt so... fixed. Unchangeable. I was always on autopilot. Now everything is shifting. Mom's job, my photography, us." She turned to look at him. "It's a lot to take in."

"Change can be overwhelming. Even good change."

"It is. But it also feels right. Like pieces falling into place after being scattered for so long."

Reed's hand found hers across the console. "I feel the same way."

For the remainder of the drive, they discussed the exhibit details—which photographs Hannah would choose, framing options, and the reception night Elaine had mentioned. Reed suggested using some of the images from their day at the river, when she'd captured that perfect light filtering through the trees.

"That was a special day," Hannah said.

Reed's expression warmed. "The first of many more special days."

By the time they pulled into Hannah's driveway, the evening light was softening toward dusk. Hannah spotted Peggy through the front window, her wheelchair positioned near the sofa, where she appeared to be reading.

"Do you want to come in?" Hannah asked as Reed parked.

"I'd like that," Reed replied. "If you're sure I'm not intruding on your evening."

"Never. You're part of this celebration."

Together, they entered the house to find Peggy looking up from her tablet with an eager expression.

"There you are!" she exclaimed. "I want to hear everything! How did the meeting go? What did the gallery owner say about your work?"

Hannah laughed, setting down her portfolio and the exhibition folder. "It went better than I could have imagined, Mom. They're offering me a spot in their Emerging Artists of Appalachia showcase next month!"

Peggy's face lit up with joy. "Hannah! That's wonderful news!" She wheeled herself forward to embrace her daughter as Hannah knelt beside the wheelchair. "I'm so proud of you, sweetheart."

"I couldn't have done it without Reed," Hannah said, glancing up at him with gratitude. "He made the connection through his father, and he was so supportive during the meeting."

Peggy released Hannah to look at Reed. "Thank you for doing this for her. For believing in her talent."

Reed's expression was both pleased and slightly embarrassed at the praise. "Anyone who sees Hannah's work would recognize her gift. I just made a phone call."

"And you helped me when I was having technical trouble today," Peggy added appreciatively. "That was above and beyond, especially during such an important meeting."

"It was no trouble. I'm glad I could help."

Hannah moved to the kitchen to put on coffee while Peggy demanded details about the gallery, the exhibition space, and which photographs Hannah planned to include. Reed joined the conversation, adding his impressions of Elaine and describing Hannah's confident presentation of her work.

"You should have seen her, Peggy," he said with unmistakable pride. "Completely professional, articulate about her artistic vision. Elaine was impressed from the start."

Hannah returned with a tray of coffee and cookies, feeling both pleased and slightly embarrassed by Reed's praise. "Enough about my day," she said, setting the tray on the coffee table. "How did the rest of your training go, Mom?"

Peggy's eyes lit up. "Once we got past that technical glitch—which Reed solved in about two minutes flat—it was fantastic and was focused on the actual insurance platforms we'll be using. It's more intuitive than I expected, and they're providing such good training."

Hannah smiled, noticing the animation in her mother's face, the excitement in her voice. "It sounds like you're enjoying it."

"I am," Peggy confirmed. "I feel so good about this, to be learning something new. And the trainer, Michael, is excellent. He's patient and thorough."

As Peggy described her training in detail, Hannah caught Reed watching them both, a soft expression on his face. When their eyes met, he smiled. A private communication passing between them—shared joy in Peggy's renewed sense of purpose and pride.

The conversation flowed easily among the three of them, touching on training schedules, exhibit preparations, and Reed's work as well. When Peggy mentioned again how helpful Reed had been with her technical problem, Hannah realized something significant: the ease with which her mother had reached out to Reed for help, the natural way he had become a trusted resource for both of them.

Eventually, as the evening deepened, Peggy announced she was tired and needed to review some training materials before bed. "Tomorrow's session starts with a knowledge check on today's content," she explained. "I want to be prepared."

Hannah rose to help her mother get settled for the evening, but Peggy waved her off. "I can manage, honey. You two enjoy the evening a bit longer. Maybe sit out on the porch swing? It's a beautiful night."

"If you're sure you don't need help..."

"Positive," Peggy insisted. "Reed, it's been wonderful having you here. Thank you again for everything you did for Hannah and me today."

Reed stood, his expression warm. "The pleasure was mine, Peggy. I'm looking forward to hearing more about your training progress tomorrow."

After Peggy had wheeled herself to her bedroom, Reed and Hannah stepped out onto the front porch. The evening was indeed beautiful. Warm without being humid, the first stars beginning to appear in the deepening blue sky. The scent of honeysuckle drifted from the bushes beside the porch, and somewhere in the distance, a whippoorwill called.

They settled onto the porch swing, its chains creaking gently as they found a comfortable rhythm. Hannah leaned slightly against Reed's shoulder, feeling the solid warmth of him beside her.

"Today was perfect," she said. "Overwhelming in the best way possible."

Reed's arm curled around her, drawing her closer. "You deserved every bit of it. Seeing you in that gallery, talking about your work with such passion—it was something special, Hannah."

She smiled, tilting her head to look up at him. "Did you notice how different Mom seems already? Just one day of training, and there's this... light in her eyes that hasn't been there in so long."

Reed nodded. "Purpose does that for people. Feeling useful, needed, and valued... it's transformative."

They swung in comfortable silence for a moment, the gentle back-and-forth motion soothing.

"Hannah," Reed said eventually, his voice taking on a more thoughtful tone. "May I ask you something?"

"Of course."

He seemed to consider his words carefully. "With all these changes happening... your mom's job, your exhibition, and our relationship growing... have you thought about what comes next? For us, I mean."

"In what way?"

Reed shifted to face her more directly on the swing. "I know we've only been together a short time, but I also know what I feel for you is real and lasting. These past weeks have shown me what I want for my future, and that future includes you."

Hannah's breath caught at the sincerity in his eyes, the quiet certainty in his voice.

"I want you to know where my heart is headed. I'm in this for the long haul, Hannah."

The simple declaration made Hannah's heart swell. "I feel the same way. What we have... it's different from anything I've ever known. Deeper. More real."

Reed nodded, taking her hand in his. "That's why I wanted to talk about practical considerations. Your mom's world is changing, your career opportunities are expanding, and I want to be certain we're thinking clearly about how our relationship fits into all of that."

"What kind of practical considerations?"

"Your mom's health and care needs, for one," Reed replied. "Her job will give her more independence, but she'll still need support. I want you to know that when I think about a future with you, that includes supporting your mom too, if it's okay with you."

Hannah felt a rush of emotion at his words. So many people would see her mother's needs as a burden, a complication. Reed saw them as a natural part of loving her.

"And there's my job," he continued. "The unpredictable hours, the occasional dangers. That's something we'd need to navigate together."

"I understand what it means to love someone in law enforcement," Hannah assured him. "I've already had a taste of the worry that comes with it. But I also see how much purpose your work gives you, how much you care about protecting this community."

"It's a calling, not just a job. But it does mean compromises occasionally. Missed dinners, late nights, and occasional danger."

"I think that every relationship requires compromises," Hannah pointed out. "What matters is that we face these challenges together, with respect for each other's needs and dreams."

Reed nodded, squeezing her hand gently. "That's exactly what I hoped to hear. Because when I look at our future, Hannah, I see us building something beautiful together—not perfect, not without challenges, but grounded in faith and mutual support."

"I see that too. And it's not something I would have believed possible a few months ago."

"God's timing is a mysterious thing," Reed said, his expression thoughtful. "When I was drowning in guilt over the Davis tragedy, I couldn't imagine opening my heart to anyone. And now I have you in my life—you and Peggy both—and everything has changed."

Hannah nodded, understanding completely. "When Mom first had her emergency, all I could see was another challenge to face alone. Instead, it opened the door to all these new possibilities—for both of us."

Reed's hand found her cheek, gently turning her face toward his. "So we're in agreement? We're building toward a future together, taking each new challenge as it comes, supporting each other's dreams?"

"Absolutely. Whatever comes next, we face it together."

Reed smiled, leaning closer. "I like the sound of that. Together."

Hannah felt a profound sense of rightness. Their lives were changing rapidly, new challenges and opportunities arising with each day. But this—this connection, this partnership, this love growing between them—was becoming the steady foundation beneath it all.

The porch swing creaked gently as they sat together, watching as more stars appeared in the darkening sky. Hannah's mind drifted to the gallery exhibition, to her mother's new job, and to Reed's growing place in their lives. So many changes, so many adjustments still to come.

Yet as Reed's arm tightened around her shoulders, drawing her closer against the cooling evening air, Hannah felt no fear of the unknown future.

Chapter 30

Hannah's wooden spoon clattered against the mixing bowl as Emma's text message lit up her phone screen.

Can't wait to see your face when you see what Reed's planned! Don't forget sunscreen!

"What on earth?" Hannah muttered, wiping her hands on a dish towel before picking up her phone. Her thumbs hovered over the keys, ready to demand answers, when she heard the familiar sound of her mother's wheelchair coming down the hallway.

She set the phone down as Peggy wheeled into the kitchen. Hannah had to do a double-take at the sight of her mother. Peggy wore a flattering teal blouse with small pearl earrings gleaming against her skin. Her hair was styled in soft waves that framed her face, making her look years younger.

"Mom, you look beautiful," Hannah said.

Peggy's smile was enigmatic as she adjusted the thin throw blanket over her lap. "I just wanted to feel nice. It's becoming a habit, I suppose." She wheeled closer, eyeing the bowl of fruit salad Hannah had been preparing. "Is that for me?"

"Yes, I wanted to make sure you had plenty to eat while I'm gone." Hannah returned to the counter, securing plastic wrap over the bowl. "I've made sandwiches too, and there's iced tea in the fridge."

"Always making sure I'm taken care of, even when you're headed out for another big adventure."

Hannah placed the fruit salad in the refrigerator, then leaned against the counter, studying her mother. There was something different about Peggy today, beyond the styled hair and pretty blouse. A sparkle in her eyes, a barely contained excitement.

"So…" Hannah ventured, "any idea what Reed has planned? He's being annoyingly mysterious. All he said was to dress comfortably and be prepared to spend the entire day with him."

Peggy shrugged, the picture of innocence. "Not a clue. You know how men like their surprises."

Hannah narrowed her eyes playfully. "You're a terrible liar, Mom. Your left eyebrow always twitches when you're not telling the truth."

Peggy's hand flew to her eyebrow, and they both burst into laughter.

"Fine, maybe I know something," Peggy admitted, wheeling over to the kitchen table. "But my lips are sealed. Reed swore me to secrecy."

Hannah shook her head, amused and intrigued. "Since when are you and Reed conspiring behind my back?"

"Since he became such an important part of our lives. He's good for you, Hannah. For both of us, really."

Hannah felt warmth spread through her chest at her mother's words. The past several weeks had unfolded like a beautiful dream. Reed's steady presence in their lives, Peggy's successful completion of her training, and Hannah's own preparation for the upcoming gallery exhibit. So much change, yet it all felt wonderfully right.

She sank into the chair across from her mother, suddenly overcome with emotion. "You know, I was just thinking about how different everything is now. Good different," she clarified. "Especially you, Mom. I'm so proud of you."

Peggy reached across the table to squeeze Hannah's hand. "Proud of me? For what?"

"For everything. Completing your training. Starting your new job this coming Monday. For being willing to try again after all these years." Hannah's voice caught slightly. "I know it hasn't been easy."

"No," Peggy agreed quietly. "It hasn't. There were moments during training when I was certain I couldn't do it—that I'd forgotten how to be a professional, how to contribute something beyond my needs and limitations. I had plenty of moments where I was frustrated or just broke down and cried."

"But you pushed through," Hannah said.

Peggy nodded, her eyes bright with unshed tears. "I did. And do you know what kept me going, even on the hardest days? Watching you come alive again, pursuing your photography, allowing yourself to fall in love. It made me realize how much I'd been holding you back."

"Mom, no—"

"Yes," Peggy insisted gently. "Not intentionally, but still. You put your entire life on hold for me, Hannah. Your dreams, your career, your chance at love—all of it—paused because of my needs. And I let you do it because I was scared."

Hannah felt tears prick behind her eyes. "You needed me."

"I did. But not to the exclusion of your own life. What I needed most was the courage to move forward, to find a new version of myself after the accident. That's what you've helped me do these past few weeks, with Reed's help."

"I'm just so proud of whom you're becoming, Mom. You're stronger than you know."

"So are you," Peggy replied, squeezing Hannah's hand. "Now, enough emotional talk or we'll both be puffy-eyed when Reed arrives. What time is he picking you up?"

Hannah glanced at the clock. "Eleven-thirty. Which gives me about forty-five minutes to finish getting ready." She stood, smoothing her hands over her comfortable jeans and tee shirt. "I have no idea what to prepare for. He's being so secretive."

"Go finish getting ready, Hannah. And wear something special that makes you feel good."

Hannah hesitated, studying her mother's face. "You're sure you'll be okay today while I'm gone? I don't know how late we'll be."

"Hannah Gentry," Peggy said firmly, though her eyes twinkled with humor. "In less than forty-eight hours, I will be a working professionally again. I think I can manage an afternoon and evening on my own."

Hannah laughed, holding up her hands in surrender. "You're right. Sorry. Old habits."

"Go," Peggy insisted, making a shooing motion. "Make yourself even more beautiful for that handsome deputy."

Thirty minutes later, Hannah emerged from her bedroom, having added a light application of makeup and styled her hair into loose waves that fell past her shoulders. She'd chosen a comfortable but flattering outfit—dark jeans, a soft green silk shirt that brought out the gold flecks in her hazel eyes, and comfortable ankle boots that could manage various terrains.

She found her mother in the living room, iPad in hand, appearing deeply engrossed in something on the screen. Peggy looked up when Hannah entered, her expression immediately brightening.

"Oh, honey, you look lovely," she said, setting the tablet aside. "That color is perfect on you."

"Thanks, Mom." Hannah checked her cross-body bag for essentials—phone, wallet, lip balm, sunscreen (thanks to Emma's cryptic hint). "Are you sure you have everything you need? I've put lunch in the fridge, and there's plenty of—"

The doorbell chime interrupted her, sending a flutter of anticipation through her stomach. Hannah smoothed her sweater nervously, then smiled at her mother. "That's Reed."

"Well, don't keep him waiting," Peggy urged, her eyes bright with excitement.

Hannah crossed to the front door, her heart doing that now-familiar skip it always did when she knew Reed was on the other side. She opened the door to find him standing on the porch, looking devastatingly handsome in dark jeans and a charcoal Henley that accentuated his broad shoulders.

"Hey, gorgeous," he greeted her, his green eyes warm with appreciation as they took in her appearance.

"Hey yourself," she replied, unable to contain her smile.

Reed's gaze moved past her to where Peggy sat in the living room. "Hi, Peggy. You look especially beautiful today."

"Thank you, Reed," Peggy called back, her voice cheerful. "Big day ahead!"

Hannah glanced between them suspiciously. "Okay, you two are definitely up to something."

Reed's expression was the picture of innocence as he offered Hannah his hand. "Ready for our adventure?"

"As ready as I can be, considering I have no idea what we're doing," Hannah replied, taking his hand and stepping onto the porch.

"That's part of the fun," Reed said, guiding her toward his truck parked in the driveway. He opened the passenger door for her with a flourish. "Your chariot awaits, m'lady."

Hannah laughed, climbing into the truck. "Such a gentleman."

"I just realized I forgot something. Give me one second."

Before Hannah could question him, Reed was jogging back toward the house. She watched, puzzled, as he reached the front door just as it opened, revealing Peggy wheeling herself onto the porch.

"What in the world?" Hannah murmured.

She watched, bewildered, as Reed positioned himself behind Peggy's wheelchair, and pushed her down the ramp.

Reed grinned as he approached the truck and opened the back door. "Small change of plans for today."

Peggy, looking perfectly comfortable as Reed set her in the back seat, smiled at Hannah's confusion. "Don't worry, dear. Reed and I have been planning a little surprise for you."

"A surprise that involves kidnapping my mother from her home?" Hannah asked, half-laughing, half-confused, as Reed carefully settled Peggy into the back seat.

"Not kidnapping," Reed corrected, making sure Peggy was seated securely before securing her seatbelt. "More like... expanding our adventure party."

Hannah watched as Reed collapsed Peggy's wheelchair and stowed it in the bed of his truck. When he slid into the driver's seat, he was greeted by Hannah's bewildered expression.

"Okay, one of you needs to explain what's going on," she insisted, looking between Reed and her mother in the back seat. "Are we going to your ranch?"

Reed started the engine, his eyes twinkling with mischief. "No, but I'll let your mom tell you what's happening... well, sort of."

Hannah twisted in her seat to face her mother, who was practically glowing with excitement. "Mom?"

Peggy smoothed the blanket over her lap, looking unusually animated. "Well, you know Holly and Loretta have been stopping by to have lunch with me lately, right? After my training sessions, while you've been at work."

Hannah nodded. Reed's sister and mother had become regular visitors over the past two weeks, a development that delighted Hannah.

"We've been talking quite a bit," Peggy continued. "About all the changes happening for both of us. And with their encouragement, and Reed's help, I've decided to do something very special today. Something to honor both of us, really."

Hannah glanced at Reed, who was navigating the truck through Laurel Ridge's quiet streets, his expression giving nothing away. "I'm completely lost. What exactly are we doing?"

"Let Reed tell you the rest," Peggy said, gesturing toward him.

Reed checked his mirrors, then made a turn that Hannah recognized would take them toward the center of town. "So, here's the thing. Your mom has been working very hard, not just on her job training, but on something even more challenging."

"What's that?" Hannah asked.

"Reconnecting," Reed said simply. "With people, with the community, and with herself."

Hannah felt a swell of emotion, understanding the significance of this for her mother, who had isolated herself for so long after the accident.

"We're almost there," Reed said, slowing the truck as the Laurel Ridge Community Church came into view.

Hannah frowned in confusion as Reed turned into the church parking lot, which was surprisingly full for a Saturday. Cars filled the parking lot, and people appeared to be gathered near the outdoor pavilion behind the main building.

"Wait, what's going on? Why is everyone at church on Saturday?" Hannah asked, bewilderment clear in her voice as Reed parked.

He turned off the ignition and shifted in his seat to face her, taking both her hands in his. "Hannah, do you trust me?"

The question was simple, but the depth in his green eyes told her this moment mattered. "Yes, of course I do."

Reed's expression softened. "Good, because your mom is about to take another big step... one that she helped plan." He glanced toward Peggy in the back seat before continuing. "The church, the community, including some of your mom's old friends that she lost touch with, have come together to have a celebration for both of you."

Hannah's eyes widened. "A celebration? For what?"

"For everything," Reed explained, his thumbs gently stroking the backs of her hands. "Your mom's new job, your gallery exhibit... the journey you've both been on. Your mom is taking a big step today, one she's prepared herself for. She's ready for a bigger future."

Hannah turned to look at her mother, who was dabbing at her eyes with a tissue, smiling through tears.

"Reed, his mom, and Holly helped me plan a little party to celebrate us, Hannah," Peggy explained, her voice thick with emotion. "I'm so proud of myself, and of you, for everything we've done. And I wanted everyone else to celebrate with us. Now, let's go join them."

Hannah sat speechless, overcome by the realization of what this meant—her mother willingly putting herself in the center of attention, deliberately stepping back into the social world she'd avoided for a decade.

Reed squeezed her hands. "Are you okay?"

"Just... processing," Hannah admitted, blinking back tears. "Mom, are you sure about this? It's a lot of people..."

"I'm sure," Peggy said firmly. "I've been working up to this for days now. I'm ready. I want this, Hannah."

The conviction in her mother's voice was unlike anything Hannah had heard in years. She nodded, a mixture of emotions—pride, love, gratitude—welling up inside her.

"Okay then," she said, smiling through the threat of tears. "Let's go celebrate."

Reed exited the truck and retrieved Peggy's wheelchair, unfolding it with ease before helping Peggy into it. Hannah joined them, still trying to process the enormity of what was happening.

The three of them made their way toward the church pavilion, where Hannah could now see colorful decorations fluttering in the breeze—streamers and balloons in shades of blue and yellow. As they approached, the gathered crowd caught sight of them.

"SURPRISE!" The collective shout rang out across the church grounds, startling a flock of birds from a nearby tree.

Hannah faltered in her steps, overwhelmed by the sight of so many familiar faces: Martha from the diner, Emma, the entire Dunbar family, Pastor Andrew and his wife Lily, and countless others from the Laurel Ridge community.

Most shocking of all were the faces Hannah hadn't seen in years, her mother's former colleagues from the insurance company, and people who had gradually stopped visiting after Peggy withdrew from society. Friends who had once been regular fixtures in their lives before the accident changed everything.

As they reached the edge of the pavilion, Martha hurried forward, her warm smile as welcoming as ever.

"Let me take over from here, Deputy," she said, moving behind Peggy's wheelchair.

Reed released the handles of Peggy's wheelchair, allowing Martha to guide Peggy the rest of the way across the grass to the pavilion. He placed a gentle hand on Hannah's back when she moved to follow.

"Wait," he said. "Just a moment."

Hannah looked up at him, questions in her eyes, but the reassurance in his expression kept her in place. They watched as Martha wheeled Peggy to the center of the gathering, turning the chair so that Peggy faced back toward them.

With hands that trembled only slightly, Peggy reached beneath the blanket on her lap and produced an object that made Hannah's breath catch, her camera, the one she kept carefully stored in its case at home.

"Okay, Deputy," Peggy called, raising the camera to her eye. "Your turn."

Hannah turned to Reed, confusion written across her features, only to find him no longer standing beside her.

Reed was kneeling on one knee in the grass before her, holding a small velvet box that he opened to reveal a sparkling diamond ring. The summer sun caught the facets, sending prisms of light dancing across his earnest face.

Hannah's hands flew to her mouth, her heart seeming to stop entirely before racing forward at double speed.

"Hannah Gentry," Reed began, his deep voice carrying clear and strong across the suddenly hushed gathering. "You've shown me what I've been missing my entire life... not just your love, but partnership. The kind of connection that makes me better, and stronger."

Hannah felt tears spill over onto her cheeks as she heard the distinctive click of her camera's shutter—her mother capturing this moment from across the pavilion.

"You've taught me that true strength isn't about carrying burdens alone, but about sharing them," Reed continued, his green eyes never leaving hers. "About finding shelter in each other during life's storms."

Another click of the camera. Hannah barely registered it, lost in the intensity of Reed's gaze, the significance of this moment.

"I love you, Hannah. I love your fierce devotion to your mother, your passion for capturing beauty in the world, and your quiet strength that inspires me daily. I love the way you bite your lip when you're thinking, the sound of your laugh when you're truly happy, and the kindness you show to everyone you meet."

Hannah's vision blurred with tears as Reed took her left hand in his, his touch steady and warm.

"I want to build a life with you. A life where we face every challenge and celebrate every joy together. Where we create a home filled with love, faith, and the beauty of everyday moments. I would like to be your partner, your support, and your shelter in every storm life brings."

He paused, drawing a deep breath. "Hannah Gentry, will you marry me?"

The world seemed to narrow to just the two of them. Reed kneeling before her, his heart in his eyes, and Hannah standing breathless with joy and disbelief. Beside them, the gathered community waited in anticipation, her mother continuing to document the moment with click after click of the camera shutter.

"Yes," Hannah whispered, then found her voice. "Yes, Reed. Yes, I'll marry you."

A cheer erupted from the pavilion as Reed slid the ring onto her finger, a perfect fit, a beautiful solitaire diamond in a vintage-inspired setting that suited her perfectly. He rose to his feet and gathered her into his arms, lifting her slightly as their lips met in a kiss that held all the promises of their future together.

When they separated, both smiling, Hannah became aware of the applause and whistles surrounding them. Reed kept his arm around her waist as they turned to face their friends and family. Hannah self-consciously wiping tears from her cheeks.

"She said yes!" Reed announced unnecessarily, his voice ringing with joy.

The celebration erupted anew as Martha wheeled Peggy forward to join them. Hannah knelt beside her mother's chair, engulfing her in a fierce hug.

"Did you know?" she asked, pulling back to search her mother's tearful, smiling face.

"I might have helped pick out the ring," Peggy admitted, her eyes dancing with delight. "Reed wanted to make sure it was something you'd love."

"It's perfect," Hannah assured her, glancing down at the ring now sparkling on her finger. "But Mom, this is huge—all these people, you being out here..."

"I know," Peggy said, her voice steady despite the emotion evident in her eyes. "It's time, Hannah. Time for both of us to live fully again. And I couldn't miss this special moment in your life." She reached out to take Hannah's hand, her fingers brushing the new engagement ring. "This is just the beginning for us—all of us."

Reed crouched down beside them, his presence completing their circle. "Your mom's right," he said. "This is just the beginning."

The three of them shared a moment of understanding before the well-wishes of the community could no longer be held at bay. Emma rushed forward, throwing her arms around Hannah with an excited squeal.

"Oh, Hannah, it's gorgeous!" she exclaimed, pulling back to admire the ring.

Martha appeared with a tray of champagne flutes. "Sparkling cider for everyone," she announced. "For the first toast of many today!"

The gathering shifted closer, forming a loose circle around Hannah, Reed, and Peggy. Pastor Andrew stepped forward, raising his glass.

"To Hannah and Reed," he said. "May God bless you both with love, faith, and joy. And to Peggy," he continued, turning slightly toward Hannah's mother, "welcome, you've been missed."

"Hear, hear!" came the response, followed by the cheerful clinking of glasses.

What followed was a whirlwind of congratulations, hugs, and introductions as Hannah found herself meeting or reacquainting herself with faces from her mother's past. Peggy, for her part, seemed to be thriving amid the attention, her initial nervousness giving way to genuine joy as she reconnected with old friends and colleagues.

At one point, Hannah found herself standing slightly apart, watching as Reed crouched beside her mother's wheelchair, both of them laughing at something Loretta, Reed's mother, had said. The sight filled her with a warmth that spread through her entire being. The two people she loved most in the world connected in their own right.

"Quite the man you've found," came a voice beside her.

Hannah turned to find Holly smiling at her. "He is," Hannah agreed, her gaze returning to Reed. "I never expected any of this."

"Sometimes the best things come when we least expect them. Reed's certainly not the same man he was before he met you. He's... lighter somehow. More his old self."

"He's changed me too," Hannah admitted. "Helped me find parts of myself I thought were gone forever."

Holly's expression turned more serious. "You know, when Reed first told me more about you and your mom, and it was becoming evident that he was spending more time with you both, I was worried he was just falling into his protective rescuer role again. That he was drawn to your situation, not to you."

Hannah nodded, understanding the concern. "I wondered that myself, in the beginning."

"But watching you together these past few weeks," Holly continued, "it's clear this is something much deeper. You don't just need each other—you complement each other. You make each other stronger."

"That means a lot, coming from you. You've been such a wonderful friend to my mom, too. I can't thank you enough for that."

Holly waved away her thanks. "Peggy's remarkable. All she needed was someone to remind her of that fact." She nodded toward where Peggy sat, animatedly catching up with former colleagues. "Look at her now. You'd never know she's spent years avoiding social situations."

"She's amazing. Braver than I realized."

"Must run in the family," Holly said with a wink, before being called away by another guest.

Hannah turned as Reed approached, two plates of food in hand. "Thought you might be hungry," he said, offering her one. "You haven't had a chance to eat with all the congratulations."

"Thank you," she replied, accepting the plate gratefully. "This is... overwhelming."

Reed guided her to a quieter corner of the pavilion, where a small table afforded them a moment of relative privacy. "A good overwhelming, I hope?"

"The best kind," Hannah assured him, her fingers finding his across the table. "I just can't believe you planned all this—the proposal, the party, and getting my mom involved..."

"It was actually your mom's idea to make it a double celebration," Reed admitted. "When I asked for her blessing to propose, she suggested combining it with a celebration of her new job and your gallery exhibit."

Hannah shook her head in wonder. "I had no idea she was ready for something like this. All these people..."

"She's been working up to it gradually," Reed explained. "First with Holly visiting, then with Loretta joining them. They've been helping her practice social interactions, building her confidence."

"All while I was at work," Hannah marveled. "Or out with you."

Reed nodded. "Your mom wanted it to be a surprise. She wanted to show you she could do this on her own, that she wasn't as dependent as either of you had come to believe."

Hannah glanced across the pavilion to where her mother sat at the center of a small group, looking more animated and engaged than Hannah had seen her in years. "She looks so happy."

"She is. She's reclaiming parts of herself, just like you've been doing." His expression turned more serious as he reached for her hand, his thumb brushing over the new ring on her finger. "I hope the proposal wasn't too public for you. I wanted to honor your mom's wish to include the community."

"It was perfect," Hannah interrupted, squeezing his hand. "Absolutely perfect. I wouldn't change a thing."

"Good. I wanted it to be special for both of you."

Hannah looked around at the celebration continuing around them—friends and neighbors mingling, laughter and conversation filling the air, her mother at the heart of it all. "It's more than special. It's a new beginning for all of us."

Reed's smile was tender as he raised her hand to his lips, pressing a kiss to her knuckles just above the engagement ring. "The first of many."

The afternoon stretched into early evening as the celebration continued. Laurel Ridge knew how to throw a party, and this one had been planned with obvious care. Tables laden with food prepared by community members lined one side of the pavilion. A small area had been cleared for dancing, where currently Reed's father Mitch was spinning his mother Loretta in a move that suggested years of practice together. Pastor Andrew and his wife had taken charge of the sound system, playing a selection of music that managed to appeal to all generations present.

As the golden hour approached, casting a warm light over the gathering, Hannah found herself seated beside her mother, both of them taking a moment to observe the surrounding celebration.

"How are you holding up?" Hannah asked softly, noting the slight fatigue around her mother's eyes despite the joy that still animated her features. "This is a lot of socializing for one day."

"I'm tired," Peggy admitted, "but the good kind of tired. The kind that comes from doing something worthwhile."

Hannah reached for her mother's hand. "I'm so proud of you, Mom. For all of this. Planning the party, reconnecting with everyone, and being willing to step back into the world."

"It was time. Watching you pursuing your photography again, falling in love with Reed—it made me realize how much of life I've been missing. How much I've held you back."

"You haven't held me back," Hannah protested.

Peggy squeezed her hand. "We both know that's not entirely true, honey." She gazed out at the gathering, a wistful smile touching her lips. "I've been hiding since the accident, using my physical limitations as an excuse to withdraw from everything that felt too hard, too painful. And in the process, I've kept you isolated, too."

Hannah felt tears prick behind her eyes at her mother's candor. "I never minded."

"That's what makes you so remarkable," Peggy said, turning to face her daughter fully. "You gave up so much for me without a word of complaint. But Hannah, that's not what I want for you. I want you to have everything... a career, your art, your life with Reed. I want to be part of that life, not the reason it's limited."

Hannah swallowed hard, emotion making it difficult to speak. "You'll always be part of my life, Mom. That's not going to change."

"I know that. Reed has made that abundantly clear. That boy loves you completely, Hannah... enough to include me in his vision for your future together."

Hannah smiled, her gaze finding Reed across the pavilion where he stood chatting with his grandfather, who had arrived late to the celebration. "He's pretty special."

"He is," Peggy agreed. "And so are you. Which is why I've been talking with him about some changes."

Hannah's attention snapped back to her mother. "Changes? What kind of changes?"

Peggy adjusted her position in the wheelchair, her expression turning more serious. "With your engagement, it's time to rethink our living arrangements."

"What do you mean? You know Reed would never expect you to move out or—"

"It's not about what Reed expects. It's about what I want for all of us. Hannah, you and Reed deserve to start your married life together without your mother as a permanent houseguest."

"But Mom—"

"Let me finish," Peggy said, raising a hand. "I'm not saying this will all happen right away. But I am saying that over the coming months, as my job stabilizes and I build more independence, we should consider options for after you get married. I could live in our house with someone living with me as a companion, or a mother-in-law suite on Reed's property."

Hannah stared at her mother, struggling to process this unexpected turn in the conversation. "You've really thought about this."

"I want you to build your life with Reed without worrying about me every moment."

Hannah reached for her mother's hand, emotion threatening to overwhelm her. "I'll always worry about you a little. That's what daughters do."

"I know. But there's a difference between normal concern and arranging your entire life around my needs. It's time for me to stand on my own more, figuratively speaking, of course." She gestured toward her wheelchair with a wry smile.

"Are you sure about this? It's a huge step."

"I'm sure," Peggy said firmly. "Not that it won't be challenging, or that I won't need help sometimes. But I need to do this, Hannah—for myself, as much as for you. I need to know I can be independent again."

Hannah was silent for a moment, absorbing her mother's words, the determination behind them. Finally, she nodded. "Okay. But we'll take it slowly. One step at a time."

"That's all I'm asking. But we do need to start planning for a future where we're both living our fullest lives."

"Deal," Hannah said, leaning forward to embrace her mother.

As they separated, Reed approached, his expression warm as he took in the sight of them together. "Everything okay here? You both look serious."

"Just having a mother-daughter moment," Peggy replied with a smile. "Discussing the future."

Reed nodded, not pressing for details. "Well, I hate to interrupt, but I have a small surprise for both of you."

Hannah groaned playfully. "Another surprise? My heart can only take so much in one day, Deputy."

Reed laughed. "Nothing as dramatic as a proposal this time, I promise. Just something I think you'll both appreciate." He glanced toward the church building, where his father, Mitch, was exiting with something in his hands.

Mitch approached, carrying what appeared to be a large, flat object wrapped in simple brown paper. "Here it is, son, all finished and ready for the big reveal."

Reed accepted the package with a nod of thanks. "Perfect timing, Dad. Thanks for getting it done so quickly."

Hannah exchanged a curious glance with her mother as Reed turned back to them, clearly excited about whatever he was about to present.

"So," he began, balancing the package carefully, "I wanted to give you both something special to mark this day. A keepsake of sorts." He knelt, positioning the package so both Hannah and Peggy could see it clearly. "This is for both of you."

With careful movements, Reed peeled away the brown paper to reveal what lay beneath—a beautifully framed photograph that made

Hannah's breath catch in her throat. It was one of her images, taken during a sunrise hike with Reed last week. The photo captured the Laurel Ridge mountains bathed in early morning light, mist curling around the peaks, sunrise painting the scene in hues of gold and purple. It was one of her favorite recent works, a piece she'd been especially proud of.

But Reed had done something special with it. Beneath the image, tastefully matted and mounted, was a scripture verse engraved on a small brass plate: "For I know the plans I have for you, declares the Lord, plans to prosper you and not to harm you, plans to give you hope and a future." — Jeremiah 29:11.

"Reed," Hannah whispered, emotion making it difficult to say more.

"It's beautiful," Peggy said, reaching out to touch the frame gently. "Absolutely beautiful."

"I chose the verse because it feels like it was written for this moment in our lives. Each of us moving toward a new future full of hope and possibility."

Hannah looked from the photograph to Reed's face, finding his eyes soft with emotion. "It's perfect. Thank you."

"The framing was Dad's work," Reed added. "He has quite a talent for it."

Mitch, who had been standing nearby, shrugged modestly. "Just a hobby. The photograph is the real art here. You have a remarkable eye, Hannah."

"Thank you," Hannah replied, feeling warmth spread through her at the compliment. "For the framing and for being here today. For everything, really."

Mitch smiled, clasping Reed's shoulder briefly before moving away to give them some privacy, leaving the three of them—Hannah, Reed, and Peggy—in their own small bubble amidst the celebration.

Reed set the framed photograph on the table beside them. "I thought this could hang in your home, a reminder of this day and everything it represents."

"It's a beautiful gift," Peggy said, her eyes lingering on the scripture verse. "A perfect reminder of God's faithfulness, even when we can't see the path ahead."

Hannah nodded, reaching for Reed's hand. "And of how far we've come."

The future stretched before them, full of promise and new beginnings. There would be challenges ahead, adjustments to make, and a wedding to plan. Her mother would start her new job on Monday, Hannah's gallery exhibit was just days away, and Reed's demands at the sheriff's department remained as unpredictable as ever.

But in this moment, surrounded by the love of family, friends, and community, Hannah knew with absolute certainty that they would face whatever came next together—not as individuals struggling alone, but as a family united in faith and love.

As Reed pushed Peggy toward the pavilion again, Hannah took a moment to herself. Standing slightly apart from the gathering, she closed her eyes briefly in silent prayer.

Thank you, Lord, for this day. For bringing Reed into our lives, for Mom's remarkable courage, for this community that has welcomed us back with open arms. Thank you for plans that are bigger than anything we could have imagined for ourselves. Help us to walk forward in faith, trusting in Your guidance every step of the way.

"Hannah?" Reed's voice drew her back to the present, his hand gently touching her arm.

She opened her eyes to find him watching her with understanding.
"I love you," she said, slipping her hand into his.

Leave A Review

If you enjoyed this book, please consider leaving an honest review on Amazon

Visit Our Website:

www.tarabaisden.com

Visit Our Amazon Author Page HERE

Find Us On Social Media:

Facebook

Facebook Author Page

Instagram